SUN AND SANGRIA

Moxey was sounding off about the advantages of
Spain, with support from Oz, who had also
taken a shine to the place.

'Like this idea of havin' a kip in the afternoon,'
he was saying. 'I think I'll really take to that.
'Cause the afternoon's the draggiest part of the
day, isn't it?'

'Also, you're foreign here, right, Mox?' Oz
agreed. 'So there's no class prejudice, is there? I
mean, back home a bloke like you just has to
open his mouth and he's pigeon-holed with the
plebs!'

Moxey looked offended. 'What about you, Oz?
Most people can't understand a tossin' word you
say . . .'

'I personally think you'll miss your roots, Mox,'
said Wayne . . .

Barry was moved. 'Breathes there a man with
soul so dead, who never to himself hath said:
"This is my own, my native land",' he quoted.

They stared at him blankly.

Also by Fred Taylor in Sphere Books:

AUF WIEDERSEHEN, PET

Auf Wiedersehen, Pet 2

FRED TAYLOR

based on the Central television series
by Dick Clement and Ian La Frenais
from an original idea by Franc Roddam

SPHERE BOOKS LIMITED
London and Sydney

First published in Great Britain by
Sphere Books Ltd, 1986
30–32 Gray's Inn Road, London WC1X 8JL
This novelisation copyright © 1986 Sphere Books Ltd
based on the television series, *Auf Wiedersehen, Pet*
material copyright © 1986 Central Independent Television plc
Central logo copyright © 1982
Central Independent Television plc

TRADE
MARK

Set in Times

Printed and bound in Great Britain by
Collins, Glasgow

Auf Wiedersehen, Pet 2

ONE

Dennis Patterson was in a hurry. These days he was nearly always in a hurry. The shiny new Jaguar he was driving raced through the busy streets, beating traffic light after traffic light, until finally, to his intense annoyance, a traffic light beat him and forced him to wait. He straightened his tie, tapped his stubby fingers irritably on the steering column, his eyes on the stubborn red light ahead. Dammit, but he was going to be late picking up Vicki...

He paid little attention to the beat-up Ford Capri that was idling alongside him at the intersection, nor did he take in the look of envy-tinged interest on the driver's face. He had got used to that lately. Since he had got back from Germany three years before, he had moved out of the world of bricklaying and into the world of easy money – easy for some, that is.

'Dennis!' a familiar voice yelled.

He continued to stare ahead for a moment, then turned slowly and examined the Capri. The other driver had wound down his window and was grinning broadly. Dennis recognised the fresh young face all right. Good grief, was all he could think. Where there should have been pleasure at meeting an old mate, he felt mostly embarrassment.

He pressed a button. His own window lowered automatically with a gentle whine.

'Aw, hell. Nev!' he said.

Neville Hope nodded, still beaming. 'Haven't seen you for ages, man!'

'No, I've been pretty busy, like,' said Dennis cagily.

'I can see that,' Neville commented, peering at the sleek lines of the Jag.

Dennis winced inwardly. 'How's the bairn?' he asked,

1

quickly changing the subject. Nev's little girl would be near-enough walking by now. Time flies. 'God, she'll be getting on, won't she?' Dennis said. 'I haven't seen her since...'

'The christening,' Neville filled in for him. The grin faded a little, and there was an edge of accusation in the younger man's voice.

'Aye, well. I'll give you a ring... we'll have a jar.'

Then the light turned green, none too soon for Dennis. He waved, stepped on the accelerator and powered away, leaving Neville's Capri standing.

Well, Dennis thought. Eighteen months. It was a long time between drinks. And it was longer still since they had all stood leering into the lens of Barry's Instamatic for that crazy group photograph outside the ruins of the notorious Hut B in Düsseldorf. Life changed, people changed, as Dennis knew only too well.

He pulled the car to a halt outside the hairdressing salon and beeped the horn loudly, settling back in his seat.

Vicki emerged within seconds, looking like a million dollars, which was probably what she cost to run. She was in her mid-twenties, slim, blonde and chic. A real rich man's toy. Dennis opened the passenger door for her, gunned the car away from the kerb as soon as she was inside.

She patted her hair, smiled at him. 'What d'you think?'

Dennis grimaced. 'Fasten your seatbelt.'

'Ooh, I hate those things.'

'Fifty pound fine,' he said gruffly.

'Well,' she said when she had managed to strap herself in. 'What d'you think?'

If Vicki's appearance was out of *Cosmopolitan*, her accent was pure Gateshead. But then a rich man didn't choose his toys for the way they talked.

Dennis sighed. 'Think of what?'

'Me highlights,' she pouted. She swivelled the driving mirror around to admire herself, adding to Dennis's irritation.

'Took you long enough,' he said. 'We're supposed to be at the airport by twelve.'

'There's a new girl works at the salon. She said she thought I looked like Stevie Nicks,' Vicki prattled on, ignoring him.

2

'Who's he?' Dennis growled.

She glanced at him suspiciously, then realised he'd really never heard of Fleetwood Mac.

'Stop at Boots, will you, Den?' she said.

'Why?'

'I need some suntan lotion.'

'They've got plenty of that in Marbella.'

'They might not have my kind. I'm not takin' any chances. I have a very sensitive skin. Remember what I looked like when we got back from Florida? I was in agony.'

Dennis shrugged. He knew he had to humour her. Christ, but the price a man paid for his share of the high life . . .

They made it to the airport on time in the end. Just. After Vicki's visit to Boots, there had been another stop. At the factory, to pick up Ally Fraser. From there on, Dennis had driven and Ally and Vicki had sat in chummy comfort in the back. Why wouldn't they? After all, it was Ally's car, and Vicki was Ally's girl, bought and paid for. As for Dennis, he was just hired help. His embarrassment at meeting Neville had been fear of humiliation, not snobbishness.

While Dennis unloaded the cases and Ally's golf clubs from the boot of the Jag and Vicki pranced around being Stevie Nicks and Farrah Fawcett rolled into one, the big Scotsman fired yet more instructions in his thick Glasgow brogue.

'Now keep an eye on Charlie Skinner. He knows I'm goin' away. An' he's a devious little bugger, so show your face around there, make your presence felt. Okay?'

'Aye,' said Dennis crisply. He had learned quickly that none of Ally's questions were rhetorical, and all his recommendations were orders.

His boss was in his middle fifties, still with a street-fighter's body and hard eyes that showed, despite his elegant, almost dandyish suits, no one messed with him. Ally prided himself on having successfully moved from the strong-arm jungle of the clubs and one-armed bandits to the 'legitimate' business world. The law couldn't touch him, he made sure of that. But no one messed with him. Especially not underlings like Dennis.

Vicki quit showing off for long enough to pipe up: 'You

said I was to remind you about your mother, Ally.'

'What? Oh, right . . .' He turned to Dennis. 'It's the old girl's birthday Sunday. She'd like to visit her sister. Pick her up about ten. Give her a breath of fresh air. Take her up the Tweed or somewhere. Berwick. She likes Berwick.'

'All right,' said Dennis.

A porter had snapped to and was stacking the cases. Dennis handed over the golf clubs.

'Enjoy your golf, then.'

Fraser shrugged. 'If we get on the course,' he said airily. 'You know what Marbella's like this time of year.'

Dennis stared at Ally. No. He didn't know what Marbella was like this time of year, and the bastard was only too aware of the fact. But Ally liked his dry little jokes, buggered if he didn't.

Five minutes later, Dennis was heading towards the suburbs. As he drove, he thought about what it meant to be working for Ally Fraser. It didn't have the romance of your own business. It wasn't even the easygoing comradeship of the site. But it sure as hell paid the bills. And these days, with jobs scarce in the North-East, even Dennis Patterson, former man of principle, had stopped being so damned fussy.

Nevertheless, his encounter with Neville at the traffic lights had disturbed him. That wild, alcoholic day in Düsseldorf, when they had said their farewells with crisp German marks in their pockets and maybe all with a secret resolution to make a fresh start, was three years in the past now. Contacts had been scarce, even between Neville and Dennis, but there had been rumours and stories: both Oz and Barry had gone overseas again; Wayne had 'settled down' with the pretty German girl he had met on the site in Germany; Moxey . . . no one knew about Moxey; Bomber had gone back to the West Country; Neville and Brenda had had the kid but precious little other luck; and, of course, Dennis was working for Ally. Maybe they were all doing okay in their different ways. Dennis certainly liked to tell himself he was. But it was going to be embarrassing telling Nev the truth about the Jag if he ever got round to ringing him up about that beer . . .

Dennis was nearing home, and feeling thirsty. More and

more these days, he was finding that a nip or two of scotch helped to deal with any qualms of conscience he might have about where he earned his living. That, and the thought of what would happen if he stopped bringing in a regular wage packet, or got on the wrong side of Ally. Self-respect was something Dennis preferred not to think about too much; except maybe now and again to dismiss it as a luxury, nice if you could afford it. Scotch was cheaper, at least in the short run. Especially for a man whose wife had just left him.

And, speaking of short runs, Ally was planning to be away in sunny Spain for three weeks. Maybe Dennis would be able to take it easy, put aside some time and get things in perspective. Forget.

Dennis poked his unshaven face around the kitchen door. His sister Norma – with whom he'd been staying since his marriage broke up – was busy making breakfast. But bacon, eggs and a fried slice were the last things on Dennis's mind this morning. He felt rough. His eyes were like two beetles swimming in tomato soup. It had been a hell of an evening, all right.

'Mornin',' he grunted. It was the best he could manage by way of conversation.

'And what time did you get in last night?' asked Norma, as though Dennis were her teenage daughter rather than younger brother.

'Not too late,' he replied evasively.

'I heard a taxi and it must have been four,' Norma went on. 'You look dreadful,' she added with a sniff.

'You don't look too delectable yourself,' Dennis retaliated.

Like a bell ringing for the end of the round, the phone shrilled. Dennis went to answer it.

'Hello,' he said cautiously, and then his face brightened. 'Oh, no Nev,' he exclaimed, 'I'm not living there any more. I'm staying with me sister ... Barry? ... No, I haven't heard from Barry for ages.'

And so Neville told him all about it.

A couple of hours later, Dennis and Neville were nursing lunchtime pints in the smart city-centre pub where Dennis did

5

a lot of his drinking these days. He was skimming through a letter that Neville had handed him.

'I'm sure he wrote to you as well,' Neville was saying, ''cos he says he wrote to all the lads.'

'Aye well,' said Dennis resignedly, 'Vera only forwards me post every so often.'

Neville looked pained. 'I'd no idea you two weren't together,' he said apologetically.

'Not for a while now,' murmured Dennis, busy scouring the letter from Barry. 'That's why I'm staying with me sister.'

Neville made sympathetic noises, but Dennis seemed not to hear.

'I wonder what she's like?' he said at last.

'Who?'

'This Hazel. Barry's intended. Hard to picture, isn't it? I mean, he's a decent enough lad, but...' They laughed. Barry meant well, but he was certainly no ladykiller. When it came to sparkling wit and repartee, Barry got left behind on the starting grid.

'Mind you,' began Neville, taking the letter back, 'he's obviously doing all right. Headed notepaper, "B. Taylor – Building Services. All Types of Work Undertaken".'

'He was always canny with his money, Barry.'

'He was going to the Gulf, wasn't he?'

'Maybe he met her out there,' said Dennis with a leer. 'Maybe she's a sheik's daughter. Does Hazel sound Arabic to you?'

'Not really,' Neville admitted. 'Anyhow, we'll find out at the wedding, won't we?'

Dennis looked surprised. 'Are you going?' he asked, nonplussed. Mates were mates, but Nev didn't exactly look as though he were rolling in it these days. It was a long way down to the Black Country, and then there was the small matter of buying a suitable present to consider. What with petrol, and somewhere to stay, that was a week's wages already – and Neville had bugger all coming in just then.

Neville ummed and aahed, toying with his pint. 'Well, I thought I might,' he said eventually. 'Won't you?'

'Possibly,' Dennis deliberated. To tell the truth, he'd been a bit taken aback by Barry's invitation to the old Hut B crew to come down and fix up his house. What a bloody cheek, Dennis thought, even though Barry promised 'a consideration'. He certainly wasn't going down a week early to knock the future matrimonial home into shape. Obviously 'all types of work undertaken' didn't include Barry's own place.

'It would be a bit of a reunion, though,' urged Neville, thinking of seeing the lads again. 'And he's offering cash...'

'I know, but...'

'Some of us could do with a bit,' said Neville pointedly. 'We're not all driving around in Jaguars.'

Dennis looked at him for a moment, and then realisation dawned. 'That's not my car, man,' he explained.

Neville's eyes lit up. 'Oh, isn't it?' he asked, curiously cheered by the revelation. Being out of a job, having to stay at home all day while his wife went to work, he'd been a bit jealous of Dennis's apparent affluence.

'No,' went on Dennis. 'It belongs to the bloke I'm working for.'

Neville tried to explain away the misunderstanding, but Dennis cut him short. It seemed very much like he wanted to change the subject.

'Howway, man!' he cried, gathering up their glasses and shoving his way through the lunchtime crowd to the bar. 'Two pints please, George! And do you want a short, Nev?'

Neville declined the offer. It was a bit early in the day to start hitting the hard stuff. But that didn't stop Dennis ordering himself a large Teacher's and slamming most of it back in one gulp.

Nev took the pint that was proffered him. Something wasn't quite right with Dennis.

'So you're a driver, then?' he ventured.

'What? No, I do all kinds of things.'

'What sort of business is he in?'

'Who?'

'The bloke you work for. The bloke whose Jag it is.'

This is getting ridiculous, thought Dennis. I'll have to come clean, or he'll be on at me all afternoon.

'It's Ally Fraser,' he said, trying to sound nonchalant.

Neville nearly choked on his beer. 'Ally Fraser!' he gasped.
'That's what I said, yes.'

Neville looked as though he was about to turn tail and run
for cover. 'What do you do for him?' he stammered. 'Go
around menacing people?'

'He's not as black as he's painted!'

'Tommy Price's brother owed Ally Fraser,' said Neville,
beginning to recover his composure. 'He sent two blokes
round. They duffed him up in front of his wife and bairns.'

'Do you want to say that a bit louder?' growled Dennis. 'I
think some people in the snug didn't get all that.'

Neville dropped his voice, and apologised. 'But I never saw
a bloke like you working for a bloke like him,' he added.

There was an uneasy silence. 'Aye well,' said Dennis softly,
'I used to be a very principled lad. It was principles that sent
me back to me wife and family.'

He knocked back the last of his scotch and took a gulp of
beer.

'Any chance of you and Vera...?' queried Neville.

'No! But I get to see the kids. That's one good thing about
living at me sister's instead of a flat.'

They both stared into their beer, swirling it round in the
glasses. What should have been a joyous reunion was rapidly
turning sourer than flat ale.

'What shall we tell Barry, then?' asked Neville finally.

Dennis grunted. 'Tell him what you like,' he said sulkily.

'I really fancy going,' said Neville, with more determin-
ation than Dennis would have given him credit for. 'I'd just
like to get away... to get away from hiking round the
building sites and babysitting, if the truth were told. D'you
know, Den, I never thought I'd say this but there's times when
I'm quite nostalgic for Germany.'

'You!' cried Dennis. He'd never heard anything like it. 'You
were a picture of bloody misery the whole time you were
there.'

'I know that,' said Neville, looking sheepish. 'But at least I
was miserable in a good cause. I thought the sacrifice was
worth it because it would make things better when I got back.
But nothing's changed.'

He fixed Dennis with a baleful stare. Dennis shifted uncomfortably, wondering what to say. He'd got enough troubles of his own without taking Neville's miseries on board as well. But he couldn't let an old mate down; he'd been the gaffer back in Germany, and he still felt responsible for the lad.

'Look Nev,' he said, jumping in with both feet. 'Ally's in Spain, so I'm not pushed for the next three weeks. So we'll go down together, eh?'

The hangdog look vanished from Neville's face in an instant. 'Yeah?' he said, his eyes opening wide.

'Why not?' went on Dennis. The change might do him good as well. 'We'll take the Jag. I'll not tell Ally if you won't.'

'Oh, I fancy that,' breathed Neville. The last time he'd been in anything posher than a Cavalier was on his wedding day.

'Might do us both a bit of good, have a few laughs, eh?' said Dennis, warming to his theme.

'You mean go early and help him out with the house?'

'Might as well. I can just about remember how to lay a brick.'

'Shall we phone him?'

'No, we'll just walk in on him. Surprise him, like.'

'"Brickies in Mercy Dash",' dreamed Neville, scanning imaginary headlines. 'Have trowel will travel!'

Dennis laughed. It wasn't just the booze that had done him good. 'Tuesday,' he said decisively. 'We'll leave Tuesday after lunch.' It wasn't such a bad scheme after all, he reasoned with himself. It would be a good break, a chance to recapture some of the old magic. So sod Ally Fraser and his 'You know what it's like in Marbella at this time of year'. Sod Vera and the endless arguments over who owned what. Bugger it, he'd go.

He raised his glass to his lips. Over the rim, he saw Neville's face beginning to settle into a frown. Oh, God, what was it now?

'I'll have to ask Brenda, of course,' said Neville bashfully.

The consultation with Brenda was both easier and harder than Neville had feared. Maybe it was hard just because it was so easy. In the old days, Brenda had been so ... sort of clinging. And in a way he had preferred her that way. Now she seemed to know what she wanted, and her new sense of confidence and security was more than a bit disturbing to a man like Neville, who still had very traditional ideas about the balance of power in his family.

'Of course you should go,' she told him over tea that night in the kitchen.

Neville toyed with his portion of casserole, made a face. 'How can I possibly go? What about Deborah?'

'Deborah'll go to me mam's.'

'But a job might come up.'

Brenda smiled sweetly. 'You'll be earning money down there.'

'I put too much salt in this, didn't I?' said Neville, changing the subject to his cooking.

'No, pet. It's lovely,' murmured Brenda patiently.

'I've made better.'

She sighed. 'If you go Tuesday,' she said, 'that's perfect, 'cos I'm not working. So I'll have the whole day with Debs. Then I can take her to me mam's first thing on Wednesday morning.'

'You want me to go, don't you?' Neville said, suddenly blurting out the accusation he had been keeping hidden ever since the beginning of the conversation. All those lifts home from young doctors. Her craze for badminton – including mixed doubles. This trendy, liberated stuff she was coming out with all the time these days.

'I said so, pet,' she told him, unmoved by his suspicions. 'D'you want another glass of water?'

He sat in silence for a while as she filled her own glass from the tap. 'A couple of years ago you'd have been dead set against it,' he muttered.

Still lingering by the sink, she turned and looked straight at him.

'Perhaps I've grown up a bit since then, Neville,' she said. 'Listen, you need a break, pet. You need to work. You must be sick of minding house and making casseroles.' She watched as he pushed his plate away. It was a childish gesture, but she just smiled faintly. 'And you'll have some time with your friends.'

'Aye. And I suppose you'll have time to play badminton with your doctor friends.'

A brief look of irritation passed over Brenda's face, but she moved closer to him. 'Neville, you're being very immature,' she said. 'You want to go, you know you do. But you've got some fixed idea in your mind that "the wife" shouldn't *want* to let you go. I thought we'd proved in the last few months that we can accept changing roles.'

Neville winced. '*You* might have accepted it.'

Brenda sat down again and took his hand. 'Neville, I like my job. I really love it. I like working and I like doing something useful. And if I'm the one who's... who's...'

'Supporting us,' he filled in for her bitterly.

'Supporting us,' she nodded, 'then that's okay. Because we're a family. And the way things are today, families have to rethink things. Most of your friends are out of work... Your brother hasn't had a job for a year. That's why Valerie went back to hairdressing. And there's something I've never told you about,' she added with a sly little smile. 'Audrey.'

Neville caught her look. 'What about her?'

'Well... listen, if you ever breathe a word of this to Tony or anybody, I'll kill you.'

'Of course I won't,' said Neville impatiently. 'What?'

'Since Tony was laid off at Consett, Audrey's been stripping.'

Neville's jaw dropped. 'Stripping? For money?'

'Not for fun, Neville. It's no laughing matter taking your clothes off at workingmen's clubs and stag parties and police benefits, is it?'

The look of shock on Neville's face was giving way to a sly smirk. 'Mind, she has got the body for it...'

Brenda smiled too, with a kind of relief at the lightening of the mood. 'Oh, mine's not too bad,' she said.

'You stick to the hospital!' chuckled Neville, and reached out for her.

It was coming to pass. The scene had been set for the Return of the Seven.

TWO

Dennis and Neville may have been the first of the boys from Hut B to make their decision, but owing to Dennis's penchant for secrecy, the boys from Newcastle were not the first to make their intentions known that fateful Tuesday.

The one who provided the first sign of life to the beleaguered Barry was none other than Wayne Norris, Dockland's answer to Don Juan. A hurried phone call from a café halfway up the M1 and Barry knew that at least one of the old gang was hot-footing it over to Wolverhampton. That afternoon found him excitedly calling his fiancée from the basement room that acted as the nerve centre of B. TAYLOR, ALL TYPES etc. etc.

'Haze?' he gibbered – hard to do in his normally slow, guttural West Midlands drawl – 'It's me ... listen, Wayne's coming! Yuh, he rang me ... well, I'll hang on for him, take him over to me mother's for a wash and brush-up, and then we'll meet you in the Way-Ling at eight o'clock ... Will you book a table there, 'cos it gets a bit crowded. All right, love. Tara for a bit.'

He put the phone down, stared around the dingy room with satisfaction. His loyalty to the Bromsgrove & District Building Society had paid off, and never mind his mates' sneers. So had his determined pursuit of Hazel. He was a determined lad, was Barry. With acne like his, you had to be. As for Hazel, she was a jewel – she had the kind of class that meant she could book him a table at the Chinese with ease, like other people crossed the road. Somewhere deep inside, in fact, Barry had a nagging suspicion that she might be too good for him.

And so he and Trev, his apprentice, got back to work. To

tell the truth, things had been a bit slack anyway, even without the need to do up the place before the wedding. He had put down his deposit when he had got back from the Falklands, where he had been working on airstrip construction with none other than Oz. But that was another story, one that could still give him a sick feeling. The house, anyway, was a solid Victorian home in a quite nice area of town. Barry and Hazel's palace, the fulfilment of a dream. But there was still a lot to be done before it would come up to scratch, and whatever help at all he could get would come in more than handy. Wayne was guaranteed, on his way . . . maybe there'd be some offers from one or two of the others. He'd spent the last two days telling a sceptical young Trev what a glorious bunch of comrades they all were – he was going to look pretty stupid if only one answered his distress call . . .

A couple of hours later, the radio was on full blare and the hammering was in full swing, when a figure slipped in through the open front door. Trev, who was working the living room and therefore was nearest, noticed nothing at first. He carried on chiselling brickwork. Then he heard a bloodcurdling yell and whipped around, a look of horror on his young face. As he recoiled from the bizarre apparition before him, he knocked his transistor off its perch on the trestle.

'Bloody hell fire!' gasped Trev.

'Is that you, Hazel?' said Barry, appearing in the doorway.

Then he saw it too. A grinning Hammer-horror mask, clawed hands pawing the air. But he'd recognise those flash clothes anywhere – and the style of that entrance. He also recognised the voice, though it was still muffled by the mask.

'Barry!' said the apparition.

'Wayne?'

Trev was starting to recover. He looked wildly at Barry. 'I nearly had a bloody heart attack!'

Wayne took off the mask, chuckling fit to bust. 'Hello, my son.'

'Hello, Wayne,' Barry said with a delighted grin.

Wayne danced a little, offered Barry his upturned palms. 'Give me five, then. C'mon, trade me some skin!'

'Oh... you've been watching the basketball on Channel Four.'

Trev, who had bent down with some dignity to retrieve his radio, rattled it suspiciously to check its condition and muttered: 'More like the Hammer House of Horror.'

Meanwhile, Barry had got into his stride: 'I dunno, always seems a bit odd to me. All them seven-foot American negroes playing for Milton Keynes... I mean...'

Wayne, however, was paying attention to the aggrieved apprentice.

'I 'ope this isn't Hazel, mate. I mean, you haven't changed that much!'

'Ah... no. This is Trev.' He made a vague gesture of introducing them. 'Trev, this is Wayne.'

'Sorry to startle you, son,' the cockney said cheerfully. 'It was meant for 'im.' He looked around, shook his head. 'So where's the lads then?'

Barry looked at Trev, who was smirking, then shrugged. 'Yuh, well. Er...'

'In your letter you said we was 'aving a big reunion. Class of '82, whatever.'

'Yuh. I wrote to all of you. Didn't I, Trev?'

The boy nodded solemnly. 'He did. I posted 'em. At the post office.'

'Yeah. I suppose that's a head start over the launderette.'

Barry shuffled his feet in embarrassment. He'd been giving Trev all this stuff about the 'Magnificent Seven', undying comradeship forged and tempered in the hell of an alien land, solidarity to the end. And all they'd got so far was one cockney in a funny mask.

'Bomber's coming. Maybe,' he said weakly.

'And what about the others?'

'I haven't heard from them yet.'

Trev smiled cunningly. 'At least you've got each other. The Magnificent Two.' He cackled evilly.

'Trevor, Trevor!' Barry said frostily – he always called him Trevor when he was embarrassed. 'Don't you have to pick up those breeze blocks?'

The boy shrugged, went out, slamming the door sullenly behind him.

14

There was a short, awkward silence.

'He's a Trotskyite, y'know. A teenage one at that,' Barry explained.

'Who?'

'Trev. He's in one of them left-wing loony groups. Sort of a political version of glue-sniffing . . .'

Wayne snorted. 'I drove all the way from Tilbury 'cos I thought we was goin' to have a knees-up.'

'It's not easy, you know!' Barry retorted. 'There's a bit of a gypsy in the soul of all of you. Moxey's always lived at No Fixed Abode. My letter to Oz was returned "not known at this address" – and that was from his wife.'

'But Dennis and Neville aren't exactly gadabouts. Wives, kids, the works . . .' Wayne and Barry didn't know about Dennis, of course.

'I must admit I'm very disappointed in them,' Barry said. 'I think my letters at least justified the courtesy of a reply.'

Wayne didn't try to hide his disappointment. 'So it's just bloody us, is it?'

'I'm very sorry if it's a bit of a let-down. If I was you I'd raff off back to Tilbury.'

Wayne shrugged. 'I just flamin' got 'ere, didn't I?'

They were interrupted by the sight of two very pretty girls standing in the doorway. This was getting like ruddy *Crossroads* – all these exits and entrances on the same set – and Barry's eyes widened in amazement. He stared at Wayne.

'Excuse us,' said one of the two girls. She didn't look as though she needed an excuse from anybody, in fact, but Barry let it pass.

'Oh, sorry, girls,' said Wayne, unable to look Barry in the eye.

The girl smiled warily at Barry. 'I don't know how long you intend to leave us in the car,' she said to Wayne, 'but we're dying for a pee!'

She had a pleasant, educated sort of voice, and naughty eyes.

'Oh yeah,' said Wayne. 'Does your house yet boast a bog . . . I mean, toilet . . . Barry?'

'First floor landing,' growled Barry with a face like granite, and already blushing deep red under his zits.

15

'Thanks,' said the girl sweetly. She and her friend tripped off up the creaking stairs without a backward glance.

'Who are they?' Barry asked Wayne when they had gone.

'Couple of girls. Linda and Pippa.'

Barry sighed. 'I can see they're a couple of girls, Wayne.'

'They're hitch-hiking. Goin' to Ireland by way of Fishguard.'

'Wolverhampton,' Barry observed coldly, 'is not a natural stopping-off place on the way to Fishguard. Even if you are desperate for a pee.'

Wayne coaxed him away from the foot of the stairs. 'I know that, Barry. But they *are* rather tasty. Even in those anoraks.'

'Wayne... I'm deeply disappointed in you.'

'Why?'

'Because you haven't changed. No growth has taken place since Düsseldorf. Marriage, apparently, has made no impact at all.'

''Course it 'as,' Wayne smirked. 'Before I was married, I'd have jumped those two by Newport Pagnell.'

Barry clucked. 'Still the same unbearable sexist conceit. Still assuming any female will be taken in by your transparent cockney charm.'

'Listen, those two ain't dim, Barry. They're at Maidstone Poly. So they can map-read. They know this is a bit of a detour, but they're quite willing to stop over.'

'Stop over where?' asked Barry suspiciously.

Wayne looked around the room appraisingly. A few packing cases. Bare wire ends. Plasterwork still needing finishing.

'Well, it ain't exactly the Wolverhampton Hilton, but at least there's a roof over our heads.'

'What!' Barry flushed beetroot, drew himself up to his full height. 'You are *not* doing it here. No one's doing it here... Not before I do!'

Another flushing – this time from the small room upstairs – indicated that the girls would soon be back.

'Take your pick,' Wayne said testily. 'I mean, I'm not fussy...'

'I mean with my bride-to-be, Hazel. This place is sacred to us.'

'Yeah, it's a temple. I can see that.'

Barry nodded. 'And you and I are meeting Hazel at eight o'clock in the Way-Ling.'

'The what?'

'The Way-Ling. Finest Pekinese cuisine in the whole of the West Midlands.'

Linda and Pippa had re-appeared. Pippa – for it was she – was still wearing the same sweet smile. 'Did someone mention Chinese food?' she asked.

The sight of Wayne's mask had left Barry unmoved. Now, at the thought of the encounters – and the bills – to come, his face froze into an expression of abject horror.

'Audrey Harmison is stripping!' roared Dennis, so astonished that he almost veered the Jag into the right-hand lane, causing a truck to beep him angrily.

'For God's sake don't tell anyone,' Neville said, '''cos I'm sworn to secrecy.'

'Jesus.' Dennis grinned and shook his head. 'And Tony doesn't know?'

'Apparently not.'

Dennis thought for a moment. 'Aye, well,' he said more soberly. 'A lot of us end up doin' things we're not proud of. Look at me.'

'You mean, working for Ally?'

'You know his reputation, Nev. Who in the North-East doesn't?' Dennis said. 'Mind you ... it's all very legitimate these days,' he added without too much conviction. 'Sauna baths, solar heating. Property.'

Neville nodded. 'Does he still do the fruit machines?'

'Video arcades it is now, son. He still has things he can skim. But there's a whole army of solicitors and nameplate companies between him and the law.'

'So what do you *do* actually?'

Dennis laughed awkwardly. 'Me? I'm just a glorified go-fer.'

'Go-fer?'

17

'Aye. Go-fer the golf clubs, go-fer the wife. Go-fer the sodding dry cleaning.'

'Oh, I see,' said Neville unenthusiastically.

Dennis couldn't miss the disillusionment in the lad's voice. This was not Nev's notion of old Dennis, not at all.

Dennis sighed. 'I mean frankly, Nev, that's why I never really kept in touch. It's like I said, I'm not proud of it.'

Neville sat in silence for a few moments, staring at the greenery. They had another hour or so's driving before they hit the West Midlands. Then they had to find Wolverhampton. Then they had to find the address Barry had given. This already felt like foreign parts, almost as alien as Düsseldorf.

'Aye well, Dennis,' the lad said then. 'It's the bloody Ally Frasers of this world that people respect. Not grafters like you and me. They see that big house at Darrass Hall with a swimming pool and the kids with their ponies. They don't question how he got it.'

Dennis could have mentioned that the local CID occasionally made enquiries in that direction – so far unsuccessfully – but he let it pass. Enough of Ally Fraser. These few days were all about forgetting the bugger.

They slowed down for a roundabout. A hulking, shabby hitch-hiker with a beard was thumbing a lift. The Jag swept past.

'Just our luck,' said Neville.

'What?'

'Did you see that bloke's face? And us off on our own in a flash Jag. Wouldn't you think fate would provide a couple of Swedish nurses?'

'Or Swedish air hostesses, eh?'

They both laughed, remembering Barry and Wayne's famous disaster at the Düsseldorf Intercontinental. It raised the mood. There'd been precious little good, stupid adolescent fun in their lives these past few years. It'd be good to see the lads.

By the time they arrived at Townley Crescent, Wolverhampton, though, it was pitch dark. Barry was not that good at giving clear instructions. And when they found a note pinned to the front door, they both remembered a few other, less rosy incidents.

The note was in Barry's neat handwriting (no guarantee of anything, of course) and read:

'We're at the Bell and Dragon. Here are the instructions, 'cos it's a bit difficult to find...'

'Aw, bloody hell,' growled Dennis.

Wolverhampton had given the world Enoch Powell and Barry Taylor. Dennis had never thought much of the former; but at least you knew where you were with old Enoch...

Meanwhile, at the Bell and Dragon Barry was having similar rosy-tinted thoughts to the ones Dennis and Neville had foolishly harboured while they were still travelling hopefully. The trouble was, he was insisting on sharing them with Linda and Pippa and Wayne. At length, as ever.

'Y'see, Pippa, it's only in retrospect that you appreciate the good times you once had. "You don't know what you've got till it's gone", in the words of the song.'

Pippa yawned. 'What song?'

'Joni Mitchell!'

'Who?' chipped in Linda.

'Before your time, I expect,' said Barry, not realising the girls were playing him along. 'I s'pose Toyah's more your mark.'

Wayne seized his opportunity. 'That's enough about us, Barry,' he said with heavy meaning. 'Now girls, another four pina coladas, is it?'

Linda nodded. 'Yes please, Wayne. And I need some cigarettes. I'll just go to the machine...'

The look on her face said: the things we have to put up with to get a few free drinks. But Barry was undeterred.

'Hey, Wayne,' he burbled on. 'Remember that funny bloke with the hare lip who took us on a day trip to Krefeld?'

Wayne stared at him. 'A golden memory,' he said dully.

'Linda, would you get me a packet of Marlboro, please,' Pippa said.

As she handed Linda a mess of change, Wayne leaned over and muttered savagely, 'You're losing them, Barry!'

'What d'you mean?'

'I mean there's other topics of conversation than German building sites!'

He stalked off to the bar to get the next round, leaving a nonplussed Barry sitting alone at the table with Pippa. He smiled glassily.

'I was in the Falklands, you know...'

Then came a cheerful Geordie voice: 'Hey, Dennis, clock her!'

Barry didn't hear it the first time. 'It was no picnic, Pippa,' he was saying. 'A hard place for hard men to do a hard job. The only thing that saved my sanity was the ping-pong table. D'you play at all. At the Poly?'

'No.'

'Oh. Just wondered.'

Then he spotted the pair of them and leapt to his feet.

'Dennis! Nev!'

They shook hands all round while Pippa, left out, looked on coldly.

Barry remembered his manners then. He turned to her, still beaming: 'These are the blokes I was telling you about – from Germany!'

Neville grinned shyly, drawing a natural conclusion. Even in the time since they'd walked into the bar he'd forgotten that nothing was natural or conclusive with Barry.

'Hello, Hazel,' he said warmly. 'Very pleased to meet you, pet.'

'Kiss the bride then, Nev,' chuckled Dennis.

Neville leaned forward to oblige. Pippa recoiled in horror.

'My name's Pippa.'

'Then where's Hazel?' Dennis asked, confused.

'Omigod!' groaned Barry. What little colour he had drained from his face. 'Hazel's at the Way-Ling.' He checked his watch. 'And has been since eight o'clock!'

As he stumbled out of the pub and leapt into his van, a cab was approaching down the street. Barry screamed away from the kerb, nearly careening into the taxi, eliciting a choice stream of Brummie oaths from the driver, who then pulled in and deposited his fare, still cursing.

'Bloody maniac! Think they own the road, some of 'em! Did you see that?'

'Oh,' said a gentle West Country voice that sat strangely with the hugeness of the man who got out of the cab with his overnight bag. 'I 'spect he just remembered his wife's birthday.'

Bomber had arrived.

In the bar, the three remaining lads were clustered at the bar. Having got through wetting themselves about Barry, they were discussing strategy.

'You've probably ruined Barry's marriage, Wayne.'

'It ain't my fault, son. We was on our way to his mum's to get booted and suited prior to meeting the lovely Hazel. We just stopped for a quick cocktail.'

Dennis looked doubtful. 'I see. Then you pulled those two,' he said, with a glance at Linda and Pippa, who were happily ensconced alone with their pina coladas at the table.

Wayne's professional pride was obviously insulted. 'No I didn't!' he said indignantly. 'I brought them with me!'

'Both of them?' said Neville, wide-eyed.

'Some things never change,' muttered Dennis.

'They're hitch-hikers, aren't they?'

Neville grimaced. 'That's typical of your luck. All we saw on the way down were Charles Manson lookalikes.'

'Aye, well,' Dennis said. 'What are you goin' to do with 'em?' Ever the practical man.

'I know what I want to do, son. The question is: where? It's all very well Barry pissing off in a panic, but where does that leave us? Where are we supposed to stay, then?'

Neville shook his head. 'Howway, Wayne. Let's face it, Barry's got a lot on his mind at the moment.'

'He brought it on himself,' Dennis said drily. 'It was his idea to bring us lunatics together.'

But at that delicate juncture, two huge, bear-like arms embraced the three of them.

'Evenin', lads,' boomed Bomber. 'Whose shout is it?'

While the barmaid began clearing away the great pile of empties from their table – which wasn't for the first time that evening – a telephone began to ring some two hundred miles away. Dennis's sister Norma, who had been busy stacking the dishwasher, rose to answer it.

'Hello,' she said. It was a bad line. She tried again. 'Hello... Yes, I can hear you, but it's a bit faint... Oh hello Mr Fraser, how's Spain?... Oh no, Dennis isn't here at the moment... Can you hold on, I'll get a pencil.'

She put the phone down and rummaged through the drawers. Dennis had fitted these units for her when he came back from Germany. He'd done a good job. The drawers glided like silk.

'Right,' she said, having found what she wanted and picked up the phone again. 'British Airways, twelve forty-five... oh, *tomorrow*!' She drew an anxious breath. 'You're coming back early then?' she asked, her voice trembling.

There were more noises from the other end. Norma's mood grew blacker and blacker. She'd told Dennis he was taking a risk, but he'd brushed her objections aside. Now he was in for it. When Ally Fraser said jump, you jumped.

'Don't worry, he'll be there,' she said without much confidence, and hung up. Now what would she do? More to the point, what about Dennis?

THREE

The Geordie contingent had always believed the beer south of
Hartlepool was gnat's pee, but this stuff at Barry's local was
slipping down a treat.

'I've always thought that wrestling was rigged,' said Neville
to Bomber as closing time approached.

Bomber's eyes swivelled round unsteadily. 'If that's the
case,' said the big feller, 'how come I always bloody lose?'

The barman shouted last orders. Dennis beckoned him
over with a fiver. Neville didn't want another, Bomber just a
half, but Dennis reckoned he could still find room for another
large Scotch. He paid for the drinks and went to the Gents.

Bomber leaned closer to Neville. 'Den's knocking back the
hard stuff, isn't he? Or is it just the excitement of the
occasion?'

'I've hardly seen him, Bomb, actually,' said Neville. 'Mind,
I had a drink with him last week and he was downing Scotch
at lunchtime.'

'All right if you can afford it,' said Bomber ruefully.

Neville's anxieties about Dennis had been simmering close
to the surface for days. Now the beer made him want to blurt
out his fears.

'He went back to his family, of course, but it didn't work
out,' he confided.

'Is that right?' said Bomber, concerned. 'So he gives up
Dagmar and he ends up with nothing. That must have hit him
pretty hard.'

Dagmar had been a pretty tasty piece, all right. There
wasn't one of the lads – except faithful old Neville – who
wouldn't gladly have gone teetotal for a month for a game of
'hide the salami' with her. Dennis had been on the verge of

23

leaving Vera for good and shacking up with her.

Their whisperings were interrupted by the arrival of Wayne.

'Look lads,' he announced, 'I've been addressing myself to the problem of accommodation. The guv'nor says there's a B and B down the street or a motel half a mile past the roundabout. I fancy the latter meself.' He leered suggestively.

'I thought we were all going for a curry,' protested Neville.

Wayne smiled. 'I think I'll give the vindaloo a miss, Nev. I've never found it much conducive to romance.'

The phone rang behind the bar.

'Is there a Mr Patterson here?' shouted the barman over the general racket. That must be Dennis, thought Neville, catching sight of a stocky figure emerging from the Gents.

'There's a phone call for you,' he called out as Dennis pushed his way towards them.

'Don't be daft,' said Dennis, reaching for his Scotch. 'Who else knows I'm here?'

'Mr Patterson!' yelled the barman, a bit more impatiently this time.

'See?' said Neville. Dennis gestured for the phone to be handed over.

Bomber, Neville and Wayne resumed their discussion about accommodation. It was beginning to look as though the motel would win. Neville was worried about the cost – after all, they weren't cheap, those places – but then he noticed Dennis by his shoulder, looking mysterious.

'Who was it?' they chorused.

'Barry,' he said simply.

'Is he comin' back, then?'

Dennis calmly finished his Scotch. He could hardly suppress a grin in the face of their expectant looks.

'No,' he said finally. 'He'd rather we went over to him.' He looked at them for a moment, and then burst out laughing.

'He's been breathalysed!' he managed to gasp between great racking sobs of laughter.

The Jag rolled slowly along the dark, unfamiliar street. Unfamiliar, that is, to its driver, Neville. Since he'd had the least to drink of all of them, he'd drawn the short straw and been forced to drive the entire gang home from the police station after they had collected Barry from his interrogators. The zit king of the West Midlands was currently sandwiched between Bomber and Wayne in the back while a well-gone Dennis growled encouragement to Neville from the front passenger seat.

'Put your foot down, Nev,' he said, his voice thick with whisky.

'I'm not used to a Jag,' Neville told him pointedly. 'I'm only driving 'cos *you're* the one who should've been breathalysed.'

'But guess who was!' Barry moaned miserably from the back. 'What a catastrophic night! First a confrontation with Hazel, then this! I was lookin' forward to this occasion, y'know.'

Dennis frowned. 'I hope you're not blamin' us.'

'No, I'm just sayin' –'

It was time for a grim-faced Wayne to put in his two pennyworth. 'You can be really bleedin' selfish, you can, Barry.'

'How d'you mean?'

'It doesn't seem to cross your tiny mind that your being breathalysed totally bolluxed up my evening.'

There was no answer to that. Neville turned into Townley Crescent and braked outside Barry's palace. Carefully, nervously, Neville manoeuvred the Jag into a tight parking space.

'How'm I doing that side?' he asked anxiously. Dennis, he noted gloomily, had now fallen asleep – if that was the kind expression for passing out.

'Bags of room, mate,' said Wayne cheerfully.

The ensuing crash woke Dennis up with a start. Within seconds they were all outside the car, staring at the damage. Nothing to the other vehicle, but a tail light gone on the Jag and a touch of body damage in the immediate vicinity.

'It's not too bad,' said Neville hopefully. 'Just the tail light, actually.'

Dennis stared blearily at the damage. 'Aw, bloody hell, Nev. Look at the paintwork. I'll have to get that fixed before Ally gets back.'

'Who's Ally?' asked Wayne.

Dennis didn't answer. The phone was ringing urgently in the house. Barry stumbled towards the door, groaning: 'That'll be Hazel...' The rest of them followed him.

The phone stopped ringing just as Barry got to it. Meanwhile, the rest of them wandered into the bare living room and gazed around in awe.

'We've got our work cut out here,' Neville commented.

'I suppose a beer's out of the question,' said Bomber.

Wayne told him there were lagers in the kitchen. Barry returned from his basement office, looking crestfallen.

'She rang off. Just as I got there.'

'Then ring her back,' said Neville.

'No. In case it wasn't her. Then I'd wake her up.'

Wayne wagged a paternal finger: 'Best not to call her in any case,' he advised. 'Don't demean yourself. You went round there, good as gold, did the gentlemanly thing, and she gave you the Spanish archer.'

'The what?'

'The El Bow, mate.'

While Barry was still disgesting that piece of information, Wayne reinforced his point: 'So now it's her move,' he said. 'But let her sweat overnight. Only increases her panic in the morning.'

Neville ignored him. 'Where are *we* going to sleep the night, then? That's what I'm worried about.'

Barry shrugged. 'Oh well... under the circs, I s'pose you'll have to kip down here.'

'I don't believe this,' snarled Dennis, who had been staring broodingly around him throughout the discussion. 'It's one thing to arrange a reunion, Barry. But do we have to recreate the squalor we once lived in?'

Neville nodded. 'At least in Germany we had a stove!'

'If you'd let me know you were coming, I'd have made some arrangements,' said Barry. 'Wayne only called me from the motorway.'

'You knew Bomber was coming,' Dennis objected.

'I made provisions for Bomber, didn't I? There's a camp bed upstairs with a duvet.'

Meanwhile, Bomber had entered with a six-pack of lager in

one paw and a quizzical expression on his face.

''Ere,' he said, 'did you leave your kitchen window open, Barry?'

''Course not.'

'Well, 'tis open now.'

Barry led the drunken dash into the kitchen. The window was wide open all right, letting in the chill night air.

'That's been forced!' Barry said in a strangled voice. He looked around the room; his eyes lighted on the stove. A greasy frying pan was sitting there with egg scrapings still warm in it. 'And who's had a fry-up? That pan's still warm!'

'What about Trev?' asked Wayne.

Barry scoffed. 'He doesn't put in a minute's overtime, him. He spends his evenings painting left-wing slogans on viaduct walls.'

They trooped back into the living room, with Barry muttering to himself: 'I don't believe it. In one night me fiancée's buggered off, I've been breathalysed and burgled.'

'Howway, man,' said Dennis. 'There's nothing here to take.'

'Oh no, Den,' Wayne said impishly. 'When I was here earlier there was a three-piece suite and a cocktail cabinet.'

'It's not funny, Wayne,' Barry snapped. 'There's tools here. And downstairs is me registered office. With all me files and records. To say nothing of the petty cash.'

Suddenly Neville hissed for silence. They stopped talking, listened.

'There's someone upstairs,' Neville whispered. And there were, in fact, footsteps above. 'And he's comin' down...'

Bomber wasted no time in placing himself by the door, and squared up to surprise the intruder.

'Hold your horses, lads,' he said confidently. 'With us he's bitten off more than he can chew.'

They waited. The footsteps came closer, tentative, furtive. Fearful, even. The door opened slowly.

Immediately the figure edged into the room, Bomber was onto him, followed by the rest of the lads in a scrimmage that would have done credit to the lowest levels of Rugby League. Finally, amid the grunts, the heavy breathing and the oaths a familiar face popped up out of the pile, looking around wildly, his limbs pinned to the floor.

'Moxey!' bellowed Barry, who had been keeping a slight distance from the fray.

The lads got to their feet.

'No one was here,' wheezed Moxey. 'So I let meself in.' He stared around at the astonished faces. 'Sorry I'm late. I had a bit of trouble getting away...'

And so there were six.

Barry sat in the corner, looking like one of those paintings of Napoleon on Elba, slumped in his armchair and dreaming of what might have been if Waterloo hadn't happened.

Neville handed Moxey a mug of hot tea.

'After Germany, things were just as desperate as ever in the UK, and I got in a spot of bother. So I joined the Merchant Navy for a while.'

'The Merchant Navy,' Neville echoed in wonder.

'See the world, did you?' said Bomber.

Moxey looked at him to check he wasn't taking the piss. 'I saw Bahrein. Twice. And I had one really desperate evening in Malta. Couldn't wait to sign off.'

Neville jabbed a thumb in the direction of the jilted lover.

'Barry's been in the Falklands.'

'Straight? I thought he was goin' to Saudi.'

Barry glanced at them. 'No,' he murmured. 'Couldn't get there, could I? Wouldn't have got breathalysed there either, would I?'

'Still, at least you saved enough to buy this place,' Neville said comfortingly. 'Start your own business.'

'An' how can I run a business without a driving licence? If you're a jobbing builder, Neville, you have to be mobile. You have to get from A to B.'

Bomber said something about a bloke's being innocent until proven guilty.

But Barry was inconsolable.

'Foregone conclusion. It's Wayne's fault. I'd never heard of a pina colada until he showed up.'

Dennis came in from the street with a face like thunder.

The shock had sobered him up a bit, just enough to give him an evil temper.

'Three hundred quid, I reckon,' he announced to no one in particular.

'What?'

'The damage to the Jag.'

'Don't blame me,' said Neville.

'And who else am I to blame? If I remember right, you were behind the wheel.'

'Only 'cos you were legless. You were knocking back scotch all night.'

'That's typical!' snapped Barry. 'And I'm the one who gets breathalysed!'

Moxey could hardly believe his ears. 'You've got a Jag, Dennis?'

'No,' said Dennis with a fierce look at Neville. 'The bloke I work for has.'

'Oh. Tricky, that.'

'Look, lads,' said Wayne, back from using the phone in the basement office, 'I just called that motel down the road and they've got accommodation, so who's for a good night's kip?' He clapped his hands, grinned. Obviously thinking of Linda and Pippa. Apparently they'd already booked in there. 'Let's resume this blissful reunion in the morning, shall we?'

'Count me in,' said Dennis, making it clear he couldn't wait to get out of here.

Bomber thought for a brief moment. 'Me too.'

'I've provided a camp bed for you,' Barry objected, cut to the quick.

'Thanks Barry. But Bomber's a big lad and needs a big bed.'

'I'll have his,' said Moxey quickly.

'Comin', Nev?' Dennis asked, already on his feet.

Neville shook his head. 'No. I'd sooner stay here. Save the money. That sofa'll do me.'

Wayne offered to drop Barry at his mum's. The lovesick swain refused. Couldn't face it, and he wouldn't be able to sleep in any case. Wayne left him with a brief reminder to hold out against phoning Hazel. '*She* has to come to *you*, son,' he said darkly, and told Neville to keep Barry to his resolution in case he weakened during the lonely watches of the night.

'Still the expert, Wayne. On affairs of the heart,' said Moxey when the other three had left.

'He hasn't changed,' Neville said, pursing his lips in disapproval. 'That's why he's gone to that motel. 'Cause those girls are there.'

'What girls?'

'Well, he only goes and shows up with two girls he picked up on the motorway.'

Barry roused himself. 'Oh yuh,' he scoffed. 'He says to me on the phone, "I'm a changed character. Married man," he says.'

'Wayne? M-married?' stuttered Moxey.

'Never!' Neville said.

'Oh yuh. He married that German girl what worked in the site office. Don't you remember he was very smitten at the time?'

Moxey looked shocked. 'I know that. But gettin' married, that's l-lunacy.'

'Here, here,' said Barry. 'I'll be walking up the aisle any day now.'

'No offence, Barry. You know what I mean. It's just that Wayne's a bloke who can jump anything. Women find him attractive, whereas you...'

'Yes?' snapped Barry.

Moxey retreated. 'Oh, I didn't mean it to come out like that.'

'I'm not a bloody gremlin, you know!'

Neville decided it was time to exercise some tact before the fiancé-in-exile went into terminal depression.

'I think what Mox means is that you're more naturally suited to marriage. Same as me.'

'Oh, you're still married, are you, Nev?' said Moxey, quick as a flash.

'Yes, why shouldn't I be?' said Neville defensively. As a diplomat, Mox was hardly your Henry Kissinger, was he?

'Oh, I was th-thinking about that tattoo you had. With the other bird's name on. That must have thrown a bit of a wobbly.'

Barry pricked up his ears. 'Yuh. How did you explain that away, Nev?'

'I didn't,' Neville said reluctantly. 'I couldn't. Just told the truth.' He wilted under their sceptical smirks. 'Sort of... Actually, I said you lot got me drunk and held me down while they did it. She believed me. Eventually. We've just agreed never to mention it.'

'Very mature of you both,' Moxey leered.

'Well, we grow up, don't we? Got a kiddie now.'

Barry nodded. 'I'm a very different person from the one you knew in Düsseldorf!' he said eagerly. 'I've saved me money. Bought this place. Started me own business. Learned elementary Spanish and joined the SDP. And I've travelled! I don't just mean the Falklands. Last year Hazel and me took a villa in Gozo,' he told them with crowning satisfaction.

'You've obviously been very upwardly mobile, Barry,' Moxey said with a hint of envy. 'Of all of us, you've really got *your* life together.'

Barry subsided back into gloom.

'I did have. Till you lot showed up!'

Early morning sunlight streamed into the kitchen. Norma, in her dressing gown, was waiting for the kettle to boil. She held a telephone receiver in her hand. The ringing tone seemed to go on forever.

At last someone answered. Please God, let this be the one, she breathed. She'd made half-a-dozen calls this morning already. Last night she'd been on the phone for over an hour.

'I'm trying to contact Dennis Patterson,' she told whoever it was at the other end. 'It's his sister here.'

There was a lot of static, and then a familiar voice came through. 'Norma? This is Neville.'

She sighed with relief. At last she was getting somewhere.

'Listen,' she said. 'It's absolutely vital I speak with Dennis. I've been trying to get hold of him since six o'clock last night.'

Neville explained how they'd been out, that Dennis had decided to spend the night at the motel.

'Then tell him Ally Fraser's coming back unexpectedly,' she pleaded. 'And have him ring me as soon as possible.'

Neville grasped the problem immediately. Even as he

31

hurriedly dialled the motel, he was glad he wasn't in Dennis's shoes.

Within half an hour, Dennis was packed and impatiently queuing at the desk to pay his bill. Just then Wayne sauntered in.

'You're keen, Den,' he exclaimed.

'What?' Dennis was in no mood to play games.

'To get to work. It's only twenty past eight. I wasn't goin' over there till ten meself.'

Dennis's embarrassment was only too clear. 'I'm not going, Wayne. Me sister rang and I have to shoot off back home.'

'Nothing serious, is it?'

Dennis sighed, shifting uncomfortably from foot to foot.

'Just somebody I have to deal with,' he mumbled. 'Look, give Barry my apologies and wish him all the best. Okay?'

With that, he picked up his change and his bag and started to make for the door. Wayne was taken aback by the other man's obvious agitation.

'Den!' he called out after him.

Dennis paused, turned. Wayne offered him his hand.

'Nice to see you again, son,' he said simply.

Dennis shook his head, realising that with so much on his mind he'd been really short with an old mate. They'd hardly had a chance to talk or find out anything about each other . . .

'Oh, I'm sorry, Wayne,' he said, shaking on it. 'Good to see you, too.'

Then he headed for the door.

'Maybe you can pop back at the weekend or something,' Wayne said to his back. 'Be a giggle!'

But Dennis was already out of the door.

Wayne looked a little wistful, then shrugged it off and began to mooch off in the direction of the dining room for breakfast. It was his turn to be called back, though. The receptionist's summons was answered promptly – especially as she was a pretty fair piece of crumpet. Wayne obediently retraced his steps, smiling.

'Sir?'

'Yes, my dear.'

'It's the two young ladies in room 216 . . .'

'Oh yeah. Give 'em a bell. Tell 'em I'm on me way to breakfast.'

The receptionist smiled sweetly. 'They've checked out, sir.'

'They what?'

'They said you'd settle their bill.'

Map-reading wasn't the only thing you learned at Maidstone Poly. The once-invincible Wayne had been outplayed at the game he had once played best. Beaten game, set and bleedin' match.

Understandably, Wayne was not in the best of moods as he drove himself and Bomber over to Barry's place later that morning, togged out in their work clothes and ready to go.

'Sorry I missed Den,' Bomber said. 'I scarcely said a word to him last night.'

'None of us did,' growled Wayne. 'He was that pissed.'

Bomber nodded. 'He never used to knock it back like that. Not scotch, anyway.'

'He never used to drive a Jag neither.'

'You can't complain,' Bomber said with a chuckle. 'What's this motor of yours? A BMW? Fancy motor, this.'

'I earned it, Bomb. Little present to meself, this was. After six months in the bleedin' Arctic Circle.'

'What were you doin' up there?'

'I worked as a radiographer on the pipelines.'

'Good money, then.'

Wayne smiled grimly. 'It's not just that. There was nowhere you could bleedin' spend it. Our only diversions were tapes and videos.'

'So what d'you do about sex?'

'Not a lot,' said Wayne, easing the responsive car into Townley Crescent with what seemed like no more than a flick of the wheel. 'You got any idea how 'ard it is to catch a penguin?'

As soon as they got to the house and met the other lads, two things were clear: Barry had caved in and cleared off to hunt for Hazel; and once the story of Wayne's motel fiasco was public, it was never going to be forgotten.

Barry had started a kitchen extension out in the garden, and that was where everyone was hard at work. Trev was sulking inside, apparently. He hated working in the fresh air except when it was in the cause of the people's struggle.

And, in fact, it was difficult for Wayne, as the resident chippie, to get to work. The plastering and bricklaying tasks were pretty much self-evident, but carpentry... you needed precise instructions for carpentry, didn't you? The cockney ended up standing around like the proverbial spare implement at a wedding, his temper still not of the best.

'Got a bloody sauce, that Barry,' he griped. 'Asks us all up here to help him out, and then does a runner.'

Neville grinned. 'He went to see Hazel, didn't he? At work. She's got a good job, receptionist or something at some conference centre. He decided to have it out with her before they got too alienated from each other.'

'Against my specific instructions, yes. All those hours in Germany I wasted, tutoring him in the ways of the opposite sex.'

Moxey paused in his plastering. 'I'm not sure they're your strong suit any more,' he said. 'Otherwise you wouldn't have had to pay for those two birds.'

Amid grins and chuckles, Wayne tried to keep up his swagger. 'Cheap at the price, son,' he said.

'B-bollocks,' said Moxey.

'You weren't there, Mox, were you?' said Wayne vehemently.

Then Bomber chipped in with a knowing smile: 'No. But I was. I was in the room next to you, and I heard 'em turnin' you away...'

'Don't know what you were thinking of in the first place,' said Neville when they had all had a good laugh at Wayne's expense. 'I thought you were married now.'

'Krista and I have an understanding, Neville,' Wayne said quickly. 'It's a modern marriage, see.'

'What, you mean it won't last?'

Bomber, in the meantime, had decided it was time for a brew-up. 'Where's that lad – what's his name?'

'Trevor,' filled in Neville.

'Trev. He prefers Trev,' cautioned Moxey.

'Oh, does he?' Bomber turned towards the house and

bellowed at the top of his well-tried lungs: 'Trevor! Trevor!'

A window opened, and the boy's sullen face appeared. 'It's Trev!'

Bomber glared at him. 'Whatever it is, sunshine, put the kettle on, eh?'

'I'm not a can boy,' said Trev haughtily.

'What are you, then?' growled Wayne.

'I'm an apprentice.'

'And we're skilled craftsmen, doin' a mate a favour, so put the bloody kettle on!'

Trev slammed the window shut again. He might have said something about 'class traitors', but no one could be completely sure.

'Obviously a graduate of the John McEnroe School of Charm and Deportment,' said Wayne.

'Yeah, well,' Bomber conceded. 'Maybe I was a bit heavy-handed. To tell you the truth, some of my skills are a bit rusty, despite all that talk.'

'You not been doin' much of this, Bomb?' asked Moxey.

'Not a lot, no. It's a treat to me, this is, layin' bricks in the fresh air, after some of the jobs I've been doing.'

The young woman who emerged timidly from the back door of the house was smartly, if unimaginatively dressed. She had a certain poise; attractive without being a stunner.

'Er... excuse me,' she said in a cultivated version of a Brummie accent.

They all stopped and looked at her politely. She wasn't one of those girls you leered at, even though she was worth a second glance.

'Do you have any idea where Barry Taylor is?' she asked.

'We wish we did, my dear,' said Wayne sarcastically.

'We think he's with Hazel, his fiancée,' said Neville.

The girl smiled faintly. 'No he's not. *I'm* Hazel.'

FOUR

Harbottle, of course, had to be the absolute picture of your respectable provincial solicitor, sober-suited and straight as all get-out. That was why he fitted Ally's purposes so well. Because Ally Fraser paid him way over the odds to be precisely the opposite of what he seemed.

The office was austere and basic, too. A few family photos, Mrs Harbottle, the kids on their ponies. One or two impressive certificates in frames on the wall. Perfect. And Harbottle knew how to keep his mouth shut. He would, wouldn't he? Otherwise how could he carry on looking like a pillar of his profession and the community?

Ally had brought some big black-and-white photographs with him from Spain, and he and Harbottle were studying them with great interest. Ally's fury at having to stand around the airport like a prune and then hail his own cab had been shelved. The big Scotsman could do that. He was always able to concentrate on the job at hand, even if there was something unpleasant at the back of his mind. Like what he wanted to do to Dennis when he found him.

'It's enormous,' said Harbottle, gazing at a photo of a large, Victorian mansion. It was bloody ugly too, but it wasn't his place to make architectural judgments.

Ally nodded. 'Thirty-two acres. It was a school before Kenny bought it.' He smiled maliciously. 'But then he had that spot of bother that forced him into exile in sunny Spain.'

'Yes . . . of course,' said Harbottle. 'And where do we come in?'

'Kenny can do sod-all with it while he's stuck on the Costa del Crime,' Ally said matter-of-factly. 'If he sets foot back here, they'll collar him. I bumped into him on the golf course last Friday – and let me tell you, Spain has *not* improved his game – and he told me about it. So I said, "Leave it to me. I'll tart it up, do a conversion, and we'll sell it off in time-sharing units." '

Harbottle looked at him suspiciously.

'So what's the panic?'

'To be frank, he'd virtually closed a deal with the Coal Board, but if we move fast he can get out of that,' Ally said with a shrug. 'I've got the number of his solicitor here so you can sort that out . . .' He paused, smiled wolfishly. 'The attraction for Kenny is that I'll take his proceeds down there in a plastic bag. In cash.'

'I didn't hear that, Mr Fraser.'

Ally's grin widened. 'That's what I pay you for. Not hearing everything I say.'

Ten minutes later, he had completed that part of the day's business. And high on his schedule was another little encounter. With Dennis bloody Patterson. Except that first he had to find the bugger.

Dennis dumped his overnight bag on the kitchen floor. Even with his foot down all the way it had taken him the best part of four hours to get home. He'd not even dared to stop for a leak until he'd hit the A1. But he'd still missed Ally Fraser's flight by a mile.

'So what's the panic,' asked Norma, coming in behind him. 'Have you seen him?'

Dennis told her how he'd gone hotfoot from the airport to Ally Fraser's factory, only to find his boss had gone out. In a hell of a temper, too, he gathered. Knowing Ally, he'd still be breathing fire when he got back – whenever that might be.

'You shouldn't have gone away and took his car, Dennis,' wailed Norma.

Dennis was in no mood to go into the rights and wrongs of the issue. 'Hey, hold up!' he protested. 'He was supposed to be off in Spain for a fortnight!'

'And there was a bloke round here earlier looking for you.'

Dennis's stomach took the plunge like an express lift gone out of control.

'One of Ally's lads?' he asked as casually as he could.

'I don't know, do I?' said Norma, busy with a dishcloth. 'He was ugly enough – a right hard case. I've said to you before, Dennis, if you're working for Fraser you're not going to be mixing in choice company.'

'I'll handle it, Norma,' he said, putting his arm around her. He was man enough to tackle Ally Fraser head-on, but he didn't want any of his family getting mixed up in it.

He took a step towards the door, and hesitated.

'Look, I'm going to the Wheatsheaf for a jar. If he phones, take a message and come and fetch us.'

'I'm going to work in half an hour, Dennis,' she pointed out. He'd clean forgotten in all the turmoil. Still, there was still time for a swift one, and the chance to think.

'I'll be back by then!' he called and slammed the door behind him.

But Dennis was as good as his word. 'Any calls?' he cried cheerily as he came into the living room where Norma was watching early-afternoon television. She could smell the public-house miasma on him, and she didn't like it.

'No,' she answered curtly.

'Better get off to work, then, hadn't you?'

Norma looked rattled. She stared at the TV screen for a long time before she finally spoke.

'I'm not going. If someone's comin' round here to brace you, I'm staying put. This is my home, and I'm not having your blood or anyone else's on that carpet.'

'Hey, Norma, I'm not in short trousers any more...' Dennis began to object, but then the doorbell suddenly trilled. Norma tiptoed over to the window and peered round the curtain.

'It's him,' she hissed. 'He's back.'

'Stay there,' warned Dennis, and went out into the hall. This is it, he thought, and took a deep breath before opening the front door.

A great bear of a man stood there, and Dennis flinched. Norma had been right – he certainly looked a hard case. And yet...

38

'Good God, man, where did you spring from?' gasped Dennis.

Oz – for it was he – gawped down at him, temporarily speechless. Norma appeared at Dennis's shoulder, glaring like a Gorgon. 'Who are you?' she snapped at Oz with all the haughty arrogance she could muster. But Dennis made reassuring noises.

'It's all right, Norma, this is a mate of mine. Oz, this is me sister Norma.'

Oz looked only marginally less baffled. 'Oh I see,' he said without much conviction.

Norma invited him in. 'Yes,' he went on, 'I saw you earlier and I wondered who you were. Didn't know what the situation was, did I?' And I still don't, he reflected privately.

'You'd better be off to work, pet,' Dennis told his sister. 'Now you don't have to worry about the carpet,' he added, feeling more like his old self.

'I'll get you a beer,' he called to Oz, knowing there was no point wasting breath asking if he fancied one. Oz had the thirst of a man who's just staggered in from the Sahara, only permanently.

Dennis disappeared into the kitchen. While he was gone, Oz came closer to Norma.

'Is he not with Vera then?' he asked in hushed tones.

'Not for a year now.' Norma was busy buttoning her coat. Her kid brother certainly knew some funny people. And there was beer on his breath.

'Ah, well,' went on Oz, undeterred. ''Cos I went round to his old house, like. There was this bloke I didn't know, but he gave me this address.'

'She sold the house,' said Norma, very much to the point. 'Her and the kids live at the coast now.'

'Dear me,' breathed Oz. What could she mean? Whitley Bay, or Redcar? There could be no worse fate.

'But I'm sure you've got *other* things to talk about,' she said with a vengeance.

'Oh, I know what you mean!' boomed Oz. 'Delicate subject, like?'

But Norma simply called out goodbye to Dennis, and left.

39

Dennis emerged from the kitchen. By the time he'd ushered Oz into the lounge, and they'd broached a couple of cans, he'd recovered sufficiently to crack a thin smile of welcome. But it was Oz who spoke first.

'Well, Den,' he ruminated, 'you must be kicking yourself, eh?'

'What?' exclaimed Dennis.

'You gave that gorgeous bloody Dagmar the heave-ho in Germany, and now your marriage is kaput and you're living with your sister.'

Dennis didn't know which way to look. 'Thanks, Oz,' he said. 'I really needed someone to come back and point that out to me.'

Oz assumed his man-of-the-world manner. 'Oh, these things happen, man,' he said expansively. 'No one knows that better than me.'

Dennis decided on a change of tack.

'Well, man, we heard you'd been thrown off the Falklands.'

Oz's chest swelled with pride. 'Aye. First person to be forcibly ejected by the Brits since the Argies.'

Dennis chuckled. Oz was a disaster area, but he had to admit it was good to see him again.

'Quite an honour, Oz. Congratulations,' he said wryly.

'Wasn't my fault, Dennis,' Oz insisted. 'Some paras picked on us in a pub one night – right head-bangers, they are – an' the next thing I knew I was bein' frogmarched onto a ruddy Hercules between a couple of MPs.' His eyes misted over at the memory of it. 'What a nightmare that journey is. You go halfway across the world, an' all you see is a bog on Ascension Island.'

'But you never showed up back here, did you?' Dennis said.

'Aye, well ... What happened was, I had meself a couple of nights in London. I deserved that. After six months in the Falklands, where men are men and sheep are nervous ...'

'And you spent all your readies?'

'No, no. I was on me way home.' He sighed. 'But you know that things between me and Marjorie have not exactly been idyllic over the years. And when I rang her from King's Cross and a bloke answered the phone, I knew they'd deteriorated

40

even further.' He took a swig of beer, licked his lips. 'But I'm not without a sense of family responsibility, Den. I posted her some cash, bought the kid a train set from Hamley's. Then I went to Gatwick and took a flight to Florida.'

'Florida!' Dennis nearly spluttered beer all over the table.

'Not expensive these days, Dennis. Jet-Save. Fourteen days, two hundred and ninety-nine pounds.'

Dennis thought for a moment.

'All right. That accounts for a fortnight. But you've been gone at least a year.'

But he would have to wait a little longer for an explanation of the missing eleven and a half months, for just then the phone rang. As though he'd been playing Jeeves all his life, Oz picked up the receiver and in his best sepulchral tones announced: 'Patterson residence.'

Dennis could have thrown a cushion at him, but Oz wouldn't be deterred. 'Who shall I say is calling?' he intoned. His eyes opened wide with surprise when he learned who was at the other end.

'It's Ally Fraser,' he mouthed.

Dennis snatched the phone from him and made keep-quiet gestures. 'Hello Ally, it's Dennis,' he began, but was chewed out by a mouthful of abuse. 'I know . . . I'll explain when I see you,' he said when he could get a word in edgeways. There was an even longer pause.

'I'll be right over,' he said simply, and put the phone down. His face had turned ashen.

'What's this?' asked Oz as Dennis struggled into his jacket.

'I've got to go,' said Dennis out of the corner of his mouth.

'What's a villain like him doin' ringin' you?' Oz knew most of the blaggers from Spennymoor clean through to Berwick-on-Tweed. Ally Fraser's name was like a gold American Express card.

'I work for him,' said Dennis simply. What else could he say?

They were rocketing along in the battered Jag. Oz still couldn't get over it.

'I'm a bit amazed,' he said when he had got the gist of

things. 'You, of all people, working for a bloke like that.'

Dennis had heard this before. He'd got the answer off pat.

'Times change, Oz,' he said. He realised they were driving through Oz's home manor.

'Where shall I drop you off?' he asked.

Oz didn't budge an inch. 'Aw, I'll just come along with you,' he said. 'I've got nothing else on.'

The gesture was there, but Dennis wanted to ride this one out on his own.

'No, Oz,' he said. 'This could be a bit tricky. I'm in for a right bollocking here.'

He should have realised this would be meat and drink for a man like Oz.

'All the more reason, then,' said the big Geordie. 'He doesn't know yet about the dent in the wing, right? So it'll impress him if you tell him you've already got the matter in hand.'

Dennis couldn't fathom it. 'How's that going to help?' he asked, clutching at straws.

''Cos me cousin'll take care of it,' said Oz triumphantly. 'We'll whip round to his garage in Scottswood. He'll have it bashed out and resprayed by midnight. Forty quid to you – nae bother!'

The Jag drew up in the yard outside the factory. Dennis checked the scene. Big Baz – Ally's minder – was standing casually just in front of the door. It was going to be like that, was it? He got out, strolled across the concrete, trying to look unconcerned. Behind him, Oz got out and made a great play of examining the damage to the tail light.

'All right?' Dennis greeted Baz as he passed him.

Baz just stood there, impassive as a bloody great violent Buddha, and nodded non-committally. Dennis could see Billy, the factory manager, also watching from the upstairs window. The bloody vultures gathering.

Ally was giving instructions to Pamela, his secretary, when Dennis stuck his head in from the outer office.

'Oh, sorry, Ally,' Dennis said hastily. 'I'll come back if you're busy...'

Ally stared at him dangerously. 'No,' he grated. 'You get yourself in here right now.'

He told Pamela to book him a table at a restaurant for the evening, then dismissed her. She smiled at Dennis as she left, but there was little comfort in it for him, especially when Ally barked: 'Close the door, Pamela. And I'm *not* takin' any calls.'

He wasted no time. Didn't even tell Dennis to sit down.

'So where did you bugger off to then?' he snarled.

'Ally, what happened was –'

But Ally wasn't listening yet. He had a few things to get off his chest.

'When I go off for a well-deserved vacation, I do not expect my *staff* to do the same.'

'Ally, it wasn't like that –' Dennis protested weakly.

'I also do not expect them to have the audacity to take my Jag. Which Billy now informs me has a crumpled left wing.'

'I've already obtained an estimate –'

Ally silenced him with a cold look. 'I thought I'd be away three weeks,' he continued, his voice now ominously calm. 'But I felt comfortable in the knowledge that I had people here I could rely on. Who could hold the fort, Dennis . . .' He was leaning forward, and Dennis could see the veins standing out in his bull-like neck. He spat out the next words slowly, with feeling: 'Who could make my presence felt even though I was in absentia.'

There was silence. Dennis cleared his throat.

'It won't happen again, Ally.'

The Scot smiled grimly. 'That,' he said, 'may be the truest thing you've ever said, pal.'

Dennis couldn't take this any more. It was time to come straight out with it and be damned.

'Look,' he said. 'If I'm here for a canin', fine. Don't milk it. Fact is, I've been to Wolverhampton, and I'll tell you for why. One of the lads I worked with in Germany called us up. He needed some help to fix his house up 'cause he's gettin' married. He called us up. So I went: a) because I wanted to see the lads again, and b) because I thought it would do my soul good to do two weeks' honest graft. Instead of brown-nosing for you because I owe you six grand.'

He'd said his piece. He looked straight at Ally, breathing heavily and with a none-too-pleasant feeling in his stomach. But there was a weight gone from him. Then he realised that Ally looked intrigued rather than angry.

'Did they all show up?' asked Ally in a quite normal voice.

'What?'

'These pals you were in Germany with.'

'Most of them,' Dennis said, nonplussed.

'And are they reliable workers, Dennis?'

'In what they do, yes. Top rank.' Where was this going?

Ally suddenly clapped his hands together, as if putting the stamp on his change of mood.

'Have you eaten today?' he asked Dennis.

'Not really ... no.'

'Nor me,' said Ally. 'I've been chasin' around like a fart in a colander.'

He went to the window, bellowed: 'Baz! Get yourself up here!'

Dennis had moved over to stand behind him. He could see Oz, still over by the car, registering some concern. Baz was heading back into the building.

Ally produced the photograph he had shown to Harbottle.

'Y'see this house,' he drawled. 'It needs a conversion. I need a bunch of reliable cowboys in there. Now, your lads could fit the bill. Right?'

'I'm not sure, Ally. I mean, they've all got their own lives to lead.'

Ally smiled in an almost fatherly way.

'Dennis, Dennis,' he said, wagging a finger at him. 'People don't do other people those kinds of favours. If they could afford two weeks out of their lives to go to Wolverhampton, that means they had sod all else better to do. So ... they sound like the kind of blokes who'd be prepared to do a lot of work, for a bit of money wi'out a lot of form-filling in or VAT. Are you hearin' what I'm sayin'?'

'I think I get your drift, Ally,' Dennis said cagily. 'I can talk to them. They might be amenable.'

'Do it, Dennis,' said Ally. 'I *need* this.'

There was no mistaking that tone of voice. This was an order, not a request.

Right on cue, Baz entered. He stood just inside the door, measuring Dennis and looking expectantly at Ally.

'You wanted me, Mr Fraser?' he grunted.

'Aye, Baz,' Ally said, suddenly all cheery again. 'We're both famished. Will Indian do, Dennis?' he asked.

Dennis was amazed at his boss's ability to switch from brutal menace to hail-fellow-well-met in a space of moments. Still, they said that about psychopaths, didn't they?

'What? Oh, fine, Ally, fine,' he muttered.

Ally turned back to Baz. 'Okay, get us some Tandoori Chicken. And the Lamb Tikka. A couple of onion bhajees. And their special rice for two.'

Before Baz had a chance to answer – or look more than just plain disappointed at not getting a crack at Dennis – there were sounds of commotion from the outer office, Pamela's voice squealing: 'Please, you can't go in there!'

Then the door was flung open and Oz lumbered in, his already battered face contorted in a threatening snarl.

'Who the hell are you?' snapped Ally.

'Never mind who I am. I know who *you* are.'

Dennis moved towards him. 'Oz, man –'

'Hang on, Dennis.' Oz faced Ally. 'I know your reputation, and I don't give a rat's! You lay one finger on me mate and you'll answer to me!'

Baz was moving in automatically to get Oz out of Ally's way. Oz backed off, but only for tactical reasons.

'Oh, aye . . .' he growled, and delivered a fine right hook straight on Baz's chin, followed up by an incredibly efficient knee in the groin. The thug sank to the pure new wool carpet, coughing and choking in agony.

'Oz, for Chrissake!' said Dennis.

Oz looked down at Baz with satisfaction. 'It's all right, Dennis. He won't give you nay bother.'

Dennis sighed. 'He wasn't goin' to, Oz. He was only goin' for Tandoori Chicken.'

'Who is this lunatic?' asked Ally.

'Ally,' Dennis explained desperately. 'it's all a mistake.

Please – this is Oz. He's a mate. In fact, he was one of the lads in Germany with us.'

'Was he now...?' Ally gazed dispassionately at the writhing figure on the carpet. 'Aye, well, not many people chin Big Baz. He could be just the type we're looking for. Make him chargehand!'

Moxey turned over his cards, while the others watched expectantly.

'P-pay eighteens,' he said.

Groans all round. A dark look from Trev, who'd thought he had the bank beat.

Moxey was gathering the cards for the next hand when Barry entered.

'What's this?' said the bridegroom, obviously in a filthy temper, ignoring their cheerful welcomes and enquiries as to where he'd been.

'Never mind where I've been. I'm not payin' you good money to play pontoon.'

Moxey looked at him, hurt. 'If you'd showed up this morning, we'd have known what to do.'

Barry's jaw dropped as he realised that there was no wall between the living room and the kitchen extension. There had been this morning first thing.

'You weren't supposed to knock that wall down,' he raged. 'Supposed to be a hatch, that is!'

'Yeah, Hazel told us that,' Neville said levelly.

'Hazel's been here?' said Barry incredulously.

'Sure. We all met her. She seemed a very charming girl.'

Bomber nodded. 'Very nice indeed. But she was a bit upset about that wall. That's why we downed tools until you got here.'

'Where 'ave you been?' demanded Trev, in a voice that implied Barry had probably been out organising economic sanctions against Nicaragua.

'It's pointless to explain now, Trevor,' Barry muttered. 'Where's Hazel now?'

'Wayne took her home.'

'Wayne?' Barry shrieked. 'Took her home? Why?'

'Because he's got a car,' Neville explain patiently.

Barry's imagination was working overtime. He rounded on his apprentice.

'Why didn't you take her home, Trev?'

'Because she preferred a BMW to the back of my bike.'

'Shall I deal you in?' asked Moxey with his usual unerring sense of tact.

'While Wayne's with Hazel? Alone? I've got to get round there!'

'Don't you want to tell us where to make a start?' Bomber suggested mildly.

Barry's eyes were wild. 'I can't think... I can't think...'

He rushed out of the room. Seconds later, they heard the door slam behind him.

Bomber shrugged. 'Go on then,' he said to Moxey. 'Deal...'

In fact, they would have been amazed at the decorum of the scene at Hazel's little furnished flat. There was Wayne, sitting among the Laura Ashley fabrics and the bijou posters, waiting for her to pour him a nice cup of tea. There was a copy of *Country Diary of an Edwardian Lady* on the bookshelf. And there was a cake that Hazel assured him was absolutely fresh. He believed her.

Hazel sat down, smiled uncomfortably.

'It was so good of you to run me home,' she said. 'And nice of you to come in for tea.' She hesitated. 'I find this ... rather difficult, Wayne, because I don't know you. But I feel as if I do, through Barry. Because you were his closest friend in Germany, weren't you?'

She seemed not to notice Wayne's look of stark astonishment at this news, and continued:

'He said you used to do things together. You used to visit museums on his motorbike.'

'Oh yeah,' Wayne agreed solemnly. 'I miss that.'

'That's why I wanted to talk to you, Wayne. About Barry.'

The cockney went into his support-for-Barry mode: 'Now look, Hazel, I explained to you about last night. It wasn't the lad's fault. It was my idea to go out for a cocktail or two, and then one thing led to another –'

'I'm not talking about the Chinese Restaurant, Wayne. I'm talking about the entire last two years. Our engagement, in fact.'

'You mean he's been going out on the piss a lot – excuse me –' Wayne was puzzled. Barry? A boozer? 'I mean, 'as he had a few from time to time? Doesn't sound like our boy...'

She shook her head. 'No, no. When has he had the chance? The poor lad went to the Falklands. And he did that for *us*. For the house, for our future.'

'I... er... don't see quite what you're drivin' at, Haze.'

'Well... sometimes I have to ask myself if he's ever had a chance to slow down, take stock, and ask himself if this marriage is what he really wants.'

'Oh, I see...'

Wayne eyed her shrewdly, took a sip of tea. He got the picture. The inflation-hit copper coin had definitely dropped.

'Or do you mean *you* haven't had a chance,' he said.

Hazel's unease was all too clear. But she pressed on. After all, she had invited him in for something, and this was it.

'Maybe,' she said slowly. 'With... with all the sacrifices he's made, my emotions are a mixture of guilt and gratitude.'

'Bit late in the day for all this, isn't it, love?' Wayne said gently.

She nodded miserably. 'It's with all you lot arriving and finishing the house. Suddenly everything seems so much more imminent.'

'How can I help?' said Wayne with a slight shrug.

'I thought while you're up here, you might have a word – just the two of you – and discover his real feelings.'

Barry's real feelings? They were no problem, thought Wayne. It's yours, sweetheart. But he just said: 'All right. No bovver.'

'Thank you, Wayne.'

He finished his tea. 'I wouldn't worry too much, Haze. All these pre-marital jitters is par for the course.'

She smiled gratefully. 'All that's behind you, isn't it? Barry showed me a picture of your wife. She's very pretty, isn't she?'

Now Wayne turned evasive. 'Very, yeah,' he said cautiously.

'Why don't you ask her up at the weekend?'

'She's in Germany,' Wayne said quickly.

'Visiting her family?'

'Yeah... well, a bit more than that. She's there sort of indefinitely.'

'Oh...'

'Look,' said Wayne, 'please don't tell Barry or the lads about this.'

'Of course not.'

Wayne took a deep breath. Confession was good for the soul.

'Probably shouldn't be telling you under the circs,' he began. 'But you don't have to worry about your Barry. Sound as a bell, he is. I'm a bit of a flake. Jack the lad. Always have been.' There was real sadness in his eyes. 'That's why she left me. "I'll come back when you've grown up," she said.' He smiled thinly. 'Might take a while, that.'

Then the intercom buzzer went. Hazel got to her feet and looked out of the window. He saw her frown.

'It's Barry.'

Wayne stood and grabbed his jacket. Confession might be altogether positive, but too much could cause more problems than it solved.

'I'd best make a move, then. I'll have a word with Barry later, OK?'

'Would you?' Hazel said. 'You're the one person I feel he'll confide in.'

He disentangled himself quickly, made his way down to the door to let Barry in. The zit king's face was not altogether friendly as Wayne opened the door and they stood briefly opposite each other. Wayne noted that he was carrying a large bunch of flowers.

'Good thinking, son. Now, if I were you I'd go straight up there and...'

'But you're not me, are you?' growled Barry. 'And you're the last person whose advice I'd listen to, thank you very much, Wayne Norris!'

He pushed his way past Wayne into the building, slamming the door behind him.

Wayne shrugged, grinned, made his way to his car, whistling softly. What would life be without its little ironies? What would Swiss cheese be without the holes? Answer: A bloody sight easier to digest...

Dennis and Oz were rattling back towards Wolverhampton in a half-wrecked VW bus that Ally Fraser had dug up from somewhere. There was no MOT, no tax, and the brakes were decidedly dodgy but, as Dennis reasoned, while it might not be in the same class as the Jag no one would get the wrong impression if they saw him at the wheel.

Alongside him Oz shifted his long legs uncomfortably. At a steady 45 mph – and no higher – this trip was taking forever. He'd chucked the last of the cans out of the window hours ago. The VW had more room up front than, say, a Fiat 126 or a Mini but he still felt squashed in like a sardine. Besides, his bladder was bustin'. He wriggled this way and that, grimaced and finally stuck up his feet on the bench seat beside Dennis.

'What do you think of these, Dennis?' he asked, pointing at his boots.

Dennis glanced down. 'Very nice,' he said. He didn't dare say what he really thought. He'd never seen anything like them outside of the local Odeon. Enormous cowboy boots, heavily ornamented, looking as though their proud owner hadn't taken them off from the moment he'd bought them.

'Amarillo, Texas,' intoned Oz. The significance was lost on Dennis, but it meant everything in the world to Oz. 'That's why I missed the plane back from Miami,' he explained. 'I wanted to buy some genuine Western boots.'

'You didn't have to go all the way to Texas,' said Dennis. They had boots like that at the shopping centre.

'I didn't know how far it was,' said Oz, dreamily. 'Bloody huge, America. You can't imagine how long it took on a Greyhound bus from Texas to Memphis.'

Steel guitars whined through his imagination.

'Oh, you've been there an' all,' asked Dennis, wishing he could kill the conversation. The deal with Ally Fraser was taking up most of his thinking time, without the intervention of Oz's born-again romanticism.

'Aw, once I was down in that direction, it seemed pointless not to. Had to see Graceland, didn't I? Pay homage to Elvis. Very emotional experience, it was. Standing by the grave of the King.'

'You've certainly lived, Oz,' said Dennis, on automatic pilot. Music for him began with the Animals and ended with Bryan Ferry, but there was no accounting for taste. 'And here's me been stuck in the North-East for the last three years, grafting away for a penny...'

'That wasn't the high point,' said Oz. Whatever next? thought Dennis. Oz was rummaging through a wad of papers he'd dredged up from his jacket.

'I went to Nashville next...' Oz declared, and held up a well-thumbed snapshot for Dennis's inspection.

Dennis flicked it a glance.

'I was in the bar and *he* came in,' breathed Oz.

'Whoever he is,' said Dennis sardonically, 'he's out of focus.' All he could see was a couple of drunks with red eyes.

'That's because of the idiot who took the photo. But that's Merle Haggard with his arm around me.'

'It could be Merle Oberon for all I can tell,' growled Dennis evenly.

'But it's him.' Oz looked thrilled to bits, as he cradled his holy relic in his enormous palm. 'Merle and Oz – live in Nashville.'

Dennis half-expected him to kiss the picture, like some love-sick schoolkid with a photograph of his sweetheart.

Barry stood in the middle of what was going to be the living room, with a big ground plan spread out on the trestles. Like a general. Napoleon was having another crack. No Waterloo for our Barry, after all. Moxey was hard at work plastering, while Bomber and Neville, the two brickies, stood by Barry's side, poring over the plan.

'Now,' said Bomber patiently, 'before we put that wall back, are you quite sure it's what you and your intended really want?'

'Yes,' Barry said firmly, back in his element. 'We resolved everything last night.'

'Including the hatch?' said Moxey over his shoulder.

Barry grimaced. 'Yes!'

Neville stared at the drawing, frowned. 'I think a breakfast counter's nice meself. That's what we've got at home.'

'I don't want any more debate about it,' Barry said imperiously. 'Just put the bricks up, then Wayne can put the hatch in.'

Wayne wandered down from upstairs, smelling the tea Trev had just brought in.

'Oho,' he interrupted. 'You're not still set on an 'atch, are you? Why don't you just 'ave one of those nice arches. Otherwise every time you want another bowl of sprouts, you'll 'ave to walk all the way round.'

Barry was getting to the end of his tether. The façade of the strategist was dropping, and Wayne was hardly his favourite person at the moment, in any case.

'Will you shut up, Wayne?' he snapped. 'Who's going to be livin' here? Hazel and I have agreed. So everyone *please* just stick to what's stipulated.'

And so they all finally got to work, with a bit of muttering but no proper mutiny. It lasted about thirty seconds before Neville said matter-of-factly:

'I'd still advise against those dimmers. I put 'em in for Brenda and I've had nothin' but trouble with them.'

Barry tensed. 'Hazel's set her heart on dimmers.'

'Suit yourself. It's just they're unreliable and dangerous . . .'

At that moment, Dennis walked in through the open door. There was a chorus of cheers, boos and other greetings.

'Didn't expect you back so soon, Den,' said Barry gratefully.

Neville was more surprised and less complimentary. 'I didn't expect you back at all!'

'Aye. I had a bit of business to take care of.' Dennis paused. 'But I came back 'cause I have a proposition that might interest some of you.'

He absorbed the ripple of interest that went through the ranks, grinned.

'Well,' he said. 'There's some good news and bad news attached to this. Which d'you want first?'

Neville's face fell. He was one of nature's pessimists, was Nev. 'Aw, let's have the bad news.'

'Okay, then,' said Dennis with a grave nod. He turned, shouted through the open door: 'Come in, Oz!'

Oz steamed in, cowboy boots and all, did a lumbering dance to yells of astonishment and delight from the lads and yells of: 'Oz!'

'Why, aye, man,' he said simply, his pudding face split by a vast, joyful leer.

Then they got down to business. Dennis had brought a big envelope containing photographs of the house 'this bloke' wanted done up. He spread them out on a packing case, and the lads gathered round.

'He wants a quick conversion,' Dennis explained. 'So's he can flog it over the odds and make a tasty profit.'

Moxey nodded. 'The unacceptable face of capitalism.'

Oz nodded too. 'Aye, that's right. Top whack for us, though.'

'I've seen the specs,' Dennis said. 'And I reckon there'll be at least a month's work. I'm in charge, so there'll be no gaffers.'

Neville looked at him thoughtfully. '"This bloke" you're talking about. He wouldn't happen to be Ally Fraser, would he?'

'Yes, Neville, yes,' said Dennis irritably.

'Who's Ally Fraser?' Wayne asked.

'Local villain,' said Neville.

Dennis glared at him.

'His money's as good as anyone else's, Neville,' he growled. 'Or are you flooded with offers at the moment?'

'I'm game!' said Bomber. 'Life saver Bomber. Bloody sight better than being bounced about the ring and having old ladies stubbing out fag ends on your arse.'

'What about you, Mox?' asked Dennis.

'I fancy it. I'm f-fairly free at the moment.'

'Wayne?'

'Can't see it appealing to him,' chipped in Bomber. 'Not with a BMW and that scrumptious little wife back home.'

Wayne was looking just a shade shifty. He pursed his lips.

53

'Yeah, I know all that, but . . . on the other 'and it might be a giggle. If it's just a month.'

'I suppose if it's just a month . . .' Neville said reluctantly.

Dennis looked relieved. 'You're all in, then.'

'If I didn't have any impending nuptials,' said Barry, 'I'd be tempted to join you. For old times' sake, like.'

'We'll miss your sparklin' repartee, Barry. The Prince of Trivia.'

'When do we start, Den?' asked Bomber.

'Monday!'

Barry stopped looking patronising and started to panic. He could represent the country at the Olympics in panicking, could Barry.

'Monday! That only gives you three days to finish my house.'

There was silence. The lads looked at each other. Bomber was the first one to speak.

'Better get crackin', then,' he said softly.

And that was what they did.

Ally had said he wanted a bunch of cowboys for his job. Well, that was what he was going to get. But Barry got quality work that weekend, and he got it fast. The lads worked out of pride, out of loyalty, and even out of a kind of unspoken love. They worked all day, and when the daylight went they worked by artificial light. There was the odd cock-up, but by and large it all went like clockwork. Seven skilled men working like a team. Something Ally would never get out of them.

It was early on the Monday morning that Hazel walked up towards the front door past piles of rubble. She went to knock, then noticed the brand new doorbell. She rang it, heard the chimes sound in the hallway.

And there was Barry opening the door.

'Come in, Haze,' he said, flushed with pride.

She stepped over the threshold and he planted a big kiss on her lips, then led her through the hallway. The wallpaper was new, and the paint smelled fresh.

'Don't touch the paintwork. It's not quite dry,' Barry said excitedly.

She was obviously overwhelmed by the fantastic amount that had been achieved in such a short time. There were little moist bits in the corners of her eyes, bless her.

'It's all done,' he said. 'The rewiring... the dimmers... paintwork. Built-in bookshelf. Music centre'll go there. Papering. Everything's ready for the carpets, and they'll be in Tuesday.'

Hazel stood in the middle of it all, shaking her head, taking it all in. Deeply moved, he could see.

'I'd never thought we'd do it,' Barry burbled on. 'And I'll tell you something, Haze...'

He crossed to the mantelpiece, where in the place of honour stood the photo of the lads that he had taken that last day in Düsseldorf.

'... Only these lads could have done it,' he said. 'Oh, I know you've laughed at me in the past when I've gone on about the special bonds that are forged between comrades in adversity. But the proof's in the pudding, isn't it?' The look on his face was intense, emotional. 'They each left their homes and families and did this for me. For *us*! We won't be lookin' for any wedding presents from those boys. Don't need any fish knives and forks from any of them. They've already given more than we could ever have asked...'

He beamed at Hazel, waited for the words of approval and gratitude. But she just stood there in the middle of the floor, started to shake, and burst into tears.

Within an instant, Barry was at her side, holding her. 'I know, love,' he said, completely misunderstanding her tears. 'I feel a bit emotional meself.'

FIVE

It hadn't been easy rousing the lads early that Monday morning. After all, the house had had to be christened in the Bell and Dragon, and there'd been the farewell rounds for Barry. Dennis managed to galvanise them onto the road an hour later than planned, amid rumblings from Oz to the effect that they might have worked like Taiwanese telly-assemblers for Barry, but Dennis needn't think they were going to do the same for that bloody villain Fraser.

Not far out of Wolverhampton, Wayne's BMW overtook Dennis's van with a blare of its horn and cheery waves from the driver, Bomber and Moxey.

'Oh, aye, what else did you get for Christmas?' muttered Dennis.

He was hung over, and he had a job to do. There'd been three days of a kind of euphoria, when he'd managed to forget everything, but now he was back into reality with an almighty bang, headed towards Derbyshire and back into the clutches of Ally.

In the BMW, things were pro tem a bit more relaxed. Wayne was explaining about his toy to Bomber, who sat beside him in the passenger seat while Moxey sat alone behind.

'I bought this car in Germany. After I did me stint in the Arctic. I went down to Düsseldorf to pick up the wife – 'cause she'd been staying with her folks – and then we drove back to England. I tell you,' he said, obviously thrilled just at the memory of it, 'on those autobahns I could be doing a hundred and thirty and I didn't even know I was moving...'

Bomber nodded. 'Well, I'd ease up now, 'cause there's a police car on your tail.'

'Oh, bloody 'ell,' mouthed Wayne, pulling the car over to the middle lane and moderating his speed.

Neither Bomber nor Wayne noticed it, but Moxey's reaction was interesting. At the mention of the word 'police car', he went down in the back seat like a soldier taking cover during an artillery barrage.

The cop car flashed past, obviously intent on pursuing some other poor bastard. Wayne sighed with relief.

'Lucky bugger you are, Wayne. They must have other fish to fry.'

Moxey re-surfaced, looking even more relieved than Wayne, though still keeping his eyes peeled to the road.

A while later, they all pulled into the café where they had agreed to meet for a late breakfast. Dennis and co. arrived a few minutes later, and they rendezvous'd in the cafeteria section.

Over sandwiches and tea, they continued the conversations they had started that morning.

'We was just talking on the way up about Barry... or at least about Hazel's postponing the wedding,' said Neville. The news had filtered through just before they'd left, too late for anything but a quick, communal 'sorry'.

Wayne paused, his ham sandwich halfway to his mouth.

'I know a bit about that, as it 'appens,' he said.

He certainly had their undivided attention. Five pairs of eyes staring at him, some of them a little on the suspicious side.

'How would you know?' asked Dennis slowly.

Wayne shrugged, embarrassed. 'When I gave Hazel a lift back to her flat, she asked me in, and before Barry showed up she'd sort of told me the 'ole situation.'

'What?' bellowed Oz, causing a few heads to turn. 'You mean, poor bloody Barry went round and found you two ensconced! Nay wonder the bloody wedding's off!'

'Bollocks, Oz,' said Wayne in an aggrieved voice. 'I'm not goin' to jump a mate's bird. Not at three o'clock in the afternoon.'

Oz stared at him coldly. 'Good job for him it wasn't three-thirty.'

'She just wanted to confide in someone,' Wayne continued, refusing to be put off his stride. 'She seemed to think I was his best mate or somethin'.'

'So what did she say?' asked Neville.

'Needed time to think. Was it for the right reasons? Re-evaluate their relationship, blah-di-blah. The point is, she was 'aving cold feet.'

Oz scoffed. 'If he knows that, he must have had his leg over.'

Wayne ignored the laughter. 'End of story,' he said. 'Should never have mentioned it, should I?'

Bomber made a face. 'Funny, though,' he mused. 'Whenever us lot are together, it spells trouble for somebody...'

'What're we doin' back together again, then?' asked Neville.

Oz had his own answer to that.

''Cause we're misfits, man. We're drifters on the highway of life, as Merle would have put it.'

'I don't see it that way meself,' chipped in Moxey with rare passion. 'We're drifters, yeah. But that's because we're free spirits. We're rebelling against the s-system that wants to grind us down. And I think comradeship has a lot to do with it. Counts for me, anyway. That's why I came. Not just to help out Barry, but to see you lot. Even you, Oz.'

'Oh ta, mate, aye.'

All of a sudden, Moxey looked embarrassed. 'Gonna get me a doughnut.'

He shuffled off to the counter. Dennis and the others watched him go.

'Strange lad, that,' said Dennis.

Neville nodded. 'D'you know, in all the time I've known him, that's the longest speech I've ever heard him make?'

'Well, if he was that keen to see us lot, his life must be bloody desperate!' said Oz.

'He's right about one thing, though,' said Bomber. 'The system *has* ground us down. We're hardly "upwardly mobile", are we? In spite of Wayne's flash motor...'

There were some uncomfortable looks around the table.

'We're all right,' Wayne answered defiantly.

Neville nodded. 'Better off than most these days.'

'Like Moxey said,' Wayne continued, 'we're free spirits. Embarkin' on another great adventure. We are the Magnificent Seven, and Dennis is Yul Brynner.'

'Don't be daft. We're not off to repel maraudin' Mexicans. We're only goin' back to layin' bricks for a month.'

Oz sipped his tea reflectively. 'Aye, but Derbyshire might as well be Mexico. It's in the middle of bloody nowhere.'

Wayne grinned enthusiastically: 'I'll be Horst Bucholtz. 'Cause he was the youngest and the best-lookin'.'

'He was also the most boring. He was always taggin' along and the other six kept telling him to piss off.'

'Barry should really be Yul Brynner. 'Cause it was him that brought us together,' Neville suggested.

That didn't go down too well.

'Can't see that somehow,' said Bomber. 'He's not a natural leader, Barry.'

Dennis smiled. 'He is going thin on top, mind.'

'James Coburn, me,' Oz said. 'Cool and laconic.'

He picked a plastic knife off the table and slipped it into his boot, turning his eyes into Coburn-like slits.

'Oh well, as the position's vacant, I'll be Steve McQueen,' said Neville.

'Oh, I forgot about 'im!' Wayne complained.

'No, no. You chose the Kraut, and you're stuck with him,' Oz insisted.

'Who does that leave me?'

'Charles Bronson, I should think, Bomb.'

'No, no,' said Dennis, who was starting to get into this. 'There was this big bloke was one of 'em. And no one can ever remember his name.'

'Aye. Den's right. I can see his face,' agreed Oz.

Bomber nodded placidly. 'Just let me know my name if you ever remember it.'

'So that leaves Bronson and Robert Vaughan for Barry and Mox.'

Moxey was on his way back, chomping on a doughnut, as yet blissfully unaware that he was being cast in a role by his peers. The others watched his approach.

'Robert Vaughan was the one who'd lost his bottle but redeemed himself by the finish,' Wayne said.

'And Bronson was enigmatic. Deadly but enigmatic,' added Oz.

Moxey arrived back at the table. Dennis looked around the rest of the group.

'Agreed, then? Bronson?'

There was a chorus of agreement.

Wayne looked at Moxey.

'You're Charles Bronson, Mox.'

'Eh? Why?'

Oz chuckled. ''Cause nay bugger can fathom you oot, man.'

So they were cast – to their own satisfaction. Let's face it, it was better than disturbing thoughts about being hard-pressed refugees from the recession, wasn't it? And it also obscured the uncomfortable fact that the man who had bought their services had no intention of saving anyone from anything – except for himself and, provided there was money in it, the deeply villainous Kenny Ames.

Ally Fraser's Jag crunched over the gravel of the drive and pulled up outside Thornely Manor. He had driven down that morning from Newcastle with Harbottle, to look the place over before Dennis and his 'cowboys' arrived.

Ally and his pet solicitor got out and stretched their legs.

'Photographs don't do this place justice,' said Ally, taking a few steps back to get a better view of the imposingly grotesque Victorian façade of the house. 'It's even bigger than I imagined.'

Harbottle made a face. 'I've always thought that Victorian architecture was an expression of their confidence rather than their taste.'

Ally set out to stroll around the house, towing his companion in his wake.

'You know, Malcolm,' he mused, 'a hundred years ago there'd have been only one family livin' here. Probably a coal owner. Picture it! There's about a hundred wretches slavin' away underground a hundred hours a week for a bowl of drippin', while he's up here suppin' claret an' playin' billiards after dinner.' He sighed with the nostalgia of it. 'Those were the days, eh?'

'In point of fact, I think most of the industry round here was steel.'

'Aye, well, times change,' chuckled Ally. 'Most of Kenny Ames's money came from pornography.'

Harbottle nodded, coughing shyly.

'Did he ever actually live in the house?'

'I think he spent a few weekends here. Before the Fraud Squad caused his hasty departure to Malaga.'

There was a brief silence.

'The Fraud Squad is my main concern, Ally,' Harbottle said tentatively. 'Any transaction involving his property is going to turn straight up on their computer.'

Ally shrugged. 'So?' he snapped. 'They can't freeze his assets. Thanks to our great British judicial system, a man is innocent until proven guilty. And Kenny Ames will be innocent until the day he dies. Providing he dies in Spain.'

They had seen enough for Ally. The place was bloody ugly, but it would do very nicely. The countryside was wonderful, and it would divide up well. They began to walk back towards the Jag.

'It draws attention to *you*, though,' Harbottle suggested mildly. 'And they're not going to fail to notice that the sale price is way below the market value. That's fraud, Ally. You're avoiding CGT. To say nothing of stamp duty.'

'My survey report will show that this house is a wreck,' Ally said airily. He ticked off the problems on his fingers: 'It's riddled with rising damp, dry rot, woodworm and probably death watch beetle.' He grinned. 'He's lucky I'm takin' it off his hands.'

They got back into the car. They were due at the Cross Keys, a posh local hostelry, for lunch with Ames's solicitor, so there was no time to muck about.

Harbottle tried one last protest, though he must have known the answer he would get.

'You haven't had a survey. I haven't even had time to conduct the normal searches.'

Ally slid the big car into gear.

'My survey will show what I want it to show, pal. I guarantee it.'

'Oh yes,' said Wayne. 'This reminds me very much of my gaff in Tilbury.' He was staring up at Thornely Manor, surveying it cockily. 'We don't have quite so much garden, o' course. On the other 'and, they don't have the pong from the lino factory.'

Moxey was by his side. 'I l-lived in a place like this once.'

'Bollocks,' said Oz.

'I did. It was a borstal near P-Prestatyn.'

He and Oz wandered off to take a look around. Dennis stood with Neville.

'What's Ally planning to do with it, Dennis?' the younger man asked.

'Time-sharing units, they call 'em.'

'All self-contained, like?'

'Aye. So we'll be puttin' in a lot of bathrooms and kitchenettes.'

Neville nodded thoughtfully. 'Lot of work.'

'Aye. There'll be a cake of readies for overtime, 'cause he wants it done fast. So I wouldn't reckon on gettin' home to Brenda too often.'

'Fine by me.'

Dennis looked at him askance, surprised by his sudden vehemence.

'Don't tell me you're heading for the broken homes club,' he said.

'Course not,' muttered Neville, recovering quickly. 'Just be glad to get me head down and get some solid work in.'

Bomber had just checked the front door and found it locked.

'What's the drill then, Den?' he asked. 'Are we supposed to wait around till he shows up, 'cause Bomber could murder a pint.'

'We passed a nice little pub in the village,' Wayne said.

'You lads go,' said Dennis. 'I'd better hang on.'

Neville paused. 'Where's Oz and Mox?'

'Waterin' the geraniums, I should imagine.'

62

But if Dennis and the others couldn't see what Oz and Moxey were up to, someone else could. Helen Bellamy had been walking her dog by the entrance to the drive of Thornely Manor when the Volkswagen and the BMW had swept in, and she had come a little closer. She was smartly dressed in country clothes, a pleasant woman who was nevertheless vigilant by nature. The old house had been empty for a while, she knew, and these days one had to mind one's neighbours' business. She saw Oz produce what was (though she didn't know it) a Forte's knife from his genuine Western boot, apply it to the window lock, and after some fiddling get the window open. As he clambered in, followed by Moxey, she decided it really was time to inform Sergeant Oakes down in the village. After all, these men did look a bit rough...

Wayne's voice echoed around the grounds: 'C'mon, Oz, Mox. We're goin' down the boozer!'

They waited. Neville said: 'Hey, Den. Listen...'

There were heavy footsteps within.

Neville looked at Dennis. 'I thought the house was empty.'

'It is...' Dennis whispered. 'Apart from the monster. I didn't mention him in case it scared you off the job.'

The echoing footsteps stopped. There was the sound of a heavy bolt being drawn back. The door opened. They half-expected to see Lon Chaney, but instead there was the leering face of Oz. Not that there was much difference. Except that Lon Chaney might have done the accent better.

'What are you peasants doin' on my property?' said Oz in a mock-aristocratic drawl. 'There's a notice out there that clearly states: "All members of the working class will be exterminated!"'

Since there were still no instructions from Ally – they didn't know he was at the Cross Keys, closing the deal and trying to get his hands on the manor's keys – they went in search of a pub. Dennis, feeling his responsibilities, stayed behind at the house.

They passed the Cross Keys first, rejected it because it looked too posh – all G and Ts and sheepskin coats – and eventually Wayne parked the BMW outside a quite quaint but reasonably shop-soiled-looking little pub further down

63

the road. It had a sign outside saying: 'Barley Mow Inn. Accommodation.' Just the ticket.

Inside it was olde worlde, though there was also a video machine and a juke box that didn't do much for the atmosphere of the place. The public bar looked neglected. It was also pretty empty. All the action seemed to be next door, where there were representatives of the lower echelons of the G and T and fancy coat set quaffing their poison. The landlord, a moustachioed ex-RAF type, clearly preferred the lounge crowd to the ruffians he got in the public. He was surly and short with the lads over their pints and pies.

'Hey!' boomed Oz to the landlord from his position by the juke box. 'How often d'you change these records?'

The landlord scowled at him. 'Nothing to do with me,' he said coldly. 'That's up to the brewery.'

Oz snorted. 'The bloke from the brewery must love Duran Duran. There's no decent music here at all.'

'Same again, is it?' said Wayne, getting up from the table where the rest of the lads were seated.

Bomber shook his head.

'No. I promised Den I'd get you all back. Just a pint and a pie, I said.'

They got ready to leave. Moxey exited to the Gents with a loud comment about 'pointin' Percy at the porcelain'.

The landlord stood and stared at them. They were not his kind of customer, that was for sure.

Spotting him standing there, Wayne sauntered over to see if they could get anything to take back for Dennis.

'Got any of those pies left, squire?' Wayne asked cheerfully.

'No. You had the last,' said the landlord, making no attempt to hide his dislike and contempt.

'Oh. Any Scotch eggs?'

'No.'

'Well, anything hot?'

'Not after two.'

Bomber intervened. 'Look,' he said patiently, 'we got this mate and he's not eaten. So what can you offer?'

'Crisps. Or that sandwich,' snarled mine host in a voice that made it clear they were about as welcome as the Pope at an Orange Lodge meeting.

64

The item of food in question was cowering in the corner of a plastic case, all alone, like a trapped animal. A dead trapped animal at that.

Bomber sighed. 'We'll have that, then.'

'We won't be comin' back here,' said Oz.

Neville frowned. 'Beer's all right. A canny drop.'

'I'm talkin' about mine host. The Wing Commander here.'

The landlord had heard him all right. He stared hard at Oz.

'Are you referring to me?' he asked.

Oz was completely unabashed. He pointed at the air force mementoes behind the bar, the photos of planes.

'You're obviously ex-RAF, aren't you? Judging by them plaques. When did they pension you off?'

'I resigned six years ago.'

Oz scoffed, looked to the others for support. 'Oh well, that was a pretty easy stretch, wasn't it?'

Neville cringed. 'Oz...'

The landlord's eyes narrowed. 'What do you mean, easy?'

'I mean, between Suez and the Falklands there wasn't much action, was there?' Oz said pointedly. 'About as much as we lot'll find around here!'

The landlord slammed the stale sandwich and a bag of crisps on the counter.

'I trust you'll go looking for it somewhere else?' he hissed.

And so ended their first encounter with the landlord of the Barley Mow Inn. But contrary to Oz's expectation – and his efforts – it was not to be their last.

For a further treat, as the BMW swung back into the drive, they spotted a police car parked outside the front of the house.

Dennis was talking to a comfortable-looking rural cop.

'Hullo, I see we've got the law here,' said Wayne.

Then came a plaintive voice from the rear.

'S-stop the car, Wayne,' wailed Moxey.

'What?'

'Stop. I gotta get out!'

Wayne braked. There were some jokey comments such as 'you've only just been!', but Moxey wasn't answering a call of nature. As soon as the car stopped, he was heading through the trees and across the grounds like a whippet.

A little later, the BMW pulled up alongside the police car and the remaining lads got out.

'Hello lads,' Dennis greeting them casually. 'Did you get us a bite?'

'Oh here,' said Bomber, handing him the notorious sandwich and some crisps.

'Oh, you shouldn't have gone to so much bother,' Dennis commented drily.

The policeman, a sergeant, smiled pleasantly. 'These your lads then, Mr Patterson?'

'Aye. This is Neville, Wayne, Oz, Bomber – where's Moxey?'

Neville looked embarrassed. 'In a minute, Den,' he murmured.

'No, but where is he?' asked Dennis, not catching on.

'He's joggin', Dennis,' said Wayne quickly. 'You know what a fitness fanatic he is.'

Dennis made to speak, but Oz got in first with his usual tact. 'What've we done wrong, sergeant?' he blustered. 'We've only been in the locality ten minutes.'

The policeman smiled easily.

'Just a misunderstanding, lads. I'm off for my lunch. Mebbe see you for a jar one night.'

'Aye. Cheers,' said Dennis.

They watched him drive away. Then Dennis turned to Neville.

'What's goin' on? Where is he?' he demanded.

'We don't know,' said Neville. 'As soon as Moxey saw the law he took off like a rat up a drainpipe.'

Wayne shrugged.

'Conditioned reflex. He's had a bit of a chequered past, has Mox.'

'Bit odd, though,' said Bomber.

'Not the way Charles Bronson would've performed,' Oz said thoughtfully. 'Maybe we should have given him Robert Vaughan.'

He held up one hand, squinted at it, doing a fair imitation of a man with the shakes.

There wasn't any more time for idle chat. The famous Jag –

last driven by Dennis in Wolverhampton – was coming up the drive. The lads watched curiously as it stopped and Dennis went respectfully over to meet it.

Ally Fraser got out, accompanied by Harbottle. The Scotsman carried some rolled-up architect's plans.

'How're you doin', Dennis?'

'Okay, thanks.'

Ally made a vague gesture in the direction of the solicitor. 'D'you know Malcolm Harbottle? Malcolm, Dennis. He'll be in charge of the conversion.'

'You've got your work cut out,' muttered Harbottle.

Dennis prickled slightly. 'Aye well, I've got the right lads for it.'

Ally looked them over, grinned.

'They look more like a bunch of mercenaries.'

Then, sweeping past the lads, he and Harbottle went into the house with Dennis. They looked around for a few minutes. It was dusty and it was damp, but mostly intact.

'How long d'you reckon, Dennis?' asked Ally as they descended the main staircase after their brief tour of inspection.

'Gimme a chance, Ally. I've only just seen the plans. I'll need a word with the architect, won't I?'

'These were drawn up for the previous owner,' said Ally, tapping the plans, then brushing some dust from his expensive overcoat. 'As for my man, he'll be down tonight. It's Howard Radcliff. D'you know him?'

'Can't say I do. I've been out of the business for a while.'

'It'll all come back to you,' Ally said. 'Now, how long?'

Dennis sighed.

'I don't know yet, Ally. That depends on whether you want everything done to first-class specifications or you're doin' a Mickey-Mouse job where we paint over the cracks for a quick profit.'

'There's nothing' wrong wi' the word profit, pal,' Ally said, his eyes narrowing. 'You come over to the Cross Keys about ten o'clock tonight. It'll save time in the morning.'

'Aye,' said Dennis, refusing to be intimidated. This was his job, and he was going to make sure Ally knew it. 'But don't think you'll be rushin' off tomorrow, Ally. Me an' you have to go into town and open a bank account. I've got to be made signatory for cheques so's I can get credit with the trade.'

Ally frowned. 'Christ, by the time I get back to Spain, I'll have lost this tan. And probably my young lady to some randy Spanish waiter.'

It was dark when the Volkswagen van pulled into the car park of the Barley Mow Inn, and it was getting cold. Which made Dennis all the more surprised when Oz said hastily: 'I don't reckon this place is a good idea.'

'Oz, we've scoured the whole district,' Dennis said wearily.

'That Mrs Armitage seemed nice enough,' Neville commented.

There were groans from the rest of the lads.

'Oh yeah,' said Wayne. 'Wipe your feet every time you come in, and please have the light out by ten.'

'Of course, we can stay at the Cross Keys wi' Ally at fifty pound a night,' Dennis suggested.

'If we don't find somewhere soon, we'll be kippin' down in the house,' Neville said miserably.

Wayne shivered. 'I don't fancy that.'

'Look,' said Dennis, 'it's just for a couple of nights. Till we find something permanent. And some of us,' he added sourly, 'are starving, 'cause some of us didn't have any lunch.'

'All right. Suit yourselves,' Oz said.

'Right. Let's go.'

Dennis made to get out of the car, but no one moved. There was silence until Wayne said quietly:

'No... you're best at this kind of thing, Den. You handle it.'

Dennis shrugged, slid open the door and got out, then looked back at the others suspiciously.

'Do you lads know something I don't?'

There were sweet denials all round, but the lads stayed put.

Dennis wandered in through the door of the public bar. It was nigh-on deserted. Just a couple of locals in the corner. The landlord – Pringle from the name over the door – was putting out some beermats on the bar when Dennis entered.

'Evenin',' said Dennis. 'Do you have some accommodation free?'

'Yes,' said Pringle simply.

'Could you manage three doubles?'

'How many nights?'

'At least a couple.'

'I think we could do that.'

'Champion,' said Dennis. What could all the fuss have been about?

He went over to the door, gave a thumbs-up sign to the waiting lads.

'It's eighteen pounds a night, and we don't take credit cards,' said Pringle when Dennis turned back.

'That's okay,' Dennis nodded. 'We prefer cash. Let's have five pints for starters.'

Pringle set to work pulling pints as the first of the lads trooped in. It was Oz, carrying his grubby overnight bag. He grinned broadly as he saw the expression of dawning horror and loathing on the landlord's face.

'Hello again!' chortled Oz.

And Arthur Pringle, licensed victualler, knew he was in for the battle of his life.

SIX

The spectral silence of the kitchen at Thornely Manor was shaken by the turning of a big key in an old lock. The back door opened and the lads, wearing work clothes, shuffled in, shivering and coughing in the early morning cold.

'God,' said Oz. 'It's like a morgue in here. Colder in than out.'

They looked around the huge, old-fashioned kitchen, with its ancient range, stone floor and dusty shelves and surfaces. It didn't bode well.

'Well, this is probably where we'll make a start,' said Dennis briskly. 'Whatever the architect decides, the guts have got to come out of this room.' He pointed to their left. 'There's a wall goin' in there, and a whole new kitchen to be fitted.'

The lads looked none too enthusiastic.

'I'm goin' into town to meet Ally, so make a start, eh?'

Oz nodded. 'Absolutely.'

Dennis looked at his watch and hurried out.

Oz promptly dug into his bag and brought out an electric kettle, a packet of tea bags and a pint of milk.

'There we are ...'

'Have we got any juice, Nev?' asked Wayne.

Neville tried it, and to their relief a bare light bulb flickered on at the touch of a switch.

Bomber, meanwhile, turned on a tap. Some nasty, rusty looking water coughed its way out into the basin.

Then, without warning, an adjoining door opened. And out of the pantry came the pathetic, frozen-looking figure of Moxey.

'H-hello, lads,' he quavered.

70

'Where the hell have you been?' asked Neville.

Moxey moved forward into the kitchen. 'I dossed down here last night.'

'You look bloody frozen, lad,' said Bomber, stripping off his donkey jacket and wrapping it around Moxey's shoulders.

Wayne eyed Moxey with rather less sympathy. 'What's the word, then?' he said after a moment. 'I think you owe us an explanation.'

Moxey hesitated, then smiled miserably.

'Well ... I've been to prison,' he confessed.

'We know that, man,' said Oz. 'But that was ages ago. Doesn't mean you 'ave to panic every time you see a policeman.'

Moxey shook his head. 'No. I mean, I've been in recently. Like last week. And I'm not due out until next March.'

Now they knew the trouble. There were some very sidelong looks.

'You've gone over the wall?' said Neville dramatically.

'It wasn't a closed nick,' Moxey pleaded. 'I was in an open prison in Cheshire. It's not as if I had to dig a tunnel or rent a helicopter. I just walked out the front door, bought a Toblerone at the post office, then got a bus to Macclesfield.'

'Why?'

'Got a mate there. He gave me a float, then I made me way to Barry's.'

'You must be mad, Mox,' said Neville.

Wayne nodded. 'Yeah, what a lunatic thing to do.'

'Well, if you was in an open prison, you must have been dealt with fairly leniently,' Bomber suggested.

'I was. I'm not a Grade A villain. Just got done for the old trouble.'

'Arson?'

'Yeah. See, with me they know that it's a psychological defect, not a criminal tendency.'

'They also don't want Walton Jail burnt down,' said Oz none too helpfully.

'But blimey, Mox. If you was in an open prison, you must have 'ad it pretty cushy.'

71

Moxey looked at him with an edge of resentment, as if to ask: who are you to tell me that?

'It's still stir, Wayne,' he said slowly. 'It's still people telling you what to do and when to do it. And I had a year of it still ahead of me.'

'You'll have a bloody sight more when they nick you,' Wayne murmured.

Bomber, the father-figure, nodded sagely.

'Wayne's right,' he sighed. 'If you give yourself up, you'll be canned for your little walkabout. But if you don't, and they collar you, you'll be lookin' at two years.'

'I'll take my chances,' Moxey growled defiantly.

The lads looked at each other. What could they say? There was no answer to that.

'All right then,' said Bomber, speaking for all of them.

'Fair enough. Say no more,' shrugged Wayne.

'We'll look after you, Mox,' Oz said.

Moxey looked around gratefully, then shivered. His skin was ice-blue with the cold. 'I'm bloody frozen.'

'Why don't we light a fire?' suggested Neville.

For the first time, Moxey looked enthusiastic about something. 'Yeah ... that's a good idea ...'

There was a slightly uncomfortable pause.

'Er ... not you, Mox,' said Wayne eventually. 'I'll take care of it ...'

The Jag was parked a short distance from the bank in the nearby market town. Dennis and Ally had been in there at opening time to go through the formalities of opening an account for the Thornely Manor work. From now on Dennis would have day-to-day control of the finances and they could really get stuck in. Sort of. From Dennis's not-so-cosy after-dinner chat with Ally and the architect at the Cross Keys the previous night, it was clear this was going to be the El Cheapo job to end all El Cheapos. God help the poor sods who had to live in the ruddy place after Ally's 'conversion'.

'Right,' said Ally as they made their way back towards the car. 'Now you won't need to bother me in Spain. Howard will be stayin' down, basically operating from the Cross Keys.

You'll control the purse strings, Dennis.' He paused meaningfully. 'You know the budget we're workin' on.'

'I know it's not enough,' said Dennis.

Ally shot him one of his sidelong glances.

'You'll manage.'

Dennis shrugged. He hadn't met Howard Radcliff before, but he knew the type of architect: youngish, pushy, none too scrupulous. Out to make a fast buck and get his practice growing at all costs. He'd be keeping an eye on the 'purse strings' on Ally's behalf, too, you could bet your life. And on the lads' work rate. Jesus, what it was to be in the pocket of a bastard like Ally ...

It felt sometimes like Ally could read a man's thoughts, and this was one of those moments. When they got to the car, he turned and smiled at Dennis. It was not his nice, charming smile.

'Oh, and another thing, Dennis,' he said very quietly. 'I know those lads are your mates. But you're the gaffer now. You're on my side, not theirs.' Seeing Dennis's non-committal look, the smile became a little warmer. 'Pull this off, and there'll be a nice wee bonus for you.'

'How much are we talking about?' Dennis asked baldly. After all, why pretend that wasn't the name of the game?

Ally shrugged. 'We're talkin' about forgettin' what you owe me.'

Then he unlocked the door and slipped into the Jag without another word.

Dennis watched him drive away. Ally knew when to put the screws on, but he also knew when to give a man the most dangerous and effective lure: the lure of hope. And he had Dennis Patterson just where he wanted him, that was the terrible thing.

By mid-morning, the lads had got a fire going in the garden behind the house, fuelling it with timber and other debris from the kitchen area, where they were at work on gutting, as Dennis had told them. Neville was just emerging from the house with five mugs of tea balanced on a plank, and the rest of them were filing outside for a deserved tea break by the fire, when Helen Bellamy came walking up the drive with her golden retriever.

It was a nice gesture, and a courageous one. And in her way she was both a nice and a courageous woman. The lads watched her approach politely.

'Good morning!' she called.

'Good morning!' they chorused.

She came up to the fire, smiling shyly.

'I'm Helen Bellamy,' she introduced herself. 'I owe you gentlemen an apology. You see, it was I who sent the policeman here yesterday. I'm afraid I thought you were criminals.'

There were one or two furtive glances at Moxey. Neville seemed to have acquired a taste for handling the gentry, so it was he who piped up:

'I suppose we did look a bit out of place around here.'

Mrs Bellamy nodded. 'Well, Mr Ames always talked about doing some work on the house.'

'No. We're not working for Mr Ames,' Neville told her. 'It's a Mr Fraser who owns this now.'

The woman registered surprise and mild consternation.

'Oh, it's been sold! I never saw any signs. None of the local estate agents had it listed.'

The lads shrugged and said nothing.

'Of course,' she continued, 'Mr Ames was a bit of a mystery man. My husband and I met him a couple of times, when we were raising money for Oxfam. He made a very generous donation.' She looked embarrassed. 'And then one day we opened the Sunday newspapers and found him described as "King Porn".'

Wayne suddenly became interested. 'Oh yeah?'

'Yes. "Is this Britain's most evil man?" one of the headlines said. And we'd always found him perfectly charming ...'

'Aye, well, you divvn't judge a book by its cover, pet,' growled Oz with satisfaction.

'Pardon?' asked Mrs Bellamy, obviously not understanding a word of his thick Geordie accent.

'He's saying that appearances can be deceptive,' Neville translated.

Wayne nodded agreement.

'Yeah. These days a lot of villains become country squires, don't they? Mingle with the local nobs, take up fox huntin', have sherry with the vicar, then once a month they pops up to the smoke and does a bullion job.'

'Aye,' Oz chipped in again. 'An' if they get nobbled, they bugger off to Spain.'

Mrs Bellamy had obviously caught the word 'Spain'. She seized on it gratefully.

'Oh, Spain, yes. Where one gathers Mr Ames now resides.'

Neville offered her a stained, cracked mug of tea. She declined as gracefully as she could.

'No, thank you. Jasper and I must be getting on.'

Moxey looked at the dog appreciatively. 'Nice dog. I like retrievers.'

'I'd a thought a retriever would be the last dog you'd like, Mox,' said Oz.

Moxey shot him a killing look.

'The old house can certainly do with a lick of paint,' Mrs Bellamy said, preparing to leave.

'Oh, it's more than that,' Neville told her. 'Big job, this. Conversion.'

There was a sudden spark of extra interest in her eyes. 'Really?'

Neville nodded. 'Aye. We'll be here a while.'

'So lock up your daughters!' Oz guffawed.

Neville told him to shut up. Mrs Bellamy fortunately hadn't understood that either, but she looked very thoughtful as she and Jasper strolled back off up the drive.

Neither the ever-helpful Neville nor any other of the lads knew that she was, in her quiet way, one of the area's most active and determined conservationists. And at the moment, Ally Fraser needed interest from conservationists like he needed the proverbial hole in the head. Less, maybe. After all, he could always pay someone to have the hole in the head for him, couldn't he?

It was around six when Dennis sauntered into the Barley Mow after a busy day touring local suppliers, ordering materials. He took in a couple of men sitting at the bar. They were wearing suits, and they didn't look as though they were from around here. Pringle appeared as Dennis reached the bar, and addressed the two men. Obviously they were guests. Their room was ready, he said.

'I think we'd rather have another pint, wouldn't we, Barry?' said one of them.

The other nodded. 'Yes indeed. Nice drop, that.'

Dennis registered their flat, suburban London accents. Commercial travellers? They weren't dressed like tourists, that was for sure.

'Don't suppose you get a lot of visitors this time of year,' said the first one to Pringle.

The landlord shook his head. 'Not until the holidays begin, no. Although this week, as it happens, I'm quite full.'

'Evenin',' said Dennis, making his presence felt. 'Large scotch, please.'

Pringle regarded him sourly. 'In a moment.' He carried on pulling his beers for the Londoners.

Dennis caught the Londoner's eye, made a face. The Londoner grinned slightly. They obviously weren't too keen on the Wing Commander either.

'Got colder, has it?' the man said, taking up the offer of contact.

'Aye. It's really chilly out there,' said Dennis, rubbing his hands together.

Pringle had the beers ready.

'Where's the rest of your people?' he asked, in a tone that implied he wished they were as far away as possible.

'Still workin' on the house. I've been into town. Sortin' a few things out.'

Pringle indicated the Londoners.

'We've got other guests staying, so I hope tonight we won't have quite so much noise.'

Dennis stiffened. 'I don't think we were all that rowdy,' he said, keeping this side of politeness.

'That crude fellow . . .' Pringle said with distaste.

'Oz?'

'The one with the broken tooth. I don't know what his name is.'

'That's Oz.'

'He was somewhat boisterous.'

76

'I don't think singin' along with the juke box is particularly boisterous,' Dennis said mildly.

'But if he doesn't approve of the choice of records, tell him not to kick it in with his hobnail boots, will you?'

The phone rang and Pringle went to answer it. Dennis turned disgustedly to the other two in the bar and jerked a meaningful thumb at the departing figure of the landlord.

'Captain Warmth!' he muttered.

The talkative Londoner grinned. 'Is that your famous northern hospitality?'

'Don't include me,' said Dennis. 'I'm from the North-East. This is the South as far as I'm concerned.'

Dennis was too intent on his scotch and his grievance to notice it, but the Londoners exchanged the briefest of interested looks at that piece of information.

'What is it you're doing here, then?' Dennis was asked.

'Buildin' job. Convertin' a big house up the road.'

'That wouldn't be a place called Thornely Manor, would it?' the man asked quickly.

Suddenly Dennis was wary. There was something about these blokes he didn't like.

'What if it is?'

The Londoner ignored his question.

'If you've got a team of lads on it, presumably it's just changed hands.'

'Mebbe. I'm just a buildin' contractor, mate,' Dennis stonewalled.

'Still,' said the other Londoner, finally deciding to make his contribution, 'you must know who's paying your wages.'

Dennis looked hard at him. 'I'd rather know why you're askin' these questions.'

Just then, the lads poured into the bar – Bomber, Neville, Oz, with Moxey following at the rear.

'Howway, Dennis!' bellowed Oz. 'Have you got 'em in?'

But Dennis was still waiting for his answer. The talkative Londoner, coolly ignoring the lads, reached into his jacket pocket and produced his identification.

'Detective Inspector Morris,' he said. 'This is my colleague, Sergeant Lawrence.'

That was when they lost Moxey again. He simply did a

silent about-turn, kept walking – straight back out of the pub and into the night.

If the Barley Mow was none too warm, courtesy of Arthur Pringle's extremely cold shoulder, it was totally brass monkey's out in the village's one phone booth, where Dennis stood chilled to the marrow, with a pile of coins beside him, desperately trying to call the airport before Ally's flight took off. Eventually, when he was halfway through his pile of change, an irritated-sounding Ally came on the phone, barely audible above the airport bustle. He must have shat himself when they'd paged him.

'Ally ... thank God,' said Dennis.

'Dennis, they're about to call my flight,' crackled Ally, 'so if you're ringin' up because you've found woodworm in the joists, I'll be less than happy.'

'Nothin' so trivial,' barked Dennis. 'It's the law.'

'Are you askin' me to bail out that big lunatic with the broken teeth? Who did he chin now?'

'Ally, shut up, will you?' Dennis said urgently. 'It's plainclothes from the Met. Asking about you and the deal on the house.'

Ally was suddenly sharp as a razor.

'What have you told 'em, Dennis?'

Jesus, this was the limit, Dennis thought. That bastard just didn't trust anyone. He controlled himself.

'I've worked for you long enough to know how to fend off questions, Ally,' he said. 'I've said nowt, but I thought you should know.'

There was a very short pause. When Ally started talking again he was crisp and businesslike. Say what you like about him, he wasn't a panicker.

'Okay,' Ally said, 'here's what you do. You call Harbottle and put him in the picture. This is his department. And tomorrow mornin' you get your team up at the crack of dawn. Get them down the house and do as much damage as you can.'

'We're in construction, not demolition!' Dennis protested.

'You need a bit of one before you start the other,' Ally fired back. 'And if they're after valuation, it'll all help to muddy the waters.'

Dennis sighed bleakly. 'So you're still goin' away?'

A hollow laugh came back to him over the line.

'Are you kidding? Spain seems more attractive than ever, pal . . .'

After Ally had hung up, Dennis walked disconsolately back to the Barley Mow. He'd better drag the lads out of the bar straight away and have a meeting. One thing about working for Ally Fraser – it certainly wasn't boring or predictable. It'd be better if it was.

It took him a little while to ease them away from the public and upstairs, but soon they were all ensconced in his room – all except Moxey, but Dennis hadn't the energy to ask where he was. After all, it was a free country, and he didn't have to go on the piss all night like the others, did he?

Dennis took off his coat and scarf, and Bomber handed him a beer.

'So what's goin' on, Dennis?' Oz demanded aggressively.

'Close the door, close the door,' Dennis said.

Neville did the honours in that direction while Wayne looked at Dennis shrewdly.

'About Moxey, is it?' the cockney asked.

'Moxey? Why should it be about Moxey?' Dennis said, genuinely puzzled.

Wayne backed off quickly, but Oz, who had had a few, continued to boom at Dennis: 'Whatever it is, I think we've got a right to know!'

'Keep your voice down!' Dennis hissed. 'There's a couple of cops down the hall, and these walls are so thin that if you fart they'd faint.'

There was a brief exchange about the truth of this between Oz and Bomber, who were next door to each other.

'Listen, man,' said Dennis, 'it's nothing to do with us. It's just a few complications have come up.'

Neville looked at Dennis accusingly.

'Aye, well, if you work for blokes like Ally Fraser, you expect complications,' he said. 'I know what's goin' on. He's done a backdoor deal where he's bought the house for way below its market value. There's a word for that, and it's fraud.'

'You don't have to work for him, Neville,' Dennis snapped. 'If you don't like his money, you can piss off back to the dole queue.'

'Don't get so tetchy, Den,' Bomber put in gently. 'We just want to know where we stand.'

Dennis shrugged. 'Same as you did an hour ago, Bomb. Business as usual. And if those bobbies come sniffin' around askin' questions, just leave it to me. *I'll* handle it.'

They all mumbled reluctant agreement.

'Fine,' said Wayne. 'Only reason we got in a bit of a panic was that we thought it had somethin' to do with Mox.'

Dennis sighed in exasperation.

'Will someone please explain to me what this business with Moxey's all about?' he asked.

'Doesn't he know?' said Oz.

'Course he doesn't. He was in town, wasn't he?' Wayne retorted.

'Don't know *what?*' Dennis bellowed, breaking his own rule about quietness.

Finally Neville sheepishly supplied the information.

'Moxey's escaped from prison. He's on the run.'

Dennis took a big pull of beer, stared dully into the middle distance.

'Aw Christ,' he muttered. 'That's all I need.'

SEVEN

The kitchen door creaked open again and in came Oz, Wayne and Neville. Oz surveyed the half-demolished, freezing room and shuddered.

'D'you know, this place is almost as cosy as our local in the Falklands.' He made a gesture of despair. 'Get the kettle on, Nev ...'

He prowled around, grinned, kicked open the pantry door. 'Howway, Mox – I know you're in there!'

Bomber followed them in, bringing the milk and the sugar. Wayne watched everything bleakly.

'If we're gettin' in this early, I don't know why we bothered to go to bed.'

Then came a timid voice from the pantry. 'Is it safe?'

'No, Mox,' said Wayne. 'The place is surrounded by the SPG with riot shields.'

'You don't 'alf flatter yourself, you do,' said Oz as Moxey appeared in the open doorway, trembling and cowed. 'You're not exactly Public Enemy Number One, you know.'

'They were cops, weren't they?' Moxey protested.

'Plain clothes from the smoke don't come lookin' for toe rags like you, son,' Wayne explained none too kindly.

But Dennis had entered now, and Moxey was eyeing him nervously.

'H-hello, Den.'

Dennis stared at him darkly. ''Morning, Papillon.' Then he softened a little and tossed Moxey a brown paper bag. 'There's a bacon-and-egg sandwich in there for you.'

'Oh ta, lads. Ta.' Moxey fell on the food like a rodent. Suddenly, with an ingratiating little smile on his face, he looked at the watching lads and said: 'By the way ... it was Brad Dexter.'

They all stared at him, completely puzzled. This information was supposed to please them in some way, but how?

'What was?' asked Wayne.

'The bloke we couldn't think of in the Magnificent Seven. Bomber's character. It was Brad Dexter.'

Wayne shrugged. 'I've never heard of him.'

'N-No-one has. That's why we couldn't remember him. I couldn't sleep last night, y'see,' he explained. 'What with frettin' about the law, and the cold, and the rats ...'

'The rats?' echoed Neville.

'I couldn't sleep either, Mox!' growled Dennis. 'Worryin' about your situation and what to do about it.'

Moxey's expression became sheepish again.

'Sorry, Den. I should have levelled with you.'

'I think he's right!' Oz boomed. They all stared at him. Oz the moralist, or what? 'It was Brad Dexter!' Oz continued excitedly. 'I remember who he was, an' all. He was the bloke what saved Frank Sinatra's life!'

Wayne looked at him in astonishment. 'When?'

'I don't know when. But apparently Sinatra nearly drowned, and this bloke Brad Dexter hauled him out. Which meant that he was in clover for the rest of his life, wasn't he? Limousines, monogrammed cufflinks. Whatever he wanted, I should think.'

'If I could drag you lot back to the real world,' Dennis said testily, 'I'd like to make a start here.'

'Start on what?' Oz demanded.

'Anything that's still standin' or intact,' Dennis said. 'Flatten it!'

They set off to their tasks in the morning's demolition derby.

'I once saved a bloke's life,' mused Neville as he and Oz started work. 'Well, sort of. He was fishin' in this reservoir and he fell in. So me and some other lads went in after him.'

'Bet he wasn't a millionaire superstar, though,' Oz scoffed.

Neville agreed sadly. 'No. He was a laid-off steel worker from Consett. So it didn't alter my lifestyle one iota ...'

It was a good few hours later when the Ford Granada came

up the drive. Moxey was working upstairs at the time, and he was the first to spot the car – and to see that the men inside were the two cops from the previous night, plus a smart-suited bloke he hadn't seen before. Moxey dashed down the stairs to where Dennis, Neville and Bomber were demolishing some wood panelling in the hallway.

'They're back!' he yelled.

'Who?' said Dennis.

'The bloody law!'

Dennis paused. 'Aw, pull yourself together Moxey. They're not after you.' He wagged a finger at him. 'Just keep doin' what you're doin'. I'll answer any questions.'

Moxey reluctantly retreated back up the stairs, muttering as he went: 'Not good for my ticker, this, y'know. This is my third heart attack in forty-eight hours!'

Dennis gave him a look like thunder.

'If anyone ends up in intensive care, it'll be me,' he snarled, and set off to receive the visitors.

'He's right on the edge, Den,' Bomber commented to Neville as they watched him.

Neville nodded.

'Hardly surprisin'. He's caught between a rock and a hard place. He's responsible for us, and he's answerable to Ally Fraser. And now he's got Scotland Yard breathin' down his neck.' He shook his head.

'Nothin' to do with Dennis, Nev,' said Bomber.

'He's Ally's man, Bomb,' Neville said doubtfully. 'And, if things get ugly, he'll be tarred with the same brush.'

Young Neville was learning a lot these days; he was getting to know how the world worked, and he didn't necessarily like it much.

The distinguished looking gentleman escorting the pair from the fraud squad was a local estate agent, Mr Punshon. He, Lawrence and Morris stalked around the outside of the house, taking their time.

'If this house had been put on the open market,' Punshon said after a while, 'I would have suggested an asking price of a hundred and sixty.'

Morris glanced at Lawrence. 'Well, according to Mr

83

Ames's solicitors, it's just been sold for a hundred and ten.'

'Really?' said Punshon with a frown. 'That does sound rather dubious. However, considering Mr Ames's reputation, I'm not altogether surprised . . .'

'That's why we're here, Mr Punshon,' said Morris.

The estate agent sighed.

'That's your province, not mine, of course. I met him once when he was trying to buy a pony for his daughter.' He sniffed. 'I couldn't put my finger on it, but I felt something didn't quite ring true about the chap.'

'Pity you didn't tell us at the time,' Lawrence muttered.

'Pity you people let him slip through the net,' retorted Punshon.

The two fraud squad men had no answer to that. It was a real sore point.

When they were ready, they made their way in through the big front door to look at the interior of the house. They entered the big main hall to see manic activity everywhere.

Wayne zoomed through, carrying a door. 'Mind your backs, please – comin' through!' he bellowed.

Moxey had found his own perfect activity, bent double with his backside to the law, fervently ripping out skirting with a chisel. He'd figured they didn't generally have identikits of bums available.

Oz was up a ladder, tearing out a great expanse of ceiling. As the two police officers and the increasingly disturbed looking estate agent moved further into the house, he sent a shower of plaster over the visitors.

'I wouldn't stand there if I was you!' he bawled.

The three of them stood there looking like they had been caught in a freak snow storm.

Punshon brushed plaster from his well-cut suit.

'Ah . . . perhaps a hundred and sixty was a little on the high side . . .' he said.

Morris looked at Lawrence. Lawrence looked at Morris. It was obvious they weren't going to crack it here. It was going to mean a trip north to Newcastle, to the guts of the Fraser empire.

Later that same day, they were having their car filled up.

'Is it far?' Lawrence said to Morris.

'What?'

'Newcastle.'

Morris smiled thinly. 'Oh yeah. Bloody miles.'

'What's it like?'

Morris thought for a moment, then asked his sergeant:
'Do you see yourself as working class, Barry?'

'What?' said Lawrence. 'I should say so. Tower block in
Leytonstone, Dad's a caretaker. Yeah, I'm solid working
class.'

'Wait till you've spent a night in Newcastle,' Morris said
ominously. 'You'll realise you're middle class.'

There were pleadings and there were arguments in the
bedroom that served as a conference centre at the Barley
Mow that night. It was in the matter of Moxey, and Dennis
had some unpleasant conclusions to draw. The lads stuck up
for Mox, of course, and it was hard for Dennis to do the job
he knew he had to do.

'Look,' he said uncomfortably, 'I have to handle this legit.'

Bomber looked sceptical.

'But this Ally's a shady old bugger himself.'

'All the more reason why he doesn't want to bring any heat
down by some petty infringement of the Employment Act,'
Dennis answered. 'I have to do your cards and your PAYE.
And Moxey's got neither.'

There was a pause while that sunk in. Then Dennis
continued relentlessly:

'If he's picked up – which God forbid, Moxey,' he said with
a weary nod to the Liverpudlian. 'They'll ask me what he's
doin' workin' without any proper documentation. And
technically I'm the employer. So when you talk about bein'
accessories, it won't be you lot – it'll be yours truly who ends
up in the clart.'

As so often happened, everyone got the point except Oz.

'Well,' he growled. 'You can baffle anyone with bloody
science.'

Moxey looked thoughtful, however. 'Den's right,' he
murmured. 'Can't compromise him. Wouldn't be fair.'

'All right, all right,' Oz blustered. 'But doesn't it strike you as ironic?'

'What?' said Wayne.

'We're all graftin' for a bloke whose reputation is dubious, to say the least,' Oz said. 'I mean, we're talkin' about a heavy-duty villain here. But Ally's hidin' behind accountants and lawyers and legal loopholes. He's so bloody cushioned, he doesn't give a rat's arse about the law or the Inland Revenue.'

He rounded on Dennis in particular. Such eloquence, and he hadn't even started drinking yet.

'And you're more concerned about poor old Moxey. Who, with all due respect, is just some low life punter. Whose only fault is that he thinks every night of the year is Guy Fawkes's night.'

That last bit was a little unfortunate, but it hit home. Moxey was a troubled man when he went to bed that night.

Morris and Lawrence were not taken in by the spartan respectability of Malcolm Harbottle's office. In fact, it brought out the worst in them. They'd seen a hundred little fat cats like this one in their working lives, and they despised them. For Harbottle, they switched into their *Sweeney* mode and pulled no punches.

Morris was thumbing through the surveyor's report on Thornely Manor while Lawrence asked the questions.

'When was this survey done?' Lawrence asked bluntly.

'When my client first became interested in the property,' Harbottle said comfortably. 'The date's on there, I think.'

Lawrence stared at him. 'And did the surveyor actually ever visit the house?'

'What are you suggesting?' Harbottle asked, all outraged professional pride.

'It's been doctored,' Lawrence snapped. 'Christ, the ink's still wet.' He leaned forward aggressively. 'We know this whole deal stinks, and so do you. You've even got a bunch of cowboys down there knocking twenty grand off the value as we speak.'

'They are renovating the property, yes.'

Morris looked up from his studies.

'They were bleeding demolishing it when we left,' he said drily.

'And even if they rip up every floorboard and discover termites in the ballroom,' Lawrence continued, 'you and I know that house has been marked down well below the odds. And your Mr Fraser is going to take a bundle of cash in a duty-free bag to Spain to make up the balance.'

'If he hasn't already,' said Morris.

Harbottle seemed unintimidated. He was cool, you had to give him that.

'You chaps,' he said plummily, 'have come an awful long way to voice these extraordinary speculations. Is there anything else I can help you with?'

Lawrence decided to give up for the moment and deal with the practical difficulties of being so far from civilisation.

'Yeah,' he sighed. 'Where do we eat in Newcastle?'

But if the boys from the Fraud Squad were drawing a blank so far, there were others who were quite capable of putting spanners in Ally's works. Like nice little women with retriever dogs – nice ladies who knew the planning laws inside out and knew how to use them.

As the lads discovered that same fine morning a hundred and fifty miles to the south.

It caused quite a stir when Sergeant Oakes's modest little country police car turned up at Thornely Manor the next day, and he and Helen Bellamy got out. Mrs Bellamy looked shy, rather embarrassed, but very determined as she asked for Dennis. The lads tried to grill her while they waited for him to arrive, but she was not very forthcoming.

'Some problem, is there?' asked Bomber.

'I'm afraid there is,' Mrs Bellamy said.

'Oh,' said Oz. 'Are the locals gettin' up a petition to expel us undesirables?'

'Not exactly.'

Mrs Bellamy was saved by the arrival of Dennis.

'Howway then,' he bellowed, seeing them chatting to Mrs Bellamy and the sergeant. 'No one said nowt about stoppin' work!'

Oz and Bomber headed back into the house.

'I'm afraid you will all have to stop work, actually,' Mrs Bellamy said to Dennis.

'How d'you mean?'

She took a deep breath.

'As I suspected,' she began, 'this is a listed building. Grade Two. I rang the council and they confirmed it. That means that nothing can be changed here without prior planning permission.'

Dennis stood his ground.

'Look, until I hear this from my boss, my lads keep working, right?'

Then Oakes intervened in support of the woman.

'I'm afraid Mrs Bellamy's right,' he said, making it clear to Dennis that he was sympathetic to his plight. 'If you don't stop, she can have a court order from the Council within the hour.'

Dennis threw up his hands in exasperation. 'I can't believe this week.'

Mrs Bellamy saw his point of view too, adamant as she was.

'There's nothing personal in this, you understand,' she said. 'And I do realise it's not your fault. But I'm sure you will agree that in this day and age we must do everything to keep the heritage of England intact.'

'I was brought up on a council estate in the North-East, Mrs Bellamy,' Dennis said with a grimace. 'I've seen precious little of the glorious heritage of England.'

But there it was. That was it. It was down tools and back on the 'phone to Ally. Pronto.

'Same again for everyone, is it?' asked Wayne.

'Why not?' said Neville gloomily. 'We've got no work tomorrow, so we may as well concentrate on our hangovers.'

Wayne headed for the bar to do the honours.

'Give us a whisky and pep, will you, Wayne?' Oz hollered. 'That curry we had's given us indigestion!'

Dennis gave a mock shudder. 'There's only one lav upstairs, and three of you 'ad to have vindaloo.'

'Same again,' a cheerful Wayne told mine host. 'And a whisky and pep, squire.'

Pringle gave him a weasel look.

'Do you mind not calling me "squire"? Or "mate", "chief", "boyo", or any of the other titles you people have bestowed on me?'

'Got to call you something,' Wayne said evenly. Like 'prick', he thought.

'Then,' said Pringle, 'I suggest you try Arthur. That was my given name.'

Wayne smiled acidly.

'As you wish, Arthur. Can I have a tot of rum on the side, Arthur? 'Cause I think I've got a cold coming on, Arthur.'

He could hear Pringle's teeth grinding as he poured the beers.

There was a sudden commotion. Wayne turned, saw the grinning face of Barry in the doorway.

'Evenin' each,' said the zit king.

'Barry! Hullo, my son!' Wayne said, amazed at his own feeling of delight. 'Just drive up, did you?'

'Yuh. Heater broke in the van an' all.'

He felt his throat, to check the glands. He was glad to see the lads, it was clear, but he looked pretty low when you looked at him closely.

'Better have a short,' said Bomber.

'I'm not havin' a pina colada,' Barry said.

'Make that two whisky and peps, Arthur,' said Wayne.

Pringle eyed Barry like a trainer checking out a dangerous animal. 'Is he another one?'

'Yeah. Last of the Magnificent Seven.' He turned to Barry, indicating Pringle. 'Barry Taylor, meet Arthur Pringle, our genial host.'

'I only have a single room,' Pringle growled. 'Fifteen pounds. Cash.'

'Whatever,' said Barry. 'I have the wherewithal.'

'Take no notice of him, Barry,' shouted Oz from over by the fire. 'Get yourself over here near the warmth.'

Bomber stood up. 'Have my seat, son. I think my vindaloo's on the move.'

'Aye, it moves fast, curry,' Oz agreed. 'I don't know why we don't just order it, chuck it down the bog, and cut out the middle man.'

Neville informed Barry there was no food at the Barley Mow.

'I'm not interested in food,' Barry said, sinking rapidly back into despond. 'I haven't eaten a proper meal for three days.'

'Oh dear, yes. Hazel, is it?'

'I thought you'd never ask.'

'Your presence here indicates that conciliatory talks have broken down, I assume,' said Wayne, bringing the drinks across.

'Pro tem, Wayne,' Barry confirmed miserably. 'She wants to think things through. Find her own space for a while, as it were.'

'I'm sure it'll work out, son.'

'I'm sure it will,' said Barry without much conviction. 'But in the meantime I felt I had to get away.'

Neville asked him about the problems of leaving his business.

'Couldn't face it. Let it slip anyhow recently, what with doin' the house.' Barry sipped at his drink gratefully. 'No, Wolverhampton's just too painful a place for me, at this point in time.'

'Too painful for me at the best of times,' put in Oz.

'I mean it's got too many memories,' Barry droned on. 'I thought: I'm best off with me mates. Get me head down and do some honest graft ...'

There was an awkward pause. The lads exchanged looks.

'Oh ... well, if you were thinkin' of easing the pain by throwin' yourself into your work, there's a bit of a hiccup there,' said Dennis eventually.

'What d'you mean, hiccup?'

Wayne took over.

'We've got one or two problems,' he said, then proceeded to tick them off on his fingers: 'The bloke we're working for has got the Fraud Squad breathin' down his neck, which doesn't inspire confidence. We've got to down tools on the house 'cause it's got a preservation order on it. And ...' He lowered his voice to a whisper. '... Apparently Moxey escaped from the nick, so we're all harbouring a fugitive from justice.'

He paused, savouring the horror that was slowly spreading over Barry's face.

'Apart from that,' he added. 'Everything's triffic.'

'What have I got myself into?' Barry groaned.

'There's no worry with Moxey now,' said Neville.

Oz nodded. 'Aye. Nay graft, nay cards, nay bother.'

Meanwhile, Bomber had returned from the Gents and had been quietly listening to the conversation.

'There is no Moxey problem,' he said gently.

'How do you mean?' asked Dennis.

'He's buggered off again. His bed's not been slept in and his kit's gone.'

Amid the general expressions of disbelief, Oz turned on Dennis again.

'What was it you said last night?' he growled accusingly. 'Can't compromise you, Dennis. Well, he hasn't. He's took off, to keep you in the clear.'

'Oh, knock it off,' Wayne said. 'Den didn't drive him away, Oz.'

'Well, *I* certainly bloody didn't!'

'Nobody did,' said Neville. 'He didn't want to implicate us. You've got to respect him for that.'

'Maybe he took Bomb's advice,' Wayne suggested. 'Maybe he's goin' to turn himself in.'

'Keep your voice down,' Dennis said. 'I just hope he doesn't get collared before he gets to the nick. They'll never believe he was on his way back.'

They all thought about that.

'Poor old Mox,' sighed Barry. 'Alone in the night. And it's bitter out.'

'Wonder where he is now. Probably sleepin' rough.'

'Aye. Curled up in a ditch. Frozen and scared.'

Barry nodded. 'I think it's terrible. Still ... as he has gone. I may as well have his bed ...'

Confronted by the others' astonished stares, the bride-groom-in-exile moved to defend himself.

'Well, there's no point in paying for a single room!'

EIGHT

Vicki was still in bed, most of her newly-tanned anatomy covered by a sheet. Not that it had been ever thus that morning. They had both had their early-morning indoor exercise and had passed on to the next stage of Another Day in Paradise. Ally stood by the window, gazing out over the azure Mediterranean, putting on his golfing clothes and mentally practising his swing. He had pretty well hammered Kenny Ames last week – and got Thorncly Manor into the bargain. He could be pretty sure that 'Britain's most evil man' would be out for revenge this fine morning, and he was mentally preparing himself. Vicki was also thinking, an activity she could never keep to herself for long.

'D'you know what I've been thinking?' she said suddenly. 'While we're out here I'd like to take tennis lessons.'

'Tennis?' Ally echoed, turning back into the room.

'Why not? I always think it's useful to have another string to your bow.'

Ally smiled grimly.

'You took up water-skiing in Florida. If I remember rightly, that lasted an hour.'

'I nearly drowned!' she said.

'What's brought on this sudden interest in tennis?' Ally asked. 'Some bronzed Australian coach down at the club, is it?'

She pouted. 'I'd like to have somethin' to do while you're on the golf course all day.'

Women ... he thought. They buy up half the shops in Malaga and still can't get happy. Never bloody satisfied.

The phone rang, and Ally felt irritation course through him. Probably Ames chickening out of the match.

'Who the devil's that?' he muttered.

It was Vicki who picked up the receiver beside the bed.
'It's long distance ... It's got that sound, y'know ...'

Ally stepped over quickly and took the phone from her, fearing the worst. He got it. Yet another call from that fatal phone box in Derbyshire, for Christ's sake.

'Hello?' he barked. 'Oh, can you speak louder, Dennis, it's a terrible line ... What d'you mean, we've got a problem?'

When he left the condominium a short while later for his encounter with Kenny Ames, his heart was black. And the only swing he could visualise was one involving Kenny Ames. On the end of a bloody rope.

Kenny Ames was there at the first tee with his caddy, waiting for Ally. All smiles, as ever. A great one for smiles, was Ames. Your modest, cheerful cockney sparrow was the façade he liked to present. He was tall, well built, and very tanned, the same age as Ally but also in very good shape.

'Good morning, Ally,' said Kenny with a charming grin. The accent was London, but a bit cleaned up; maybe influenced by his brief period as a member of the English landed gentry.

'No, Kenny,' snapped Ally. 'It is not a good morning. It is not a good morning at all.'

Kenny shrugged, every inch the relaxed lotus-eater. The Perry Como of Porn.

'Oh well,' he said evenly. 'If your mood's going to affect your game, we'll double the ante.'

'You are the cause of my mood, Kenny,' Ally said. 'You could say I'm a little bit peeved with you.'

Ames didn't even react. Ally could chill normal blokes to death with a look, but not the likes of Kenny. Kenny hadn't become the Sultan of Smut without being able to look after himself very well in a ruthless world.

'Didn't you like that little masseuse I sent you?' he asked innocently. 'She did wonders for *my* swing.' Ames motioned politely to the tee-off. 'You won last week, so you have the honour.'

Ally carefully dug his tee.

'I'm talkin' about the house,' he growled. 'Why did you

ver tell me it was a listed building?'

Ames chuckled. 'You never asked me.'

'How can I convert it into time-sharing units with a preservation order slapped on it?'

Kenny waited while Ally selected his driver.

'You never told me that was your intention,' he said then.

'Aw, piss off, Kenny. You didn't think I was gonna live there, did you?' Ally said.

'I did, actually ...' Ames pointed behind towards the clubhouse. 'And you'd better play. There's some more behind us.'

There was another golfing party approaching. Ames was right. Ally addressed himself to his game, trying to give himself that swing he had practised so often in his head – and sliced the ball pretty horribly, to Ames's obvious delight. His mood certainly was not helping his game.

'Oh dear,' said Kenny, with all the heartfelt sincerity of an encyclopaedia salesman who finds out your son's just failed his 'O' levels for the second time. 'What bad luck!'

He selected his own driver, prepared to play, keeping up a constant chat as he went.

'Oh yeah ...' he said. 'I was going to live in it when I first bought the drum. I saw myself as a country squire. Really appealed, it did. Got myself all kitted out – y'know, guns from Purdie's, suits from Daks. Bought a fishing rod and a Range Rover ...'

He struck the ball squarely, watched it soar towards the green with evident pleasure, allowed himself a modest, satisfied nod. They began to walk towards the green with their caddies trailing along behind. Revenge was indeed sweet for Kenny Ames, in golf and in other areas of life. He milked it for all it was worth.

'I went up there for a few weekends,' he continued placidly. 'To ingratiate myself with the local populace. Had the neighbours over for sherry. Went to the church fête and enrolled Katie in the local riding school.'

'The local populace, I assume, did not know that you were London's leadin' pornographer,' said Ally archly.

'No,' Ames grinned. 'I kept that schtum. Left things fairly

vague. Hinted at the rag trade.' He sighed at the memory of it all. 'I was really getting into it, actually. I woke one morning, and thought: I'd quite like to end my days here! I wasn't being morbid, more philosophical. Thought if I snuff it I'd like it to be in a typical English rural setting. Preferably with a cricket match in progress on the village green. And the distant sound of church bells ...'

'And is there honey still for tea?' Ally quoted sarcastically.

'Pardon?'

'Rupert Brooke.'

'Who's 'e?' asked Ames, suddenly forgetting his elocution practice.

'He was a poet,' Ally told him. 'He shared your recently acquired affection for the joys of England.'

Ames nodded enthusiastically. 'Oh. I must give him a read. Is he one of the modern ones?'

'He's long gone. Died in a foreign field.' Ally smiled unpleasantly. 'And so will you, Kenny. Unless you return to your beloved country. You won't be hearin' church bells, though. It'll be the clangin' of a cell door.'

They were getting close to the green.

'I was set up. That's the tragedy,' Ames said defensively.

'I feel a bit the same way,' muttered Ally.

Ames laughed.

'Oh, come on, son. You've acquired a beautiful house, well below market value. All you have to do is guarantee to restore it to its former grandeur.' He grinned boyishly, enjoying the fact that Ally's ball was a lot farther from the hole than his own. 'Why don't you turn it into a fat farm ...?'

Ally braced himself. Another seventeen bloody holes of this. But he'd find a way to wipe the grin off Kenny Ames's face and make a killing on Thornely Manor. Somehow. He'd find something for Dennis's cowboys to do to that place if it damned well killed him ...

While Ally was enjoying – if that was the word – his early game of golf, the now idle lads were having a late breakfast at the Barley Mow, and pretty soon they were all aware that they were entering a new stage of their war with Arthur

Pringle, licensee. Until now they had been like an invading army, making occasional raids. Now they were stuck around on occupation duties, and preparing for what promised to be a drawn-out war of attrition.

Neville and Wayne were sitting around the electric fire in the public. Pringle had grudgingly consented to put on one bar to ward off the morning chill. Oz and Barry entered as mine host was plonking down tea and toast for breakfast.

'I suppose it's too much to ask for one boiled egg, is it?' Oz asked loudly.

Pringle glowered at him. 'Tea and toast. I told you that when you registered. I'll get you some Marmite.'

'Oh, don't put yourself to that much bother, mate.'

'Here, Oz,' said Wayne, fuelling the fires. 'Remember what Arthur told you – he doesn't like bein' addressed as "mate", "chief", "squire", "boyo", "admiral", "petal", or "bacon-balls".'

Pringle retreated, soundly regretting he had ever brought up the subject of modes of address the previous night.

Barry was looking refreshed. He had slept well for the first time in days, apparently.

'Back in the bosom of your family, isn't you?' cooed Wayne.

'There's a lot of truth in that, Wayne,' Barry agreed solemnly. 'I can't tell you how much the thought of bein' with my muckers sustained me at my time of grief.'

Oz snorted. 'Howway, man ... your fiancée hasn't died. She's got cold feet, that's all.'

'Pro tem,' added Wayne tactfully.

'I think there's something that exists between men that doesn't exist between men and women,' Barry continued.

'Hey, who's sharin' a room with him!' bellowed Oz.

Barry glared at him.

'I'm not talkin' about *that*, Oz,' he said. 'That's typical of you, that is. I'm talkin' about comradeship, not turd-burglin'!'

There was a short interval while Pringle slapped a jar of marmalade and a jar of Marmite down on the bar for them to fetch. Then Barry resumed his little lecture.

'I don't think women understand that, y'see.'

'What?' Neville asked.

'Comradeship! What I'm talkin' about. I think that's what freaked Hazel out when you lot showed up. She felt threatened somehow. She felt excluded.'

'Oh, don't lay that on us!' Oz protested.

But Wayne was nodding. 'No, no, I think Barry's right. It's a classic syndrome. Any of our old ladies would react the same. They resent our shared past.'

'I don't think Brenda feels left out 'cause she didn't share a wooden hut with us in Düsseldorf,' Neville said sardonically.

'No, of course not, Nev,' said Barry. 'But imagine if all of us lot had shown up at your place. All laughin' and jokin' and full of the joys of spring. Bound to have an effect on her, wouldn't it?'

'She probably wouldn't notice,' said Neville. 'Too busy at the hospital. Or playing badminton with the doctors.'

The unexpected bitterness in his tone surprised and shocked them all. There was a moment's embarrassed silence. Then Oz jumped in with both feet.

'Oh aye? What's this?'

'I mean, she's got her own career,' Neville said. 'She's her own woman, like. I'm all for it.'

His obvious misery and lack of conviction was so stark that even Oz failed to follow up.

'I think that's a good approach to living, Nev,' said Barry, moving to save the situation. 'I think a changing role for women is inevitable and right in this day and age. Can't chain them to the kitchen sink. I've always encouraged Hazel in her career.'

Oz nodded sagely.

'I never discouraged my Marjorie in a career,' he said. 'I'd've been perfectly happy for her to bring a penny in.' He sighed. 'However, change to her meant somethin' different. It meant changin' from knockin' off the TV repair man to a bloke in the rates office, or a welder in Wallsend slipway.'

Another awkward silence. Talking about male-female relationships was a real minefield in present circumstances.

'Are we to take it that things between you and Marjorie are

not altogether tickety-boo?' Wayne enquired gently.

'Would you be with her, after that lot?'

Barry put on his talking-about-relationships face.

'I'm sorry about that, Oz,' he said. 'But quite frankly, you brought it on yourself.'

'How?' demanded Oz.

'When you and I were in the Falklands, you never wrote to her. Never phoned her, never sent her any money.'

'Same as when we were in Germany,' Neville agreed.

'That's because of the kind of woman she is,' Oz insisted. 'She's been slaggin' half of Tyneside while me back's turned.'

'Ah,' said Barry, who was on his high horse and wasn't about to get off it in a hurry. 'But which came first, the chicken or the egg? Your neglect or her promiscuity? "And in the end, the love you take is equal to the love you make", as John Lennon said – though I was never quite sure what he meant, actually ...'

Barry's moral musings were interrupted by Dennis's return from another visit to the village phone box.

'Where've you been?' asked Neville after Dennis had settled down in a chair.

'I've been talkin' to Ally's brief,' he told them. 'He says that if there's a preservation order on the house you can always appeal to the Department of the Environment.'

'Oh, the government!' scoffed Oz, back on the offensive. 'Then we'll be here for eternity. They can't make their mind up about sod all, that lot! Except for closin' pits ...'

'We'll be wrapped up in red tape for ever,' Barry said bleakly. 'I tried to get me granny a rebate on her gas bill. It took eighteen months and it was only twenty-two pound.'

Neville, as usual, had seen the worst possibility.

'If we have to down tools, we can't afford to hang around here indefinitely,' he said. 'We won't get paid, will we?'

'Look, I'm in charge of the cheque book,' Dennis assured them. 'I'm the signatory on the account. You'll get your whack.'

'Aye, but for how long?' Neville murmured. 'How long before Ally rings up and cancels the account?'

'That could be quite a while, Nev,' said Oz cheerfully.

'Thanks to British Telecom, he'll never get through.'

Pringle had wandered into the bar and, unnoticed by the lads, had been listening to their conversation. He was smiling, actually smiling.

'Am I to take it you're leaving?' he asked brightly.

Dennis looked at him sourly. 'Not yet we're not.'

'Better get a dartboard in, Arthur,' Wayne goaded. 'And a pool table and a couple of videos. All those amenities which your hostelry so sadly lacks.'

'You're not hanging around here all day. And I'm not doing lunches!' Pringle said with a scowl.

Wayne watched him stalk out of the bar.

'He's a diamond, our Arthur, isn't he?' he observed, smiling maliciously.

They didn't see Pringle again until later that morning. They were playing an improvised game of football against the wall of the Barley Mow, with Bomber in goal and the rest of the lads cantering energetically around the car park, showing off their skills. Neville had just crashed a neat right-footed drive against the garage door when the landlord appeared with a crate of empties and winced at the sight and sound of them.

'Look, you people,' Pringle called over. 'Do be careful!'

'Don't fret, Arthur,' said Oz. 'There's a lot of skill out here. There won't be any loose balls.'

'Why don't you go into a field if you want to do that?'

'It rained overnight, Arthur,' Wayne put in. 'Don't want us traipsin' into your luvverly hostelry with muddy boots, do you?'

Pringle beat another retreat.

Dennis's van drew up. The lads stopped their game and moved to greet him, clustered round like kids when dad comes home.

'Where've you been?' asked Oz.

'With the architect. He's got an appointment with the council this afternoon. Then he'll find out what we can do and what we can't.' Dennis shrugged. 'Look, nothing's goin' to happen for a couple of days, so if you want to take off, that's up to you.'

'Are you?' Neville asked.

'No. I've got to be around here, haven't I? I rang Norma and told her to come down. Be a break for her. Breath of fresh air. Might stay at the Cross Keys.'

Wayne smirked. 'I 'ope you told her to bring you a tie.'

'I could go home,' said Bomber. 'But it's a bloody long way to Bristol. And if we gets the go-ahead, it don't seem worth it.'

'Bit of a pisser, though, innit?' Wayne said.

Barry was unmoved.

'Suits me,' he drawled. 'This is just what I need after what I've been through. A sort of "time out" as they say in those American football games.'

Oz put on a show of irritation.

'It's a fine kettle of fish as far as I'm concerned,' he complained unconvincingly. 'I mean, you told me there was a good gig down here, Dennis. So I cancelled all my existing plans. And I've been here – what is it? – forty-eight hours, and I'm laid off already.'

'What bloody plans have you cancelled?' demanded Dennis angrily.

'I had a few irons in the fire. 'Course, they're all blown now ...'

'Look, you're bein' paid, Oz,' Dennis said.

'For a week.'

'During which time things'll be resolved. I'm sure there'll be work of some kind for us.' Dennis looked at the lads almost pleadingly. 'Who knew this was goin' to happen?'

'Yes. 'Tis not Den's fault,' Bomber supported him. 'It won't do us any harm to have a couple of days free.'

'There's some very nice scenery around here,' Neville said. 'Apparently there's a famous waterfall within driving distance.'

'Waterfall? Who wants to see a tossin' waterfall?' roared Oz.

'Bound to be action somewhere. Just a question of sniffin' it out,' Wayne suggested.

Dennis reacted quickly.

'Aye, well. If you do find some, be discreet, eh? I mean, people around here already think we're the Wild Bunch, so don't give 'em any cause to prove they're right. Just restrain yourselves. OK?'

'So I suppose lootin', pillagin' and ravagin' is out of the question, is it?' Oz asked.

'You know what I'm sayin', Oz. Just try to behave like adults.'

With that, Dennis went on into the pub.

'Great, this,' said Oz. 'We had more fun in the Falklands, didn't we, Barry?'

'I think it's goin' to rain again,' muttered Barry, ignoring him.

Bomber looked thoughtful.

'I wonder what sort of state poor ol' Mox will be in now.'

'I just hope he doesn't start a fire to keep himself warm,' Oz said darkly.

They turned as one man. Another vehicle was pulling into the carpark, a Mini Metro, and as it came close they could see that there was a young girl behind the wheel, an attractive one at that.

The girl got out. She was in her early twenties, dressed in casual student style, but smart. She moved round to the boot to get out her case, giving the lads a curious look as she did so.

'Looks like we've got another resident,' said Neville.

Wayne leered. 'She can move in with me any time she likes.'

'Fat chance you've got.'

But Wayne was already moving in.

'Nothin' ventured, nothin' gained,' he hissed, and set off towards the girl.

'He never changes, does he?' said Barry. 'It's pathetic.'

Then they got back to their game of football.

Wayne, meanwhile, had made his approach to the new guest. She was struggling with her suitcase, as he had known she would. 'Here, let me take that. It's far too heavy for a girl like you.'

'Oh, thanks,' she said. She had a pleasant, middle-class accent, hard to place where she came from.

'Stayin' here, are you?' Wayne began as he manhandled the case towards the inn – not too quickly, of course.

'Just for a couple of nights, yes.'

'Oh well,' Wayne smiled. 'You'll bring a little ray of sunshine into our drab existence. My name's Wayne.'

'Carol,' she answered readily.

'Well, welcome to our humble abode, Carol,' he continued smoothly. 'It's a bit of a naff place, mind you. And the landlord, he's a right bloody misery. I think he took this pub when they turned him down for the Wheel Clamp Unit ...'

He didn't have time to react to the slight blush that spread across her face as he spoke, for from the rear of the pub emerged Arthur Pringle.

'Hello, Carol,' he said with something close to affection.

'Oh, hello, daddy!'

'Oh, fuck me,' muttered Wayne.

Pringle saw Wayne, accelerated rapidly, and almost wrestled the suitcase from him.

'I'll take that ...' he said firmly.

At precisely that moment, there was the sound of breaking glass from the soccer pitch-cum-carpark ...

Wayne scraped off the last of the excess putty, skilfully wiped his prints off the glass. If he hadn't been on the top of a ladder, he would have stepped back to admire his handiwork. As it was, he practically fell off when he heard a female voice from down below:

'I brought you some tea.'

Wayne looked down and recognised Carol Pringle below him, smiling sweetly and far from shyly.

'Oh great,' he said. 'Just finished, actually.'

He was down the ladder in no time.

'Is that your job? Windows?'

He shook his head. 'Only when the lads have got a ball. I'm a chippie.'

She handed him his tea and he decided to do his fence-mending straight away.

'Ta. Here, I'm sorry about rubbishin' your old man. Basically, me an' Arthur get on great.'

She gave him a sceptical look. 'More than I do.'

'Oh? Bit iffy, is it?'

'More than a bit,' she answered with a nod. 'Since my

102

mother left, he's got worse, really. All his children are a terrible disappointment to him.'

'How come?'

'Because none of us joined the Air Force,' Carol said. 'My sister lives with a lecturer. My brother's gay and runs a health-food restaurant.'

Wayne got the picture. All kicking over the traces. Promising.

'What do you do?' he asked.

'I'm studying sociology at Nottingham University. Last year.'

'Then where?'

'As far away as possible,' she answered quickly, with a tight half-smile.

Wayne offered her a cigarette, and she accepted.

'I used to like it round here,' she went on. 'When I was a kid. I can't stand it now. The people have changed. They're not loyal any more. They're all the rich overspill from Sheffield. Or retired Tories who've got nothing better to do than complain about declining values and Arthur Scargill.'

'Yeah. I think our presence here has raised a few eyebrows,' said Wayne.

Then Pringle appeared from the pub, glared at Wayne and called Carol in.

'I'll talk to you later,' Carol murmured hastily before she followed her father back inside.

Oh, she's eager, thought Wayne. A nice girl, and a naughty one too. Who wouldn't be with an old man like that?

These were going to be an interesting few days of respite, these were, and no mistake.

NINE

In the lounge of the Cross Keys, Dennis was anxiously minding a tray of tea things. Away in the lobby he could see Howard Radcliff, Ally Fraser's very smooth and very competent architect, deep in conversation on the lobby payphone. Smiling enigmatically, the smarmy little bugger put down the phone and strode elegantly towards him.

'So what's the form then?' asked Dennis with some trepidation. 'What did the council say?'

In the manner of those accustomed to dealing with bureaucracy, Howard was non-committal. 'It's much as I expected,' he explained. 'The procedures on listed buildings are fairly standard. I could appeal to the D of E but that would take a year.'

'So we've had it, then?' asked Dennis in a monotone.

'No,' drawled Howard, 'there's a degree of flexibility. I mean –' he gestured expansively – 'there's no way we can rip the guts out of the house and convert it into sharing units. But if I can convince the Council that we plan to *restore* the house, without changing the original façade ...'

Dennis was getting weary of this mullarkey. So OK, maybe you couldn't afford to pick and choose nowadays, but in his book a job worth doing was worth doing well. He had no faith in schemes that promised the earth to gullible local councillors and in the end meant little more than leaky roofs for the tenants and a villa with a swimming pool for the contractor. Resignedly, he was spooning sugar into his tea when he saw Norma standing by the reception desk.

'Excuse me a moment ...' he murmured, 'but my sister's just arrived.'

Howard watched him dash over to the reception desk. He

doesn't know what side his bread's buttered on, he reflected.

Dennis greeted his sister effusively. 'Hello, pet!' he cried. 'You made good time.'

Norma returned his greeting warmly. 'I've got your clean washing in the car,' she told him as the receptionist handed her the book.

'Yeah,' said Dennis gratefully, 'but not now. Look, I'm with the architect. Just check in, eh, and I'll get you some tea.'

As Norma completed the formalities, Dennis went back into the lounge to rejoin Howard. He still couldn't rid himself of those nagging doubts about the loophole they'd identified.

'But is that what Ally wants?' he resumed, not entirely sure of his ground.

'I don't know, Dennis,' said Howard with practised ease. 'But I do know that Ally bought the house as an investment. He did *not* buy it to live in. Can you see him and Vicki as Lord and Lady of the Manor?'

Dennis saw the logic. 'No, I can't,' he confessed. 'It's too far from her hairdresser's.'

Howard signalled a passing waitress and ordered a fresh pot of tea. 'And another cup, please,' added Dennis.

'Mind you,' he went on, 'whatever Ally decides to do with the house, it's going to take you a while to draw it up, isn't it? So there's not much point in my lads hanging around?'

'Not necessarily. Whatever we do, there's a certain amount of spare work has to be done.'

'Then the quicker we put them to work the better,' interjected Dennis. "Cos God knows what they'll get up to around here.'

That evening, in the discreetly-lit dining room at the Cross Keys, Norma was feeling more than usually expansive.

'That was delicious, thank you,' she whispered as the waiter took their main-course dishes away.

'D'you want a sweet?' asked Dennis. They both glanced round at their surroundings, feeling slightly overawed. There was a low, indistinct murmur of conversation. This was Egon Ronay land, right down to the low-key, expensive decor and the classic country prints.

'I shouldn't,' said Norma, 'but I'm sure I'll be tempted. Let's wait a few minutes.'

Dennis caught the eye of a passing waitress. 'I'll have a brandy, please,' he said, eyeing with pleasure the seams on her stockings.

Norma leaned forward conspiratorially. 'This is a rare treat for me, Dennis,' she intoned.

'It's a thank you, Norma,' said Dennis frankly. A couple of bottles of the house red had made him feel generous. 'A thank you for giving me bed and board, doing me laundry and putting up with me moods. And helping me look after the kids when I have them over.'

'This place can't be cheap,' Norma murmured.

Dennis smiled mischievously. 'I'll lay some of this off on Ally as "consultations with architect",' he said, but he couldn't help remembering the times – either with Vera or with Dagmar – when a blow-out like this would have been followed by a no-holds-barred session afterwards.

Norma looked pensive. 'Yes,' she said eventually. 'He won't notice any difference. I saw that Vicki in Fenwick's about a month ago. The coat she was wearing could have bought this hotel.'

'Aye, she's done all right for herself, young Vicki,' said Dennis with a twinkle in his eye. 'Mind you, she was bound to go far with legs like hers.'

'How long, though, Dennis?'

'I just admire them, Norma,' he chuckled. 'I've never measured them.'

But Norma wasn't in quite so playful a mood.

'I mean, how long before he dumps her?' she asked. 'Before he dumps you, come to that?'

Dennis didn't need this. 'Aw, don't start on Ally again,' he pleaded.

But Norma wouldn't be put off. 'He just makes me uncomfortable, that's all. I can't help it Dennis, I hate you working for him.'

You and me both, kid, thought Dennis. He could sense the good feeling evaporating as the old family arguments reared their ugly heads.

'I think you do too,' went on Norma. 'I know why you do it. You do it for your kids.'

'I wouldn't be here if I didn't,' said Dennis, indicating their surroundings.

Norma was warming to her theme. 'I know you're not happy,' she confided. 'I know that's why you lost touch with Neville and lots of our friends. 'Cos you didn't want them to know. You keep things inside but I notice. You're under a lot of strain, Dennis!'

Where was that bloody waitress, thought Dennis, the anger surging inside him. 'Well, this isn't helping!' he snapped.

'You're so quick-tempered,' breathed Norma, as though she'd uttered a universal truth.

Dennis flashed an angry glance at her. He grabbed her half-empty wine glass, and drained it at a gulp.

'And you're drinking more than you should.'

Dennis looked at her askance. 'Just 'cos I ordered another brandy,' he sneered.

'I'm going by the number of empties I throw out every week,' implored Norma.

Though his temper was rising, Dennis didn't want to escalate the argument.

'Look Norma,' he said, using all his self-control, 'let's not have an argument, eh pet? At least the job I've got now suits me fine. I'm doing what I know and what I'm best at. I've got a team of lads and we're doing a hard day's graft, six days a week. So there's no problems, OK?'

He made a big conciliatory gesture, looking round for the waitress, but suddenly his expression changed.

'Oh, Christ!' he breathed, crestfallen.

'What is it?' asked Norma. She hadn't a clue what was going on. Not trouble with Ally Fraser again?

'Problems,' muttered Dennis, and hunkered down in his chair.

Oz was standing by the entrance to the dining room. It wasn't his flashy boots that were causing heads to turn – it was the jacket that went with them. He looked like a refugee from the Grand Old Opry.

Worse still, he'd spotted Dennis and Norma, and was

coming over. 'Hello, Den,' he called loudly.

'Hello, Oz,' said Dennis, rather more quietly.

The Scottswood Road Kid gave Norma a peck on the cheek – coolly received – and gazed in admiration around the room.

'Canny place, this,' he observed. 'Good grub, is it?'

'Very good,' said Norma, tight-lipped.

The waitress came over with the sweet trolley. Oz caught sight of a bowl of plump strawberries.

'They look good!' he cried, and popped a couple into his mouth.

Norma and Dennis exchanged uneasy glances. 'Are you all here?' the latter asked warily.

'Aye . . .' mumbled Oz through a mouthful of fruit. 'This is the last port of call. We've been scouring the area looking for some action.'

'And did you find any?' Norma asked out of politeness.

'Got more chance of findin' a nun in a knocking shop!' boomed Oz. Dennis wished a hole would open up and swallow him.

The maître d' came over. 'Is this gentleman joining you, sir?' he asked.

'No,' Dennis quickly retorted.

Oz got the picture. 'Oh! Right!' he said, wondering what he'd done wrong. 'We'll be in the bar if you fancy one. Nice to see you, Norma.'

He left the room, much to the relief of everyone.

Now Dennis could give his undivided attention to the waitress. Mercifully, she hadn't fled at the approach of Oz.

'What will you have, pet?' he asked Norma, turning to the sweet trolley.

'The cream caramel looks very nice,' she said. The waitress served her.

'Nothing for me, thanks,' said Dennis, patting his stomach, 'but can you chase up that brandy?'

She moved off. Norma busied herself with her cream caramel. After a few mouthfuls she carefully put her spoon down.

'I was in the video shop the other day,' she began, 'and I ran into Audie Charles.'

'Oh yes?' said Dennis, not really interested.

'She'd been talking to some woman and your name came up. And she said – this woman – that you owed Ally Fraser money.'

Dennis felt the bile rising in his throat.

'What?' he blustered. 'Which woman? Who said this?'

'I've no idea who it was. A friend of Audie's. The question is, is it true? Is that why he's got such a hold on you?'

'He's not got any kind of hold on me!' snarled Dennis. 'The reason I work for Ally Fraser is because he trusts me. He's surrounded by so many arse-lickers. They'd be pushed for an answer if he said hello.'

'Dennis, please!' hissed Norma. Heads were beginning to turn.

'I don't know if you've noticed,' growled Dennis, lowering his voice, 'but these days people can't be too choosy about the work they get. Specially up our way.'

The brandy arrived. Dennis grunted his thanks. Norma could see his hands balled into fists, the knuckles turning white.

'I'm not getting at you, Dennis. I'm just concerned. About your state of mind . . .'

He downed the brandy in one gulp.

'. . . and your health.'

'Don't be!' snapped Dennis. A right old cock-up this evening was turning out to be.

Sooner than Norma might have liked – another coffee would have been nice – her tense-looking brother was steering her out of the dining room.

'Everything all right, sir?' asked the maître d' as they passed.

'Very nice, thanks,' smiled Dennis. More and more these days he was having to put on a brave face, and the strain was beginning to tell.

There seemed to be a commotion in the bar. Dennis would have given the place a wide berth, but then he heard a familiar voice bellowing in anger.

He sighed, signalling to Norma to wait in the hallway, and moved quickly into the bar. From the doorway he was able to witness the last act of a tragedy that he should have seen coming: the lads preparing to leave, a defiant Oz still thrusting himself foward despite Bomber's restraining arm, determined to have the last word to a bemused, irritated crowd of county types.

'You can all relax!' Oz was firing at them. 'we're off! And we won't be back, neither! Where I come from, we're hospitable to strangers. But you lot have made us about as welcome as a fart in an astronaut suit!'

There were disgusted murmurs from the locals. People turned away as the lads left, with Oz now leading. Dennis cringed. Jesus, what it was to have charge of a batch of bored cowboys in the middle of the countryside. In many ways they were more alien here than they had been in Düsseldorf. This was another country, another world.

Not that all contacts with the locals had been so hostile or demoralising. The Cross Keys fiasco had been a clash of cultures – the lads' ebullience and lack of inhibition versus ingrained local habits of the quiet, incestuous drink. But Neville had met one of the local county types in the shop the previous day, had been identified as a builder, and had been very pleasantly asked to pop over and do a bit of moonlighting. For him, at least, the country wasn't all bad.

'It's not too far. About two miles, he said,' Neville told Barry, who had agreed to run him over to the possible job.

Barry shrugged. 'I'm not bothered. I've got nothing on, have I?'

Neville was mildly embarrassed. 'I hope the lads don't mind,' he said. 'I'd just rather occupy me time workin' than anythin' else, y'know?'

Barry nodded. 'Quite right, Nev. I've always found work very therapeutic.'

They had just reached the van when Oz appeared.

'Hey! Where are you two off to?' bellowed the big man.

Barry explained Neville's stroke of luck.

'Hang on,' said Oz. 'I'll come with you. Sod all else to do.'

Ten minutes later, the van drew up outside a handsome, though unpretentious country house. More a superior farmhouse than a stately home, but impressive for all that. A sort of workaday elegance about it.

'Lovely place, eh?' commented Neville.

'Must have made a bob or two to have this,' Barry agreed. It certainly touched the upwardly-mobile soul within.

'Listen,' Neville said carefully. 'If he needs some more hands, would you lads be interested?'

'Naw,' said Oz emphatically.

'But it's always pocket money, though, isn't it?'

'Money may be your God, Nev,' Oz said. 'But it's not mine.'

With that he and Barry drove off in the van, leaving Neville to make his way into the house.

He knocked on the door. It was opened by a pleasant, attractive young woman dressed in an old sweater and jeans. Hardly the image of the gentry he'd had, but a very nice surprise.

'Good morning,' he said shyly. 'I'm Neville. I spoke to your husband in the shop ...'

'Oh,' she said with a relaxed smile. 'You've come to help us out. Yes. Why don't you come in?'

He hesitated, aware of his dirty boots.

'Don't worry about your feet,' she laughed. 'The house is full of dogs and babies.' She ushered him in. 'James won't be long. He's in the barn. Would you like some tea?'

'Oh, wouldn't mind,' Neville answered gratefully.

He found himself in a big, ancient kitchen with a flagstone floor and an Aga in the corner. There were toys everywhere, dirty dishes still piled by the sink from breakfast, and a baby playing placidly on the floor. A venerable dog woofed amiably at him as he entered.

'Sorry the place is in such a mess,' said the woman, introducing herself as Celestia. Neville smiled at the baby, who was at the crawling stage and staring at him from its playpen.

'That grubby thing's Lucy,' said Celestia.

'I've got a little girl,' Neville said eagerly. 'Deborah. She's almost two. I miss her, actually.'

She nodded. 'I like them when they're two. They're really boring at *this* age.'

Neville looked around in slight awe.

'It's a lovely house.'

She smiled. 'It's not very practical. And a bugger to heat.'

Neville almost blushed át such earthy words coming at him in cut-glass tones. But he was enjoying himself. These were nice people. Maybe the gentry weren't so bad, after all.

His impressions were underlined by James's entry, in clothes similar to Celestia's, wearing a pair of very dirty gumboots. James was about thirty, well spoken, but with a no-nonsense air that was like a breath of fresh air. Within minutes, he and Neville were outside, humping junk and debris from an old stable building and loading it onto a trailer hitched up behind a not very new tractor. James worked just as hard as Neville. He was accustomed to physical work, that was clear, for all his obvious breeding.

'So many of these houses have these old stables and barns which just stand there doing nothing except decay,' James explained as they worked. 'I thought I'd put this to some use. Make a games room for the kids, or an office for myself.' He smiled embarrassedly. 'Sort of thing one's always planning to do but never has the time or the money to get round to it.'

'I know what you mean,' agreed Neville. 'I've been promising to retile our bathroom for the last two years.'

James nodded, motioned at the old stable building.

'What d'you think, Neville? Would it cost an absolute fortune?'

Neville stepped back, examined the building critically, shook his head.

'I don't think so. You'd need to run power in. And you need insulation and a new roof. But the structure's in amazingly good nick.'

James pointed to a broken-down wall.

'I'd have to repair that.'

'I could do that,' said Neville with a hint of satisfaction.

'Could you?'

'I'm a brickie. That's my trade.'

'Really? How come your trade brings you so far afield?'

It was a slightly naïve quesiton, however well meant. Neville grimaced slightly as he introduced James to one of the realities of northern working-class life.

'Oh, you go where the work is,' he said gently.

Neville had his own way of dealing with the Magnificent Seven's enforced idleness. Dennis's was also clear, and in character: fencemending Norma while at the same time staying on the end of the all-important telephone connection to Spain and Ally. As for the other lads, there was a certain tragicomic predictability to their activities too.

Bomber sat in the bar of the Barley Mow, reading a paper to while away the morning, with the others gone out and Wayne not yet surfaced from his bed.

Carol appeared with a mug of tea for him and a sweet smile. No Arthur this morning, which couldn't be bad.

'Thank you my dear,' purred Bomber. 'Service with a smile makes a change round here.'

Carol shrugged. 'Father's hopeless. Then he wonders why the place is always empty.'

Then Wayne shuffled into the bar from upstairs, still bleary and less than alert.

'Mornin', Bomb . . .' he suddenly moved a swift few notches up towards wakefulness. 'Oh, hello, Carol.'

She smiled at him. 'Someone had a good time last night.'

'Yeah, we emptied six pubs,' said Wayne with a crooked smile.

Bomber nodded ruefully. 'I've had more exciting evenings.'

'Mind you, Bomb, that was a blinding game of skittles in the Green Dragon. Right cliff-hanger, that was.'

'Do you want some tea?' Carol suggested brightly. It was obvious she had a soft spot for Wayne, plain as day, Bomber thought with interest.

'Oh, magic,' Wayne said, flashing her a boyish grin.

'This place is on the up and up, Bomb,' he said as Carol moved over to the bar to fetch a mug – loud enough for her to hear. 'We'll be havin' bunny girls next.'

'It's only for a day,' Carol said. 'Dad's gone into Sheffield, so I said I'd look after the place.'

'Oh, I'll give you a hand if you like,' Wayne suggested quickly. 'I can pull pints.'

Bomber looked at him, then at Carol. 'That's not what you want to pull . . .' he murmured.

And Wayne's imploring look, his plea to Bomber not to

queer his pitch, told the man from Bristol that he was spot on the right track. Wayne was into his seduction routine – and nothing was going to stop the machinery now it was going.

A few miles away, Oz and Barry had stopped the van by a green meadow that ran down to a seductive-looking stream. Oz had had this brilliant notion that there might be trout in the water, and in this case he had been right. Within minutes of their making a stop, Oz was in the stream with his trousers rolled up while Barry watched dubiously from the bank.

'You can't do this without rods and flies and suchlike,' Barry insisted.

Oz grinned. 'You just wait and see.'

'What d'you do?'

'You tickle 'em,' Oz told him. 'Used to do this when I was a lad up in Northumberland. There was this stream near where I spent me holidays.'

'There was a stream near us when I was a lad, too,' Barry said with a frown. 'Nothing lived in it, though.'

But Oz was no longer listening. 'I've seen one,' he hissed. 'See, they rest by the side of rocks.'

'Where is it?' Barry whispered.

'There's no need to whisper. It can't bloody hear us!'

'Well, I don't know that, do I?'

'Take your coat off!' Oz ordered.

'What for?'

'When I hoy it on the bank,' Oz explained, 'drop your coat on it. Stop it wrigglin' back in the river. They fight, y'know. They're gutsy little devils.'

'Me coat'll get all fishy ...'

'Listen, d'you want a fish supper, or don't you?'

'All right,' Barry conceded.

He reluctantly took off his coat. Oz, meanwhile, kneeled in the water, slipping his handkerchiefed hand under the surface.

'Here we go ...' he said, giving a running commentary. 'I'm strokin' it ... gently ... just like a woman really ...'

He hushed Barry into silence now, continued the delicate movements, then suddenly pounced. His hand cleared the water, gripping a quite large fish, which he hurled onto the bank to Barry's total amazement.

114

'Bloody hell, Oz, it's a flyin' fish!'

'Get it! Get it!' Oz growled.

Barry grabbed his coat, shrieking as he gripped the material with the writhing fish inside it, 'It's all wriggling and alive!'

Just as Oz was scrambling back to the bank, the fish squirmed out of the coat and leapt back into the stream.

'Oh, you pillock!' oathed Oz.

Barry looked shamefaced.

'I'm sorry. It took me by surprise. I've never done this before.'

'Aye. Well, next time don't just stand there like a paralysed matador!'

As time went on, they perfected the technique. They had two expired and fat trout laid out on Barry's coat, and Oz was going after a third, when Barry glanced up the bank and saw a burly man in a patched sweater, cord trousers and gumboots approaching fast.

'There's someone coming,' he said casually after a couple of moments.

'What?' said Oz, leaving off his task and suddenly alert.

Barry pointed. 'Over there, heading this way.'

Oz waded rapidly to the bank.

'Right, gi' us the fish,' he commanded, and promptly stuffed them in the pockets of his anorak.

'He's wavin' at us,' Barry said, still unconcerned.

'Howway, man!' hissed Oz, already heading for the bushes.

Barry stared at him. 'What's the rush all of a sudden? I wanted to have a go meself.'

'He could be a gamekeeper!'

Barry followed, and they headed back towards the van at speed.

'Are you sayin' this isn't legal or something?' Barry panted.

''Course poaching's not legal!'

'Poaching? You never said anything about poaching!'

Oz glanced at him contemptuously.

'You don't think these streams are open to the public, do you?' he said. 'People pay thousands for a rod of river.'

'How serious is it?' Barry asked nervously.

Oz carried on running. 'Put it this way,' he told Barry. 'If they catch us, we'll never make it to the Crown Court.' He pointed in passing to a nearby oak tree. 'They'll string us up from that branch!'

They made it to the van, and Barry started it up and put his foot down. The country was a terrible place; it was run by unspoken codes, while in the city signs and officials were constantly telling you what and what not to do. The country was a bloody trap ...

They drove as far as the market town, where they parked in the main square. They were both famished, so they found the only eating house in sight – a twee little tea shoppe – and wandered in.

The place was one of those jumped-up cafés that did light meals and teas. The tables were small and impractical, especially for Oz, who looked like a huge kid trying to sit down at a kindergarten play table. They squeezed in – the only men among a batch of worthy local matrons and three bored-looking waitresses – and ordered the lunch of the day, with double portions of chips. After a while, despite the strangeness of the place, they started to relax. Until Barry looked up from the remains of his cottage pie and his eyes widened.

'Oz!' he moaned. 'There's that bloke.'

He could see the big man in the sweater and cords standing by his own Landrover, staring with interest at the van parked outside.

'What bloke?' asked Oz lazily.

'The gamekeeper!'

Oz looked, mouthed an obscenity that turned several heads.

'Get the bill!' he said urgently, pushing back his chair and moving over towards the coatstand where they had left their outdoor clothes.

Barry had just finished paying at the cash register, and Oz was putting on his anorak, when the doorbell tinkled and the gamekeeper moved purposefully inside.

'Excuse me,' the man said pointedly.

Oz looked at him as if he had never seen him before in his life.

'Aye?'

'About half an hour ago, you and your mate were down by the river, weren't you?' the man asked.

'What river?'

'You know perfectly well what river.'

Oz, all angelic innocence, turned to Barry.

'Did we pass a river, Barry?'

'I think we did. When we were having our walk,' said the zit king, his pockmarked face white with terror.

The gamekeeper stared at them both implacably.

'You had no right to walk there. That's private land.'

'We weren't to know that,' said Barry. 'We're not from round here y'see.'

'There's notices posted. You can read where you're from, can't you?' growled the gamekeeper, whose whole manner gave a new meaning to the word 'dour'.

'Hey, hold your horses, son!' Oz retorted angrily.

But the burgeoning conflict was interrupted by the icy tones of a county lady who wanted to get her tweed coat from the coatstand behind him.

'Would you excuse me, please?' she asked, in the kind of voice she obviously used for training red setters.

Oz moved wordlessly, still intent on his duel with the gamekeeper.

'Are you tellin' me,' he snapped, 'that there's all these acres around here – and we're not allowed to walk on them?'

'There's public footpaths.'

'I'm not talkin' about footpaths. I'm talkin' about all those miles of fields and moor.' Oz indicated Barry. 'Him and me were in the Falklands, y'know. And one of the things that kept us goin' was the thought of walkin' in England's green and pleasant land. Which we fought to preserve.'

Barry looked embarrassed.

'We weren't actually there during hostilities,' he explained with his usual touch of pedantry, rather ruining the effect of Oz's words. But the big Tynesider carried on regardless.

'We was there rebuilding the land what had been ravaged by the invader!'

'That doesn't give you the right to go poaching,' the gamekeeper persisted.

'Poachin'? Poachin' for what?'

117

'Trout.'

'Oh aye,' said Oz, all righteous anger. 'Where's our rods, then? You got a fishin' rod stuck down your trouser leg, Barry?'

The gamekeeper ignored Barry's anxious cackle.

'There's other ways. There's tickling them.'

'"Ticklin'" 'em?' Oz turned imploringly to their audience of matrons. 'Have you heard this?' he demanded. 'I suppose you tickle them until they're so weak with laughter you just pick them out of the river and toss them in the pan, is that it?'

The gamekeeper sighed. 'Have you any idea how serious an offence it is?'

'Look mate,' said Oz. 'Before you talk about an offence, I think you should provide some evidence. I'll tell you what I'll do. His van's out there. You can search that. And you can search me and me mate, an' all.'

Barry's lip started to tremble. Oz was playing a very dangerous game with this remorseless henchman of the landowning classes. The gamekeeper stared at the deep pockets of Oz's anorak. In response, Oz lifted his hands, offering himself to a search.

'Go on!' he said. 'This is typical, this is. Typical of the attitude of all you people towards strangers. But if you don't find nowt, we'll expect a public apology.'

For a moment it looked as though the gamekeeper might back off, but eventually he moved forwards and thrust both his hands into the anorak pockets. No result. He glowered at Oz, still reluctant to concede an apology.

'Check the van next, shall we?' he said.

'Right! Right!' agreed Oz, ignoring Barry's amazed looks, still maintaining a perfect expression of outraged innocence.

They got as far as the van. It was then that the lady who had just retrieved her coat from the stand and left the tea shop failed to find her car keys in her handbag and began to check her pockets. The three men turned as there was a squeal from a few yards away. The lady who had just delved into her pockets was holding up a fat, dead, very cold and slippery trout in one well-manicured hand ...

*

Dennis and Norma were sitting in the lounge of the Cross Keys, having tea. The atmosphere had improved again, perhaps now that Norma had some appreciation of the real immediate strain he was under. And it was nice to have a relaxing few days in the country and enjoy a taste of how the other half lived. Dennis was looking through the food guide to find a nice place for dinner.

He saw Bomber enter the lounge, and they greeted each other amicably.

'What've you been up to?' Dennis asked.

Bomber grinned, as if to say: I've got a surprise for you.

'Oh, I've been driving around the countryside,' he said. 'And I picked up a hitch-hiker.'

He gestured towards the door, and Moxey entered, looking even more sheepish than usual.

'H-hello, Den.'

Dennis smiled warily.

'Er . . . I don't think you lads have met my sister Norma. This is Bomber, and Moxey.'

They exchanged greetings.

'Everything all right, is it?' Dennis asked then, with a clear hint of meaning.

'Oh yeah,' Moxey said quickly. 'I had to go down to the smoke. Sort things out. Got me cards.' He produced his documents, flashed them at Dennis. 'So there'll be no problems in that department.'

Moxey didn't have to go into which Irish pub he'd hung out in, or how much it had cost to take on his new identity. Dennis was experienced enough to have a rough guess, and wise enough not to ask. It didn't matter. So long as Moxey had those cards, Dennis was in the clear.

'Champion,' said Dennis. ''Cause the architect tells me with a bit of luck we'll all be back at work on Monday. You've timed it rather well, Moxey.'

'Er . . . it's not Moxey now,' the Liverpudlian corrected him. He checked the documents. 'It's Brendan Mulcahy.'

Dennis sighed. How the hell had he got himself mixed up in all this?

Norma suggested some more tea. Dennis looked at his watch.

119

'Oh, I think it's almost time for a drink, isn't it, lads?'

There was enthusiastic agreement.

'Why not, eh?' Dennis said comfortably. 'Things seem to be shaping up all right for once.'

As they rose, one of the waitresses came in, looked around the room, spotted Dennis.

'Mr Patterson?'

'Aye?'

'Could you come to the telephone, please? It's the police. A couple of your lads have been arrested ...'

Neville had been enjoying tea and scones in James and Celestia's kitchen after a day's plastering when a phone call had meant that his host had to go into town – something about some poachers. James had offered to run Neville back to the Barley Mow after the unfortunate piece of business at the police station, and Neville had readily agreed. Another interesting aspect to a really pleasant and interesting day.

When he followed James into the police station, there were two surprises for him. One was seeing Oz and Barry sitting on the bench behind the desk, looking very downcast and foolish. The other was the burly gamekeeper's greeting to the young farmer Neville had spent the day with.

'Good afternoon, Sir James,' the gamekeeper said respectfully. 'Sorry about this.'

James looked at the two poachers. 'Are those the chaps?'

'Yes, sir. Caught them red-handed.'

The gamekeeper unfolded a piece of newspaper on the desk, revealed the two trout.

'Oh dear,' said James wearily. 'So what do I have to do?'

Neville moved forward and whispered in his ear: 'Er, excuse me, Sir James. Could I have a word?'

'Certainly, Neville.'

Neville could see the lads' amazement at his being on first-name terms with the Lord of the Manor, but he pressed on: 'In private, like ...'

'Those two poachers, sir,' he said on the pavement outside. 'They're my workmates.'

'Really?'

'I'm sure they didn't know what they were doing. They

120

wouldn't have known it was your property.'

'No, I suppose not.'

'I mean, we're townies, aren't we?'

Sir James stroked his chin doubtfully. 'I suppose so. The trouble is, they take a rather dim view of that kind of thing. And as I'm the landowner I'm expected to set an example.'

'They could make amends,' Neville said quickly.

'How?'

'Instead of payin' that fine, they could help me fix the wall.'

Sir James looked downright relieved. 'It does seem a lot of fuss about nothing . . .' He smiled. 'And Celestia and I could have that trout for supper.'

At that moment, Dennis and Bomber got out of Bomber's BMW in front of the police station. Dennis looked at Neville.

'What's happenin', Neville?'

Neville smiled smugly.

'Don't worry,' he said. 'Sir James and I have taken care of everything.'

The lads were in a state of euphoria as the BMW and Barry's van turned into the Barley Mow carpark. Oz was convinced that with the local nob on their side, they would never be outcasts again. Bomber agreed: 'They'll certainly think twice about pushin' us around now!'

The bubble burst when they saw Wayne sitting on a pile of luggage stacked outside the pub – their luggage. He was smoking a cigarette, trying to look nonchalant.

'Where've you all been?' he asked. 'I'm bloody freezin', I am.'

'Never mind that. What's happening?' demanded Dennis. Wayne smiled thinly. 'Arthur's kicked us out, hasn't he?'

'He can't do that!' Oz roared.

'Yes he can. It's his pub, and he's done it,' Wayne said.

'He's gotta have a reason, though,' Bomber chipped in.

'Well, he's always been a bit beady about us bein' here, hasn't he?'

'Aye, we're payin' customers, though,' Neville said.

Wayne was beginning to look more and more shifty. 'Yeah, but we do make a lot of noise . . .'

He began to pick up the cases. 'Better load up, hadn't we?'

'Hold on a tick!' said Barry. 'I'm not takin' this lyin' down.'

'Nothing to do with me,' Moxey said. 'I've never slept here once.'

Dennis suddenly grabbed Wayne's arm. 'Wayne, if he's turfin' all of you out, you must have put up some kind of black. Now, what was it?' he demanded.

Wayne realised the game was up. He sighed.

'Well . . .' he said slowly. 'I suppose him findin' me in bed with his daughter did have *something* to do with it . . .'

TEN

History, it has often been said, repeats itself. Well, now it had happened to the lads. There had been Hut B, and now there was Thornely Manor. The few hours after their expulsion from the Barley Mow by the outraged Arthur Pringle had seen them tour most of North Derbyshire desperately seeking alternative accomodation, to no avail. Old Arthur had obviously been on the blower to his fellow-licensees and innkeepers; everywhere they asked, there was no room. Hordes of commercial travellers had coincidentally descended on the district, booking out every hostelry within a twenty-five mile radius. There had been one or two guest houses where the blacklist wasn't operating, but who wanted to be in by ten, keep their boots clean, and sleep in a double bed with Oz?

The squalid comradeship they had known in Düsseldorf drew them back to the grim, mock-gothic halls of Thornely Manor like moths to a flame ...

'It looks worse by night than it does by day,' said Neville miserably as they rounded the curve in the drive and spotted the looming outline of the house.

Moxey, sitting next to him in the back of the VW van, nodded.

'It's not too bad once you get inside, though – bit like prison, really.'

And the sad convoy of VW, van and BMW made its way towards the only roof they were going to get over their heads that night – and maybe for some time to come.

The bags were piled up just inside the door of the old drawing room. And there was no mistaking the fact that Wayne was in disgrace. He'd been handed a broom and told

123

to sweep the place out. It had once been warm and elegant; now the room was about as welcoming as a set from a Frankenstein movie.

Bomber shuffled in with a big carpet over his shoulder, interrupting Wayne's lonely task.

'I found this upstairs, Wayne – should take some of the chill off this room,' he said.

The cockney was subdued, to say the least. He shivered miserably.

'I think I'm gonna need a blow-lamp to take the chill out of the atmosphere, though.'

Bomber looked at him with a distinct lack of sympathy.

''Tis true you wouldn't win any popularity contests at the moment.'

He lowered the carpet to the floor, began to unroll it.

'If I'd known old Arthur was goin' to react that badly,' Wayne said, 'I'd have had second thoughts about strumpin' his daughter – honest.'

'Yes, and havin' had those second thoughts, you'd still have gone and done it,' retorted Bomber, unconvinced. 'Knob Law – that's what you're ruled by, Wayne. As soon as there's a fire in your loins, there's a freeze-up in your brain.'

'Normally, it's only me that suffers, though,' Wayne said in his own defence. 'Grazed knees from shinning a drain-pipe, the odd pulled muscle from doin' it to the *Bolero* at 45 instead of 33 ...' He sighed. 'I may have dropped my mates in it because I couldn't say no to an afternoon of passion,' he added, leaning on his brush and going a bit misty. 'But she wasn't half worth it!'

Bomber glowered at him.

'That's some consolation to us, Wayne,' he growled. He finished laying the carpet. 'Right. While you finish your jankers here, I'll go and have a scout around. See if I can't find some mattresses or cushions ...' He got as far as the door before he turned back and fired his final salvo: 'And you'd better decide which of the twenty-two bedrooms you're going to lock yourself in!'

In the kitchen, the rest of them were hard at work unloading the necessities of life. Oz and Moxey were piling cans of beer into the fridge as Dennis came in from the grounds.

'Been shopping?' he asked.

'Just stopped off at the village store to get a few supplies in,' said Oz.

Dennis looked at the fridge and the massed ranks of beer cans, then asked Oz for the keys to the VW camper. Oz obliged, and at the same time handed him the receipts for the 'supplies'.

Dennis looked at them and his eyes widened. 'Twenty-seven pounds, sixty-two pence!'

'Yeah,' Oz said calmly. 'But that includes a toilet roll . . .'

Eventually the drawing room was more or less fitted out as a makeshift dormitory: piles of groundsheets as mattresses, a fire of debris and bits of old beams in the grate, lit by Wayne.

'There,' the Londoner said, stepping back from the fire he had made. 'Should make Moxey feel at home, at least.'

He stared at Bomber's handiwork.

'I don't want to disparage your efforts, Bomb,' he said, 'but I have to say that this place looks like a bleedin' mortuary.'

Bomber eyed him coldly.

'Wayne, if I was in your position, I should restrict my comments to "yes sir", "no sir", and "three bags full sir". Otherwise, this room might look more like a mortuary than you think!'

'Point taken,' Wayne backed down hastily. 'A low profile for a few days, then?'

'As low as the pile on this carpet . . .'

Barry and Neville walked in. Barry, in fact, looked cheered by the relative order and the fire.

'Oh yuh,' he said. 'Not too bad at all, really. I can see us settlin' in here. What with the idyllic country view, the elegant room and the flickering glow from the fire – this could be Brideshead Revisited . . .'

Neville lashed out at the dust sheet with a foot. 'Reminds me more of Gateshead Revisited . . . all it needs is a tin bath in the hearth.'

'Never mind. We can probably get some sleeping bags at Asda tomorrow – it's amazin' what you can buy in

125

supermarkets these days,' Barry said cheerfully.

'Yeah, they've certainly come a long ...' Wayne began, making an attempt at being included in the conversation.

The other lads jumped on him like a ton of bricks.

'We don't want your opinions, dick-brain!' snapped Barry.

Neville nodded. 'Yeah – we could do with a rest from you, Wayne, OK?'

'Fine ... fine ...' Wayne said after a short silence, looking really crestfallen. 'I've said I'm sorry, lads. I can't do much more.'

'No – but don't go expectin' instant forgiveness,' said Neville.

'It's all right,' Bomber murmured. 'I've told him – a few days in the dog-house, and if he keeps his nose clean and stays out of trouble, he might get remission.'

Wayne opened his mouth to protest, but at that moment Dennis entered with Oz and Moxey. The last two chucked cans of beer to everyone except Wayne.

'Right, lads!' Dennis called out. 'If I can just have a minute ...'

'Have as much as you like, Dennis,' Oz said, fixing Wayne with a hostile stare. 'We're not goin' anywhere.'

'Now,' Dennis continued, ignoring the in-fighting, 'considering the short notice with which our previous tenancy agreement was terminated, we haven't done too bad to get this place habitable. I know it's not perfect by any means ...'

There were looks of angry agreement from Oz and Neville.

'... But at least it's a roof over our heads. Now, as far as the work goes, we've got clearance to start again. But, dependin' on what Ally Fraser has in mind for the place, the architect'll need a bit of time to come up with some new plans.'

Dennis turned to Bomber and Oz.

'So if you can concentrate on clearing out the cellar ...'

To Wayne and Moxey:

'Wayne, Moxey, make good that panelling and plastering we've ripped away – and that should keep you busy till we get the next word.'

He noticed that Moxey was looking pained, as if he wanted to say something.

'Aye, what's up, Moxey ... oh.' He understood, grinned. 'I forgot, we've got a new man workin' with us now – tell 'em, Mox ...'

Moxey stood up and searched for the words.

'W-well, as some of you already know, I've got a new identity.' He reddened with embarrassment. 'As far as officialdom is concerned, I'm now Brendan Mulcahy ...'

Neville and Barry couldn't help bursting out laughing.

'So,' Moxey said, pressing on, 'it would help if you all started callin' me Brendan. So I get used to it, like.'

'What I don't understand ...' Wayne began, and was howled down in seconds. He went to his 'bed' and lay down in disgust.

Dennis left to go back to the Cross Keys – for tonight, at least. Norma was off back home in the morning. Then he would move in with the lads, he said.

'Not now you're a gaffer, you won't,' said Oz belligerently.

'What?'

'I was goin' to say, even though we're livin' on site now, we still want travellin' time. You tell Ally Fraser that.'

Dennis stared Oz down. 'Aye. An' what if he wants to charge you rent for livin' on his property?'

Oz turned away.

'Right, lads,' said Dennis. 'I'll be back tomorrow afternoon after I've seen the architect. Sleep well. All right if I take your car, Wayne?' he added. ''Cause the lads'll need the van for shopping.'

'Well, hang on ...' said Wayne, put out.

'Right, thanks!' Dennis cut him off, holding his hand out for the keys. Wayne tossed them over disconsolately.

It was a tough experience for Wayne, being sent to Coventry. After all, he didn't even know where the bloody place was, except that it was somewhere north of Watford.

Kenny Ames had breakfasted well, and was lounging, as usual these days, by the side of his pool, reading a well-thumbed copy of *Country Life*. A large union jack – the right way up, because he was very careful about those kind of things – fluttered in the gentle breeze that caressed the grounds of his villa. It was a perfect morning. It didn't even put Kenny out when Ally Fraser suddenly emerged through the French windows, unannounced.

'Morning, Kenny,' said Ally curtly. 'Don't get up.'

Ames smiled affably. 'Ally, my son!' He checked his watch, feigned surprise. 'This is a bit early for you, isn't it? Don't tell me an earthquake has struck the Casa del Fraser?'

'No, no,' said Ally. 'But, as it happens, it's property I'd like to discuss wi' you, Kenny.'

Kenny sighed, laid his *Country Life* to one side, gestured for Ally to settle down in the lounger opposite him.

'Certainly,' he began easily. 'I take it from the briskness of your manner that it's your manor giving concern again?'

Ally stared at him. 'It's funny you should anticipate that – it's almost as if you knew about the problems I'd have with the house before you sold it to me ...'

'No, it wouldn't be that,' Kenny said, refusing to take the bait. 'I think I'm just in a perceptive mood today. Now, how can I help?'

'I spoke to my architect last night,' Ally said. 'It would appear that we now have reasonable but limited scope for redeveloping the *interior* of the house, provided we do not molest the *exterior*.'

'Sounds a bit like having an arse-lift without the face-lift,' Kenny chuckled.

Ally was not amused, however.

'Quite,' he said heavily. 'Indeed, I am reliably informed that my time-share apartments are a non-runner so far as the local council are concerned. Nor would a fat-farm be any more generously considered.'

'Perhaps you should threaten to flog it to one of those Bagwash religious sects? The council might change their tune then,' Kenny suggested helpfully.

'I'd be interested in more practical suggestions.'

Kenny nodded, picked up his copy of *Country Life* again. He leafed through it thoughtfully.

'Here we are,' he said after a while. 'Just the job. Private nursing homes for, as they term it, "retired gentlefolk". Sprouting up all over the place, they are.'

Ally moved over to examine the page Kenny was reading from.

'It sounds a bit of a switch from my "country pads for city slickers" idea,' he said doubtfully.

'Don't knock it, Ally. You're simply going from exploiting disposable incomes to exploiting disposable people.' Ames smiled, pleased with the comparison. 'And there's actually more purse in the latter.'

'How d'you reckon?'

'Well, for one thing,' Kenny said, 'there's a faster turnover of guests, obviously. And the other beauty of these homes is that you not only get fees from the DHSS but also from grateful couples whose granny you're taking off their hands – it's win *and* place, son!'

Ally looked at him suspiciously. 'You seem remarkably well informed about all this, Kenny.'

'Yeah, well,' said Mr Sunshine. 'One of these was high on my investment portfolio before my enforced exile.'

Kenny reached over and took hold of Ally's arm enthusiastically.

'Ally, it's a cinch!' he said. 'Once you've done your building work, your only overheads are for the soup, the walking frames, and some old matron to give you a bit of window-dressing. And what council with a heart is gonna refuse permission for an old folks' home?'

Ally was obviously impressed. He looked at Ames thoughtfully.

'I'll talk to my man-on-the-spot. See what he says.'

'I'll tell you, Ally – you pitch in for this, and Bob's your uncle!'

'Or my grandad in this case,' said Ally drily.

Kenny laughed heartily.

'There we are, y'see. I told you I felt perceptive this morning. And if there was any lingering grievance, which I'm sure there wasn't, over my selling the house to you, then now – well, we're sweet, aren't we?'

Ally smiled, recognising the velvet-cased threat in the laughing boy's little speech.

'Aye – for the time bein'.' He picked up the copy of *Country*

Life. 'D'you take this regularly, then?'

'Oh yes ...' Kenny nodded in the direction of the flag. 'I get terribly nostalgic for the old country, you know, Ally. Being abroad doesn't half make me miss some basic English things – the gee-gees; me executive box at Spurs; cold misty mornings, and fried breakfasts ...'

His wistful recitation was interrupted by the appearance of a leggy blonde in a bikini, carrying glasses of Buck's fizz and a bottle of champagne on ice for refills. Ally savoured her, then chortled humourlessly.

'Then again,' he said. 'There are compensations ...'

'There you go, Norma,' Dennis said, loading the last of his sister's bags into the car and slamming down the boot with a kind of grim finality. 'Safe journey, pet.'

He leaned over and kissed her on the cheek. Norma's visit had been a pleasant change of routine – if he forgot the embarrassing incidents and the odd argument – but now it was back to realities.

'Are you going to be all right, Dennis?' she asked anxiously.

'What?' He shrugged wearily. 'Oh, aye. Just got to sort out the new work for the lads, make sure they're OK in the house, talk to the architect, and then let Ally know that his prime development property is now being squatted in by my six tearaways. Apart from that, I haven't got much on my plate ...'

Norma managed a painful smile.

'You could just get in the car and come back with me to Newcastle,' she said.

'I can't deny it's crossed my mind, Norma,' Dennis answered slowly. 'But ... well, I've never walked away from a job yet, and I'm not going to start now.' He paused, dead-pan. 'I'll *run* from this one.'

'So that's all that's keeping you here, then – professional pride?'

'What else would there be?' asked Dennis sharply. He had decided to brazen this particular question out.

'So if I hear any more rumours about you being in debt to Ally Fraser, I should ignore them?'

Dennis looked her straight in the eye. 'That's up to you, Norma,' he began. 'You know what it's like up there. Especially after all the ups and downs I've been through in the past few years. I'm surprised there aren't *more* rumours about me ...' His voice assumed a high-pitched, gossipping-housewife tone. '"Dennis Patterson's in debt, drinking too much, seeing different women, turning queer, gone born-again Christian." You could pick any one, long as it keeps the tongues wagging.'

'You're not that special, you know. It was just the one particular rumour I heard.'

'Aye well – maybe you should ask whoever's doing the talking – 'cos they seem to know more about it than me. Now come on Norma, stop mothering me. I've got graft to do.'

He ushered her towards her car.

'I'll give you a ring later in the week,' she promised as she strapped herself in.

'I'll have to call you, pet. I'm moving in with the lads tonight. Just like old times.'

Norma didn't know whether this was a good thing or what. She turned the ignition. 'Take care, Dennis,' she said with a hint of warning in her voice, and then she was off. Dennis watched her car until it was out of sight, and then turned back towards the Cross Keys.

After he had sorted things out at the inn, he drove into the town in Wayne's 'borrowed' BMW. He parked it in the centre of town, found his way to an olde worlde building nearby and made his way up some stone steps.

Howard Radcliff had certainly settled in quickly and with a characteristic sense of style. The offices were quite small, but very comfortable: a sofa and a desk, a filing cabinet and the obligatory drawing board. And in the middle of the room, an architect's scale model of Thornely Manor, complete with little plastic trees and cars.

'Very nice, Howard,' said Dennis, taking it all in. 'I hope Ally's picking up the bill for this.'

Radcliff grinned complacently.

'Well, I did manage to persuade him that it was cheaper to

131

rent offices down here than to travel from Newcastle every week . . .'

'Pity he didn't feel so obliging towards my lads – they're having to squat at the manor at the moment,' Dennis told him.

'That's the way the cookie crumbles,' Radcliff commented with a shrug. 'Coffee?'

He got two cups from a percolator, sat at his table and observed Dennis examining the scale model.

'Any word from Ally, then?' Dennis asked.

'Yep. He phoned from Spain this morning. He was in a very businesslike mood.'

'Sounds ominous.'

'On the contrary, Dennis – he's made a very shrewd decision, as it happens.' Radcliff gestured at the unfinished drawing on his board. 'Thornely Manor is now to become an old folk's home.'

'Really? Bit of a change. Suddenly feeling his age, is he?'

Radcliff chuckled. 'I'm not sure what his motives are. All I can say is that planning permission will be a breeze.' He counted off the advantages on his fingers. 'Government grants will be available for some of the work, and, once completed, the premises will be rate-free.'

'Sounds like a good hand,' Dennis agreed cautiously. 'Doesn't it change your plans, though? I mean, this rules out the jacuzzi and the Nautilus gym. And the squash court in the barn'll have to go . . .'

'*Some* alterations will be necessary, obviously,' Radcliff said with a patient smile. He moved over to the model, removed the roof to show a new facsimile interior. 'Essentially we'll be altering the balance of the design from large, self-contained units with some communal facilities, to a reduced, less private unit space per person, but with larger areas for group activity . . .'

'Small bedrooms and big cludgies, right?' Dennis translated for him.

Radcliff looked pained. 'That will be the strand of the redevelopment, yes.'

Dennis asked him when the new plans would be ready and

was surprised to hear that Radcliff was reckoning on the end of the week. He had done old folks' homes before, and they were a 'piece of cake'.

'Growing old is a growth industry, obviously,' remarked Dennis. 'So, is there anything in particular we can work on in the meantime?'

Howard looked at the model. 'Well, the kitchens will have to be extended to accommodate mass catering equipment, and I should imagine I'll take out that second stairwell and build in a lift.'

'Always assumin' that Ally crumbles the cookie that way, of course.'

'We shall have to see . . .' Radcliff said, missing the sarcasm completely.

Dennis looked unlovingly down at the model, with its tiny rooms. Jesus, who'd get old? Who'd become so helpless they were commodities for the profit of the likes of Ally Fraser and this eager-beaver young man on the make?

'Little boxes, eh, Howard?' he mused. 'Before they get stuck in the littlest boxes of all . . .'

They had been to the supermarket, and this time they had actually bought some food. Tons of it. Hardly gourmet provisions, but nourishing enough. Oz had also spent a lot of time testing out Moxey *alias* Brendan Mulcahy, to make sure he had his new identity right. Oz's helpfulness had even extended to buying Moxey several cans of Guinness for cultural reasons.

And it was 'Brendan' who now appeared with the lunchtime sandwiches. It was a warmer day now, and they were sitting around on benches under the trees. Cheese and chutney, and ham.

Wayne made to take one, and the plate was deliberately withdrawn and passed on. He was not yet considered to have done his penance. The others got served first; he got the leftovers.

Barry had been giving a lot of thought to Moxey's new identity.

'Who is Brendan Mulcahy, anyway?' he asked, munching

133

on a sandwich. 'I mean, does he really exist, or is he just a creation?'

'Nah – he's probably a dead man, isn't he?' said Oz.

'I know how he feels ...' muttered Wayne.

'All that happens,' Oz continued, 'is that his family flog off his passport for a few quid so that some other Mick can come over here and get a job.'

'That's not all he might get up to, either,' said Bomber darkly.

Neville started. 'You mean the IRA, Bomber?'

'IRA bomber is right,' growled Oz. 'You want to watch it, Brendan, or you might find the Anti-Terrorist Squad on your tail as well as the ordinary Plods.'

'You're really reassuring, you are, Oz,' Moxey moaned.

Dennis appeared around the side of the house to a chorus of greetings. Neville tossed him a can.

'Just having our statutory lunch-break, Dennis,' Oz pre-empted any enquiry. 'Of which we have roughly thirty-eight minutes left ...'

'What's happenin' then, Dennis?' Neville asked. 'Any word from Ally Fraser?'

Dennis took a swig of beer. 'Aye. As from now, lads, we're working on Thornely Manor Rest Home for Retired Gentlefolk.'

The news sunk in.

'Oh, that's nice, isn't it?' said Barry. 'Something of service to the community.'

'Perhaps all his customers will be retired villains!' suggested Bomber.

'Knowing my luck, they'll be retired coppers,' Moxey sighed.

Oz's eyes narrowed as he looked at Dennis.

'Sounds a bit rum to me. I know Ally Fraser – if he helped an old lady across the road, he'd be after her pension book. So what's really goin' on, Dennis?'

Dennis shrugged. 'As far as I know, Oz, this is just a straightforward property development. If you have ob-jections to working for Mr Fraser, all you have to do is leave ...'

'Yeah, and go back to the dole queue,' said Neville.

Oz got to his feet. 'Just because there's nay work, Neville, doesn't mean you have to work at anything. Integrity comes into it, and all.'

'Oz,' Dennis said mildly, 'you know Ally Fraser spends a lot of time in Spain now. Suppose he wanted to develop an old people's home out there, and suppose he wanted us lot to build it for him. How would you feel then?'

Oz did his best to maintain his self-righteous stance.

'I'd judge that job the same way as I'll judge this one,' he said nobly. But he couldn't really hide his interest, as neither could the others. 'Would this ... would this be in Marbella then ...?'

ELEVEN

That day they got down to their first real experience of hard, directed work since the lay-off. Bomber and Oz went to their appointed task of clearing out the debris from the cellar, piling it into tea chests and anything else that came to hand, moving it out into the garden. Barry began rewiring upstairs, working behind the skirting boards that had been so thoughtfully ripped out. Moxey plastered; and there was genuine pleasure in restoring the areas around the beautiful old cornices. Wayne, still in solitary, worked alone on the bannisters on the main staircase, replacing and sanding. Dennis and Neville set to outside the house, measuring and trenching for the extension that would give the kitchen capacity for the kind of mass catering Ally now had in mind. It was a good feeling for all of them, though they would never have admitted the fact.

It was dusk when they all crowded into the kitchen. A dust-blackened Oz dived straight into the fridge for the beer and began handing out cans to the lads that wanted them – all except Barry, who was getting into healthy living and decided on tea.

'Dear me,' growled Oz. 'That cellar's a dusty hole. Bomber and me definitely got the short straw.'

Bomber, also guzzling beer thirstily, agreed: 'Very true – the place rather put me in mind of some punk club I bounced at for a couple of days. The Rat's Arse, I think it were called ...'

'So you didn't come across any priceless oil paintings or racks of vintage wine down there?' said Neville.

'I'd have settled for a few bottles of Château Exhibition meself,' Oz said. 'Nah ... Bomber found a couple of old video-cassettes in a tea chest – that's about all that was recognisable ...'

'Video-cassettes?' echoed Wayne.

Oz ignored him for the moment. 'Are we talking to him yet?' he asked the rest of them.

There were murmurs of 'suppose so', shrugs.

'Yes, London,' said Oz then, keeping it as short as possible. 'Video-cassettes. What of it?'

Wayne grinned. 'Well, they might be a bit tasty, that's all – bearin' in mind that the former owner of these premises was a major porn-merchant. Isn't that right, Dennis?'

'Aye, I believe so. Kenny Ames, I think his name was.'

Moxey's eyes lit up. 'Maybe we'd better have a look at 'em – just in case they're depraved!'

'Sorry to disappoint you, *Brendan,* but Bomber and I chucked them into the skip with all the other rubbish,' Oz said.

There were groans from Wayne and Moxey.

'Don't be too disappointed, lads,' said Dennis. 'We haven't got anything to play them on, anyway.'

'No, that's true,' Wayne admitted. 'But we've got to start thinking about giggles for the evenings now the Barley Mow's out of bounds ...'

He was on dangerous ground there, especially with Oz. The big Tynesider could bear grudges very well.

'Yeah,' he snapped. 'And whose fault is that?'

Neville sighed, unwilling to sit and listen to more Wayne-bashing.

'Well,' he said, looking at his watch. 'I don't propose to spend my nights lookin' for a pub we haven't been barred from. I'm goin' to pop up to Sir James's and do a bit of work around his house. Any of you lads feel like helpin' out?'

'Bollocks, man,' growled Oz. 'I thought serfdom was over now ...'

'He'll be payin', Oz – and besides, you still owe him for those two trout you nicked from his stream.'

'Aye. I would do if we'd ended up with 'em. But the bloody law hung onto the bastards for fish supper down at the nick.'

Neville could see there was no point in arguing and made a

dignified withdrawal with his bag of tools.

They sat supping their cans for a while, then Bomber broke the silence.

'Well,' he began, 'I don't know about anyone else, but I'm game to try the Barley Mow again. After all,' he said with a withering glance at Wayne, 'only one of us strumped the daughter. Even somebody as unreasonable as Arthur Pringle should see that.'

'I wouldn't bank on it,' said Dennis. 'But it's worth a go.'

'Yeah,' Wayne objected. 'But what about me? I can't show me face, can I?'

Oz leered at him maliciously.

'Certainly not. You can stay here and play with yourself . . .'

The van drew up outside the Barley Mow, with Dennis at the wheel and Bomber, Moxey and Oz inside. Barry, still on his clean-living kick, had gone off to do some brass-rubbings.

'Right,' said Dennis. 'Leave this to me – let me have five minutes to reason with him.'

Oz nodded. 'And if that doesn't work, give *me* two minutes to rip his lungs out.'

Dennis shot him a cold glance, steeled himself and got out of the camper, watched by the other three as he made his way towards the pub.

The place was damned-near empty, as usual. Arthur Pringle did not inspire customer loyalty; he got the desperate and the uncritical.

His shortage of paying drinkers, however, did nought to improve Arthur's reception of Dennis. He glared at the new arrival with implacable hatred.

'Thirty seconds to get out,' he barked, 'or I'll call the police!'

Dennis made a good job of appearing both unmoved and diplomatic.

'Arthur,' he said mildly. 'Please. Hear me out for a moment.'

He moved closer to the bar, drawing on all his skill and tact.

'Arthur, look . . .' he began. So far, so good. 'We know the thoughtless behaviour of one of our group has caused you much heartache. And, believe me, we feel the same way about him as you do. That's why we've disciplined him ourselves in a way you would have approved of ...'

'Castration?' Pringle snarled.

'Of the social kind, yes. He's confined to base, in the glasshouse – as you brave fighter pilots might say!'

'That still leaves the rest of you to create mayhem,' said Pringle. He was slowly calming down. Dennis knew that if he went carefully, he had him ...

'Arthur,' he continued, 'I'm a respectable married man. Outside in the car I've got three other men, who've done a hard day's work and simply want a pint and a quiet evening's conversation by your fireside as a reward. They're not rapists, thieves or vagabonds!'

It was a brilliant little speech, a masterpiece, even. Pringle's face had softened as he spoke. He could see that all that stood between them and an evening's drinking in the warm was a little matter of pride, and Pringle just might be about to swallow that.

Then a familiar voice piped up from just outside.

'Has the bastard give in yet, Dennis?' enquired Oz in a loud whisper.

That did it. Silently, his face once more a mask of hatred, Arthur Pringle pointed Dennis the way to the door ...

Ally and Vicki were sitting on the patio in the early stages of a game of chess. Ally enjoyed the game, it appealed to his notion of himself as a master-strategist. And if Vicki was no Boris Spassky, she was the only opponent he had at the moment. Anyway, it was good ego-massage. Ally always won. Safer than golf with Kenny Ames, that was for sure.

'Did you ever see *The Thomas Crown Affair*?' asked Vicki suddenly.

Ally didn't take his eyes off the board.

'I never went to pop concerts, Vicki. I was too busy working.'

'It was a film,' she explained with a pout. 'And in it Steve McQueen and Faye Dunaway seduced each other over a chess board ...' She looked at him meaningfully. 'It was a very sexy scene.'

'Really?' murmured Ally. 'I think *you* might find that a

little uncomfortable, Vicki – all these pieces sticking into your bum ...'

She pulled a face. And the phone rang. Ally got up to answer. He came back with it, timidly moved another pawn as he picked up the receiver.

'You live dangerously, don't you?' Vicki muttered.

But Ally was already into the call. It was Howard Radcliff, ringing from Derbyshire.

'I'm well, Ally, thank you,' said the architect's voice over the line. 'I just thought I'd let you know that our planning application's in, and that my personal contact on the council says there'll be no trouble.' He paused to collect Ally's approval. 'And my new drawings are also coming along nicely.'

'Good,' said Ally, keeping one eye on Vicki's vagaries on the chess board.

'And I just thought now would be an opportune time to discuss the costing of the materials. I've drawn up three different budgets for fittings, surfaces and other interior details ...'

'Oh yes. And what do they run at?'

'At £22,000, £48,000 and, top of the range, £65,000 ...'

Ally winced at Howard's estimates, and also at the fact that Vicki was enthusiastically hopping her bishop around the board as if it were a knight.

'Well, Howard,' he said quickly. 'In view of the revised nature of the premises, I think it would be a pity to waste all your fancy-dan trappings on people with one foot in the grave. I think we should err on the side of caution, don't you?'

The young architect knew Ally's rhetorical question was more in the nature of a command, but he put up a token fight.

'As you wish, Ally. But the first figure I quoted is an absolute rock bottom, using the cheapest materials available.'

'That's all right, Howard – I've already laid out enough cash on this project. It's time I started earning a little nest-egg for *my* old age.' Ally's voice was decisive, brooking no objections. 'So I want no corner left uncut, Howard – understand? And you can pass that on to Dennis, too.'

140

No argument.

'Will do,' said Radcliff. 'Incidentally, it may interest you to know that he and his boys are currently staying at the house,' he said conversationally.

'Are they now?' Ally growled. 'Well, don't mention it yet, but later on I think we might broach the little matter of rent with them ...'

'I'll get the meters read as well, if you like,' chuckled Howard.

'I was not jokin', Howard,' said Ally with a hard edge to his voice.

'Right.' Very serious again. 'I'll get the plans out to you by the weekend, Ally.'

They said their goodbyes, and Ally put the phone down. He looked at the board, then at Vicki, with a lordly disdain. The game was a mess.

'If Faye Dunaway played like you,' he muttered, 'she'd have been lucky to get a goodnight kiss ...'

Back at Thornely Manor, another day's work had reached its close. The lads were working hard, and they were getting very restless, with nothing to do at the end of their grafting. Wayne had disappeared off in his BMW on some mysterious errand he wouldn't discuss. Dennis had promised the lads a trip into Chesterfield, the local metropolis, to catch some action, with him doing the honours at the wheel of the camper. They all assembled, scrubbed and well-togged, in front of the house an hour after work finished.

Then they all piled into the camper. Dennis got into the driver's seat, started the engine – or tried to. He turned the ignition a number of times, and each time the motor spluttered and died.

'Dennis man,' growled Oz. 'We're not gettin' any breaks at all! We must be cursed!'

They waited. A lot of anxiety and no response from the engine. The starter motor was obviously jammed.

'If the worst comes to the worst, we can probably all squeeze into the back of my van,' suggested Barry.

'Barry,' said Oz irritably, 'a twenty-five mile trip in the back

141

of a builder's van, slidin' around in cement dust, is not the ideal prelude to a big night out!'

'Just a thought,' Barry mumbled.

'Typical of Wayne to bugger off just when we need his motor,' Bomber said.

Then Moxey spoke up: ''Ere, I've just been thinking, you know. This Arthur bloke at the Barley Mow has never really met me.'

'You've missed nothin'.'

'All I ever did was run in and out to collect me bags,' Moxey continued determinedly. 'My head never touched a pillow. Maybe *I* could get served!'

'That's right,' Oz said. 'Think of yourself first.'

'No. What I mant was, maybe I could get drinks for you lot, provided you stayed out of his sight ...'

'What are we supposed to do? Sit in the children's room?' asked Neville gloomily.

Dennis intervened. 'Calm down, eh?' he counselled. 'There's no need to get desperate yet.'

He tried the ignition again. A horrible grinding noise issued from under the bonnet.

'*Now* can we get desperate?' Oz asked.

They arrived at the Barley Mow again half an hour later, in Barry's van. Chesterfield was out. Desperation was in.

'Good evening,' said Arthur Pringle as Moxey entered the bar. Not particularly pleasantly, not unpleasantly. A good sign.

'What'll it be?'

'Pint of bitter, please. Straight glass.'

Pringle was, actually, a little bit suspicious, said he knew Moxey's face. Moxey told him he'd popped in one lunchtime a few weeks back. That seemed to satisfy him.

Moxey paid for the beer, then, as if he had an afterthought, said: 'Er, is it all right if I take a drink out to my kids?'

'I should think so – provided you bring the glasses back, and provided they don't break any.'

'Oh no,' said Moxey, in the slight Irish lilt he had affected since he had become 'Brendan Mulcahy'. 'They're very well behaved.'

'What'll it be, then?' said Arthur. 'Coke, orange juice . . . ?'

'Er . . . five pints of bitter, please . . .' Moxey grinned stupidly. 'They're growin' lads . . .'

Arthur was smiling now. Like a shark.

'They must be . . . five kids, eh?' he said. 'You Irish, by any chance?'

'Yeah,' said Moxey eagerly. 'Brendan Mulcahy's the name!'

Pringle stared at him.

'Right – you can piss off out of here, then. We don't serve Micks in this pub!'

A crestfallen Moxey crept out of the pub. He admitted his failure to the thirsty lads waiting in the carpark.

'Did he recognise you?' asked Dennis.

Moxey shook his head. 'No. He won't serve Micks, apparently.'

'I don't believe it,' Oz moaned. 'The man has all the charm of a mass grave!'

It was cold, dark, and Gothic – and so was their mood – when the lads pitched up back at the manor. Barry led the disconsolate group in through the door and started up the stairs. Then he paused, whirled around to face them.

'Hey, listen!' he gabbled, staring wildly at the drawing room door. The rest of them fell silent and listened. There were voices all right.

'Oh, London's got a bird in there, that's all,' growled Oz. He was so miserable, even sarcasm was beyond him.

'No, no,' said Barry wildly. 'They're *male* voices!'

'Well, it's either a ghost, or Wayne's on the turn,' commented Bomber.

Oz grunted furiously, pushed past Barry and threw open the door of the drawing room.

The sight that greeted him was cosily domestic. Wayne ensconced in an arm chair with a television set on in the corner.

'Hello, lads,' said the cockney with a crafty grin. 'Just havin' a quiet night in with the goggle-box.'

They were as appreciative as they had been desperate a few

minutes before. Wayne had done the right thing if he wanted to restore his popularity, and there was no doubt that had been his intention in popping down to 'ye olde video shoppe' and fixing up a TV and VTR system ready for their return.

Wayne had been working his way through one of the tapes he and Bomber had found in the cellar. It was by no means impressive. A film of Kenny Ames having a golf lesson – and not doing too well.

'About as exciting as the carpark at the Barley Mow,' Oz scoffed.

Wayne grinned even more broadly, leaned forward and killed the golfing tape.

'Fortunately I did take the liberty of renting a video tape especially for the night.' He held up a box so that they could read the title. THE BITCH. 'I thought somethin' with a bit of culture might be appreciated ...'

There were cheers, the opening of cans, and the lads settled down for some good dirty fun. The tape began to play. With strange, very doggy barking noises.

'I don't remember this bit,' said Barry cautiously. 'Not that I've seen this before, mind ...'

The barking was combined with jolly, Walt Disney-style music. Curiously, Oz was the first to really catch on.

'This isn't THE BITCH,' he moaned. 'It's 101 DALMATIANS!'

Wayne reddened. 'Bugger – they must have given me the wrong bloody tape.'

'Easy mistake to make – they've both got dogs in the title.' Dennis consoled them as the screen went blank again.

'Hang on!' said Wayne, eager to avert yet another swing against himself on the lads' part. 'We've still got the other one of those tapes we found – might be somethin' on that.'

'Yeah. Tennis lesson, probably,' Moxey sniffed.

He was wrong, so wrong. Wayne pushed the 'play' button, and they found themselves looking at a tape of the very room they were sitting in now – with expensive furnishings, and full of people. There was party music, and ... lo and behold ... some very heavy-duty villainous types surrounded by a bunch of model girls in their underwear and not much else.

The 'action' on the tape was sporadic, obviously filmed

144

with a hand-held camera at irregular intervals throughout a very debauched evening. Kenny Ames kept appearing, groping a girl or shoving one in the direction of a crony, like a tipsy sultan doling out his harem to favoured friends. The girls lost even more clothes as time went on, and the guests got drunker.

'This bloke Ames seemed to have the right idea about life,' said Dennis drily, to murmurs of agreement, especially from Oz.

Then it happened. The camera focused rather shakily on a 'two-shot' of a topless girl and a moustachioed middle-aged man whose identity was unmistakable, despite the poor quality of the tape.

'Bloody hell! It's Arthur!' Oz bellowed, nearly falling off his chair in his excitement.

'The dirty old sod!' Bomber chortled.

The fuzzy sound-track picked up the girl's voice: 'I'm Pee-Wee,' she mouthed. 'Who are you, darling?'

The face of mine host turned a deeper shade of pink, cast a furtive glance at the camera.

'Pringle. Arthur Pringle,' he muttered throatily.

The girl giggled. 'Hello, Arthur. What do you do?'

'I run the local pub – Mr Ames invited me over.'

'Local, eh?' the girl crooned. 'Kenny says we've got to be nice to you. Do you want me to be nice to you, Arthur?'

No response. Arthur's jaw dropped, his mouth worked soundlessly.

The girl laughed. 'Come on, Arthur. Let's have some more champagne,' she pouted, pouring some in his glass. 'Come on. I'll show you the house ...'

'Call me Tiger,' Pringle said, recovering his wits and obviously beginning to enter into the spirit of things. 'It was my nickname in the RAF ...'

The lads howled in disbelief. 'Tiger!'

'Bloody hell,' said Oz when the camera left Pringle and the girl to whatever came next. 'There's him lookin' down his nose at us, and he's more debauched than we are!'

And already, of course, they knew exactly what to do next.

*

145

The next lunchtime, the lads pulled up in the carpark of the Barley Mow in Barry's van. The place was quiet, which was probably just as well. Dennis sighed.

'Right,' he said. 'Come on, lads. Let's get this over with and get back to work.' He produced the infamous video cassette, handed it with some ceremony to the Londoner. 'I think this is your moment, Wayne.'

Headed by a grinning Wayne, the lads trooped into the empty public bar. Arthur was in there, as it happened, and his face transformed into a mask of hatred when he spotted the cockney daring to trespass.

'Before you say anything, Arthur,' Wayne began smoothly, 'I want you to know that we understand. We'd probably have done the same in your position. You know,' he continued, rubbing it in, 'wife's done a runner and some topless crumpet is wrapping its legs round you ...'

'You not only are rubbish, you talk rubbish as well ...' Pringle snapped. 'I'll just call the police!'

Just as he was about to exit towards the phone, Wayne fished the cassette out of his pocket. 'I wouldn't do that, old son,' he purred. 'They'd probably be very interested to see this ...' Arthur's face was darkening in a way that gave Wayne enormous satisfaction. 'Remember a party at Thornely Manor, Arthur? Remember Kenny Ames and Pee-Wee and a man with a video camera?'

The look of anger changed to one of horrified surprise on Arthur's part.

Wayne put the tape down lovingly on the bar.

'Yes!' he intoned. 'Arthur "Tiger" Pringle – This Is Your Life!'

And that, he might have added, was the lads fixed up with a place to drink again ...

TWELVE

The man behind the counter at the building merchant's office in the town had got to know Dennis very well in the past few days. He was getting on, he had seen some cowboys in his time, but he was basically a decent man, and he knew his trade, as Dennis was well aware.

'Hey up, Geordie,' he said cheerfully when Dennis walked in. 'Back for some more, are we? Must be a right palace you're building out there in the country.'

Dennis shrugged, handed over his latest list of materials requirements.

'More like a doll's house from now on, Pop. Take a look at this.'

There had been a visit from Howard Radcliff, and the pushy young architect had once again pared things right down to the bone in terms of quality on the job. The very shoddiest materials, and now even the plans for a lift had been ruled out. Something about Ally needing to watch his cash flow. An old people's home with no lift! The only people who would be able to live there would be folks who were so fit they didn't need to be in there in the first place ... To tell the truth, Dennis was becoming more and more ashamed, and he was aware that the lads would also be aware of the kind of dump they were building. There had not been too many laughs for Dennis since the reckoning with Arthur Pringle.

'Any chance of getting this lot out to us tomorrow?' he asked the old man.

The merchant checked his delivery roster.

'Aye, I should think so,' he said. Then he smiled cynically. 'Might have trouble stopping some of it blowing off the lorry, though. It's not what you call substantial, is it?'

'That's why they call 'em breeze blocks, I suppose,' Dennis retorted, dead-pan. The merchant laughed. 'Oh aye,' Dennis added. 'We'll need a plumber for a week or so. Know any good lads locally?'

The merchant looked at a notice board behind him that was covered in trade cards. 'Aye, let me see . . .' He plucked a card from the board. 'This bloke from Derby's a top man. Hard grafter, reasonable rates, pleasant disposition.'

'Sounds ideal.'

'Use the phone, if you like.'

'That'd be canny. Sure it's no trouble?'

The merchant was impassive. 'No, none at all. He's me brother-in-law.'

Dennis paused in the middle of his dialling. 'Nepotism, eh?'

'What?' said the merchant. He flexed his hand quizzically. 'No, just a touch of arthritis . . .'

'Two more pints here, please, Arthur!' Wayne called to mine host.

Pringle glowered at him.

'When you're ready, of course,' the Londoner added with exaggerated politeness.

'Certainly, *sir*,' Pringle snarled through clenched teeth.

'Now, now, "Tiger" – don't overdo the sarkiness, otherwise we'll have to do a little video screening for your brewery, show 'em what their tenant gets up to in his spare time.'

Pringle shoved the pints down on the counter, stared at Wayne.

'Did I ever tell you about the time I was taken prisoner in Malaya?' he rasped.

'I don't think so, no,' said Barry.

'Those little gooks with coloured hair,' mine host continued with a meaningful glance at Wayne. 'They put me in a bamboo cage. They used to poke sticks at me, humiliate me and abuse me. They thought they were safe, see, because I was behind bars. Then, when I was rescued by my pals in the SAS, I took my revenge by stringing the little bastards up by their ankles and horse-whipping 'em . . . One pound seventy pence, please. Or do you want them on the house?'

'No, certainly not, Arthur,' Wayne answered cheerfully. 'All we want from you is a modicum of civility and access to your pub. Long as you provide those, we have no need of humiliation.'

'Yeah,' Barry agreed. 'Magnanimous in victory, we are, Arthur. I mean, we could demand our rooms back if we wanted to be really awkward.'

It was Pringle's turn to be smug. 'Just a pity I'm fully booked again, isn't it?'

'How much are you actually payin' em to stay?' was Wayne's parting shot.

In the corner, Neville, Bomber and Dennis were sitting over pints, watching Oz and Moxey play darts.

'Still a bit of atmosphere in here, isn't there?' said the big Bristolian in an attempt at cheer.

'Aye,' said Neville. 'Reminds me of a funeral parlour.'

'Come on,' Dennis said. 'We were moaning when we were banned from here, and now we're moaning 'cos we're back. Just be grateful for small mercies, eh, Neville?'

Neville nodded miserably. 'I am. It's just a bit depressing to round off your working day by going somewhere you're not really welcome.'

'Could be worse for me,' Bomber put in. 'Could be goin' home to the wife.'

'My wife's not like that,' Neville said, refusing to be jollied along. 'Makes me feel welcome whenever I come in from work ... Always give me a kiss and cup of tea, and we talk about our day, and then play with the baby for an hour ...'

'Er ... are you homesick, Neville?' Dennis asked.

'Me? What makes you think that?' the younger man shot back defensively.

'Look – why don't you take the weekend off and go up and see Brenda?'

'I don't think I could afford to lose the money.'

'It's only one day, Neville. We won't be working Sunday.'

Neville's face brightened. 'Could I? I mean, you won't be short-handed on Saturday?'

'I think Den would rather be short-handed than have you long-faced,' Bomber suggested.

A delighted Neville bounced off to the bar to get some more beers in. Dennis shook his head.

'Suddenly lost his money worries . . .'

Bomber frowned. 'I thought Nev's missus had gone all independent on him – you know, leaving notes saying: "Playing squash, your dinner's in the deep freeze."'

'Aye, she has turned a bit that way by all accounts.'

'Then what's all this pipe and slippers bit?'

Dennis smiled sadly. 'I dunno, Bomb. Nostalgia?'

The next day they made the acquaintance of Harry Blackburn, the plumber Dennis had hired through the building merchant.

He growled up the drive in an American four-wheel drive that was not exactly humble or inconspicuous. It had his name, trade and phone number in big letters on the side, plus, in even bigger, red letters: 'I'M PLUMB CRAZY!' Harry, a craggy looking character in his mid-thirties wearing dungarees and a battered cowboy hat, opened the cab door and perched on the running board as if gazing out over the wide plains of the Mid-West.

'Is Dennis Patterson around?' he asked in a broad Derbyshire accent.

Dennis, who was supervising the unloading of the materials that had arrived from the merchant, strolled over.

'You the plumber?' he asked.

Harry jerked a thumb at the legend on his truck. 'That's what it says.'

They shook hands and introduced themselves.

'I've got all the gear in the back,' Harry said, and winked. 'Special discount from the bro-in-law, of course.'

'Every little helps,' said Dennis drily.

'Right. Where do you want me to start?'

'Well, you could give us a hand with this stuff, if you don't mind a bit of labouring.'

'Not me, Dennis – always ready to muck in.'

'Good lad. We'll have a break soon as we've finished unloading, and then I'll introduce you to the rest of the team.'

The work went on, and the lads were beginning to realise

the quality – or lack of it – of the materials they were going to have to finish the job with.

'Aye, Ally Fraser's budget obviously doesn't stretch too far,' said Oz balefully, taking in the stuff he and the others were stacking in one of the ground floor rooms.

'It'd better stretch to cover our scratch, or there'll be trouble,' muttered Bomber.

'Yeah, definitely cowboy material, this,' Moxey agreed. 'We'd probably be better off usin' Lego.'

Just then, Harry entered through the door, carrying the front end of a bundle of timber that he was sharing with Dennis.

'I'll keep on workin',
Long as my two hands are fit to use,
I drink a little beer each evening,
And sing a little bit of these workin' man blues . . .'

He sang lustily, though not exactly tunefully, and Oz whipped round when he heard the sound.

'Hey, listen to that,' said the Geordie incredulously. 'Merle Haggard song, that!'

Harry grinned, stopped next to Oz. 'Aye – you a fan too?'

'A fan? I've met him, man – in the flesh! And in Nashville!'

Harry's face was consumed with a kind of wild ecstasy. 'Bloody hell – let me kiss your feet, old mate!'

At the other end of the bundle, Dennis was looking decidedly sour at the hold-up, but the two instant friends weren't bothering. They were swapping song titles:

'"Honky-Tonk Night Time Man"!'

'"If We Make It Through December"!'

Then in unison: '"Okie from Muskogee"!'

'What's the hold-up down there?' Dennis growled.

'Naw,' said Oz. 'Merle never sang that one, Dennis. Sounds more like Johnny Cash!'

At the lunch-break, Oz showed an astonished Harry his famous snapshot taken in the bar in Nashville.

'There y'are,' he bragged. 'Me and Merle, live in Nashville.'

Harry squinted at the photo. 'I thought he shaved off his beard years ago.'

'That's not a beard,' Oz said quickly. 'It's just a shadow

across his face.' Then he took the photo back and examined it closely. 'Aye, maybe it is a beard. Anyway, he's a canny bloke – he was very pleased to hear I'd been in the Falklands, 'cos he's a patriot, like.'

'A Falklands veteran who's met Merle Haggard,' said Harry, overcome with admiration. 'You're just about the most famous person I've ever come across, Oz.'

Meanwhile, Dennis sat with Bomber, Wayne and Neville, discussing the remaining part of the job.

'What's the word then, Den?' Wayne was asking. 'Do I set about restoring that second staircase to its former glory, or is the lift going in?'

Dennis concentrated on his sandwich, tried to appear casual and avoid the issue at the same time.

'I should leave it till after the weekend, Wayne. I don't think Howard's had the final approval of his plans from Ally yet.'

'I shouldn't think there's much chance, judging by the gear that came in this morning,' the Londoner said doubtfully.

Bomber nodded. 'Seems a pity to skimp on such a solid building, doesn't it?'

'Look,' snapped Dennis, suddenly rattled. 'It's Ally's money. It's up to him how he spends it, isn't it? If he wants to do the place in mud and straw, it's his decision.'

There was a moment's embarrassed silence.

'Yeah,' Neville said then. 'But it's a bit of a cheat on an old people's home, Dennis ... you should give them the best.'

Dennis got to his feet. 'You're getting well paid, Neville, so quit moaning, eh?'

With that, Dennis drained his beer and stalked off in the direction of the house.

The lads watched him go.

'Getting a bit tetchy, isn't he?' said Bomber.

'Strain of being a gaffer, I guess,' Wayne mused.

Neville shook his head. 'Strain of being employed by someone like Ally Fraser, more like.'

The days at Marbella were not filled with hard graft, and neither were the nights dark and gothic. Nor were Ally and

Kenny and their companions unwelcome at the Marbella Club Restaurant, though they had probably never done an honest day's work in their lives.

While the lads went 'home' to their chill billets at the manor, Ally sat with Vicki and Kenny and the porn king's bronzed, blonde beauty of the moment at a table overlooking the pool on a balmy Spanish evening after an excellent dinner, taking in the gentle croak of bullfrogs and the relaxing rhythms of a guitar player.

Vicki drained her wine glass and peered at the bottle.

'Nice drop of wine, that,' she drawled. 'I didn't know they did a white Rioja.'

She pronounced it 'ree-oh-jar'. Ally winced.

'I think ye should go and powder your nose, Vicki,' the Scots villain grated. He had business with Kenny. A little plan for which he had already done the groundwork.

'Why, gone all shiny, has it?' said the girl defiantly.

'I was talkin' euphemistically ...' Ally received her spoilt pout with a steely glare of his own. 'Now, go an' have a slash while Kenny and I talk business.'

'Order us a brandy while we're gone, eh?' Vicki said. She and Kenny's companion rose and strode huffily off, leaving the two men alone.

'Birds can be a right liability sometimes,' Ally sighed, and offered Kenny a cigar.

Kenny nodded thoughtfully. They both knew what this little tête-à-tête was about. Ally had picked up on the fact that there had been contacts between the British and Spanish Home Offices about the problems of all those bent Brits-in-exile – a colourful community of whom Kenny was a leading member. And Ally was determined to take advantage of his situation, as one of the few resident heavies who didn't – yet – have the law on his tail.

'I've talked to some of the Brit community this afternoon,' Kenny said after a while. 'Your story's got a few of 'em making travel plans already.'

'They've got a wide choice of countries who don't have extradition treaties with Britain,' Ally said with a satisfied chuckle. 'Costa Rica, Afghanistan, Mongolia, Libya ...'

The cockney thug grimaced. 'I can just see myself playing golf with Gaddafi.' He puffed on his cigar. 'So what's your plan, Ally?'

Ally took his time. 'Did you ever play Monopoly as a kid, Kenny?' he asked.

'Not often, no. I didn't like that "go to jail" bit. Even at an early age it gave me a shiver.'

'But you remember the broad principles of the game? Buying property at advantageous prices. Making offers to people who needed the cash to stay in the game.'

Kenny's eyes narrowed. He hadn't got where he was by being slow on the uptake.

'I think I see what you're getting at.'

'Good,' Ally continued with a hint of condescension. 'You see, if a dozen or so of your similarly-placed colleagues were in need of quick cash and even quicker exits, I could be in a healthy position to take their properties off their hands ...'

'At knockdown prices, of course.'

Ally grinned. 'You *have* played the game more than you admit ... And as most of the properties are in choice sites, I would then be well placed to develop them as holiday homes for those Brits who *can* move freely around the world.'

There was another pause. Kenny was starting to bristle. His eyes were now slits.

'And what happens,' he said slowly, 'if, as I suspect it might, your property speculating schemes get up the collective noses of those poor, hunted people?'

'That's where you come in, Kenny,' Ally coaxed. 'As a partner and general public relations expert. I'm sure that, between us, we can smooth things over. After all, we'd be helping them out. And there's no telling what might happen with this Spanish government,' he added darkly. 'They're socialists, y'know – they might just repossess the houses and kick you all out without a bean.'

'I'll need a few days to think about it,' Kenny said.

Ally knew he was over the initial hurdle.

'Of course,' he said smoothly. 'We're only throwing the dice to start at the moment. But we should be ready to move quickly ... on the deal, that is.'

Kenny looked troubled.

'It's a real choker this, you know,' he said then. 'I bet people back home think people like me have a great time out here. But without the freedom to go where you want, when you want – it's just another prison, isn't it?'

Kenny was getting maudlin, which was all to the good. Silly sod. There were no restaurants, or German blondes, or good booze in the Scrubs, and Kenny knew it.

Ally flagged down a passing waiter with a masterful wave.

'Four brandies, *por favor*,' he said. He pointed to Kenny. 'And make his a large one ...'

He'd soon be home and hosed. And he had those lads finishing the job in Derbyshire up his sleeve, too. They were part of his Spanish plans, whether they knew it or not.

And then in England, the parcel of earth that figured so large in the dreams of the Kenny Ameses of this world, Saturday came around.

Saturday afternoon found Neville at home – Dennis had let him have the van for his flying visit to Newcastle – and in bed with his bride. There was passion, excitement, the thrill of athletic performance ...

Then the radio lost its reception. Neville leaned over to twiddle with the tuner. Newcastle had just been moving nicely from mid-field.

Brenda sat with her arms folded, scowling.

'It was hardly worth coming to bed if you're going to listen to the football all afternoon.'

'I'm sorry, Brenda. It just seems ... a bit unnatural ... trying to do it during the day. Besides, I can't concentrate when Newcastle are playing.'

'There was an article in Cosmo last month about how married couples should use as much variety as possible in their love-life,' she said sullenly. 'Times, places, clothes ...'

'What's Cosmo?' Neville asked vaguely.

'*Cosmopolitan* magazine – for the woman of today.'

'Oh. That's where you get your fancy ideas from, is it?'

'They're not fancy,' Brenda snapped. 'Just interesting. Things are changing for women, you know, Neville. Even on Tyneside.'

He stared gloomily at the radio.

'I know, pet, I know. I was just brought up in a very traditional way, though.'

'Yes,' she said. 'Wife at home looking after baby, pub with the lads, Saturday night on the nest and Sunday afternoon asleep on the sofa after a big lunch ...'

Taken aback by her vehemence, Neville went on the defensive.

'I've never been that bad. I'm not a chauvinist, Brenda.'

'No. But you're not a feminist either.'

'Look,' he said slyly, 'if it'll make you happy, you go to the pub tomorrow lunchtime and I'll cook the Sunday dinner for you and Debbie.'

'You're going to have to; I'm doing a couple of hours at the hospital tomorrow.'

It was Neville's turn to sulk. 'Some weekend off ...' He wilted under the force of Brenda's stare. 'Sorry, pet ... I'll be happy to do it. I'll give Debbie some cookery lessons ...'

'Neville!'

'Sorry ...' He cocked an ear to the radio. 'Half-time.'

Neville switched off the match, made an attempt to snuggle up to his wife, explaining that he suddenly had ten minutes free. She refused to respond.

'About those clothes you can wear,' he said then. 'To make things more passionate.'

'What about them?' she asked suspiciously.

'Well, how would you feel about wearing some?'

'Depends what they are – there's a fine line between eroticism and kinkiness, Neville.' She paused. 'What did you have in mind?'

He leered in triumph. 'A black-and-white football shirt ...'

The pillow hit him hard in the face.

A few hours later, in another part of the Sceptred Isle, the remaining lads were pulling into the carpark of an unknown pub in the remotest reaches of the Derbyshire countryside. As Wayne parked his BMW, muffled sounds of country music drifted out on the air.

'Listen to all that twanging,' said the Londoner. 'Sounds like a load of cats in a yard.'

'You've nae taste, London,' growled Oz.

'Are you sure they're not just tuning up?' Barry asked helpfully.

Dennis pointed out Harry's truck.

'Suppose that means we have to stay,' chuckled Bomber.

'Come on,' Oz said, determined to convert them all before the night was out. 'It'll sound better with a couple of pints.'

'Yeah,' muttered Wayne. 'One in each ear!'

In the fetid depths of the pub – largely peopled by characters in full Marlboro Country gear, including the audience and the band – Harry spotted them immediately. It wasn't too hard for him. After all, they were looking totally bemused and, except for Oz's Nashville gear, they were the only ones not dressed like extras from *High Noon*.

'Howdy pardners!' boomed Harry.

'Sorry we're late,' grinned Oz. 'We ran into Apaches on the way over.'

Harry ushered them through the crowd. 'Come on. I've reserved us a table near the band.'

'I was afraid of that,' said Wayne.

Just then Moxey grabbed hold of Barry's arm. 'Hey, look at that!' he cried in amazement. 'Shoot-out at the O.K. Corrall!'

Barry followed the pointing finger. A bunch of cowboys were taking on an electronic game in a last-ditch shoot-out, a kind of Wild West version of Space Invaders.

But Barry wasn't impressed. 'Looks more like the O.K. Co-op,' he mumbled.

'And the funny thing is,' said Harry, appearing at his shoulder, 'two of those guys are rozzers.'

'I don't think I find that funny, somehow,' said Bomber, edging away from the scene.

'But it brings a whole new meaning to the term "pub-fight", doesn't it?' Dennis pointed out cheerily. After all the disappointments of the past weeks, he was determined to enjoy himself tonight, even if some of the others didn't look too pleased at the choice of venue.

But, in fact, their mood did improve after a few pints. The band wasn't that bad, especially when you'd deadened your aesthetic sense a bit, and the local Country fanatics were a cheerful, welcoming crowd. Even Wayne had cheered up. His sharp eyes had picked up signs of some possibly unattached crumpet, and as Oz moved to get another 'pitcher' of beer (they did it authentic here), he sidled off to chance his arm.

He found one girl he had been eyeing standing in a relatively quiet corner of the bar. She wore a Rhinestone jacket, but he was way past being fussy. A week at Thornely Manor did things to a man.

'Glenda Campbell, isn't it?' he opened. 'The original Rhinestone Cowgirl.'

'You what?'

'Sorry, it was a joke,' Wayne persevered. 'I'm called Wayne. After John, of course.'

'What?' the girl said again, straining to hear him above the din of the band and the drinkers.

He moved forward and spoke right into her ear: 'I said, are you always so chatty up here?'

'Oh, I'm sorry,' the girl said guardedly. 'I was listening to the music.'

'Masochist, are we?'

She smiled at him for the first time. 'I only come 'cos my brother's playing the fiddle.'

Wayne clocked the brother. Over six foot and a bushy beard. Like Bluto from the *Popeye* cartoons.

'Looks like a sensitive type,' he said. 'Can I get you a drink – Horlick's or something?'

'No thanks. I've got to drive him home later,' she said, looking at the brother again.

'Oh yeah. I saw the series. *Rawhide*, wasn't it?'

He was working well. She'd laughed again. He pressed home his advantage.

'Look, is there another bar or anything in here? You know, one with a broken jukebox, preferably.'

'Sorry. If you want a break from this, you'll have to go out in the carpark.'

'Shall I see if they've got a table for two?' Quick as a flash.

She thought about it, and she went.

On the stage, the music died down. After a few whispered consultations, the band's singer stepped back up to the mike.

'Boys and girls,' he said in a voice that was half-Marlboro, half-Chesterfield, 'We have a very special guest with us this evening ... Apparently he appeared with the great Merle Haggard in Nashville last year, and is a close personal friend of Merle's ...' Excited whoops from the audience. 'What's more, he's offered to come up on stage to perform one of Merle's greatest hits. Would you please give a down-home welcome to ... Big Willie Osbourne!'

The remaining lads had been ignoring the goings-on on stage. Suddenly they were all attention. Horrified, Dennis clapped his hand over his eyes in time to shut out the image of Oz lumbering up to the mike, now jacketless and wearing a bloody great cowboy hat.

It was incredible. The band struck up, and Oz started to sing. Really sing. The lads' mouths dropped open. The bugger had something. And the locals were lapping it up, absolutely rapt at the sight and the sound of him.

'How could someone so ugly make a nice noise like that?' asked Bomber in amazement.

'Perhaps he's only miming.'

'What was it he called himself?' asked Moxey.

Barry grinned. 'Big Willie. It's true an' all – I shared a shower once with him in Düsseldorf.'

'That man's wasted laying bricks,' said Harry, overcome with admiration.

Over by the door, if they had been looking, they would have seen the Rhinestone Cowgirl, returned from the carpark at the sound of Oz's dulcet tones, and a disgusted-looking Wayne. Oz was the hero now.

And after, he returned to the plaudits of the lads.

'Sorry about that,' he said coolly. 'Couldn't control me urges any longer.'

Harry had come back from the bar.

'Oz,' he said reverently, 'you were so great, the landlord's standing us drinks for the rest of the night.' He checked his watch. 'We've got about five minutes ...'

Well, it was better than the Barley Mow, and somehow they'd earned it. There was an innocence about them that evening, a drunken one, but an innocence all the same. And they were united. Which was just as well, because there were storms ahead. Being a cowboy for a night in the pub was good fun: to be one on work for an old people's home was another matter entirely.

THIRTEEN

'Pretty poor show, this, Arthur,' Oz growled. 'No hunks of cheese, no gherkins.'

'I like to treat my customers the way they treat me,' retorted Pringle.

The lads were munching crisps to help a basically liquid Sunday lunch go down.

'Surprised there aren't little bowls of rat poison, in that case,' Moxey observed.

But Pringle was already off down the bar to serve another customer, leaving Moxey oathing under his breath.

Barry, meanwhile, had been studying the Sunday papers.

'Here, look at this. Very interesting, this is,' he said. There were groans from the rest of them. Another of Barry's 'interesting facts' . . .

'Life's too short, Barry,' said Oz. 'Whatever it is.'

'No, listen . . . The *Sunday People* here's done an investigation into the scandal of unregistered old people's homes. Apparently there's lots of them springing up without anything bar the basic facilities, and they're cleaning up by pocketing fees from the Social Security!'

'Can we not just have a quiet pint, eh, Barry?' Dennis said uncomfortably.

But the others were already gathered around the paper, interested. Dennis stayed where he was, hoping for the best.

'I hope that's not goin' to apply to our place,' said Barry.

Oz glared at Dennis. 'You'd better ask *him* about that, Barry. He knows what Ally Fraser's up to.'

Bomber was reading, and looking more and more concerned. 'Some of the places condemned here have got more facilities than Thornely Manor, by the sound of it.'

161

Wayne nodded. 'Couldn't have less, could they?'

Dennis decided to try to head off the worst.

'We haven't finished the job yet,' he said none too convincingly.

'No,' said Oz, 'but the way it's going isn't too promising. I mean, is he going to put in proper heating and a fire escape Dennis?'

'I wouldn't know,' Dennis grated.

'Because I'd hate to see our skills wasted on some wide-boy scheme of Ally Fraser's ...'

'Look, Oz,' Dennis said, rising to the bait. 'As I remember, you weren't too wild about some of the quality that went into those flats we built in Germany. But it didn't stop you finishing the work.'

The big Tynesider shook his head.

'That was different: it was for Germans. What we're doin' here is for Brits. Old-aged Brits at that. I don't want to feel I'm creatin' slum conditions for grannies to live in. We're supposed to have left that stuff behind in the Fifties.'

'I've dealt with Fraser from the start on this,' Dennis answered with deliberation. 'As far as I'm concerned, the job's above board. Your precious pride will not be abused. Okay?'

'It's not okay,' said Oz, his eyes narrowing. 'We've all seen the rubbishy material coming in over the last few days. You wouldn't build a garden shed with most of it ...'

'The job is sound,' Dennis barked.

'So you say ...'

'Yes, I do,' Dennis insisted. He paused. 'And I'm the gaffer.'

Oz wasn't going to stand for that.

'Ally Fraser's gaffer,' he sneered. 'And the way it looks at the moment, he only has to fart and you go for a shit!'

Dennis got to his feet, faced Oz. For a moment it looked as if he was going to throw a punch. Then he thought better about it and stormed out of the pub.

'Bit strong, Oz,' Bomber said mildly in the ensuing silence.

Oz shrugged.

'Yeah, well,' he mumbled with a kind of embarrassed defiance. 'There's a strong smell of rat about this ...'

162

*

hez Neville, meanwhile, the dominant smell was of roast
ef and Yorkshire pud, prepared by the man himself. He was
eeling by the open oven door, turning over the roast
tatoes, when the doorbell rang. Seconds later, Brenda
hered Norma into the kitchen/diner.

'It's nice to meet you at long last, Norma,' she was saying.
ve heard a lot about you through Neville.'

'It's very nice of you to invite me over, pet.' She produced a
ottle of wine with a flourish. 'I've heard a lot about *you*
rough Dennis.'

She looked down, and saw Neville hard at work. Brenda
lt a nudge in her ribs. 'I'd heard that you'd got things
operly organised in the kitchen,' Norma said admiringly.
ooks like it's true!'

Neville cringed with embarrassment. He didn't mind doing
e work – in fact there were times when he really enjoyed it –
ut what got his goat was the song and dance routine women
ad to go through when they caught him with a colander in
s hand. Swallowing his pride, he stood up. 'Hello Norma,'
e said with a brave attempt at cheerfulness. 'How are you
et?'

'Fine, thanks.'

'I hope you'll still be after eating this lot.'

Brenda made as if to swipe him round the ear. 'Stop being
pologetic,' she told her husband playfully. 'You're a good
ook ... when you give yourself the chance.'

She winked at Norma and asked her to sit down.

'Will you have a drink?' she enquired.

'I think I'll go mad and have a gin and tonic, please,' said
Iorma. Neville grimaced. We've got a real piss-artist here, he
hought, and wondered what the boys were up to.

As Brenda busied herself with glasses and bottles Norma
urned to face Neville. 'I must say this *is* a treat,' she began.
Having Sunday lunch cooked for me – never happens when
ur Dennis is at home!'

'Well, it's the least I could do really, after he'd lent me his
an,' he explained, and then checked himself. 'Not that we
vouldn't want to have you over anyway, Norma,' he added
urriedly. 'Dennis sends his love, by the way.'

163

He put the roasting tin back into the oven and came over the table. Norma eyed the wine glasses, the napkins in the silver rings, the neat place settings.

'I don't suppose you live this well now you and the la have moved into that derelict house, Neville?' she venture

'Well actually,' he said, and remembered to think before said anything else out of place. 'Sunday lunch is a b occasion for us usually. One time of the week when we ca relax and push the boat out ...'

A hundred and fifty miles to the south, a silent and wrathf Arthur Pringle watched as Bomber and Oz put away enoug booze on which to float a small skiff. He cursed the day he ever let this lot into his pub. He cursed that cockne smartypants with his ear-ring and non-regulation hairc whom he'd caught *in flagrante delicto* with his daughter. I cursed her too. But most of his rage was turned inwards c himself, as he rued the time he'd got drunk at the party up the big house. Tiger indeed! If one word of that whole sordi business were to leak out, he'd never be able to face th annual squadron reunion again. And that, to Arthur Pringle would be the cruellest cut of all.

It was getting on for three o'clock when Neville was finall able to clear the plates away.

'Sorry about the Yorkshire pudding,' he mumbled.

'Don't worry, pet,' sympathised Brenda. 'I can't always ge it to rise myself.'

'It *tasted* very nice,' chimed in Norma. 'It just looked a b flat, that's all. Perhaps you should call it Lincolnshir pudding.'

'I'll put the coffee on,' said Brenda, squeezing past into th kitchen. As Neville sat down again, Norma seized he opportunity.

'I'm actually very glad you asked me over,' she whispere to him, '''cos it gives me the chance to talk to you abou Dennis ...'

'What about Dennis?' asked Neville, looking puzzled.

'Is there anything bothering him, do you think?'

Neville's brow furrowed. 'No, I don't think so,' he announced. 'I know some of the lads can be a problem now ?'s the boss but . . .'

Norma cut him short. 'I don't mean work, Neville,' she said pointedly.

Neville paused before answering. What was Norma driving ? 'Well . . .' he began, 'if it was anything else he wouldn't say, knowing him. Why?'

Brenda came back with the coffee cups, eager to get into the conversation. She, too, noticed Norma's anxious expression.

'Is there anything wrong?' she asked.

Norma felt edgy. Should she leave things at that, or try to push on in the hope of getting to the bottom of it? She opted for the latter course. After all, Neville was the only one out of Dennis's lot whose brain wasn't just there to stop his ears banging together.

'Look, I'm sorry to bring this up,' she plunged in, 'but I'm sure we're all concerned for Dennis's welfare.'

Neville and Brenda looked at each other, nodding assent.

'A few weeks back, I ran into Audie Charles. Do you know her?'

Brenda knew her all right. The Jodrell Bank of Tyneside. Audie Charles listened out for everything. She could guess what was coming.

'Well,' went on Norma, 'she'd heard that Dennis was badly in debt to this Ally Fraser, and that was why he was working for him.'

Instinctively Brenda pushed a protective hand across the table. 'Oh no, pet,' she soothed, 'I'm sure it's not true.'

But Norma wasn't to be deterred from discovering the truth. 'How do you feel, Neville?' she asked. 'Is there anything in it?'

'He's never mentioned anything . . . but I suppose it's possible.'

Norma smiled awkwardly. 'Whenever I've tried to confront him, he's snapped my head off,' she confessed.

'I don't want to be personal,' said Brenda, pursing her lips, 'but I have to say I was a bit surprised when I found out that

Dennis was involved with Ally Fraser. I mean, he has g
something of a reputation as a ... well, you know ...'

Norma spared her the trouble. 'Don't beat about the bus
Brenda,' she said. 'He's a crook. We all know that. And if
relative of yours was working for a crook, wouldn't you
worried?'

'Don't forget I'm working for him as well,' interjecte
Neville, but Norma cut him short.

'I'm sorry I brought this up,' she sighed. 'There's probably
simple explanation. Let's not spoil the day by talking abou
it, eh?'

But as Neville and Brenda exchanged looks it was clea
that the lunch had been spoiled. Neville coughed and fidgete
before speaking out.

'Look Norma, if it's any help I'll have a word with hir
when I get back tonight,' he promised. Norma patted hi
hand, murmuring her gratitude.

The phone rang. 'That's probably Interpol now,' sai
Brenda, trying to drive away some of the dark clouds that ha
gathered over the table. Neville didn't know where to look
She leaped up and answered the call.

'Hello,' she said with a quizzical note in her voice. Then he
tone brightened 'Oh, hello, Ali ...'

Neville shot her an agitated glance. 'What's he doin,
ringing here?' he mouthed. This didn't sound too good
Maybe Ally Fraser had been up to something while he wa
away.

'It's Ali, my squash partner,' she said with her hand ove
the phone. 'He's an Egyptian doctor.'

That's all right, then, thought Neville, as she made
arrangements for the following Tuesday. Suddenly he sho
bolt upright in his seat.

'Egyptian!' he cried.

So much for a peaceful Sunday afternoon at home.

Neville parked the van outside Thornely Manor and humped
his bags through the darkness into the house. The lads were
sitting around in the drawing room, reading and watching
TV. There was a pleasant but low-key welcome for their
returning mate.

'Hello, Nev,' said Bomber. 'Nice weekend?'

Neville smiled self-consciously. 'Yeah. Great, thanks.' He patted his stomach. 'Ate too much, of course.'

'Can't beat the wife's cooking, eh?' Oz put in.

'I'll say,' responded Neville bravely. If only they knew ...

He looked around. 'Dennis about?' Best get it over with.

'Yeah,' said Wayne. 'He's sulking upstairs in his office.'

'Sulking?'

Oz spoke up: 'Yeah. We had a bit of a go at him about Ally Fraser and this poxy job. Didn't take it too well.'

'Oh,' said Neville. He put his bag down and sighed. 'Anyone want tea?'

A chorus of approval. Neville made his way out of the room.

He found Dennis at work behind his makeshift desk in the gloomy room that served as the gaffer's office.

'Neville,' Dennis gave him the briefest of acknowledgments. 'Good time?' He went back to his work.

'Not bad,' Neville said. 'Had a nice lunch with Norma this afternoon.'

Dennis half looked up. 'Oh aye? She all right?'

Neville took a breath and went for it: 'Well, no. No, she's not all right.'

Dennis's attention was on him now, and there were signs he was worried.

'Why? What's the matter?'

'She's worried about you ... and Ally Fraser.'

'I'm not havin' an affair with him, if that's what she thinks,' Dennis said, trying to laugh it off.

Neville stuck to his guns. 'No. But you're more than just an employee, aren't you?'

'What are you getting at, Neville?'

'Debt. You owing him money.'

'Oh aye,' Dennis countered with just a bit too much sarcasm. 'Audie Charles been jangling again, has she? There's nothing in it, Neville.'

His eyes were restless, evasive, Neville thought. Well ...

'Isn't there?' Neville said. 'It'd explain a lot of things.'

'Oh yes. Such as?'

'You bodging this conversion for a start. It's not like you to

167

put up with shoddy work, Dennis. Unless that's what Ally Fraser wants from you.'

Dennis got to his feet at last. He stared straight at Neville and his face was reddening.

'Neville, in case you hadn't noticed, the construction industry in this country is finished!' he said heavily. 'We can't afford to be too choosy about the work we do any more, 'cos it may be the last we get. Now, if I can stay alive by skimping on a conversion for Ally Fraser, I'm gonna do it – and so are you, man!'

Neville looked at him levelly. 'You must owe him an awful lot of money to talk like that, Dennis.'

The older man stared at him, and Neville met his gaze coolly, though his heart was thumping.

'How much?' he asked firmly.

There was a pause. Dennis began to crumble visibly. He sighed.

'At the last count – six grand,' he said then. 'Not including interest.'

Neville nodded. 'Which, knowing Ally Fraser, will be about fifty percent. Why, Dennis?'

'You wouldn't understand, Neville,' he sighed. 'You have a happy marriage. That's why. I never did – even when I came back from Germany. For a while I thought I could make things better by throwing money about. I was wrong, but by the time I found that out, I was in a hole with Ally Fraser looking down at me.'

'Why didn't you tell us?' Neville said with feeling. 'We're your mates!'

Dennis shook his head. 'It doesn't concern you – not directly, anyway.'

'It does if we're going to have to compromise ourselves as well.'

'Neville,' Dennis snapped, 'it's just a piddling four-week job! If I bring it in on time and to Fraser's meagre budget, I'm in the clear. And if I don't, I may wind up in the Tyne with me pockets full of bricks!'

So the truth was out. Neville went back downstairs to make the tea, deeply troubled. Something was going to have to be done, if anyone was going to keep any self-respect around here. Especially Dennis. And if he couldn't do it for himself, maybe his mates were going to have to do it for him.

Dennis was at the front of the house, collecting a load of bricks from the pile there, when Howard Radcliff's Range Rover came up the drive. The trendy young architect was sporting a pair of fancy sunglasses. He got out, and Dennis noticed he was carrying more plans under one arm.

'Morning, Dennis,' Radcliff said breezily.

'How do,' Dennis returned the greeting guardedly.

'Been another slight change,' Radcliff said, waving the plans at Dennis. 'The kitchens this time.'

'Don't tell me – they only have to be big enough to take one microwave ...'

'Close. Now, let's go and see how far your lads have got, shall we?'

Radcliff strode off into the house. Dennis put down his bricks and followed sullenly in his wake.

When they arrived at the kitchen extension, where the lads were supposed to be working, Radcliff was troubled, and Dennis embarrassed, at the sight of everyone sitting around doing nothing, Harry the plumber included.

'Bit early for a tea-break, isn't it?' said Radcliff.

Dennis nodded. 'Yeah. Come on, lads. Shape up, eh?'

No one moved, and he realised there was something going on.

Oz finally deigned to look at Radcliff.

'If you took those stupid glasses off, Hedgehog, you'd see there's no tea around,' he snarled. 'That's because this isn't a break, it's a strike.'

Radcliff laughed incredulously. 'A strike?'

'Yes, sunbeam,' said Bomber with soft menace. 'A strike.'

The architect backed down. 'Well,' he said, turning nervously to Dennis, 'you'd better sort this out with your gaffer.'

Now it was Neville's turn.

'No, you sort it out with yours,' he said. 'You tell Ally Fraser that nothing gets done here till he upgrades the conversion. And more importantly, till he takes the squeeze off Dennis ...'

Dennis groaned. 'Neville!'

'It's all right, Dennis,' the lad said stubbornly. 'We're all determined about this.'

Radcliff looked bemused and irritated. 'What's going on here?'

'You've got the message, Hedgehog,' Oz hissed. 'Now pass it on to Fraser.'

'All right,' said the architect with a sidelong glance at Dennis. 'If that's what you boys want ...'

He turned on his heel and went. Dennis stood looking at them all, shaking his head.

'Thanks a bunch.'

'Neville told us,' said Oz, ignoring the sarcasm.

'So I gather.'

'It seemed like a choice between being loyal to you, Den – or doing this job properly,' Bomber said.

'So what happened?'

Oz grinned. 'We reckon we can do both, Dennis. Fancy a cup of tea?'

Radcliff could hear Vicki twittering by the poolside when he got through to Ally in Spain. The big Scot was not in an especially good mood, and his humour deteriorated completely when he was told the news about the workers' revolt at Thornely Manor.

'Right – leave it to me.' Ally said crisply over the phone. 'I'll send a few of my industrial relations advisers down there. Sort the bastards out. Bye now.'

That last 'bye now' before he slammed the phone down on the hapless architect had a harshness in it that was pure Gorbals kill-or-be-killed. Howard felt a shiver go through his dapperly attired body as he stood listening to the heavy silence.

It was the next morning that the peaceful atmosphere of the strike-bound Thornely Manor site was broken. They had been expecting it. Harry was sitting out on the front step, his cowboy hat tilted over his forehead, smoking a cigar and singing quietly to himself: 'Do not forsake me, Oh my darlin'...'

Very appropriate. The theme from *High Noon*.

Harry may have looked as if he was half-asleep, but he noticed all right when the big Jag zoomed up the drive and squealed to a halt in front of the house. It spewed out Big Baz and four equally monstrous heavies. Ally's 'industrial relations advisers' had arrived.

Keeping his cool, Harry straightened his hat, threw away his cigar and ambled over to lean in through the doorway.

'I think the boys from the brown stuff just arrived!' he called out.

He turned back to see Big Baz and friends moving towards the house. Suddenly their advance was blocked by a phalanx emerging from the interior: Bomber and Oz looming to the fore, the others just behind, lining up for a classic stand-off.

Big Baz paused, grinned wolfishly.

'We're here to persuade you back to work,' he growled.

Oz looked him in the eye, nodded. Both of them remembered the little set-to in Ally's office a few weeks before. This was a needle match.

'Well, you just failed,' Oz said deliberately.

Baz gave the nod to his helpers. An assembly of iron bars, coshes and other instruments of violence appeared from inside their coats. There was a little flicker from the weaker ranks of the lads, namely Wayne and Barry.

'Did I ever tell anyone I was a Quaker?' muttered Barry.

Wayne winced. 'Are you sure we can't reason with them?'

'I think it's too late for that,' said Bomber grimly.

Then Harry delved into his dungarees and produced an ugly looking plumber's wrench. Dennis whistled. 'So that's why they call you "Monkey Wrench" on your CB channel.'

Harry nodded cheerfully. 'I know how to use it, an' all.'

For a moment, the two groups faced each other out. Then, without warning, Big Baz charged forward, leading his band of thugs into action, and battle was joined.

Big Baz unwisely chose to tackle Bomber first. He took a hefty swing with his cosh at the towering Bristolian which Bomber calmly ducked before grabbing Baz's arm and expertly thowing him flat on his back, as if he had been in a wrestling ring. Baz moaned, winded.

Oz, meanwhile, was not using methods from the wrestling ring – or at least not legal ones. He floored one heavy with a well-judged boot in the privates. Moxey sprung onto the toppling thug to finish him off. Harry tossed his wrench at another, missed, and put it right through the windscreen of Ally's beautiful Jag. Undeterred, Harry put his head down and butted his assailant in the midriff, sending him flying.

Dennis and Oz, meanwhile, had jumped a thug who had Barry by the nice Marks and Sparks jumper Hazel had given him for Christmas and was about to belt it and him to destruction. Wayne dodged in and out of the mêlée, delivering skilful kicks at hostile forces, like a little terrier.

Big Baz staggered to his feet, facing Bomber, only to be tossed bodily onto the roof of the Jag, inflicting a large dent on the car and himself.

'Watch it – my face isn't insured!' yelled Wayne.

'Ah, "The Fightin' Side of Me", Oz,' said Harry as they met among the mayhem. 'Remember that? One of Merle's best ...'

Moxey was calling out for a box of matches to set alight the particular bastard he had on the ground.

'I bet you're sorry you did this now,' said Dennis to Neville with a sly grin.

'Beats layin' bricks for exercise,' said the lad.

The hired heavies were either walking wounded or lying down playing dead when Ally's limousine pulled up outside the house. He'd driven like the wind from the airport, and this was not the scene he had expected to greet him: his troops bloodied, bowed, and beaten.

The Scotsman got out of the limo slowly and made his way towards the carnage with a look of anxious distaste on his face.

'Sorry, boss,' mumbled Big Baz thickly, still nursing a cut lip.

Ally said nothing, didn't even pause as he slowly edged towards the house, where the lads were standing, dirtied but undefeated. Suddenly his expression changed from anxiety to a respectful smile. He gestured to the vanquished heavies.

'Very impressive,' Ally stroked his chin thoughtfully. 'Er, I don't suppose you want to take this to ACAS . . . ?'

'Not a chance!' said Oz, savouring their triumph.

Ally nodded reluctantly for Dennis to join him in the back of the limo. They would discuss the trouble somewhere 'more civilised'. Soon the car had swept off up the drive towards town. From now on, the lads would have to sweat it out for a while. And trust Dennis.

Later that morning, Arthur Pringle was astonished and more than a bit put out by the sight of seven lads trooping into his deserted pub, many still bearing the marks of their encounter with Big Baz and co.

'Morning, Arthur,' said Oz. 'Seven pints of best as quick as you can, please.'

'Bit early, isn't it, even for you lot?' mine host snarled.

Wayne grinned. 'Yeah, well – we're taking industrial action, aren't we, Tiger?'

'Get that beer out in support,' roared Bomber.

Pringle reluctantly began pulling pints while the lads found seats.

'I thought strikes had gone out of fashion with you working classes ever since Scargill got his arse kicked,' he sneered conversationally.

'This was a unanimous decision, though, Arthur,' retorted Neville. 'No need for a ballot or anything.'

'Yeah,' agreed Wayne. 'Besides, we're strikin' on a matter of principle. The care of the elderly. You should be flattered.'

'One day our names will be as famous in the great tapestry of organised labour as the Tolpuddle Martyrs,' intoned Barry.

'Perhaps you'll suffer the same fate – transportation to Australia,' Pringle hit back.

'How about the Thornely Manor Magnificents for a name?' mused Bomber, undeterred by Arthur's insults.

Neville suddenly looked worried. 'We'll be the Derbyshire Dummies if Ally Fraser closes the job down without paying us,' he said.

'Now, now,' said Harry, returning from setting up a darts match with Moxey and scooping up a couple of pints to keep them going. 'No despondency, please. We've won a great victory this morning. And I'm about to thrash Brendan here at 501.'

'It's all right for you to be cheerful, Harry,' Moxey said. 'You've got work lined up for ever – as long as there's a blocked drain or a cracked bog, you're in clover. A plasterer's a high-risk occupation.'

Oz looked at Moxey meaningfully. 'Certainly is the way you go about it, *Brendan*.'

Pringle had finished doing the honours and was standing waiting to be paid. 'Right. That's six pounds thirty. Or am I expected to contribute to the strike fund?'

Wayne handed over the notes. 'Here you go, "Tiger". Might as well have it while we've got it.'

There some banter about the Londoner's usual reluctance to stand his round. Then Oz wandered off to chalk for the darts players. Neville sidled up to Wayne.

'Going to be a bit of a blow if Ally Fraser pulls the plug on us, isn't it?' he said.

'Yeah, I suppose so,' the cockney conceded. 'I don't imagine he'd be over generous with his redundancy payments.'

'Have you managed to save anything up so far?'

'Er, let me think . . . no. Which, considering I've been living like a Trappist monk, is quite an achievement. Still,' Wayne sighed, 'you give me any income you like, and I'll live beyond it.'

'Where's it all gone, then?' Neville probed. 'Sent some home to Krista, have you?'

Wayne started to bluster: 'Yeah. A few bob here and there. I dunno – it just seems to slip through me fingers, same as always. I don't think the car helps, mind.'

'Aye. Thirsty motors, them BMWs. Still, if the worst comes to the worst, you could always flog it . . .'

'Yeah. I could probably get seven or eight grand for it,' Wayne agreed. Then he grinned. 'Mind you, I can't unload it here 'cos it's still German registered, and there's the small matter of import duty which I . . . inadvertently overlooked.'

Neville nodded gloomily.

'There's always complications in life for us workin' blokes, isn't there?' he said. 'As soon as you claw your way up the cliff-face, there's always someone waiting to tread on your fingers. Probably Ally Fraser's turn today.'

In the other corner, Barry and Bomber were also considering the problem of redundancy, Fraser-style.

'What'll you do if we get laid off, Bomb? Head for home?' asked Barry.

'I should think so. Throw meself on the mercy of the wife and the DHSS.' Bomber grimaced. 'Mind you, it's a toss-up as to who'd give me a harder time. How about you? Would your young lady keep you?'

'She won't even *have* me at the moment, never mind keep me,' Barry said sadly. 'Nah. I suppose I'll give me business another few months, and if it still don't take off, I'll try and get in on one of those sunrise industries . . .'

Bomber looked at him strangely. 'Can't see you as a milkman, Barry.'

Barry chuckled. 'Nah, Bomb – they're high-technology jobs. You know, microchips, computers and all that. With my electrical background I might stand a chance. Then again, I'd probably be replaced by a smidgeon of silicon with ten million faculties and an Oxbridge accent.'

'Nothing could take the place of you, Barry.'

'Aw, Bomber. Thanks very much,' said Barry, who thought it was a compliment . . .

'Hey up, lads!' bellowed Oz from his place by the dartboard. 'The shop-steward's back!'

Dennis walked into the bar. Wayne signalled Arthur for another pint.

'What's the word then, Den?' the cockney asked. 'We out of a job or not?'

Dennis smiled. 'No. On the contrary – he's agreed to put more work in at the manor.'

The lads' relief was tremendous. Dennis was a hero.

'I knew we'd twist the bastard's arm all right,' said Oz.

Dennis nodded. He knew what it had taken – a few threats

about what would happen if the Customs and Excise found out about Ally's VAT fiddles, plus the rest.

'There is a small snag, however,' he added.

Neville winced. 'Here it comes – he wants us to take a cut in wages!'

'No, actually,' said Dennis slowly. 'What Ally wants is for us all to do his next job for him. In Spain!'

Amid the amazed cheers and eager questions, Arthur Pringle was pulling pints. With a broad smile on his face.

'I'll get these, lads,' he beamed. 'Just to wish you *bon voyage* ...'

FOURTEEN

The prospect of señoritas and Sangria at the end of the long, hard haul at Thornely Manor put a zest back into the lads' appetite for work, and a spring back in their steps – and none more so than Wayne, to whom what he referred to as 'Eurocrumpet' was the stuff of life. Thus it was that early in the morning he bounded joyfully from the manor to run an errand in the village in his beloved BMW.

Wayne pulled up short when he saw a sober-suited middle-aged gent examining the car with great interest. The cockney approched the incongruous scene with a frown.

'Can I help you, squire?' he asked with an edge of warning.

'Oh, hello,' the man said mildly. 'No. Well, I was just admiring the car. Yours, is it?'

'That's right.'

The man nodded, pointed to the number plate. 'German, I notice.'

'BMWs usually are.'

'I meant the registration. DS – that stands for Düsseldorf, doesn't it?'

'Probably,' Wayne said testily. 'Since we're good on initials, how about "F.O."?'

'Don't know that one,' said the man, still in the same quiet, imperturbable voice.

'Didn't think you would. Now, look, what's this about, old mate? 'Cos the vehicle's not for sale ...'

'I'm glad to hear it – because having already avoided import duty, you'd then be breaking the law again. Mr Wayne Winston Norris.' The visitor produced a warrant card. 'Customs and Excise ...'

Two hours later saw Wayne walking disconsolately away

from the customs compound at the East Midlands Airport. He threw one last, sad glance at the vehicle inside the chainlink fence, now imprisoned and festooned with customs stickers. For all the world he was like some grief-stricken owner leaving a dog behind in quarantine.

'What's the damage?' asked Dennis gruffly, getting out of the waiting van.

Wayne shrugged. 'Well, I've got to find about eight hundred quid duty before I can reclaim the car. Until then, it stays put in there.' He nodded in the direction of the car pound.

'You haven't got the money, presumably?' Dennis said.

'I'm about seven hundred and ninety-nine short of the mark, to be honest.'

'Well, now we're working again I can pay you something tomorrow,' Dennis said. 'With another couple of weeks and Ally's bonus for finishing, you should more than cover it.'

'I'll find the money all right. I'm just annoyed with myself for getting caught out. I told 'em I was just a visitor when I brought the motor in through Harwich, you see.'

Dennis raised an eyebrow. 'Well, you *are* just a visitor, aren't you?'

'What?' Wayne said, but recovered quickly. 'Oh yeah – right,' he babbled, covering his tracks rather clumsily. 'But I suppose I should've told them it was me wife's car and left it at that.'

'Can't it be registered in Krista's name now?'

'Too late for that now, Den,' Wayne murmured evasively. Then he grinned. It took a lot to keep Mrs Norris's boy down. 'Still, I suppose they were due a result against me, the old Customs and Excise ...'

'How d'you mean?'

'Well,' Wayne said confidentially, 'when I came back from Germany I had a little bag of dope stashed in the spare tyre, but they were so busy with the paperwork they missed it!'

Dennis did a double take, then shook his head in despair.

'Sometimes I wonder about your progress towards maturity, Wayne,' he said with a sour smile. He looked at his watch and clucked disapprovingly. 'Come on – nose to the grindstone for you.'

It was nose to the grindstone for all of them – right through to the end of the working week.

'Come and get your scratch, lads!' bellowed Dennis, wandering into the drawing room at the manor with the lads' paypackets clutched in his hand. It was Friday night at last, and dirty work clothes had been discarded. Most of them had already had baths. They clustered round while Dennis handed out their wages.

'Here, Den,' said Neville after he had opened his. 'Take a tenner for petrol money.'

Dennis accepted the note. He and Neville were both off home for the weekend, as was Barry – still trying to patch things up with Hazel.

'Don't piss it against the wall now, Wayne,' he told the cockney as he handed him his envelope. 'Otherwise you'll never get your motor back.'

'Yeah, well. I've gotta spend a bit – me big end needs servicing.'

'I think I'll treat Hazel to dinner somewhere posh in Birmingham this weekend,' vowed Barry, breaking off from putting Savlon on his pimples to collect his wages. 'Reaffirm the troth I've plighted to her.'

'What's a troth, for God's sake – and why would Hazel want one?' asked Oz.

'It's a pledge of fidelity, Oz,' Barry explained haughtily. 'No wonder you've never heard of it.'

'I've been faithful to my Marjorie, Barry – I've never been with another bird within a month of seein' her.'

'Well,' Moxey chipped in, 'as you haven't seen her for over a year that gives you plenty of scope ...'

'Right – see you Monday, lads!' Harry said on his way to his truck. 'Remember, if you get desperate, it's country and western night down my local again!'

'Wild horses wouldn't drag me,' said Wayne.

Harry exited. Meanwhile, Dennis and Neville had their overnight bags ready and were saying their farewells.

'Have a really boring time in Newcastle, lads,' Oz mocked. 'We'll do some strumping for you.'

Dennis just grinned, for some reason.

'You're all gambling, though,' said Neville. 'Us married lads are on to certainties.'

'Barry's not,' said Moxey slyly.

'Don't be so sure, Moxey,' Barry insisted. 'When Hazel hears about my various exploits and my impending foreign travel, she'll probably beg me to ravish her. "But no, Hazel," I'll say to her. "Only within the sanctity of marriage will I countenance such behaviour." I'm gonna be hard with her.'

'Usually helps, Barry,' said Oz with a leer.

Then Barry went out, following Dennis and Neville.

Wayne reached over and put on a smart jacket. They were gong to splash out tonight, drive somewhere a bit upmarket.

'Right,' he chortled. 'Now the devoted husbands and fiancés are out of the way, it's time for us philanderers to get to work!'

Bomber checked his tie in the mirror. 'Bomber's primed and ready to go off!'

It was a few minutes before they realised why Dennis had been grinning when they had talked about their big night out. They'd forgotten that he and Neville were taking the VW, Barry was taking his van – and Wayne's BMW was in the customs pound. They were marooned at Thornely Manor, all dressed up – with no wheels and therefore nowhere to go ...

Norma was busy tidying away plates and an empty wine bottle from the coffee table. Dennis had been tired, and she'd had no time to prepare anything other than a quick snack supper, but they'd both enjoyed the meal. It was good for him to get away for the weekend and see his kids.

'Yes, all right, all right!' Dennis called up the stairs as he came in from the hall. 'I'll do it now!'

He took a pile of plates from Norma. 'The kids want "Hill Street Blues" recorded, if you don't mind,' he said. 'So leave them pots – I'll do 'em later. Pour us a brandy instead, eh?'

'*I've* had enough to drink, Dennis,' Norma told him pointedly.

But Dennis took no notice. He was down on his knees in front of the TV set, fiddling with the video. Norma folded her arms and stood there in silence, waiting for the moment to pounce.

'When I was a kid,' he said to no one in particular, 'I used to spend my Sunday mornings either playing football or on church parade with the Boys' Brigade. Nowadays, they come straight downstairs and watch sex and violence on the telly. Can't be good for them.'

He stood up, red-faced from the effort of crouching down.

'I blame the parents myself,' said Norma.

Dennis decided to ignore that little dig. But Norma wouldn't be fobbed off.

'I don't want to nag, Dennis,' she began, meaning the opposite, 'but you are putting the drink away these days. Is there anything bothering you?'

'I only drink when I'm winding down from work, Norma. It helps me relax. Anyway, there was an article in the paper the other week saying drinkers were less likely to have heart attacks than those who didn't tipple. I knew I was right all along.'

He knew he couldn't bluff his way out of a paper bag with Norma. She looked at him with a severe expression on her face.

'Did Neville mention our little chat to you at all this week?' she said archly.

'What chat's that?'

'About Ally Fraser. And money.'

'Aye, he did mention it. I was able to put his mind at rest.' He changed the subject abruptly, giving her the news about the trip to Spain.

'Oh yes,' said Norma, clearly unimpressed. 'This is by choice, is it?'

'Norma, look,' said Dennis, feeling exasperated. 'Once and for all, I'm straight with Ally Fraser. Once we finish at the manor, and complete the Spanish work, that's probably the end of our association.'

'Only probably?'

Dennis sighed, wanting a drink. 'If he keeps coming up with employment for me and the lads, we'd be daft to say no, wouldn't we?' he started to explain. 'I mean, we can't go down the Job Centre and say "Sorry, we've been offered work but we didn't fancy it, have you got anything?"'

It didn't work. She took a step closer to him.

'Dennis,' she said, 'Look me in the eye and tell me you don't owe money to Ally Fraser.'

He didn't turn round. 'Bloody hell, what is this? The Spanish Inquisition?' he spat over his shoulder.

'I just want to find out what's going on!'

'Well it's none of your bloody business, pet!'

'Oh, isn't it?' snapped Norma. If it came to a shouting match she was determined to get the upper hand. 'But it is my business if you want somewhere to live, or somewhere to bring the kids when it's your weekend, or somewhere for your bloody mates to crash out! If you want me to keep helping you out, Dennis, you'll have to be straight with me.'

'I am straight with you, Norma,' protested Dennis.

'Then why do I keep hearing the same story on the street?'

'If it's just the gossip that's bothering you, why don't you move house?' He was getting malicious now, knowing he was losing.

'Dennis,' she cried in supplication. 'You don't understand! We're family! For all your years and your travel, you're still my little brother! I care about you!' She was close to tears. Dennis shifted his feet, and looked hard at her.

'How much do you owe him?'

'Six thou,' he mumbled.

'How much?'

'Six thousand pounds,' he said, louder this time.

'Oh, Dennis!' she sobbed, looking pained.

'For God's sake, Norma, it's not that bad. Half the bloody country's in debt or living off credit. When you come down to it, there's not that much difference between Access and Ally Fraser.'

'Except that he's got power over you, Dennis – power to make you do things you might not want to do.'

'Norma! I'm only a brickie! All I'm doing is working on a house for him. I'm not a contract killer or something! And when this job's done, I'll be in the clear. That's the deal. I promise you – I'll be off the hook within three months.'

Norma nodded slowly. 'Promise?' she said after a while.

Dennis knew the worst was over. 'Would I lie to my big sister,' he asked, 'knowing the belting she'd give me when she found out?'

He could feel the relief running through his body. Norma looked at him, and smiled.

'I think I fancy a brandy now, pet,' she said.

FIFTEEN

The last day of work at the manor arrived. The lads knew they had done a good job, even though the materials had still not been top quality, despite the upgrading caused by the strike. It certainly looked good. Whatever beauty the ugly gothic building had once had, Dennis and his team had restored. There was a decent-sized kitchen, a lift, small but sound rooms. No one needed to feel the old folks had been short-changed – though how Ally proposed to run the bloody place was another question, mercifully beyond their control.

When Ally Fraser's Jag swept up the drive towards the house, they were ready for him. Dennis warned the others and emerged to greet the boss.

'Looks very impressive from the drive, Dennis,' said Ally, taking in the newly-painted exterior.

'Wait till you get inside,' Dennis grinned, unable to conceal his pride.

The lads meanwhile, were filing out like a reception committee. Ally smiled, went to the boot of the Jag, hauled out a case of champagne.

'Here we are, lads,' he announced, all bonhomie. 'A little refreshment to celebrate completion. And it's Spanish – thought it might get you in the mood.'

The lads crowded round. Oz was eager enough, too, but he also cast Ally a suspicious glance.

'We were hopin' for summat a bit more solid,' he muttered.

Ally knew what he meant. 'Oh yeah. Here we go ...' He reached inside his well-tailored jacket and produced a wad of fat envelopes. 'Pass these around among your men, Dennis,' he said.

Soon they were all flicking through £20 notes with delighted smiles. Especially Wayne.

'Very nice,' said the cockney. 'I can get my beloved motor back now. Can I borrow your van for an hour, Den?'

Dennis tossed him the keys. Oz, announcing that champagne was not really his tipple, offered to go with him to keep him company.

While the rest of them waded into the champagne, Wayne and Oz set off for the airport and the customs and excise shed.

When they arrived, Wayne checked that the car was still there, mournfully observing the film of grime that had quickly collected on the paintwork.

'They could at least have given it a clean,' Wayne moaned.

'They've probably been joyriding in it – did you check the clock before you handed it over?' said Oz in his usual know-all fashion.

'No, didn't think to,' Wayne murmured.

'I'll come in with you,' Oz offered. 'Pretend I'm your legal adviser. If there's any trouble, I'll nut the bastard.'

A couple of minutes later, they were ensconced in an office with the official who had orginally collared Wayne. Now in uniform, the man exuded bureaucratic self-satisfaction as he took his time in reading through Wayne's file.

'Right,' he said when he had kept them waiting long enough. 'Shouldn't take long, Mr Norris. You have the full payment with you, I presume?'

Wayne handed over the envelope. 'Here you are. It's in pounds, not Deutschmarks. That okay?'

The man stared at him frostily. 'No need for any sarcasm, thank you.'

'It's all there, mate,' said Oz as he stolidly counted the notes.

'I have to check,' said the official with a pursing of the lips. 'Just in case you've given me too much.'

Wayne waited a few moments, then asked conversationally: 'Now that I've paid up, I don't suppose you could tell me how you found me?'

'Certainly not. That's privileged information.'

185

'Thought it might be.'

The counting continued, while Oz prowled around the office and Wayne waited. Then the official got up.

'Right,' he sighed. 'I'll just get you a receipt for this ... won't be a moment, Mr Norris.'

When the man had left the room, Wayne leaned forward and picked the file up from the desk while Oz stood guard by the door.

'Any luck?' the Tynesider hissed.

Wayne nodded. 'Here we are,' he said, reading from the file. '"Acting on information received from a Mr Arthur Pringle of the Barley Mow Inn ..."'

Oz chuckled grimly. 'Pringle! I might have guessed it'd be that bastard.'

Wayne nodded. 'I suppose it's his idea of revenge for me boffing his daughter.'

'Aye – and at eight hundred quid, it's probably the most expensive poke of your life!'

The completion party was in full swing when they got back. The rest of the lads were several sheets to the wind with champagne, Ally was all smiles and amiability – not all induced by alcohol – and loud music was blaring from a cassette in the corner.

'I'm really pleased with the work, Dennis,' Ally was saying. 'You and your lads are top men. Shall we consider your debt repaid?'

'I'd like to think so,' said Dennis with dignity.

They shook hands, and Ally toasted: 'Here's to Spain!'

Wayne and Oz stood on the fringes, taking in the celebration with serious mien. Oz grabbed Bomber as the Bristolian raised a glass to him.

'Here,' he said. 'Guess who shopped Wayne to the Customs – Pringle!'

'Slimy old sod,' Bomber oathed. 'Tell Den ...'

Oz sauntered over to Dennis, whispered in his ear. Dennis nodded, thought for a moment, then wandered over to the cassette player and snapped off the music.

'Lads' he said to get their attention, 'I'm sorry to interrupt the party. But when we've finished the drink, we've got a little bit of work to do!'

There were groans all round. It was getting dark, and they were all in party mood. What the hell could he be talking about?

Dennis ignored the 'what fors?' and grinned cunningly.

'Well,' he said at last. 'I've just had an idea for a little leaving present for Arthur Pringle ...'

The village was peaceful, swathed in the mists of early morning. The only sound was that of rooks, cawing their tribute to the day. The strange little convoy of loaded-up vehicles outside the phone box by the green sat mute. And six weary but triumphant men stood around the cubicle while Wayne dialled a number and stood with a coin ready to close the connection.

The phone answered. Wayne pushed his coin into the box.

'Hello, Arthur,' he said pleasantly. 'This is Wayne Winston Norris with your early morning call ...'

The line crackled. An irritable, half-asleep voice said: 'Is this your idea of a joke, you cretin?'

'Oh no,' soothed Wayne. 'We wouldn't joke with you, Arthur, 'cos we know you haven't got a sense of humour. The reason we're calling is to say goodbye, because we're all loaded up and ready to leave. And to tell you about the leaving present we got you ... if you'd care to look outside your front door ...'

At the Barley Mow, a dressing-gowned Pringle cursed, put the phone down on the bar and shuffled off to his front door. Wearily he unbolted and unlocked it, opened it. For a moment he was dumbfounded. Instead of the morning light flooding his porch, there was only a darkness that, as his eyes accustomed themselves, revealed itself as a freshly-built, bare brick wall that had been neatly constructed across the entrance to his pub.

He stumbled back to the phone, and his oaths were terrible to hear, ancient curses born of impotence and frustration. And as he poured venom over the phone, there was still Wayne's mockingly calm voice saying: 'Now, now, Arthur.

Don't be ungrateful. We're even going to sing you a song . . .'

Over the line from the village, Arthur's final contact with the lads from Thornely Manor was of seven tuneless, raucous voices singing lustily to the tune of the old Vera Lynn song:

> *'Wall meet again,*
> *Don't know where, don't know when . . .'*

The Revenge of the Seven was complete, and no one could deny they had gone out in style.

SIXTEEN

A car pulled up outside Norma's house. There were two occupants. One was Dennis, the other – at the wheel – was a very attractive lady in her early thirties. Her name was Christine, and for the past few days she'd been tap-dancing her way into Dennis Patterson's heart.

Dennis had enjoyed himself in that brief period between finishing up at Thornely Manor and getting ready to fly out to Spain. He'd looked up Chris – whom he'd known a long time, and who'd helped him pick up the pieces after his marriage to Vera finally fell apart – and he'd had a few jars with some of his old mates, but most of all he'd relished the sense of freedom from the responsibilities of keeping the old Hut B Brigade in order. Bomber was coming up in a day or two to stay with him and Norma while they made the final arrangements with Ally; the other lads had sorted something out for themselves. Moments like this were to be cherished, he thought as he turned towards Chris. Within a week he'd be back to the old routine.

'Thanks for a lovely evening,' she said, and smiled. There was hardly any hint of Tyneside in her voice, even though she'd been born and bred in these parts.

'Not over yet is it?' asked Dennis, in mock surprise. He'd had enough wine with the meal to make him feel mellow and amorous, but he'd been careful not to get too far gone. After all, he might be in with a chance, tonight. It had been a long time . . .

'I thought if you came in . . .' he ventured.

'I don't think so,' said Christine with easy grace. 'I start work at eight.'

'It's not even half-past eleven!'

'It's not just that ...'

'Don't worry about me sister,' said Dennis. 'I'll put her in the cellar and chain her to the wall.' Christ, he thought, I should be working the clubs as a stand-up comedian.

Christine laughed. 'You know what I mean,' she said provocatively. 'It's her house and I don't feel comfortable.'

'Look, I haven't seen you in ages, Chris. And I'm off to Spain in a few days. I'd just like to talk a bit more, y'know.'

She glanced across at him, weighing up the risks. 'Well ...' she demurred. 'Perhaps a coffee.'

'Great,' cried Dennis. 'Just let me undo your seat belt.' And anything else I might find, he fancied to himself.

Suddenly Christine screamed. Dennis froze in alarm.

'What is it?' he hissed.

'Two horrible men!'

He followed her frightened gaze. Two men were staring into the car. Their faces were horrible indeed, and their names were Oz and Moxey.

They grinned. Dennis couldn't believe it.

'So who's the lass, then?' Oz demanded to know once they'd got inside.

Dennis cringed. 'Keep your voice down,' he growled. 'Me sister's asleep.'

'I hope we didn't sabotage your romantic tête à tête,' said Moxey.

'You didn't help.'

'Who is she?' Oz insisted.

'No one you know, Oz.'

'Obviously,' said Oz. It was like talking to an idiot. 'If I knew who she was I wouldn't have asked ...'

'Her name's Christine,' Dennis conceded.

Moxey said he was impressed with the motor.

Oz meanwhile had found a bottle of Scotch.

'Where's your sister keep her glasses?' he asked.

Dennis reluctantly went to fetch them. He didn't want Oz running riot among the household gods.

'To whom do I owe the dubious pleasure of your company?' he asked over his shoulder.

'I've had a very fraught day, Dennis. Haven't I, Mox?'

'He has Den. Very traumatic.'

What is this, mused Dennis. A variety act?

'Was the Spread Eagle closed for renovations?' he asked sarcastically.

'It's his Marjoric,' Moxey explained, taking the glass Dennis handed him. 'She's done a runner.'

'What are you talking about?'

'You know me flat?' Oz broke in. 'Me home, like?'

Dennis was well aware of the Oz residence. The place looked like football hooligans used it for their pre-match warm-up.

'Well, Marjorie doesn't live there anymore.'

Oz looked mighty aggrieved.

'Didn't you try her mother?' suggested Dennis. 'She must know.'

'Oh aye, she knows. But she wouldn't tell us!'

Moxey's voice assumed a hectoring tone. '"Marjorie's got a chance to better herself now". "Marjorie wants to improve her life, after years of your neglect".'

'All right, all right,' cried Oz, putting his hands over his ears.

But Moxey wasn't to be so easily displaced from his new role as on-the-spot correspondent.

'She said she doesn't want him showing up at this point in time and bolloxing it up for her,' he went on.

'It's me lad – Rod – I'm concerned with,' Oz confessed. 'I want to know he's being took care of.'

'Bit late in the day for that, isn't it?' Dennis suggested.

'What d'you mean?'

'You've hardly been the doting parent, have you?'

Oz thought hard about this. 'But I've been overseas, man,' he protested. 'Working for the lad's future.'

'Oz, when you got back from the States you came back up here. But you couldn't have gone near the flat or you'd have found all this out then.'

'That's where you're wrong, Dennis,' cried Oz in a tone of righteous indignation. 'I'd only been back in town four hours so I was still in the Spread Eagle, right? And I met Steve Platt.

And he told me that Marjorie and the lad were over in Blackpool stayin' at her sister's. So I stayed at me mother's that night. Then I met you, you told me about the job, and the rest is history.' And with that he rested his case.

But Dennis still felt Oz could have shown a bit more willing. 'Tomorrow you can check with Marjorie's friends,' he urged, 'or that place she used to work.'

Oz had more immediate worries. 'It's tonight I'm concerned about,' he said.

'What do you mean?' asked Dennis.

'We need a place to crash. I mean, I promised Mox a bed, didn't I?'

'D'you mean here?' asked Dennis in shocked surprise. 'We've already promised to put Bomber up.'

'In a day or two,' Oz pointed out. 'Not tonight, though.'

'Why don't you go to your mother's?'

'I can't wake her up at this time of night!' he cried. 'She's nearly seventy, Dennis.'

'But you could have gone there *before* the pubs closed,' Dennis berated him.

'I haven't got her a present,' said Oz, as though that settled the matter.

In a corner of the living room an academic looking man was speaking knowledgeably about the principles of higher mathematics. Sprawled across a sofa, Oz and Moxey formed a rapt, if uncomprehending audience. Neither had shaved, or progressed much beyond the early stages of getting dressed. The room smelt of beer, and worse.

In front of them, on the coffee table, was a tray laden with breakfast things. There were mugs, a teapot, plates covered in greasy crusts, bacon rinds and blobs of ketchup.

'We didn't have an Open University when we were lads,' said Moxey, not taking his eyes from the screen. 'It was Secondary Modern for us. With the wind coming in through the broken windows and teachers who didn't give a toss if you got your O-levels or ended up in Borstal.'

Oz nodded sagely. 'We're victims of the system, Mox,' he said.

'Nowadays you just get up, put the kettle on, sit in front of the telly and four years later they give you a degree in physics. Great!'

But Oz wasn't so sure that was quite how it worked.

'It takes a bit more than that, Mox,' he explained. 'Gettin' up this early's not easy, is it? And if your dad's laid off and they keep repossessing the telly, I mean where are you?'

'Education, though, that's the key,' breathed Moxey, warming to his theme. 'You tell your kid that when you find him.'

'Oh absolutely!' agreed Oz, who'd left school the instant he was legally entitled to. 'Computers, that's the thing these days. The silicon chip has transformed life as we know it. Technology, industry, manning levels . . .'

'Don't they also use it to make women's tits bigger?'

'Oh aye,' said Oz. 'It's got lots of applications.'

Their philosophical discussion was interrupted by the arrival of Norma. The sight that greeted her was not a pretty one. She sniffed.

'I see you found yourself some breakfast,' she said, acid-voiced. The kitchen was still full of greasy smoke.

'Aye, well, we'll replace it, like,' promised Oz.

'Where's Den?' asked Moxey.

'He's with Ally,' replied Norma.

'We thought you'd gone to work, like,' said Moxey, feeling a trifle guilty about the mess.

'No!' snapped Norma, stabbing her finger at Oz. 'I've been on the trail of his Marjorie.'

Oz looked embarrassed. 'Oh, Norma, that's not your problem, pet!' he cried. 'I'll be on to that as soon as I've had a shave.'

'What I have found out,' Norma went on undeterred, 'is that your Rod is at Middle Street School. So if you can get yourself into some sort of shape by four o'clock you can get round there.'

Oz looked at his watch. It seemed a distinct possibility, assuming they didn't get too distracted over a lunchtime jar. Why, he noticed with a start, it was nearly opening time already!

*

The days passed in an alcoholic haze. Even as renowned a fixer as Ally Fraser was finding it difficult to get a flight for all of them at the height of the tourist season. Truth to tell, the lads were getting restless. Moxey had disappeared, desperately looking for someone to kit him out with the right documents. The others were keen to get down to a job of work once more.

To soothe those still remaining, Ally decided to honour them with an invite to his place for the night. Butter 'em up and keep 'em out of harm's way while Harbottle greased a few more palms at the Spanish end and he figured out how to get them into the country relatively unobtrusively. With things getting a little warmer for him in the UK these days, and such rich pastures over among the criminal classes in exile in Spain, Ally was going to have some cheap, efficient work done on the villa he had bought – three weeks there and then back for the lads. They were going to be holidaymakers if they did but know it, an irony that gave the George Raft of the Gorbals considerable satisfaction.

Ally was very much the gracious host when the first lot of the uncouth multitude turned up: Wayne, Oz, Barry and Neville. Christine was coming with Dennis, which hadn't been part of the original invitation, but what the hell? Now Vicki had someone to chew the fat with. She'd been showing signs of boredom lately. Maybe Christine would help show her which side her bread was buttered on.

Darrass Hall was built postwar, but tasteful. It could have been in Bel Air but for the chill north-easterly that could tear through its well-tended grounds when Tyneside was unlucky. The outside was classy, and the inside was opulence, Fraser-style.

Naturally, he gave the first four proles a guided tour. They were particularly impressed with his gymnasium. Ally played with the dimmer switch while they took in the treadmill, the exercise bike and his weights machine. The whole set-up oozed money – what it costs to work off the effects of wealth.

'This is where I keep mesel' in shape,' said Ally casually. There were whistles, murmurs of appreciation.

'D'you do this every day, Ally?' asked Neville.

'I try to.' Their host grinned self-deprecatingly. 'Three times a week I have this Danish bit comes over and gives me a massage as well. I tell you, she gets the kinks out,' he added with a leer.

Barry put down his drink and examined the treadmill, asked how it worked.

'You set the speed to whatever you like,' Ally explained.

He switched it on. Barry's eyes lit up. He stepped onto it.

'Oh, it's great, this,' he enthused. 'Jogging without ever leaving the house. Very therapeutic, I should imagine ...'

Ally indulgently left him to it. 'There's a sauna through there. And out the back I've got the swimming pool.'

Neville muttered approval.

'A swimming pool up here?' said Oz. 'I should think it's about as much use as a chocolate fire-guard ...'

'I do twenty laps a day, all weather,' Ally said with careful emphasis.

Neville, meanwhile, had spotted the ultra-violet apparatus above the massage table.

'Is that to give you a suntan?' he asked.

'Aye. But you lads'll get plenty of that in Spain. Come on through an' bring your drinks.'

He began to lead the way out, but as they filed away Oz reached out and turned up the speed on the treadmill. Barry's little legs thrashed vainly to keep up with the new tempo. His face reddened.

'I'll do you, Oz!' he shrieked.

Downstairs the doorbell rang, and Vicki tiptapped across the parquet floor of the hallway to answer it, swaying slightly on her impossibly high heels. A Filipino woman appeared but Vicki dismissed her.

'It's okay, Maria,' she told the maid. 'I'll answer it!'

Waiting outside were Dennis and Christine.

'Oh, hello, Dennis,' Vicki gushed. 'Come in.'

They entered.

'I don't think you know Christine Chadwick,' Dennis said a little stiffly.

Vicki's brow puckered. No, she *did* know her from somewhere. 'But, it's been a long time though ...'

Christine smiled. 'I used to get me hair done at Maison André's and you were the manicurist,' she said.

'Eee, that's right!' Vicki giggled. 'You're looking lovely!' She led them through into the living room to join the others.

Sausages on sticks were being offered to the rest of the lads by a Filipino man – Maria's husband, it seemed – when Dennis, Christine and Vicki entered the room.

They paused on the threshold to survey the scene; the lads in jackets and ties, obviously on their best behaviour, seated around a large imitation log fire, surrounded by expensive stereo and television equipment, with Ally serving drinks from a bar that was amass with chrome and mirrored glass.

'Oh, he's brought the tart along,' Oz remarked, giving Christine the once-over.

'D'you know her?' asked Wayne, showing interest. Teenage jailbait was his usual line, but he could always make an exception.

'I've seen her,' said Oz, but Dennis hadn't been too upfront with the facts about the new love in his life.

Ally Fraser came bustling over and greeted the new arrivals effusively.

'Is it Christine or do you prefer Chris?' he asked cheerfully.

'I don't really mind, Mr Fraser.'

'Ally, Ally! What's this "Mr Fraser"? Come and get a drink down you!' He steered her away, leaving a tight-lipped Neville to confront Dennis with the question he'd been burning to ask.

'So you've brought a date?'

'So?'

'Yesterday you said it was just the lads. No wives, you said specifically.'

'Well, she's not me wife, is she?'

'That's not funny, Den. I could have brought Brenda. She wanted to come, y' know.'

'I'm sorry, Nev. I just didn't think of it.'

Neville was determined to vent his spleen. 'She'll be well

pleased when she hears there were women here,' he moaned.

Dennis had just about had enough. 'So why don't you give her a bell and send a mini-cab?' he asked.

'And where's she going to get a babysitter at this time of night?'

'Aw look, don't get on my case, Neville! Give us the night off, eh?'

On the other side of the room, Vicki was trying to open a tin of cocktail nuts. Wayne moved in.

'Here, let me do that,' he suggested.

She smiled at him gratefully. 'Oh, thanks very much. I'm bound to tear a nail.'

They introduced themselves.

'Are you coming out to Spain then, Vicki?'

'Oh yes. We've just got back, actually. I love it there. It's almost me second home.'

He nodded. 'D'you get a lot of tourists there?'

'Yes, in the season it's packed. But where we are, we don't get the common ones.'

'Oh well, you won't be seeing much of me then,' said Wayne with a chuckle.

She nudged him playfully. 'I didn't mean that.'

Ally missed little, wherever he was, and he didn't miss the little intimacy between Wayne and Vicki. But he just filed it away and banged on the bar for everyone's attention.

'Now we're all here,' he announced, 'I'd like to say a few words.'

They gathered round. As they assembled, Vicki discreetly withdrew 'to show Christine the house'.

'Now,' Ally began when the women had gone. 'I'm sorry if you lads have been farted around a bit, but these things happen. Unexpected contingencies. However, everything's sorted out and I've booked you all to fly out there on Saturday.'

There was a murmur of interest.

'Is that from here or Heathrow?' asked Dennis.

'From here. 13.45.'

'I didn't know there were any scheduled flights from here on a Saturday,' said Dennis.

Ally nodded. 'It's not a scheduled flight as such, Dennis. You could say it is our own luxury charter.'

'What? Our own plane?' Oz chortled. 'I fancy that. The brickies' special!'

Ally smiled condescendingly. 'I haven't gone that far, Oz. A pal of mine owns this travel company. He's got this tour going down there and happily there's a few spare seats.'

Oz grimaced. 'Oh, it's an economy measure, is it? I see.'

Ally raised a hand. 'It's more than that, if you'll hear me out. Y'see, officially you lads are not goin' there to work. Because I could'na get the work permits. The reason I want you there is because I trust the British workforce.'

'Very patriotic,' commented Wayne, but the irony was lost on Ally.

'I think if one is in a position to help the working man, one should do it,' Ally continued. 'Also, your Spanish workman is not exactly up to scratch. When I'm there it's mañana, mañana. Once I've gone it's siesta, siesta . . .'

Barry nodded. 'They do tend to indolence, the Latins. Maybe joining the Common Market will change their attitude, though.'

Ally stared blankly at him, then picked up the threads of his speech:

'All I'm sayin' is, you're supposed to be there as tourists. So arrivin' on a charter will reinforce that impression. D'you get my drift?'

'So we'd better take buckets, spades and waterwings, then,' said Oz.

'Aye. And show up to work in a cossy, that's the idea. I'll give you some pesetas out there for walkin' around money. This will be deducted from your wages. Which will be in readies, as usual, back here.'

Bomber dug Dennis in the ribs and told him to ask Ally about digs. Dennis asked Ally whether they were still going to stay at the hotel they had originally been booked into.

'Unhappily they can no longer take you,' Ally said.

Dennis was firm. 'Look, Ally, the lads have had enough of barrack room conditions.'

There were murmurs of agreement. Ally made a gesture as

if to say: 'What do you take me for?'

'All has been taken care of. You'll be staying in the same place as the rest of the tourists. Very charming hotel, apparently. Only a stone's throw from the beach.'

'Aye, well,' grumbled Oz. 'The Spaniards are famous for how far they can hoy a stone!'

It got a laugh. Even Ally joined in.

'They're also famous for how badly they can lay a brick,' he said, turning the joke to his own advantage. 'That's why we're off to sunnier climes. So *"hasta la vista"* and *"vaya con Dios, mis amigos"*!'

He raised his glass in a toast. They all joined in enthusiastically, except for Neville, who was still a little sour about the business with Christine.

Ally suggested a game of pool and found willing takers in Dennis, Oz and Bomber. But Neville cornered Bomber just before he was about to head into the pool room.

'I've been thinking,' he confided. 'As it's a charter, it can't be too pricey. So it might be a good idea to take the wives. D'you fancy takin' yours, Bomber?'

'Oh, I don't know, Nev. She's got her hands tied with all our kids.' He winked. 'Besides, Bomber quite fancies getting amongst all those señoritas.'

Bomber made off to the pool room. Neville stared gloomily into the middle distance. Was he the only decent married man in the world? Then he saw Barry, still slumped in one of Ally's deep sofas, wallowing in the unaccustomed luxury. He sighed and approached the zit king.

'I could grow accustomed to evenings like this,' commented Barry as Neville neared him. He gestured to the bar. 'Hazel and I talked about puttin' in a bar. There's space enough in that downstairs area, if you remember. Nothing on this scale, of course, but there's enough room for me to stand behind something.'

'Have you spoken to Hazel about Spain?' Neville asked.

'I have, actually. She's quite keen. But you know, Nev, she's in a very senior position in her job. She can't drop everything just like that.'

'But there's a possibility, is there?' Neville persisted.

'Oh yes. But I prefer to get out there and see the lie of the land first.'

Neville then drifted over to where Wayne was leafing through record covers by the stereo.

'What about you, Wayne?'

'What about me, then?'

'Any chance of you asking Krista out to Spain?'

Wayne did a double-take, turned to Barry.

'Didn't you tell him?'

'How could I? I haven't had the opportunity,' Barry protested. 'I haven't seen sight nor sound of Nev since our little confab.'

Over a Chinese, Wayne had finally spilled the beans about his splitup with Krista to the zit king.

'What's this?' Neville asked anxiously.

'Now's your chance, right?' snapped Wayne.

He picked up his glass and waltzed out to watch the pool game. Neville looked enquiringly at Barry.

Barry pursed his lips. 'This may come as a bit of a shock to you, Nev . . .' he began, feeling about a hundred and ten years old.

When he had explained the basics, Neville nodded sadly.

'You must admit, he's got no one to blame but himself.'

'Oh, he knows that,' said Barry.

'He never lets it alone, does he?' Neville continued. 'He'd slept with half Düsseldorf before he met Krista.'

'I think the experience may have changed him,' Barry said optimistically. 'And I mean he's got people like you and me, Nev. That's got to be a stabilising influence.'

Neville shook his head. 'I don't think I've ever been an influence on Wayne. I think he thinks I'm dull.'

'Mature. That'd be *my* word for it,' Barry said.

Vicki ushered Christine along plush corridors and through expensively furnished bedrooms. Proudly she showed off her walk-in wardrobe, bigger than many a living room. There was money here right enough, Christine thought, but their taste was a bit, well . . .

'How long have you known Dennis, then?' asked Vicki as they were coming downstairs.

'About a year, on and off.'

'When I did your nails, weren't you going through a divorce?'

'That's why I was biting them a lot.'

The joke was lost on Vicki. She'd always thought Christine had ever such nice nails.

'No, I just remember you mentioning it,' she went on.

'Well,' said Christine confidently. 'It's all behind me now.'

'Dennis is divorced now, isn't he?'

'Yes. Is Ally?'

Vicki hesitated. 'Not technically. She won't hear of it. She's a very staunch Catholic, you see. And she's not going to give up the money either.'

'Doesn't that bother you?'

'Oh no, Christ, marriage is just a bit of paper these days, isn't it?'

'Perhaps ...'

They paused at the pool room door before rejoining the lads.

'Well, it's been lovely talking to you again after all this time,' said Vicki. Truth to tell, she missed the company of women like Christine. 'You ought to come to Spain, y'know. We'd have a good laugh, out there. And I get so bored on me own with him on the golf course all day.'

Christine was a bit circumspect. 'I'm not sure Dennis would want that,' she said warily.

Vicki winked. 'I'll have a word with him,' she said.

But Christine wished she hadn't. Whatever happened between Dennis and herself, she wanted it to come about of its own accord, without other people's interference. Yet as soon as she'd joined him, she knew what the answer would be if he did ask her to go with him.

Ally had just potted the eight ball to win the game.

'That's one to us, Bomber,' he grinned, polishing his cue.

'Aye, well, early days yet,' countered Oz. 'Best of seventeen, eh?'

'Rack 'em up!' cried Bomber. 'You rack 'em, I smack 'em!'

And so it went on. Actually Christine enjoyed being with Dennis in this male stronghold – she hadn't a clue where Vicki had got to, dabbing at her already immaculate make-up, probably, or phoning one of her friends – but she wasn't so sure about enduring this kind of thing night after night. And that was probably what the rest of the wives had had to put up with for most of their lives.

Just then Vicki came in, wrapping herself in a luxurious mink.

'I'm off, Ally!' she called. 'I'm going to meet Karen down the club.'

'Aye, okay,' grunted Ally, lining up on the bottom pocket. She bid the rest of the party goodnight, and skittered off.

Wayne hadn't stayed long in the pool room with the boys. Feeling restless, he had decided to take a look around the grounds, get time to think. He had spoken to Krista a couple of times since arriving on Tyneside. She was going to have a baby – and she still didn't want him back. That was enough to make even him think a bit, whatever the other lads might say. There'd been the momentary flicker of electricity with Vicki, of course, to take his mind off things, but she'd apparently cleared off to meet some friend somewhere. Suddenly, as he rounded the corner of the house, the cockney heard an engine turning over wearily. He homed in on the garage and saw Vicki sitting in the driving seat of Ally's Jag, vainly trying to start the beast.

'Got a problem?' he said with a grin as he strolled into the garage.

Vicki looked up, smiled back, then furrowed her pretty forehead in frustration.

'Oh, it often does this,' she said. 'Makes me mad.'

'Give it a moment,' Wayne advised gently. 'You may be floodin' it.'

She obediently put the choke in. 'It did this in the middle of Northumberland Street last week. I was so embarrassed.'

Wayne nodded. 'Where you off to, then?'

'I'm goin' down to Annabel's. It's this disco Ally owns.'

'Oh, we was there last night,' Wayne said.

Understatement masked a multitude of sins. They had got into a fight, with poor old Moxey at the centre, which was why their fire-raising friend had done another of his runners:

always terrified of the fuzz getting hold of him and checking his ID.

'D'you want to come down later?' Vicki asked coquettishly. 'I could leave your name at the door.'

'Do you mean me, or all of us?' Wayne probed.

'Why?' she asked, all innocence. 'Do you always do everything as a group?'

'No,' said Wayne, 'there's a lot of things I do on my own. But maybe tonight would look a bit off. I mean, I am Ally's guest, aren't I?'

'Suit yourself,' she pouted.

'Maybe we could leave it till Spain.'

'Leave what?'

Wayne shrugged. 'A bit of dancing or something.'

She looked at him, smiled. 'Have to see.'

They'd gone about as far as they could for the moment, Wayne thought. And he was on Ally's territory.

'Let's try it now, then,' he said. He reached in through the window to turn on the ignition, bringing his face very close to hers. 'Don't give it too much pedal ...'

The engine fired into life. Wayne straightened up, and with a wave Vicki moved off out of the garage and increased speed down the driveway.

Wayne watched her go, then sighed and turned back towards the house. A shape was blocking the lit doorway now. The unmistakable, large shape of Ally Fraser. Impossible to tell how long he had been there, but the expression on his face told the story.

Wayne strolled towards the door, keeping his cool.

Ally waited until he was close to the entrance, then said very quietly: 'That's mine.'

Wayne nodded. 'Yeah, lovely motor, squire,' he answered just a little too cheerfully.

The Scotsman's craggy face did not change expression. But his eyes bored into Wayne's like lasers.

'I didn't mean the car,' said Ally.

The following day, Dennis's face wore a worried expression as he busied himself fixing a shelf for his sister.

'What do you think I should do, Norma?' he asked.

'I'm amazed you asked her.'

'Christine brought it up, actually. She said she'd got some holiday due and she'd love to come. And I agreed at the time. I mean, I'd had a few and I was feelin' fairly mellow.'

Norma looked at him in amazement. 'I don't know what you're looking so worried about,' she began. 'She's a lovely girl and if she wants to go to Spain with you, you should feel very flattered.'

In the cold light of day Dennis wasn't sure it was such a good idea. Especially with the lads – and Ally Fraser – around. He said as much to Norma.

'It's not them that's giving you cold feet, it's you!' she exclaimed when he'd got it off his chest.

'How d'you mean?' Dennis was a bit puzzled by all this amateur psychology.

'It's not just at work you build walls, Dennis. You build them round yourself. You're scared of facing your own feelings.'

Dennis conceded that his track record wasn't any too great in that particular department. Norma let him have the rest of it.

'Take her with you!' she urged. 'You've been fence-sittin' with this one for a long time. If she goes to Spain with you it's going to force a decision one way or the other. What's the worst thing that can happen? You'll find out that you're not compatible. But you might have some fun . . . and God knows you could do with a bit.'

Dennis could see the logic. 'You should write one of them agony columns, Norma,' he chuckled.

'I care about you, pet!' Norma cried warm-heartedly. 'I worry about what's going to happen to you.'

She looked at the big pile of washing sitting by the machine, at the tools scattered over the worktops, where Dennis was fixing the shelf.

'And as me husband's back from the Gulf in two months, I'd like the house to meself,' she added drily.

And so Christine came too. It made Neville happy – he could see Brenda getting a bit fractious having to cope with Oz and

Co. all day and all night as well as with Debbie – and for Barry it was useful bait to lure Hazel along later.

Moxey had managed to fix things up for himself pretty well. The following Saturday found them at the airport weighed down with luggage, just like authentic holiday-makers. A right party. Not that the women travelled free; Ally had been glad enough for them to tag along – increased the lads' credibility as tourists – but they paid charter rates for flight and accommodation. He couldn't afford to hand out freebies. Especially not with the boys from the Fraud Squad on his tail.

As they milled around the check-in, a blazered character with a clipboard walked up and hailed Dennis.

'Party of ten for Swallow Tours,' he said cheerily. 'Are you all here?'

Dennis confirmed they were. The tour leader collected in their tickets and passports so they could be checked through as a group.

Christine and Brenda went off to buy magazines while Neville minded Debbie. Wayne wandered up and grinned at the little girl.

'I think it was very noble of your dad to bring you and your mum,' he told her. ''Cause you'll keep him out of temptation. While the rest of us are samplin' all the pulchritude down there.'

Neville frowned. 'There won't be all that much,' he said. 'It's not the tourist season.'

'There'll be enough,' Oz said firmly. 'And even before we get there, we'll have somethin' sorted out.'

Wayne nodded enthusiastic agreement. 'You're not telling me this charter tour's not got its fair share of secretaries, shopgirls and hairdressers.' He rubbed his hands in glee. 'We'll have it all locked off before we're even landed, won't we, Oz?'

The tour leader waved for them to go over and check in with the rest of the party. Oz and Wayne moved eagerly towards the queue, exchanging lascivious grins. Then they saw the Swallow Tours party. Every single one of them was over sixty-five ...

'What's this lot?' Wayne asked in a strangled voice.

205

'The Spennymoor and District Senior Citizens' Society,' the guide explained with a grin. 'They go every year. You were lucky to get those seats.'

Neville took in the looks of horror on Oz's and Wayne's faces and smiled broadly.

'I wouldn't waste any time, Wayne,' he mocked. 'I'd steam in now!'

SEVENTEEN

The trip from the airport to the hotel, for which, mercifully, Ally had provided the lads with a separate minibus, took them through the hills around Malaga, and they were all awed. Not by the scenery, though it was impressive enough, but by the amount of building that was going on – hotels, villas, towerblocks. It was the kind of boom area the lads hadn't seen in England for ten years or more.

'What was it Ally said?' Oz commented loudly. 'He wanted to bring a team down here so he could help the British unemployed. Bollocks! We're here 'cause there can't be a Spanish brickie free from Malaga to Gibraltar!'

Bomber nodded. 'I've never seen so much building in my life.'

'Mind, I think it's ruined the view,' Brenda commented.

'Aye,' said Neville ruefully. 'But think of the lads they're employing. They must all be millionaires.'

The hotel itself was not new, but, as the tour guide had already told them, at least it was finished. His name was Russell, and he was always cheerful, always optimistic. He handled wild grannies with an expertness that had even Oz respectful.

Not that there was any shortage of building activity around them. When Neville, Brenda and Debbie went upstairs to their room, they looked around – Brenda pretty disconsolately, for the place was small and there was only a shower, which would cause problems for the baby. It seemed secluded enough. Then Neville opened the shutters and was faced with two Spanish brickies working not five yards away on the new hotel next door. '*Buenos Días*!' his Spanish colleague greeted him cheerfully. 'Bloody hell!' said Neville.

Dennis had also checked out his and Christine's room. He came down into the hotel bar to find all the lads ensconced, packing away Heinekens and brandy chasers.

'Hello, lads. Your rooms all right?' he asked.

Wayne grinned. 'Dunno. We ain't seen 'em yet.'

'By the time we do, we'll be too legless to care,' chipped in Oz.

Dennis sighed. Bomber offered him a drink.

'Aye. What are you lads on?'

'I think it's brake fluid,' said Oz. 'But it's cheap.'

'Fundador,' Bomber explained.

'I'll give it a go, then.'

Bomber did his shout.

'Another one, Carlo,' he told the barman. 'I came to Spain when I was a lad,' he added, turning back to the others. 'First holiday abroad. Tossa del Mar. Went with me mates from Bristol. Drank a lot of Fundador then. We were never sober. Did all our boozing in an English pub called the Lord Nelson.' He chuckled fondly at the memory. 'Ate our grub at the Tudor Tea Rooms, run by a couple from Beckenham. So I never saw an inch of Spain.'

'This part of Spain's overrun by Brits, apparently,' Dennis said.

'Suits me,' Wayne said. 'Got more chance of getting strumped by a couple of birds from Birmingham than you have by some señorita. 'Cause they're staunch Catholics, the Spanish, aren't they? If you do take one out, she'll bring her granny as a chaperone.' The cockney suddenly registered Carlo, the barman, staring at him challengingly. 'Which I respect!' he added hastily to appease the Spaniard's feelings.

Barry entered. He had already bought a guidebook and a handful of postcards.

'I've just been scoutin' out the area,' he droned. 'We're not exactly in the most picturesque part of town. As far as I can see from this street map, this hotel's got a bullring on one side and an abbatoir on the other.'

Oz feigned horror. 'I hope they don't use this place as a short cut! Fancy sittin' down to your dinner when they drag a bleedin' carcass through the lobby!'

Time passed, and Wayne looked at his watch. Time to move on. With the oldies gathering here, there wasn't much chance of action, was there?

The rest agreed and downed their drinks, except for Dennis.

'You comin', Den?' asked Oz.

'No. I'm happy, thanks.'

'Well,' goaded Oz. 'I'm sorry you can't come out with us and have a laugh. But it was your decision to bring the girlfriend.'

Dennis bridled. 'I'm waiting in for Ally's call.'

'Suit yourself.'

They exited, with Barry, guidebook in hand, already saying: 'The guide recommends the Bar Mediterranée . . .'

Dennis watched them leave and continued to sip his drink. As he sat there, two old ladies from the Spennymoor pensioners' group came in, all freshened up and clutching their handbags. Dennis had already been introduced to them by Russell. Their names were Beatie and Alice, if he remembered rightly, and they were in their late seventies.

'Are you warm enough, Beatie?' said Alice as they approached the bar. 'You should have put your woolie on.'

'No,' said the other old dear stoutly. 'I'm not tired at all.'

Watching them, Dennis felt a tug in his heart for all the world's old ladies, those homemakers in the twilight of their years. Their needs were modest, their demands of the world few . . .

'Hello, ladies,' he said. 'Can I offer you a drink?'

Alice looked at him and giggled. ''Ere, Beatie – this young man's trying to get me drunk.'

'Go on. First night of your holidays. Glass of wine or something?' Dennis persisted. A little touch of the exotic. He could afford it.

Alice examined him with interest.

'No,' she said decisively. 'I'll have a large gin with very little tonic, and she'll have a brandy and ginger . . .'

'I think that's it ahead,' said Barry, who was sitting beside Dennis in the front of the minibus. It was early morning and on the way from town they had already passed a dozen villas that might have fitted the description of Ally's, most of them brand new or uncompleted.

'What d'you mean, you *think*?' Dennis barked. 'Is it or isn't it?'

Barry peered at the envelope on which Dennis had scribbled the instructions the previous night.

'I'm not sure,' he confessed. 'None of these roads have names. We turned left past the Tennis Ranch, took the left-hand fork, then it says here half a mile, a white villa on the right, so that should be it ...'

There was indeed a white villa ahead.

'What's the name of his villa?' asked Bomber.

'The Villa Mimosa.'

'That must be it, then,' said Barry excitedly. ''Cause that shrub in front's mimosa, isn't it, Oz?'

Oz scowled. 'You're askin' me? I never saw a tree till I was twelve. The only flower I recognise is a dandelion ...'

So they pulled up alongside a stone wall. Dennis opened the door, got out to look around. There was no sign of life.

'Aw, this must be the one,' he said with a sigh.

'There's nay car around,' Oz cautioned.

'Might have popped into town,' Dennis insisted.

'Maybe they're round the pool,' Bomber suggested.

The place was, in fact, deserted. No one at the pool. No response when Dennis knocked on the windows.

'Very nice,' said Barry.

'Pool's a bit small,' Wayne scoffed.

'Oh, yours is Olympic size, is it? The one in your back yard in Tilbury,' growled Neville, who had had a hard night, what with Debbie crying and Brenda complaining about the noise from the demented OAPs ripping it up downstairs.

'Ooh ... what's wrong with her?' Wayne shot back. 'Get out of bed the wrong side, did you?'

'Seventeen times, yes,' said Neville bitterly. 'D'you think I slept with the noise you lot were making? Then at seven those Spanish brickies were back on the job.'

'Where's this?' asked Oz.

'About three feet from me pillow.'

'We don't get that,' said Moxey helpfully. 'We're all on the other side of the hotel.'

'Who arranged that?' demanded Neville, incensed.

'I did, Neville,' Dennis explained. 'I thought the further you and Brenda and the bairn were from the lads, the more peace you'd get.'

Neville sighed at the bitter ironies of life.

'So what's Ally want us to do, Dennis?' asked Bomber.

Dennis jerked a thumb at the side of the house. 'He wants to enlarge the pool and the terrace area.'

Bomber appraised the job with an expert eye. 'He can only extend the terrace *that* way. Have to cantilever it.'

Dennis nodded. 'And he wants a brick barbecue built.'

'We should do that first,' suggested Wayne. 'Then we can have barbecued chicken for lunch every day.'

Oz rocked on his heels, surveying the luxurious surroundings.

'Well,' he admitted, 'you've come through for us this time, Dennis. This is the pleasantest building site I've ever worked on.'

'Beats Düsseldorf hands down,' agreed Barry.

Oz checked out the pool. 'We can have a dip every day, an' all.'

'Well, no,' said Barry. 'We can't do that, because we'll be extending the pool. Unless you want to dive into a heap of rubble.'

Oz's eyes lit up. 'All the more reason to use it now, then.'

There was enthusiastic agreement. Dennis expressed his doubts. After all, it wasn't their pool.

'We're not lepers,' said Moxey, hurt. 'We won't pollute it.'

'Even if we do, we'll be pulling the plug this afternoon,' added Oz.

Everyone else put in their two bob's worth and Dennis finally agreed. No cossies, but what the hell? They were all lads together.

'I don't want that Vicki comin' out on the terrace and findin' seven brickies' dongs floatin' on the water ...' Dennis cautioned, but by then they were stripping. Within moments the first were splashing around.

Some time later, an ageing Rover, right-hand drive, with Spanish number plates, pulled up in the drive. A neatly-dressed English couple got out. Geoffrey and Pauline Oxlade had moved from the Home Counties to Spain when he had retired from the firm, and they were pillars of the extensive English community on the coast. Pauline fetched the shopping from the back of the car while Geoffrey peered in a puzzled fashion at the minibus. When he spoke it was with the authentic voice of the English middle class.

'Who's that belong to?'

'I've no idea,' Pauline sniffed.

'Is it whatsisname's day to do the pool?' wondered Geoffrey.

'No, darling. He comes Thursdays.'

'Yes,' her husband said doubtfully. 'But you know what they're like . . .'

Pauline was firm. 'No, I'm sure he has a little yellow car.'

Geoffrey shrugged, made to move up towards the house, then froze when he heard the sounds of splashing and loud voices from the pool.

'Can you hear something?'

They approached the pool cautiously, with Geoffrey to the fore, and saw six naked, lily-white and *working-class* bodies thrashing around in the water. A seventh was watching, fully dressed, from the sidelines.

'Good God!' bellowed Geoffrey. 'Pauline, don't come any further!'

'Who . . . who's in our pool?' she squealed.

Geoffrey steeled himself. 'I'll take care of this.'

Dennis was the first to see them coming. He greeted them with a polite good morning.

'Never mind "good morning",' Geoffrey blustered. 'Can you explain who you are and what you're doing here?'

Dennis shrugged. 'We're just waiting for Mr Fraser.'

'Who?'

Suddenly doubts clouded Dennis's brow. 'Hold it down, lads, will you!' he called to the swimmers. The noise level subsided sufficiently for him to ask in a normal voice: 'Er . . . is this Villa Mimosa?'

'No, it is not,' Geoffrey snapped. 'This is Dunedin.'

'Oh God!' muttered Dennis.

Pauline, meanwhile, gingerly made her way to Geoffrey's side.

'Geoffrey!' she shrieked. 'They're all naked!'

Oz, who had been bobbing like a great seal in the water, glowered up at her. 'It's not customary to wear a morning suit when you have a swim, missus!' he growled.

Geoffrey turned puce. 'If you're not out of here immediately, I shall call the Guardia Civil!'

Dennis could feel the anger rising inside him, but he kept his temper. 'Look, pal,' he said, 'there's been a legitimate mistake, all right? No need to go over the top. I mean, we're all Brits here.'

'You,' Geoffrey sneered, 'are the type of "Britisher" that caused my wife and I to retire here in the first place.'

That was when Dennis gave up.

They finally found the Villa Mimosa. Ally came out to greet them with a face like thunder.

'Where the hell have you been?' he snarled.

Dennis faced up to him. 'I'm sorry, Ally. We got lost.'

Ally took in their wet hair. 'Looks more like you've been swimmin'.'

'It's a long story,' Dennis sighed.

'It was my mistake, Mr Fraser,' Barry said. 'We took the wrong left-hand turn after the Tennis Ranch ...'

'Yes, yes, yes,' Ally waved away the explanation impatiently. 'Get your hairy arses round the back!'

Round by the pool, there were signs of preparation. It had been drained, and building materials, bricks, sand and a concrete mixer were in evidence. The lads took in the view while Dennis checked the plans with Ally and a Spaniard, Hector, who had been waiting for them to arrive.

'Hector here went over the specs,' Ally explained. 'He's got in what he reckons you'll need. Check it out and anything else you require, let him know. Because Hector is the one who has to buy from the trade. Because *officially* Hector is the contractor.'

Hector nodded enthusiastically. '*Si.*'

'He's the front, right?' said Dennis sourly.

'Exactly. Mind, he's a builder in his own right. He's got a team doin' a villa down the road.'

The rest of them were still staring out over the terrace.

'Be nice to think you could retire to somewhere like this,' Bomber said thoughtfully. 'I suppose the best I can hope for is a caravan at Clevedon, overlooking the Bristol Channel.'

'At least there people would talk to you,' Neville said. 'You'd have neighbours and friends. Here you might be surrounded by people like that couple who hoyed us out their pool today.'

'Aye,' said Oz. 'I know we were trespassing, like. But as soon as I saw his face I hated him. That's the kind of person makes you ashamed to be English.'

Barry frowned. 'In all fairness, he probably feels you're that type of person, Oz.'

'Well, I'm not,' Oz growled. 'He is, though. Every time I see his sort, the hairs curl up on me spine.'

'The bourgeoisie,' contributed Moxey.

'A prick in my language,' Oz continued. 'He's the type who's always moanin' in the golf club, or writing to the papers about people not pullin' their weight. What's he do when he cops his pension, eh? He goes to Spain so he won't have to pay any taxes!'

'When did you last pay income tax, Oz?' asked Barry.

'That's not the point, as you well know ...'

Just then, Vicki came out of the villa carrying a tray of beers. She was also wearing a bikini that, if you had had the pleasure to disassemble it, would hardly have remade into a pocket handkerchief. Wayne was the first to notice, predictably.

'We interrupt "Any Questions" to bring you a news flash ...' he leered. 'Well, a flash of some sort, anyhow.'

The others' eyes swivelled to watch Vicki, and if their tongues started to hang out, it was only partly for the beer.

'I thought you boys might be thirsty,' she smiled.

They thanked her, transfixed.

Ally had seen it all. He told her to put the tray down and excused himself. A minute later he and Vicki disappeared into the house. The lads watched her go.

'I always wondered what our Vicki would look like unwrapped,' mused Wayne.

'Pathetic!' said Barry, shaking his head at Wayne's obsession with the female form.

Wayne twinkled. 'I disagree,' he murmured. 'I'm not disappointed at all.'

Inside the house, Ally reared to face Vicki. There was a hint of danger in his eyes.

'Look, while we've got those cowboys around the house, it might look better if you didn't go flauntin' yourself,' he said.

'Who's flaunting?'

'D'you think that bikini's the height of discretion? Christ, I've used bigger band-aids when I've cut meself shavin'!'

Vicki pouted. 'You don't complain as a rule ...'

'As a rule, I don't have seven randy brickies out in the garden.'

'There's no point in going out there, is there?' said Vicki sullenly. 'I can't sunbathe. I can't swim because there's no water in the pool. And I can't stay here playin' me records because I won't be able to hear them for the concrete mixer.'

Ally's eyes had been narrowing as she spoke.

'Are the arrangements not to your liking, Vicki?' he asked then.

'I'm just saying –'

'Is the villa no longer up to scratch?' he continued harshly. 'May I remind you that two years ago when you were a manicurist at Maison André, your idea of the holiday of a lifetime was a fortnight in Redcar ...'

'I'd travelled before I met you, Ally!' Vicki retorted. 'Me and my friend Barbara spent two successive summers in Magalouf!'

Ally smiled humourlessly, pointed to the phone.

'D'you want to give Barbara a bell?' he suggested with deceptive mildness. 'See if she's still got the tent?'

And meanwhile, as work began at the Villa Mimosa, and Ally's troubles increased, Geoffrey and Pauline Oxlade entered the local police station to make a formal complaint about those *terrible* people who had invaded their swimming pool. Captain Fuentes of the plainclothes branch was about to enter the lives of Ally Fraser and the lads in a way that was to prove ultimately fateful.

EIGHTEEN

By the time the sun was high, the lads were hard at work. Stripped to the waist or in t-shirts, they were grafting on extending Ally's piece of paradise. For now, Barry was acting as lookout at the front of the house while the others laboured.

'I'm very relieved, Nev,' said Moxey-Brendan-Francis to Neville as they worked.

'What about?'

'This country,' Moxey told him. 'I really like it.'

Neville looked at him warily. 'We've seen nothin' of it yet.'

'No,' Moxey conceded. 'But based on what I've observed, it'll do me. Everyone speaks English, so you don't have to learn the lingo. The English papers get here by tea time. The bars sell English beer and the sun's always bloody shining.'

'I suppose there's worse places for a holiday,' said Neville.

'I'm not talking about a holiday,' Moxey said with sudden passion. 'I'm talkin' about a new life.'

Neville stopped work in his amazement. 'You're staying on?'

'Certainly. As far as I'm concerned, England's finished. They should slap a bloody great notice on it: "Out of Order"! I've no desire to stay on and watch it going through its death-throes.'

'This has nothing to do with the fact that if you go back they'll slam you in clink?' Neville asked, getting the picture.

Moxey reddened under his developing tan. 'That had affected me decision, yes.'

A few moments later, Neville found a chance to move over to where Oz was working.

'Moxey says he's never going back!' he told the big man urgently.

Oz shrugged. 'You can't blame him, Nev. This is where all the English villains come. No extradition treaty with Spain, is there?'

'I know that ... I can't imagine never seeing home again, though ...'

'Moxey hasn't got a home,' Oz said gently. 'The nearest he's ever had to one was livin' with us in that poxy hut in Düsseldorf. He's been adrift all his life, man.'

Meanwhile, Barry had managed to cover his arms and legs with suntan oil and was applying some Nose-Cote when he spotted a Spanish police car approaching. He clucked anxiously and headed round to the pool area.

'Lads! Dennis!' he squawked. 'It's the bloody law! The Old Bill!'

Moxey blanched. The rest just panicked a bit.

'Can you believe it?' said Oz. 'They must have signed that extradition treaty. Just your bad luck, Mox.'

Moxey didn't think that was funny. Dennis was already bellowing orders for them to start the prepared drill. They moved with practised precision, scrambling out of the empty pool, erecting deckchairs, laying out rubber mattresses, stripping off their work clothes and hiding their tools. A piece of new brickwork was hidden under towels that were made to look as if they were drying in the sun. Wayne slammed a tape into a cassette player, and music started blasting out over the patio. Sunglasses were put on, and beers were being passed round as Fuentes arrived from the front of the house to find seven men reclining by the (drained) pool, with drinks and music.

The Spanish cop looked at them long and hard. '*Buenas tardes*.'

Dennis glanced up as if he had only just noticed him. 'Oh, *buenas tardes*. Can we help you?'

Fuentes ignored the question. 'What are you doing here?' he asked in slightly stilted English.

'Tourists ... vacatione ...' said Dennis easily.

'You staying here?' Fuentes said, indicating the villa.

'Er ... no, no ... Hotel Miramar,' Dennis explained. 'Just visiting for the day. We're friends of the owner, like.'

'Señor Fraser?'

'Aye.'

'*Si*,' added Barry. 'Old friends. *Amigos* . . . from a long way back.'

Just at that moment, Ally appeared from the villa, drink in hand.

'To what do we owe this pleasure?' he asked Fuentes with a broad smile. 'It must be fairly serious for you to forego your siesta.'

Fuentes reacted stonily. 'Señor Fraser . . . today I get a report from people who also live in this area.'

'Report about what?' Ally asked pleasantly.

'They say they see seven men in their pool,' the Spaniard said, and his eyes were counting the number around Ally's. 'English men,' he continued. 'They think maybe they are thieves.'

The lads looked suitably embarrassed. Ally tried to laugh it off.

'Sounds highly dubious to me. What are they known as – The Swimming Bandits?'

Wayne laughed, but Dennis judged the situation and thought it best to come clean. You didn't muck around with blokes like this cop.

'Look,' he began, 'there is an explanation, like. It was us.' Noting Ally's nervous reaction, he plunged on: 'We went to the wrong villa.'

'My fault really,' burbled Barry. 'You know that right fork past the Tennis Ranch –'

'Shut up, Barry,' Dennis cut in crisply, then turned back to face Fuentes. 'We thought it was Mr Fraser's, y'see. But no one was at home, so we just took a dip . . .'

'I see,' said Fuentes.

Ally moved in quickly. 'I'm sorry you've wasted your time, captain. Would you like a drink?'

Fuentes continued to stare doubtfully at the seven men round the pool. There was something not right . . .

'Thank you, Señor Fraser, but no,' he refused with quiet dignity.

One last, penetrating look. Then Fuentes sighed.

'Enjoy your holiday, gentlemen,' the Spaniard said with unmistakable irony, then turned on his heel and strode away.

A graciously smiling Ally watched him all the way back to his car, gave him a cheery wave as Fuentes turned one last time before climbing into the driver's seat. When the cop was safely off down the road, his expression changed. Ally's face was dark with anger as he turned to confront Dennis and the lads.

'I don't believe this!' he snapped. 'Your first day here and already you've got the police on your case for terrorisin' the neighbourhood!'

'If you gave your streets names and your houses numbers, this would never happen,' Oz shot back defensively.

Ally treated him to a cold, Gorbals-style stare.

'It'd better not happen again, pal!' he grated. 'How many times do I have to tell you? You keep a low profile. While you're here, you keep your heads down and your mouths shut!'

The alarm was over at Ally's villa, but unknown to either the lads or their boss, the matter had not stopped there after all. Early evening saw Captain Fuentes enter a café in the port of Marbella. This was the hunting-ground of the beautiful people, far from the half-completed hotels and the cheap package tours; there were expensive yachts at their moorings on the nearby quay, chic boutiques and pricey restaurants. And the place was coming alive for the evening's delights.

Fuentes shook hands with a man in his mid-thirties who had been waiting for him at the café, then ordered some appetisers and a scotch from the waiter in Spanish. When he spoke to the other man at the table, however, it was in English.

'You don't mind if I eat?' he said. 'No lunch today.'

Nick Wheeler nodded reluctantly. 'Make the most of it, Miguel,' he warned. 'It's the last meal the paper's paying for.'

Fuentes looked at his English journalist contact in surprise. 'Why do you say this?'

Wheeler sighed, took a pull at his large drink. 'Because they want me back in London. My editor thinks I spend all my time sitting in the sun, drinking Scotch and looking at pretty girls.'

The two men paused to ogle a couple of especially fine examples of leggy female beauty who happened to be passing.

'This is not true?' Fuentes asked then.

'It certainly isn't,' Wheeler said with mock indignation. 'Anyone who knows me well will tell you I'm strictly a vodka man!'

Fuentes smiled politely at the Englishman's little joke. Then he got down to business.

'I have something for you,' he confided.

Wheeler's lived-in features arranged themselves into an expression of scepticism. 'That'll make a change. I've been back-handing you for a month with precious little to show for it.'

'Hey!' Fuentes retorted, looking pained. 'You look for English criminals, yes? I tell you where they live, where they drink. Is not my fault they do not talk to you.'

Wheeler grunted. 'So have you found one who will?'

'I find seven,' Fuentes told him proudly.

'Seven?'

'*Si*. They stay at Hotel Miramar.'

'That doesn't make them villains,' said Wheeler, still unconvinced.

'Ah. They are friends of Señor Fraser. I see them at his villa.'

With that the hack's interest quickened dramatically. 'Ally Fraser?'

'*Si*. They say they are tourists, but I smell they are not. They sit round pool, it has no water. I am police. In any country it is the same. I know they hide something.'

Wheeler grinned, clocked another couple of passing girls. He leaned back in his chair and toasted them.

'You never know, Miguel,' he chortled. 'This might keep me here another week . . .'

'So what have you girls been up to today?' Bomber asked Beatie and Alice.

They were clustered at the bar – except Neville, who was

upstairs having his sunburn worked on by Brenda, and Dennis, who was giving Christine a bit of attention. The oldies were already hard at it, and the lads were coming to accept that unless they went into Marbella Port, there was more action with the Spennymoor OAPs than anywhere else within walking distance.

'Thank you,' Beatie responded, ignoring his question. 'I'll have a gin.'

'She gets worse!' Alice guffawed.

'She can have what she likes,' Bomber chuckled. 'You're only young once. What about you, my dear?'

Alice said she would confine herself to sweet sherry.

'Very wise,' said Bomber solemnly. 'I don't want you getting too pie-eyed before our first fox-trot.'

No one noticed Nick Wheeler sidle into the room and take a seat at the end of the bar. He ordered a vodka tonic and sat watching. And listening.

Moxey was sounding off about the advantages of Spain, with support from Oz, who had also taken a shine to the place.

'Like, this idea of havin' a kip in the afternoon,' he was saying. 'I think I'll really take to that. 'Cause the afternoon's the draggiest part of the day, isn't it?'

'Also, you're foreign here, right, Mox?' Oz agreed. 'So there's no class prejudice, is there? I mean, back home a bloke like you just has to open his mouth and he's pigeon-holed with the plebs!'

Moxey looked offended. 'What about you, Oz? Most people can't understand a tossin' word you say ...'

'Hey, I might have a slight accent,' Oz growled, 'but I know a lot of grammar and vocabulary, don't I, right? I can dazzle anyone, me.'

'I personally think you'll miss your roots, Mox,' said Wayne. 'I mean, these tax exiles like Rod Stewart, Roger Moore, David Bowie. I often ask myself: are they happy?'

Oz scoffed. 'Well,' he said firmly. 'If they're not, there's sod all hope for the rest of us!'

'Michael Caine went back, didn't he?' Wayne continued. 'And shall I tell you why? Because in spite of his millions, his palatial mansion and his jacuzzis, he couldn't get a decent English sausage in Beverly Hills.' He waited for them to digest that information, then added a little lamely, 'Apparently.'

Barry was moved. '*Breathes there a man with soul so dead, who never to himself hath said: "This is my own, my native land",*' he quoted.

They stared at him blankly.

'You what?' said Moxey.

Barry smiled proudly. 'Sir Walter Scott said that.'

Oz shrugged. 'Aye well,' he said dismissively, 'you're bound to feel a bit homesick, aren't you, if you're holed up in an igloo in the Antarctic.'

Nick Wheeler chose that moment to move across and join them.

'Hi!' he said cheerfully. Their response was guarded, so he persisted. 'Just arrived, have you?'

Oz measured the new arrival up and decided he didn't much like the look of him.

'Aye,' he said reluctantly.

Wheeler nodded towards the pensioners at the other tables. 'The under-thirty travel club, is it?'

'Aw, we're not with them,' said Oz, loosening up a bit. 'We just came on the same flight.'

'Holiday, is it?'

'Well,' confessed Oz, 'you could call it a holiday. I mean –'

Barry hissed a warning. Oz looked at him in surprise.

'Loose lips sink ships,' muttered the zit king through clenched teeth.

'What's he on about?' said Oz, bewildered.

Wayne had got Barry's point and was staring pointedly at Wheeler, who naturally hadn't missed a trick. He knew he was on to a winner. These boys were hiding from something, it was obvious.

Barry had decided to take over as spokesperson.

'We're on holiday, yes,' he said. 'We're a club, y'see.'

'Oh yeah?' said the journalist.

'Yes.'

'What club's this?'

Oz and Wayne looked at Barry. His mind raced for a few seconds, then he blurted out: 'The ... the Wolverhampton and District Aqualung Society.'

There was an uncomfortable pause.

'Long way from the sea, Wolverhampton,' Wheeler observed.

'Yes,' Barry agreed energetically. 'How true. That's why this annual trip is so important to us, y'see. 'Cause the rest of the year we have to make do with the reservoir, don't we, lads?'

'Oh yeah!' they chorused.

Within minutes, Wheeler was on the hotel phone to London. Yes, he was still in Spain. Listen, had there been any arrests in the Sheffield payroll job yet? No? Well, there were seven involved in that, and he'd just come across seven suspicious characters. The paper needed to get a photographer down here quick and, no, he wasn't pissing them around.

Wheeler turned and saw Dennis, Neville, Christine and Brenda join the others at the bar.

'Ian,' he crowed down the phone. 'There's a new bunch of British bandits in town, and I'm looking at them!'

So much for Ally's 'low profile' ...

NINETEEN

By shortly before noon the next day, Nick Wheeler had found his way to Kenny Ames's tennis club and was installed at a table, drinking a casual espresso, when Kenny came off the court after his usual session with the club pro. He called out as the porn king made his way to the changing room.

Ames turned, registering Wheeler without particular pleasure.

'Oh, blow me,' he said. 'You still in Spain? Hasn't your paper got somewhere more useful to send you? They haven't definitely found Dr Mengele yet. Why don't you piss off to Paraguay?'

Wheeler smiled weakly. He had been up till three buying cheap brandy for those yobbos at the Hotel Miramar. Still hopeful, but he needed a bit more to hang the story on, which was why he had braved Kenny Ames at this ungodly hour of the day.

'I'm still deductable, am I?' said Ames sourly when the journalist offered to buy him a coffee.

Wheeler finally got him to join him at the table.

'Good job you don't work for the *Mirror*,' Ames commented. 'Old Maxwell closed his foreign desk, didn't he? Put all his money in Oxford United...'

'I must admit my days here are numbered,' Wheeler agreed.

Ames nodded. 'I'm not surprised. The Costa del Crime's old hat now. A lot of the chaps have moved on. Judah Binstock was last seen in Haiti.' He grinned. 'I expect he's got all them voodoo priests sticking pins into wax effigies of Leon Brittan.'

'You're still here, Kenny,' said Wheeler.

Ames frowned. 'You've had two exclusives with me, Nick,' he said. 'Terry Leather's the lad you should be talking to.'

'He won't play ball.'

'Well, Terry's got his old mum in Hainault with a heart condition. He don't want her getting upset by reading anything derogatory.'

'He said if I printed one word about him, he'd rip out my liver and feed it to the seagulls,' Wheeler said with a grimace.

Ames chuckled appreciatively. 'He must have liked you, then, 'cause sometimes he can get a bit stroppy with hacks.'

Wheeler sipped his coffee, then fixed Ames again. 'I'm more interested in this new lot.'

A veil came down over Ames's face. He had no idea what the hack was talking about, but he wasn't about to give anything away. 'Oh yes?' he said coldly.

'Come on, Kenny,' Wheeler said with a snort. 'If there's a new chap in town, you know who it is – let alone seven of them!'

'Who told you this?' Kenny hissed, still none the wiser but keen to find out.

'I was with them last night.' Wheeler sighed. 'Until three in the bloody morning.'

'Three in the morning? That should've loosened their tongues.'

Wheeler nodded. 'I do know they're friends of Ally's . . .'

Suddenly the penny dropped for Kenny Ames. 'Oh *that* team!' he said with an emphasis that was bound to excite the journalist's curiosity.

Wheeler was on to him like a hawk.

'Come on, Kenny – give us a break. No one else is on to this one.'

Ames smiled enigmatically, back in control and beginning to consider his options. There were several birds could be killed with this particular stone, my word there were . . .

It wasn't until Kenny Ames's Mercedes was almost at the top of the front driveway of Ally's villa that Ames noticed the big man asleep on the grass. He didn't know it, but the sleeping sentry was Oz, who had succumbed to the effects of last night's bottle and a half of Fundador (courtesy of Nick

226

Wheeler) while supposedly keeping watch outside the 'building site'. Ames brought the car to a halt, got out and stared at Oz curiously. He slammed the door. Oz continued to snore loudly. He shrugged and walked past him to the pool area.

By the pool, the rest of the lads were hard at work, and music was blasting from a cassette player. As a result, no one heard Ames's approach, and they were all too busy to see him. The pornographer-in-exile stood by the cassette for a moment, watching them with amusement, then snapped the music off.

The lads looked up and realised they had been caught red-handed.

'Oh, er... *buenas tardes*,' mumbled Dennis. 'We're just er... er...'

'I can see what you're doing,' said Ames with a chuckle. 'Good job I'm not from the Ministry of Works, isn't it?'

'How did you get past our look-out?' asked Barry.

'Oh, I just took the precaution of not waking him up.'

Dennis turned and bellowed down the hill: 'Oz! Get yourself up here!'

'Sorry to throw you a wobbly, lads,' Ames said mildly. 'Is Ally in?'

Wayne told him the owner wouldn't be back till four.

Ames sighed. 'Well, can't be helped.' He smiled. 'I'm Kenny Ames, by the way.'

He got the expected response, half-shock, half-fascination.

'You've heard of me, then?' he said.

Neville nodded. 'Yes. We did up your house in England.'

'Mind, it looked a bit different by the time we'd finished with it,' Bomber said.

'I hope you didn't destroy its essential character, though,' said Ames. 'I loved that house. When you stood in the library and looked out across the landscape, it gave you a sense of timeless continuity.'

'I know what you mean,' Barry agreed keenly, sensing a kindred-spirit in appreciating beautiful things. 'That particular view reminded me of a Constable.'

Ames winced. 'Bit of a dirty word, that. If it wasn't for the constabulary, I'd have still bloody been there.'

A bleary-eyed Oz shambled round the side of the house.

'Here he is,' said Moxey. 'Well done, Hawkeye.'

'No harm done,' Ames said cheerfully. 'I'm not the enemy.' He surveyed the work in progress. 'You lads've got your work cut out here.'

Neville said drily that they had worked in plenty of worse places.

'What about your spare time?' said the genial seeming racketeer. 'Found yourself a laugh, have you?'

'Haven't had time yet, really,' said Dennis.

Ames shook his head sympathetically and then, apparently quite spontaneously, an idea occurred to him.

'Tell you what,' he suggested, 'I've got this yacht down at the Marina. Why don't you pop by on your day off? My pleasure.'

The lads were surprised, and it showed.

'A yacht? Us?' Moxey said wonderingly.

'Don't worry. We won't put to sea,' Ames assured him. 'Nothing that hazardous. Just have a bit of a chin-wag and get pissed in the port, eh?'

Put like that, how could they refuse? A date was set for the weekend. A *yacht*, for God's sake.

'We were here yesterday,' said Christine as the party strolled along the quayside, heading for Kenny Ames's yacht. 'Vicki showed us round. You see that restaurant with the yellow tablecloths? That's where we saw Sean Connery!'

'Well, it *could* have been Sean Connery,' Brenda chipped in.

'It *was*, Brenda!' insisted Christine.

Barry, Moxey and Wayne were following up behind the couples.

'This is more like it, eh, Mox?' said Wayne, looking around with pleasure. 'Here's your Porsches and your playboys...'

Moxey, hiding behind a pair of thick sunglasses, seemed less comfortable with his surroundings.

'Bit too extravagant for me, this side of it,' he said.

Barry was enjoying himself, though. 'Oh no. I'll bring Hazel straight down here.'

'Oh, she's coming, is she?'

'Almost certainly.'

Christine, in the meantime, had run ahead to take a photograph of the party. She called on Oz and Bomber to speed up and get in the picture with the others.

'Nothing like this at home, eh?' said Neville to Oz when the last two had caught up.

'Well, there's the North Shields Fish Quay, Nev,' Oz corrected him.

Christine took the picture, and they moved on.

'If he wants to go out to sea, like, I'm not going,' said Brenda to Neville. 'Not with Debs.'

'It's just drinks,' he reassured her.

'Well, if she gets sleepy, I'll take her back to the hotel.'

Neville sighed. 'I thought you'd be thrilled with this, Brenda. I mean, how often do we get asked on a yacht?'

'It's *whose* yacht that bothers me,' she said primly. 'This man's a wanted criminal. What would my parents think? What would your mum think?'

Then they were there, alongside a gigantic gin-palace of a motor cruiser. They spotted Kenny in the stern, his arm around a sun-tanned blonde and a bottle in his other hand.

'Here we are, lads!' he called out.

They clambered aboard. Ames helped Brenda and Debbie aboard and cooed over the baby as he found her a spot to sit in a fishing chair.

When they were all on deck, Ames indicated the blonde. 'Now, I don't know all your names, but this is Inge. Put your stuff down below. There's tubes in the chest, or Sangria if you prefer. Come on, Inge,' he told the girl. 'There's thirsty men here . . .'

Dazzled by the opulence of the yacht and its surroundings, the group of guests obeyed Ames' every instruction.

And a way away, on another boat, sat Nick Wheeler. By his side, the photographer he had requested from London had set up a camera on a tripod with a zoom lens, and he was clicking away frantically, to Wheeler's great satisfaction. His deal with Kenny had brought a bonanza. The Sheffield payroll gang! After this, he'd be in clover at the office for weeks, even months to come.

*

The lads had learned to be careful of the Spanish sun. They wore hats and neckerchiefs to protect themselves from its noontime intensity, and they worked in the shade where possible. And they were working hard, making good progress.

Oz paused, wiped the sweat from his brow. 'Hey, Den! Siesta time, surely? That sun's bloody murder!'

Dennis checked his watch. 'Aye, I guess we could take a break about now.'

Then Bomber came panting round from look-out duty at the front of the house.

'No,' he said, overhearing the conversation. 'Put your back in it, lads. Governor's home.'

Dennis looked surprised. 'Ally? He was playing in a golf tournament.'

'Doin' a crafty check on us, perhaps,' suggested Bomber.

Moxey grinned. 'Or he doesn't trust Vicki. Not with Wayne around.'

Ally's car roared to a halt. He got out quickly, slammed the door and strode towards the villa.

'Hey, Den, something's up,' said Neville. 'He looks furious.'

Dennis shook his head. 'It can't be us. We've done nothin'. Heads down...'

They all got down to work again, and succeeded in feigning quite convincing surprise when Ally arrived.

'Afternoon, Ally,' Dennis greeted him pleasantly. 'Didn't expect to see you back.'

Oz noticed Ally was carrying an English newspaper in one paw. 'Oh, you've got the paper. Great!'

Ally froze him with a diamond-hard glare.

'I have a paper, yes,' he said through clenched teeth. 'Yes. Now, get round here, you lot. I'd like to read you something. Something interesting.'

They all gathered round, exchanging puzzled glances. Ally opened the tabloid to its centre pages and read slowly and with great clarity:

'"Spain's Costa del Crime is still a haven for the growing

band of Brits whom Scotland Yard are 'anxious to question'. Kenny Ames, 47, who persists in denying that he was Britain's King of Porn, continues to sun himself on his luxury yacht in Marbella ..."'

'Er!' gulped Barry. 'That must've been the one we were on ...'

Ally silenced him with a stony glance.

'"No doubt his companions, newly arrived from England, are business associates ..."'

Ally could read no more. He angrily thrust the paper at Dennis, and the others clustered around him to read the sordid details.

There wasn't just a story. The lads gasped when they saw a large photograph of Kenny Ames with his arms around Inge – and a group picture of the entire seven of them. The picture had obviously been taken on board Kenny's yacht two days earlier. The headline read: 'LIVING IT UP IN SPAIN. KENNY AMES AND FRIENDS'.

The lads reacted with a mixture of surprise, indignation, and amusement.

'That's us!' moaned Moxey.

Oz smiled delightedly. 'Hey, look at that. Centre spread!'

Wayne had seen better photos of himself and said so. Neville wondered what Brenda's parents would think.

'Read on!' Ally rasped.

Dennis obeyed.

'"I spoke exclusively to the new arrivals in their luxury hotel ..."' he began.

'Their what?' hissed Moxey.

'"They were evasive about their reasons for being in Spain, one of them claiming that they were members of a Wolverhampton Aqualung Society. Research has shown that no such club exists."'

They all looked at Barry, who winced visibly.

Dennis continued:

'"Meanwhile, police continue their search for the gang who pulled off the daring payroll robbery in Sheffield last week ..."'

He lowered the paper, horrified.

'Who wrote this rubbish?' demanded Bomber.

Dennis consulted the by-line. 'Er ... Nick Wheeler.'

'Nick!' Oz bellowed. 'That was the name of that fellah who kept buying us drinks in the bar!'

'This is your idea of "keepin' a low profile", is it?' Ally said.

Dennis shrugged. 'Howway, Ally, this story's a load of bollocks.'

'*I* know that. And by now the rest of Fleet Street will know that,' Ally said patiently. 'And in their anxiety to discredit this story, they'll be down here buzzing round you lot like bees in a jam jar!'

Neville looked worried. 'We'll just have to tell 'em we're ordinary gadgies –'

'Workin' in my villa, I suppose?' Ally snapped. 'That's precisely what I've been tryin' to avoid!'

There was a brief silence. Then Dennis smiled. 'Wait a minute, though,' he said slowly. The rest looked puzzled. 'We can still be working lads down here on a holiday.' His grin broadened. 'We just have to make it look convincing.'

Ally glowered. 'And how do we do that?'

'Well, Ally ...' said Dennis. 'You'd better give us the rest of the week off!'

Kenny Ames seemed just as relaxed as ever. 'Ally, Ally! Why would I want to embarrass you?' he asked.

Ally was still standing on the deck of Kenny's yacht, pacing irritably to and fro.

'I often ask myself that question, Kenny,' he snarled. 'If you'd wanted to draw attention to my situation, you couldn't have stitched me up better.'

Ames raised a soothing hand.

'You weren't the mark, my son. I wanted to rubbish that Nick Wheeler. He's been a right pain.' He grinned cunningly. 'Now his credibility's down the crapper, they'll haul his arse back to Fleet Street. Which is a great relief to me and Terry Leather and the rest of the chaps.'

Ally shook his head.

'And I've had to lay my lads off till the heat dies down.'

Kenny Ames's Cheshire cat expression did not alter. It was

obvious he was glad to see some heat on Ally Fraser, the smug bastard. Just a few weeks back, the Scotsman had been trading as 'Mr Clean', ready to launder the out-and-out villains' possessions – for a price. Well, we'd see now.

'Must hurt a bit, I can see that,' he said with transparent insincerity.

'You could help,' Ally grated. 'You could reinforce the impression they are tourists, after all.'

'How?'

'Invite them back on the yacht!'

Ames' grin evaporated and suddenly he looked pained.

'You must be joking!' he said. 'Have you seen how that lot drink?'

Oz, Barry and Moxey trudged down a side street, lugging towels and suntan lotion. The beach had been too much. Even in the relative shade of the street and wearing shorts and t-shirts, the heat was still getting to them.

'This is the place,' said Oz, jerking a thumb at a bar bearing a Union Jack and the sign 'The Britannia'. 'Someone told me a lot of Brits hang out here.'

'Anywhere to get out of this sun,' Barry panted.

Inside, it was more like an East End drinking club than a continental bar. There were plaques of English soccer clubs and team photographs on the walls, plus pictures of English celebrities, including Alvin Stardust, Mike Yarwood, Terry Venables and Jimmy Tarbuck. There were English beers, English beermats, and a dartboard. Even Senior Service ashtrays. The three lads peered around in wonder.

'Three pints of lager here, pet,' Oz told the landlady, an obvious Brit.

The place was suddenly rather silent. There was the rustle of a newspaper. Then a middle-aged gent at the bar checked first the centre spread, then the new arrivals.

'Hey, look, Lionel!' he said to the other half of the bar-owning team. 'Some of the Sheffield mob!'

Heads turned. People began to whisper. The lads reacted sheepishly.

'We're goin' to get a lot of that for the next few days from the English tourists,' muttered Barry.

'I've got a good mind to sue,' said Oz.

'Sue?' queried Moxey.

'Naw, naw – seriously. I mean, it's libel, isn't it?' Oz maintained. 'We could cop a fortune! End up with a yacht ourselves!'

Barry shook his head morosely. 'They cover themselves,' he said. 'Teams of lawyers to check it all out. They never say anything directly. We still get the stigma, mind. It's guilt by association.'

'This has settled it, of course,' Moxey groaned. 'I couldn't go back now, even if I wanted to. The die is cast!'

'Toss off, Moxey,' said Oz, undaunted. He reached into his jacket and took out a copy of Wheeler's article, already dog-eared from constant perusal. 'Naw,' he said. 'You're the only one nay-one *can* recognise. You're wearin' aviator shades and you're out of focus.'

The landlady put the beers on the bar. Oz made to pay, but the middle-aged man who had first drawn attention to them leaned over first.

'Here, I'll get these, Tania,' he said.

Oz stared at him coldly. 'Aw, thanks all the same, pal, but we've got into enough trouble accepting drinks from strangers.'

'No ulterior motive mate,' said the man, who had a strong cockney accent. 'Just saw your picture in the paper, didn't we, Li?' he added, appealing to the landlord.

'Yeah,' Lionel confirmed. 'I'm thinkin' of sticking it up on the mirror.'

Barry was blushing.

'I'd sooner you didn't, if you don't mind,' he said. He turned to the stranger. 'Quite frankly,' he continued, 'this has been a great embarrassment to me. Y'see, I don't subscribe to this unhealthy glamorisation of the criminal fraternity. I'm a lawabiding taxpayer. I've no wish to be lumped together with the Kenny Ameses and Terry Leatherses of this world.' He warmed to his theme. 'Behind the façade of their luxury villas and their blonde lady friends, you have to remember they are despicable people. As far as I'm concerned, the sooner they're

234

shipped back to England to serve twenty-five years in Parkhurst, the better for all of us!'

When he had finished, the man nodded politely.

'That's a point of view, of course,' he said evenly. 'And very well argued, er . . . ?'

'Barry,' the zit king introduced himself. 'Barry Taylor.'

'Pleased to meet you. My name's Terry. Terry Leather.'

TWENTY

The little Spanish taxi struggled up the incline that led to Ally Fraser's villa. It pulled up in front and Dennis, Christine, Neville, and Brenda got out, with baby Debbie in her mother's arms. The taxi driver walked round to the boot and started to unload the luggage as his passengers stretched after the cramped drive from town. Ally had spotted them and was on his way down to meet them.

'Hello, playmates!' he boomed.

'All right, Ally,' Dennis acknowledged him.

'Hello, Mr Fraser,' said Neville.

Their host grinned, very hail-fellow-well-met. 'Just call me Billy Butlin for the moment, eh?'

Brenda smiled awkwardly. 'It's very good of you to let us have your villa for a few days, Mr Fraser.'

'My pleasure, dear,' Ally said heartily. 'I know how boring those tourist hotels can be at this time of year – especially when you've got a young family.'

Dennis and Neville exchanged glances. They knew Ally's real motives.

'And how expensive they can be with us lying around doing nothing . . .' Dennis retorted.

Ally forced a smile.

'Well, I did bring you out here to work, Dennis . . . and if the unwelcome glare of publicity prevents that, a few economies are always welcome.'

He called out for Vicki to give a hand getting their things up to the house. He obviously had no intention of straining himself, of course.

'And where will you be staying while we're in your villa, Mr Fraser?' Brenda asked.

'Oh, I've taken a little suite over at the Marbella Club ...' the Scotsman said casually.

'That's the rich playboys' place, isn't it?' said Neville. 'Golf courses inside the room and that.'

Ally looked a bit uncomfortable. 'I've always thought it over-rated, personally ...' Vicki was making her way down towards them, dressed in a fetching new outfit, and Ally seized on the distraction. 'But I thought young Vicki could do with a break,' he added quickly. 'After all, there's not much point us staying here with the pool out of commission and the place looking like a building site.'

'Still, it'll be nice and quiet for baby,' Brenda said. 'Hello, Vicki, pet ...'

Vicki greeted them. The three girls had spent quite a lot of time together and had got on surprisingly well.

'Lovely outfit again, Vicki,' Christine said with genuine admiration.

'Aye,' answered Vicki, pleased. 'Got it this morning in that Italian boutique we found in the port ...' She showed them the quality of the material. 'It's organic silk, whatever that means...'

'The worms are free range,' said Ally impatiently. 'Now, you take the girls up to the house for a drink, eh, Vicki, while I have a word with the lads.' He nodded in the direction of the bags. Vicki took a couple, with difficulty, and Christine and Brenda managed the rest.

While the women made their way up the steps to the villa entrance, Ally turned businesslike.

'Right,' he said. 'You've got two days off, Dennis. Then I want your mob back grafting.'

'All right, all right,' Dennis answered testily. 'It's not our fault there are so many criminals round here for us to get confused with. Maybe you should have chosen a better area...' he added with a sly smile.

'We didn't court the publicity, Mr Fraser,' Neville said. 'We were just tricked.'

'Aye. Maybe. But trouble and you lot seem to go hand in hand. Now, what are the other Herberts up to?'

'Following my instructions to the letter,' said Dennis

crisply. 'Acting like simple, law-abiding tourists.'

Ally looked worried. 'Hum,' he mused. 'Maybe a two-day lay-off is pushing it a bit...'

At that moment, four 'law-abiding tourists' were clearing themselves a space on the beach. Oz, Wayne, Bomber and Barry were all geared up for a day in the sun, unpacking towels, holdalls, all the time with half an eye on the surrounding topless talent. Wayne, deciding a body commercial was in order, had already stripped down to a pair of very brief swimming trunks that did little to conceal his major gift to the world.

> *'On the beach ...*
> *You can dance and sing and shout,*
> *On the beach ...*
> *You can let it all hang out ... !'*

'I wouldn't if I were you,' Barry said in response to the cockney's cheerful singing. 'It may be a topless beach, but I'm certain it's not bottomless.'

'Aye,' said Bomber with relish. 'The local coppers have probably got a special bare bum patrol ... big Alsatians trained to kill at the first sight of something round and white.'

'Pity, really,' Oz mused as he settled down to sunbathe. 'I've always wanted to have a sun-tanned arse instead of a spotty, working-class one. No matter how far you rise in society, dress smart, talk proper ...' He gestured to his own behind. 'There's always this, back here, to give away your true origins.'

'That's probably how they make the final selection for *Who's Who*, Oz,' Barry mocked. 'Line the candidates up and ask them to drop their trousers ...'

Wayne laughed. 'Yeah. It'd be a kind of *spot*-check, I suppose!'

'God,' groaned Oz. 'Sand, Germans everywhere, and bad jokes from Wayne. It's just like bein' back in Düsseldorf again.'

Bomber wasn't standing for any of that.

'Don't you start moaning, Oz. You must have dreamt of

days like this when you were stuck in that bloody hut. We've landed on our feet here, boy, and no mistake!'

Oz shrugged. 'Yeah, well – we're not gettin' paid for this, are we? This is still Ally Fraser's time – he should be forkin' out.'

'I think he's been quite generous in the circumstances,' Wayne objected. 'He could've shipped us all back to Blighty.'

Barry, busy leafing through his Spanish phrasebook, glanced up. 'Like they said in *Guantanamera* – *"es un hombre sincero"*. He is a sincere man...'

'Yeah, well,' said Oz. 'The Spanish police think we're illegal workers, and the British press think we're just illegal. So now we have to pretend we're just tourists.'

'What's wrong with that?'

'Because, Wayne – tourists have money, and we are largely skint!'

Barry sighed in exasperation. 'You don't need money to have a good time here, Oz,' he intoned. 'There's natural beauty, sea and sand, a new culture to absorb. Even Moxey appreciates that.'

'That's why he's still in that bar with those English villains, I suppose,' Oz said cuttingly. 'Absorbing cultural notes about how to live on the run.'

'Yeah,' Terry Leather was telling Moxey. 'He really had me goin', your Brummie Mate – I thought he was serious about that "bring back hanging for bank robbers"!'

Moxey downed some more champagne. 'Well, he's got a really dry sense of humour, has Barry,' he said. He leaned forward confidentially. 'Between you and me, he even had time for a joke while we were transpiring our little business with the security van ...'

'He never did?' said Leather.

Moxey nodded. 'Asked one of the guards if he had change for the parking meter!'

Terry Leather was professionally impressed.

'You need a cool head in those circumstances,' he agreed. He raised his glass to toast Moxey again. 'Anyway, cheers... What was it again?'

'Moxey ... Cheers, Terry.'

'Welcome to Spain, Moxey. Er ...' Leather dropped his voice discreetly. 'And though I don't wish to pry, if you and your firm need any business advice, there's a few investment people I can put you in touch with...'

'Thanks for the offer, Terry,' said Moxey quickly. 'We're just finding out feet at the moment, really. Gettin' used to livin' out here.'

Leather grinned encouragingly. 'You'll soon make the transition, son – don't worry. You get a bit homesick now and again, but the thought of a cell in Wandsworth soon cures you of that.'

'Yeah, I know that...'

'Done a bit of bird, have you, Moxey?'

'Yeah,' said Moxey without thinking it through. 'Few years for arson, like –'

Leather's expression suddenly darkned. 'Arson?' he growled. 'Not really a kosher line ...'

Moxey gulped. Then the villain came to his rescue.

'Oh, I get it!' Leather chortled. 'Insurance job!'

Moxey grabbed the lifeline offered. 'Yeah. That's right – just to raise money for this other job.'

'Very shrewd,' said Leather admiringly. 'Last year *we* were busy, we financed the gig with a loan, then went back and turned over the same bank.'

'Bitin' the hand that feeds you, eh?' quipped Moxey, surprising himself with his own wit. This was the life ...

Terry guffawed, called to Lionel, the landlord of the Britannia: 'Here, Li, why don't we have a bit of a sing-song tonight, in honour of these lads?'

Lionel nodded. 'Yeah. All right, Tel.' He smiled at Moxey. 'If you bring your mates round about six, we'll knock over a few bottles of Moët, eh?'

'Yeah, right,' said Moxey.

'And in the meantime, if there's anything we can help you with, just give us the wire,' Leather offered.

Moxey looked thoughtful. 'Well,' he began, 'this is probably a daft question, but do you know if there's many jobs for plasterers goin' round here?'

Leather's jaw dropped. 'I thought you mob picked up nearly four hundred thou?'

'I know, but ... well ... got to do somethin' to keep yourself busy, haven't you?' Moxey gabbled, trying desperately to cover his tracks. He edged off the stool. 'Anyway, better go and meet up with the rest of the lads . . .'

Terry Leather indicated the photo from the paper, which now had pride of place on the mirror.

'Here,' he said as a parting shot. 'You had any more bother from the press yet?'

'Don't think so,' said Moxey, still moving towards the exit.

'You will do, don't worry,' Leather told him. 'Like bleedin' sand-flies, they are.'

Moxey was on his way out. 'Right – thanks for the warning, Terry. See you later ...'

With that he was gone. Leather looked at Lionel quizzically, then sighed.

'They're all headbangers, these northern lads,' he said with a mixture of puzzlement and amusement. 'Fancy wanting to go back to work for a living!'

Lionel shrugged. 'Must be all that Hovis they eat.' He fished a bottle of champagne out of the ice bucket and offered it to Leather. 'Top-up?'

Wayne had just got back from an attempt at chatting up three nearby Norwegian girls, and he and Oz were planning the resumption of the campaign, when they spotted a couple of seedy-looking and very pale middle-aged men approaching across the sand towards them.

'Hello, lads!' said one, panting slightly from his exertions and adjusting his ill-fitting summer gear.

'Sorry to interrupt you when I can see you're busy,' said the other, leering in the direction of the Norwegian girls.

'Who are you?' asked Oz warily.

The two men produced yellow press cards and gave their names as Sid and Ronnie.

'Have you got a few words for the press, please?' asked Sid.

If they had expected their press cards to get an awed response, however, they had come to the wrong place.

'Yeah – two,' muttered Oz laconically. 'And the second one if "off".'

'Right,' Bomber said. 'Go on and beat it. We've got into enough trouble with you buggers!'

Ronnie judged both men's size and decided it would be better to soft-pedal. 'Yes. We know – but we're here to help you, lads,' he soothed.

Wayne smiled sourly. 'All right,' he said. 'What's the Norwegian for "I want to dive into those blue pools called eyes"?'

Sid laughed politely. 'Look,' he said, 'the more you stall us, the more difficult it'll be for you in the end ...'

'What are you on about, man?' Oz snarled in exasperation. 'That story in the paper wasn't true. *We're* not armed robbers!'

'Lovely, mate. We want to believe that too, so we can run spoilers on that crap Nick Wheeler wrote,' Ronnie said.

Sid nodded. 'So just tell us who you really are and what you're doing here, and we'll go home!'

'Mind your own business.'

'You're not helping us ...' Ronnie threatened.

'Look, my boyos,' said Bomber, rising to tower over them. 'What the other bloke wrote was cobblers. We know that. Why should we have to prove it to you?'

'So we can deny it on your behalf,' Sid persisted.

'I've finished reasonin' with these bastards,' said Oz at last. 'Let's just bury them head-first in the sand, eh?'

The two crime reporters began to back off.

'All right, all right,' murmured Sid. 'It'll probably take a day or two for you to realise that talking to us is for your own good...'

'Yeah,' gibed Ronnie. ''Cause otherwise we'll head back to England and write you up as holidaying scroungers from the dole queue...'

They finally disappeared when Bomber really started to show signs of getting riled.

'Remind me to stop buyin' papers when I get home,' said Bomber as they watched the journalists' retreat.

'I know how people like George Best must have felt now,'

Oz agreed bitterly. 'Hounded from dawn to bloody dusk – or dusk to dawn, in his case ...'

Moxey approached at that moment, having watched the final stages of the encounter.

'Who were they?' he asked.

'More journalists,' said Wayne.

'Shite-hounds, you mean,' said Oz.

'What did they want?'

Bomber pulled a face. 'Apparently we've still got to clear our names in that great popular court known as the press!'

'Maybe we should talk to 'em,' Wayne conceded, having had time to think about it. 'Put the record straight about why we came here.'

'In that case, the bloody job goes up the Swanee, doesn't it?' Oz warned.

'Yeah,' Moxey added nervously. 'Besides, I've already told Terry Leather that we really *are* the Sheffield payroll robbers ...'

The others stared at him incredulously.

'You've done *what*, Moxey?' Oz said finally.

'Well, I just thought it'd be a good idea to play along – help get us established round here.'

'You're the only one who's staying, Mox,' Bomber corrected him. 'It's not goin' to help us when we get back to Britain!'

'*If* we get back!' Wayne said. 'These geezers aren't noted for tolerance where wind-ups are concerned, y'know.'

'Anyway, he wants us all to go down to their bar this evening for a sing-song...' Moxey said, as if that made everything all right.

'Oh, terrific!' roared Oz. 'A sing-song in Sing-Sing! I think I'll stay on the beach...'

Meanwhile, Barry had reappeared, looking agitated. He had been off down the beach with his phrase book, checking out a sign nearby for interest's sake.

'What's the flap, Barry?' Bomber asked.

'Nothing, nothing!' Barry said in a strangled voice. 'Just that the sign over there is a warning about terrorist bombs on the beach ...'

So much for sunbathing in Sunny Spain ...

'This is Marbella's poshest gaff, Vicki,' warned Ally as he got out of his car at the elegant entrance to the Club-Hotel. 'So don't talk unless you're spoken to, and then just nod, okay?'

They began to walk towards the door, carrying their chic hand luggage.

'Sometimes I think you're ashamed to be out with me, Ally Fraser,' Vicki said accusingly.

'Not ashamed Vicki – but frequently embarrassed.'

'Why? What have I done wrong?'

Ally put his bag down, turned to face her.

'You've got an hour to spare, have you?' he asked sarcastically. 'Take last night then, as a brief example. A dinner at a Michelin one-star restaurant. International playboy customers. I order you a beautiful dish of steamed turbot stuffed with scallops – and you complain to the waiter 'cause you think your fish-knife is a cake-slice!'

Vicki pouted and flounced off towards the reception desk in a huff.

'So stick to spaghetti tonight, eh?' Ally called after her.

Meanwhile, at the Britannia the sing-song was in full swing. The bar was packed out with dubious-looking cockney exiles in expensive leisure-wear, some with wives and kids in tow, all whooping it up self-consciously and trying to pretend they were still back down the Elephant and Castle. A man was dancing on the table with a pint balanced on his head. Lionel and Tania were flogging champagne like it was going out of fashion. Moxey was at the bar with his mate, Terry Leather, while Oz and Bomber watched from the sidelines. Wayne and Barry were seated at a nearby table.

'I've never known the words to this one ...' Bomber sighed as the rest of the room went into yet another loud chorus of 'Maybe It's Because I'm a Londoner'.

'Aye,' said Oz. 'I thought about lettin' rip with "Blaydon Races", but I don't want to draw attention to meself with this mob around.' He leaned over and muttered to Bomber: 'One of them asked if we were tooled-up on our last job, and I told him we had four trowels and a spirit level!'

Bomber stroked his beard. 'I hope he took it as a quaint north country joke.'

Oz shrugged and looked in Wayne's direction.

'Look at London,' he said. 'Even he feels out of place.'

'Really,' Barry was saying. 'It's quite insulting that they believe this newspaper story, and all this guff Moxey must have told them. Er ... I don't look think *I* look like a criminal, do you, Wayne?'

'Not a robber, no,' Wayne answered with a smirk. 'Child molester, possibly.'

Barry looked around. 'God, what a futile existence they must lead, eh?' he said, taking in the false jollity. 'No need to work, but no real way of enjoyin' themselves apart from gettin' pissed on champagne and gettin' maudlin about London.'

Wayne nodded. 'For once I have to agree with you, Barry,' he said quite seriously. 'I know these people, y'see. Grew up with them all around me. They're fish out of water here, I can tell.'

'Yeah. You just know they're deeply unhappy.'

The singing reached a boozy crescendo.

'Makes you feel quite sorry for 'em really,' Barry added. 'Outlaws, living away from their homeland, with no hope of ever returning.'

As it happened, that was the subject Terry Leather had just got on to with Moxey at the bar.

'O' course, I'll go back one day and clear my name,' he was telling his willing listener. He nodded in the direction of the kids sitting on the other side of the room. 'Take the kids to see the Hammers on Saturday, go down Petticoat Lane on a Sunday morning, have a big lunch of mash and eels ...'

The cockney villain was almost in tears. Moxey changed the subject.

'What do your kids do for schooling, like?' he asked.

'Me an' the wife teach 'em ourselves,' Leather confided. 'English an' maffs an' that ...'

'I can just see it,' Moxey chuckled. 'If Tel, Del and John

find a van with a million quid in it, how much does each of them get?'

Leather glanced at him oddly. 'Yeah, that's the sort of thing ...'

Then he looked past Moxey, gestured to the door. ''Ere,' he said. 'That's your gaffer, isn't it?'

Moxey saw Dennis and Neville, both looking confused and a bit taken aback, and called them over.

They were out again within no time, Dennis practically dragging Moxey bodily from the Britannia.

'You bloody idiot, man!' he thundered at Moxey in the street. 'We're supposed to be keepin' our heads down for a few days!'

'It's all right for you lot,' Moxey protested. 'You've all got homes to go back to.' He jerked a thumb in the direction of the bar. 'This is gonna be my home, so I've got to get some new friends, haven't I?'

'That's all very well, Mox,' said Oz, 'but we've got the press on our backs tryin' to prove one thing while you're goin' round tryin' to suggest the opposite.'

Dennis nodded. 'None of which will help Ally Fraser's blood pressure.'

Moxey looked chastened. 'I'm sorry,' he muttered. 'It was probably a bit selfish of me.'

'Right,' Dennis said, softening in response. 'I suggest you try and have a quiet night back at the hotel.'

'Suits me,' said Bomber. 'I've had enough of champagne.'

'An' I've had enough of payin' for it,' said Oz, staring meaningfully at Moxey. 'What do they think we are? Made of money?'

Dennis grinned. 'Yes, probably. Come on – no harm done ...'

Not that they did, in fact, stay back at the hotel for long. The OAPs had become markedly less friendly since the robbery story, and all of them were feeling the need to let off steam. But how could they go out and have a good time, at the same time keeping a low profile and avoiding being recognised yet again?

The disco was Wayne's idea. It was certainly pitch-dark. They could hardly see each other, let alone anyone else, and you needed a guide-dog to find the bar. Eventually they stumbled over towards it, following their noses.

'*Buenas noches, señores!*' a trendy young Spanish barman in a black silk shirt with a medallion greeted them cheerfully out of the gloom.

'You wouldn't know it but it's still daylight outside, mate,' said Oz. 'Five beers, *por favor*.'

Bomber surveyed the dance floor – what he could see of it – while the beers were being fetched.

'There's no chance of makin' an introduction, by the looks of it,' he observed. 'I suppose you just dive in and grab something.'

'You certainly feel anonymous in here, don't you?' said Moxey.

Barry snorted with disgust. 'Yuh. Always the same, these pleasure-domes. You sacrifice personality and communication in favour of superficiality and posturing. Very depressing.'

An attractive girl appeared suddenly and glanced tentatively at Wayne.

'I'm not depressed, Barry,' he said with a laugh.

The girl sidled up to the bar, caught Wayne's look, started to turn away again, then got bold enough to dart forward.

'It's you, isn't it?' she said.

Wayne smiled. 'That's right,' he said, going into a routine. 'The new man in your life...'

The girl gestured at all of them. 'No – I mean, it's you lot. The robbers!' She moved forward excitedly. 'Can I have your autograph, please?'

So much for anonymity.

If the other lads couldn't avoid notoriety, Dennis and Neville thought they had it made. After retrieving the others from the Britannia and delivering them back to the hotel, Dennis and Neville had returned to the villa, where, with Debbie safely in bed, they had begun to enjoy a good supper and wine with Christine and Brenda.

'This is the life, eh?' said Neville, still capable of being amazed by his luxurious surroundings.

'Aye,' agreed Dennis. 'Make the most of it – you'll be back on the outside lookin' in day after tomorrow...'

As he made his wry comment on their situation, he nodded towards the patio doors.

Brenda followed his nod, then let out a squeak.

'There's a bloke out there!'

Dennis and Neville were on their feet within a second, but not before Sid and Ronnie slid open the glass doors and swanned in.

'Who the bloody hell are you?' demanded Dennis.

Sid flashed his card. 'It's all right. Press.'

'No, it's not bloody all right,' Dennis roared. 'What the hell are you doin'...'

'"On my property", were you going to say?' chipped in Ronnie. 'That wouldn't be true – this well-upholstered drum belongs to Ally Fraser.'

'You know,' Sid said with satisfaction. 'The Newcastle-based Scottish gangster.'

'He's not a gangster, he's a businessman,' said Christine.

'You've still got no right to be in here, mate,' said Neville.

Sid smiled nastily. 'I hardly think villains on the run should be squealing about rights, do you, Ronnie?'

'Certainly not, Sid. Unless they're *not* villains, of course.'

They were a great double-act. Made Cain and Abel look like Butch Cassidy and the Sundance Kid, thought Dennis.

He motioned for the women to calm down.

'All right,' he asked the two reporters. 'What do you want?'

'Just the truth,' said Sid.

'Will you know what to do with it?' Neville muttered.

Ronnie rounded on him. 'Listen pal,' he sneered. 'Smarten up, eh? Tell us who you are and what you're doing here, and you're off the hook.'

A bewildered Neville just looked helplessly at Dennis.

Dennis sighed. Carrying the can again...

'All right,' he began. 'I'm Dennis Patterson and this is Neville Hope. These ladies are Christine and Brenda. Neville and I are brickies from Newcastle and we're here on holiday. That's it.'

Ronnie, who had been scribbling notes on a scrap of paper, looked up: 'What about the rest of the gang?'

'They're all buildin' workers too. We met out in Germany a few years back, and this is a sort of a reunion, isn't it, Neville?'

'Aye,' the younger man agreed. 'We were all in the SS together during the war,' he added stroppily.

'Don't take the piss,' snapped Sid. 'You were doing well up till then. Right, I'll need names and home addresses so our desk in London can check the backgrounds.'

A look of alarm flitted between Dennis and Neville.

'Aye, all right,' Dennis said reluctantly. 'Some of the addresses might be a bit vague... Let's see, there's a Mr Osbourne, Mr Taylor, Mr Norris, Mr Bushbridge, and er...' he stalled obviously wondering what to do about Moxey. 'What's the name of your mate with the spotty face, Neville?' he asked in desperation.

Neville's turn to carry the can...

TWENTY-ONE

Oz took another swallow of strong Spanish coffee.

'I never thought I'd be grateful for the fact that I can't get a fry-up!' he moaned.

Bomber winced at the thought of all that grease. 'I know how you feel, Oz,' he said. 'What *was* that bloody stuff we were drinking last night?'

'Never mind what *we* were drinking – what about what those groupies were drinking! That's what caused the damage.' Oz emptied his pockets, slapped a pitiful little pile of notes and coins down on the breakfast table in the hotel bar/dining room. 'Look at this . . .' he muttered, staring at the remains of his Spanish currency. 'Probably about two pound fifty left!'

'Maybe we *should* rob a payroll wagon after all,' mumbled Moxey.

'That remark's in pretty poor taste, if you don't mind me saying so, Moxey,' Barry said. 'If it wasn't for you subscribing to this cult of glamorising criminal activity, we wouldn't have found ourselves being exploited by those vacuous females.'

Moxey bridled. 'You didn't seem to mind at the time!'

There was no denying it. While it had lasted, being a notorious bunch of criminals had been fun. Then the bill had come for all the champagne those admiring girls had been drinking . . .

Wayne edged into the room to join them, his eyes protected by dark glasses. There was a limp, hungover greeting for the cockney.

'Anybody get anything last night?' Wayne asked first of all. 'I mean, apart from drunk and broke?'

'Naw,' said Oz. 'It was a definite case of look but don't touch. How about you?'

Wayne shook his head. 'I tried to strump that dark-haired one in the lift, but I couldn't get it to go up – the lift, that is. So I was hauled out by the night porter and given a right telling-off.'

He didn't get much sympathy.

'You know what's beginning to happen, don't you?' Barry said mournfully. 'Our lives are beginning to mirror those of the villains. We're not tourists, nor are we workers; we're caught in a foreign country, in limbo –'

'They don't limbo in Spain, man – they flamenco,' Oz pointed out.

Bomber nodded solemnly. 'Barry's got a point, though. Leisure without graft is a pretty hollow experience.'

'What's it to be today, then?' asked Wayne, helping himself to coffee. 'I don't think I can face sunlight or Sangria.'

Moxey agreed. 'I don't think I can face any more tourists saying "haven't I seen you in the paper?"'

There was a gloomy silence.

'Costa del Sol,' muttered Oz. 'More like Costa del Arsol...'

Then Barry brightened. 'Hey, why don't we go to Gibraltar for the day?' he suggested. 'It's only about sixty miles down the coast – the border's open now!'

'Aye, well – I don't mind,' said Oz. 'I've always wanted to have me photo taken with one of them baboons.'

'There'd be cheap British beer, duty-frees and today's paper, too!' Bomber said, rising to the occasion.

Moxey pointed out that papers were still a sore point, but for the moment they were all swept up with the enthusiasm. Let's face it, it was something to do.

They scraped together a kitty for hiring a car.

'I fancy one of them big four-wheel drive Chevvies with an eight-track stereo and an open roof ...' Wayne fantasised.

'Wonder if they do a five-seater Porsche?' Oz matched him.

An hour later, they were fixed up. The kitty, however, had not been quite as grand as they had hoped, and accordingly neither were their chariots for the day's adventure. What they ended up with were two identically tiny and battered white SEATs, Spanish-made Fiats.

'I'd take out some life insurance as well if I were you, Bomber!' Oz called out to the big man, who was sorting the details out, along with Barry.

'Who fancies driving, then?' asked Moxey.

Wayne frowned, still staring in horror at the tiny cars. 'I don't think you drive,' he said. 'You just pedal.'

'Right,' said Barry decisively, 'anybody mind if I take the wheel? I've always wanted to motor on the continent, ever since I bumped into Pat Moss once in Halford's...'

'Bomber's on! I'll do the trip down, 'cause I'll be too pissed to drive comin' back.'

'Aye, all right then,' said Oz. 'Mox, you get in with Barry – that way only one car will have a really boring journey.'

They poured themselves into the cars, Moxey and Barry in one, Wayne and the two big lads in the other. Bomber told Barry to take the lead – if there was any trouble, they'd flash their headlights.

'Hey, hang on!' said Moxey to Barry as the zit king started the engine. 'Barry! Didn't you get breathalysed a few months back?'

'Yes, I did, Moxey,' Barry said irritably. 'But I have not yet been convicted. And even if I had been, as you well know, worse criminals than drunk drivers are turned loose in this poxy country!'

They moved out onto the main Malaga-Cadiz highway in convoy.

Back at the villa, Neville and Dennis had cans of beer at their sides, were sprawled out on sun-loungers, at peace with the world and still enjoying their chance to see how the other half per cent live.

'Wonder what the others are up to,' Neville said lazily.

Dennis looked at his watch. 'Well, there's been no sign of them for nearly eighteen hours now, so they must actually be keeping out of trouble.'

'New world record!'

Dennis chuckled, took another swig of beer.

'Fancy a trip into town later?' he asked. 'Have a game of pool or something?'

'Aye,' said Neville. 'Great.'

Suddenly, however, Debbie appeared, suspended over her father by a smartly dressed Brenda.

'Here you are, Neville,' his wife said. 'Your daughter would like a little attention...'

Debbie was lowered onto Neville's chest.

Then Christine appeared, also dressed up for an outing and with a determined expression on her face.

'Don't get up, Dennis,' she said. 'We can find our own way out.'

'Out?' echoed Dennis.

'Yes,' Christine said, laughing. 'Brenda and I are going into town for lunch.'

''Bye, pet!' said Brenda brightly, ignoring the expression of shocked disappointment on her husband's face.

''Bye, Dennis,' said Christine. 'We'll be back in time for afternoon tea on the terrace.'

With that, the two women were off. And Debbie began to pull at her father's hair, making odd little squealing noises.

'I wonder what the others are up to?' said Dennis disgustedly.

The main highway was certainly busy. And it was also full of white SEATs. Bomber had a lot of trouble keeping Barry in view. Not that that was the only problem. Just out of Marbella, he glanced at the dashboard and muttered an oath.

'Hello – bloody petrol gauge is readin' low. That Spaniard said he'd just filled her up.'

'A likely story,' said Wayne.

Oz scowled. 'Yeah, well – pull over and I'll piss in the tank. After what I had to drink last night, it's like rocket fuel!'

Bomber looked back at the road and registered a familiar seeming white SEAT pulling off the road.

'Looks as though Barry's having the same trouble – they're pulling in.'

He slowed down, frowned in a puzzled fashion as the lead car drove straight into a forecourt that was, if he had but known it, the very plush entrance to the Marbella Club.

'Must be the classiest petrol station I've ever seen.' Wayne said. 'They've even hid the pumps.'

Bomber halted right behind the other SEAT, leaned out of the window.

'What the bloody hell have you stopped for, Barry?' he yelled.

There were indeed two people in the SEAT, and the driver had blond hair like Barry's. But when the driver got out, they realised they had made a blunder: she was blonde, beautiful and very desirably female, as was her companion.

The two girls strolled haughtily into the Club, ignoring Bomber's shouted apologies.

'Sorry, lads,' said Bomber with a sigh. 'There's just too many of these little white buggers on the road!'

'Well, we'll just have to catch up with 'em in Gib...' said Oz.

But Wayne was already climbing out of the cramped little motor.

'Sod Gibraltar,' he growled. 'It's rocks-off here for me!'

'Bomber fancies a beer now too...'

'Aye well,' mused Oz, taking in the surroundings. 'There must be worse gaffs to stumble on than this.'

So out they all got, crumpled, still hungover, and very unlike the Marbella Club's usual clientele – which, of course, included at the moment one Ally Fraser and friend...

Ally was taking pre-lunch cocktails with Vicki when the lads rolled in. Plunged in a deep Chesterfield, he had his back to the door, so he didn't immediately register their arrival.

'Any thoughts about lunch, my petal?' he said easily.

Vicki smiled craftily. A good session in bed had cured Ally's gripiness.

'Your mood's lasting surprisingly well,' she said. Then she saw the arrivals. 'Ooh, look! There's some of your lads!'

Ally whirled round, and his expression darkened when he saw the three most disaster-prone men on his team ambling up to the tastefully-upholstered bar.

'What the bloody hell are they doing?' he snapped. 'They can't afford to drink here on the wages I pay 'em...' He sank deeper into his chair. 'Don't let 'em see you,' he hissed to Vicki. 'I don't want 'em coming over here...'

'It's nice to know there's someone else you're ashamed of bein' seen with apart from me!' gibed Vicki.

Meanwhile, Oz, Bomber and Wayne had installed themselves at the bar and were waiting for the barman to finish a long conversation he was having in Spanish on the place's cordless phone.

'Oi, Manuel!' boomed Oz after a while. 'If you can walk and talk at the same time, how about pouring us some beers?'

The barman scowled, but after a short time he replaced the phone and sauntered over to them, making it obvious he didn't like their look.

'Yes, gentlemen?' he asked in a voice tinged with disdain.

'Three beers, matey,' said Bomber. '*Por favor...*'

The barman shrugged. '*Tres cervezas, si.*'

He gracefully took the tops off three bottles of Löwenbräu, keeping one eye on the lads all the time.

In another corner of the room sat Geoffrey and Pauline Oxlade, the two pukka expats whose pool the lads had desecrated that disastrous morning after their arrival. Since then, of course, they had seen their worst suspicions confirmed by the newspaper reports about the 'Sheffield payroll gang'.

'How they've got the brass neck to turn up in here, I don't know,' sniffed Pauline, watching the three men at the bar with loathing and fascination.

'I suppose it's their idea of fun to sport their ill-gotten gains in this manner,' said Geoffrey.

Pauline rounded on him. 'Are you going to *do* something, Geoffrey?'

'Yes,' he said. 'I'm already composing a strong letter to the *Times*.'

The barman put down three bottles and glasses on the counter, ignoring Wayne's request for him to pour the beers. Then he went to work on a fearsome sounding electronic till, which seemed to go on blipping for long enough to sort out twenty-five-year mortgage repayments.

'I don't like the sound of that,' said Oz.

The barman turned back to them. 'Will the gentlemen be staying for lunch?' he asked.

'The gentlemen haven't decided yet,' retorted Bomber.

The barman reached out and handed over a bill. 'In which case, if the gentlemen would be so kind...'

Oz took the bill and glanced at it. He blanched. 'Bloody hell! We've only had three beers, man – not thirty!' he bellowed.

'The gentlemen are free to drink elsewhere if they wish,' the barman pointed out coldly.

It was then that Wayne spotted Vicki, who despite Ally's warnings couldn't help staring at the lads' antics.

'Hello,' said the cockney. 'Our fairy godmother is at hand – with our godfather.'

Oz grinned.

'Howway, Mr Fraser!' he called out loudly. 'Can we put these on your account, please?'

There was no help but for Ally to get to his feet and come over, running the gauntlet of the other members' disapproving looks.

'What are you tearaways doing in here?' he growled, barely controlling his fury.

'We're acting like tourists,' said Bomber. 'On your orders!'

Oz nodded agreement. 'Only we could do with a sub out of our wages...' he said in a stage whisper.

Ally threw some money onto the bar in payment for the beers.

'Now drink up and move out,' he hissed. 'Before my reputation in Marbella is ruined.'

But he was too late. Fuelled by another pre-prandial Bloody Mary, Geoffrey Oxlade had got up the gumption to confront the trio at the bar.

'Let me guess,' he sneered as he approached them. 'Planning another bank robbery, are we?'

Oz looked him up and down. 'I remember this prick...' he snarled.

'For Christ's sake!' said Ally through gritted teeth. But no one was interested in sparing his feelings, on either side.

'Now look here,' Geoffrey bleated, 'you may enjoy

immunity from arrest in this country, but you are not immune from our contempt as decent British citizens!'

Bomber looked at him warningly. 'Careful, boyo – you're way off the mark!'

'Am I now? And I suppose the newspaper story was, too!'

'I'm surprised at you, reading a rag like that, mister. I usually have it hanging up on a nail in the bog!' Oz taunted.

'The matter is in the hands of our lawyers, actually, squire,' Wayne added. 'And they'd be happy to take action for slander as well.' He gave the nod to the barman. 'Pass us your blower, Manuel...'

'I refuse to be intimidated by you,' Geoffrey blustered. 'You may have wealth now – criminally acquired, of course – but that doesn't entitle you to strut around here.' He shot a poisonous look at Ally. 'Even if you were invited...'

Oz got down from his stool. 'I've had enough of this!'

'It's all right, sir,' Ally said ingratiatingly to Geoffrey. 'They're leaving...'

'I'm not leaving!' Oz roared. 'I meant I've had enough of him!' He stared daggers at Geoffrey. 'Just suppose we were armed robbers,' he told the man. 'At least our crime is honest, it's upfront. We get our money at the end of a gun – but you sneaky bastards get it at the end of a balance sheet or income tax form!'

Oz was just getting into his stride. And Oxlade was turning a vivid shade of puce.

Ally smiled weakly, turned to Vicki.

'I think we'll skip lunch...'

Dennis lifted himself up on one elbow, peered down towards the front of the villa. Ally's car had just screeched to a halt, and their boss was on his way up to the house, striding along the path with a paper under his arm and a face like thunder.

'Why do I suddenly have a bad feeling, Neville?' Dennis sighed. 'As though Oz was stickin' pins in a Dennis Patterson doll?'

Ally arrived just a few moments later.

'Your boys are wasted on buildin' sites, Dennis,' he

snapped. 'They should be organisin' military uprisings in banana republics!'

'Have they been causin' trouble, Mr Fraser?' asked Neville mildly.

'No! No!' Ally fumed. 'They've just spent a happy half-hour slagging off some of the most important people in Marbella society – of which I am no longer a member!'

Dennis winced. 'I thought it was too good to last.'

Ally slapped the paper down. 'Anyway, you can whistle them back in now, 'cause the heat is off. Your true humble status has been revealed to a grateful nation...'

Neville picked up the paper and looked at the story under Sid and Ronnie's by-line. It was headlined: 'HOLIDAY BRITS SLAM ROBBERY SMEAR'.

Dennis nodded. 'Right, I'll get 'em cracking first thing tomorrow morning.'

'I've got a better idea,' Ally said. 'How about a night shift?'

Moxey and Barry were slumped at separate tables in the hotel bar when Oz, Wayne and Bomber trooped wearily in. There was a distinct chill between the two incumbents, but maybe Oz was too wiped out to notice or care.

'There you are,' he growled. 'What happened to you? We've been lookin' all over Gibraltar for you!'

Barry cast a hate-filled glance at Moxey. 'Well, you were wastin' your time, because we didn't get there!'

'Why? What happened?' asked Bomber. 'Puncture or breakdown?'

'Neither,' said Barry. 'Thanks to the superlative map-reading skills of Marco Moxey here, we couldn't find Gibraltar!'

Oz frowned. 'But it's a five-hundred-foot high chunk of rock, man! Ye cannot miss it!'

'Moxey can,' said Barry.

Moxey shrugged. 'Be fair, Barry – we did get there eventually...'

'Yes,' Barry barked. 'And then you saw a British bobby at the border gates and we had to turn back!'

'You haven't suffered a great loss, Barry,' Wayne told him.

'It's a bit like Canvey Island with chimps.'

Bomber nodded. 'Aye, and it's full of Jocks left over from the 1982 World Cup.'

'So where did you end up?' asked Oz.

'Oh,' said Barry, 'we stopped off at a picturesque little dog-hole called San Pedro and got wheel-clamped.'

The general amusement at that did not improve his mood.

'I didn't know they had the Denver Shoe here,' said Bomber.

Barry nodded. 'Yuh, well. It's called the Catalan Clog in Spain.'

'How did you find that out?'

'Oh,' Barry answered, 'from a light-hearted discourse with the educationally-subnormal peasant who put it on our car. I knew my Spanish lessons would come in handy.'

'Well, if it's any consolation, Barry, we haven't had much fun either,' Oz said.

Barry held up the long postcard he had been writing, allowed it to unfold onto the table under the effect of gravity.

'Bet your day wouldn't fill one of these, though,' he said. 'I only hope this catalogue of dejection will melt my Hazel's heart and bring her rushin' to my side.'

'Well,' Oz asked, 'has anyone got any cash for a beer?'

Moxey gestured helplessly. 'The bar's closed 'cause the waiter's got diarrhoea.'

Bomber put his head in his hands. 'Sufferin' Ada!'

Dennis walked straight into the black silence that descended on the room at this final straw of news.

'Hello,' he sid, looking around sourly. 'No riot police, no water cannon? Finished for the day, have you?'

Oz glared at him. 'Watch it, Dennis. We've all had a poxy time here.'

'Well,' said Dennis, 'I've got some more bad news for you – Ally Fraser wants you back at work at seven o'clock sharp tomorrow morning.'

To his amazement, there were cheers and grins, back-slapping. By God, he thought, these lads are nothing if not unpredictable.

TWENTY-TWO

'Hi-ho, hi-ho, it's off to work we go...' sang the lads as they swarmed around the pool and the patio. There was shovelling going on, cement being mixed, an ornate wall arising like a little miracle. Dennis had never seen the lads work so hard or so willingly as they had after this lay-off. He shook his head, wandered off around to the side of the house, where Brenda and Christine were sitting in deckchairs, bikini-clad look-outs.

'All quiet on the southern front?' asked Dennis.

'Aye,' Christine told him. 'Not that I'd recognise a Spanish Ministry of Labour official if I fell over one...'

Brenda asked Dennis if the workers would like some tea.

'I'm sure that'd be appreciated, Brenda.' He winked. 'Best-looking can-lad we'll ever have had ...'

He returned to the pool area and announced that fresh tea was on the way, courtesy of Brenda.

'What are the rest of you having?' asked Neville, deadpan.

'She's doin' it for all of us, Neville...'

'Here, Den,' called Bomber, 'what's Fraser having on the walls of his pool?'

'Ceramic Andalusian tiles, apparently.'

Barry smirked. 'From "Habitacion", no doubt,' he quipped, showing off his Spanish and his general class.

'It's gonna be like a big bath, in't it?' Moxey commented.

Oz grinned. 'You've never seen a bath before, have you, Mox?'

'Nice to see you back at your bitchy best,' said Dennis.

'Nah – it's just banter, Den,' Wayne explained. 'A sure sign of improved morale among the troops!'

'My morale's gonna be even higher if my Hazel turns up in the next week or so,' said Barry.

'You finally got that great wodge written, did you?'

'Yes,' said Barry with satisfaction. 'Posted it last night.'

'Don't know why you bothered,' Oz remarked. 'You could've used it as a raft and paddled it back to England.'

At that point, Christine and Brenda arrived on the patio, carrying trays of tea and biscuits – and still in their bikinis. There were appreciative whistles from everyone bar Dennis and Neville.

'Hey, hey!' Dennis protested. 'That's our women you're whistlin' at.'

'Only me an' Dennis are allowed to do that,' said Neville possessively.

Christine looked at him sceptically. 'Are you really?'

Neville reddened. 'Well no, actually...'

Jeers all round. A break and then back to work. A fair day's work for a fair day's pay. Honest graft for a villain's sake.

At the Tennis Ranch, the villain in question was talking to his most intimate enemy over a soft drink in deference to the early hour. Kenny Ames, bronzed and kitted out in snappy tennis gear, was waiting to go on for a coaching session with the pro. The conversation between him and Ally was strictly side-of-the-mouth, for this was not the Britannia or some other thieves' kitchen but one of the strongholds of the straight, moneyed community in Marbella.

'No,' Kenny murmured, 'of course I didn't ask you here to watch me play tennis – though you can stay if you want...'

'Thank you, Kenny,' said Ally Fraser frostily. 'But I don't think I could stand the excitement. Now, what was it you wanted to see me about?'

Kenny leaned forward confidentially. 'Well,' he began, 'you know this firm of yours that's doing the building?'

'They've been arrested for sinkin' a yacht?' asked Ally, alarmed.

'No, no – they're workin' up at your place, aren't they?'

'You never know with that mob...'

'Well, anyway – now that this payroll robbery nonsense has subsided, I think they could be of some use to me ... I mean us ...' Kenny corrected himself hastily.

Ally looked at him suspiciously. 'How's that, Kenny, since they're about as useful as a match in a firework factory?'

Ames smiled. 'Well,' he said, 'I presume that after they've finished tarting up your villa, they're all goin' back to Blighty ...'

'I doubt they'll be welcome, but yes.'

'Er ... because me and a few of the boys in the Britannia have a few things we'd like returning to certain people in London ...'

Ally's eyes narrowed. 'Let me guess – like keys to safe-deposit boxes, that sort of thing.'

Ames was impervious to sarcasm.

'I'm saying nothing, Ally,' he said smoothly. 'But the point is, now they're in the clear, and more importantly, seen as victims of press smears, The Old Bill and the Customs won't dare get the hump with them.'

'Which makes 'em useful couriers?'

Ames grinned wolfishly. 'Play it as it lays, son!'

'So what's my cut, if I pass 'em your way?'

'Goodwill and such,' Ames said airily. 'We'd work something out ...'

Ally looked highly dubious.

'Just ask 'em to pop down the Britannia in the next few nights ...' Ames persisted.

Ally said he would see what he could do – and an idea was forming in his own devious brain. No one knew it yet, least of all Dennis and the lads, who were expecting to get paid, but he was in deep schtuck, and Kenny had prompted some very interesting thoughts about how to get out of it again.

Just then, the tannoy crackled into life: 'Will Mr Ames please go to Court Number Eight.'

Kenny got to his feet, looking pained. 'I do wish they'd insert the word "tennis" before saying court ...' he said.

It was with a new sense of deserving that the lads made for the bar at the hotel that evening. They had earned a beer or two, or three, or ...

But one of them suddenly pulled up in the general rush for liquid refreshment. Barry stopped, did a double-take. For sitting at the bar was none other than Hazel, his lady-love.

'H-Haze,' he gasped.

She smiled sweetly. 'Hello, Barry. Sorry to shock you...'

There were some jeers and nudges, but the rest of them were sensitive enough to leave him and Hazel to it.

'Hazel, I'm amazed that you could be here so quickly!'

'Well,' she said matter-of-factly, 'there's two flights a day from Birmingham International, and it only takes two and a half hours, you know.'

'I don't mean the flying' time, Haze – I'm amazed by the fact that you should respond so promptly to my emotional appeal. I only posted it yesterday evening...'

She looked at him quizzically. 'Posted what?'

'A jumbo picture view of the Costa del Sol – with a jumbo love-letter on the back!'

'I'm sorry, Barry – I haven't seen it at all. I booked the flight a couple of days ago. Teresa Mackintosh in our accounts department had a last-minute cancellation through a family bereavement.'

Barry was crestfallen. 'Oh – oh, I'm sorry.'

'Well, it was only an old uncle of hers in Mexborough, but she felt she had to go...'

'No, no – I'm sorry you didn't come out here in a fit of passion rather than through Teresa Mackintosh's misfortune.'

'Well...' Hazel smiled. 'I admit I was a bit curious about that newspaper story describing you all as payroll robbers.'

'Oh,' snorted Barry. 'What a load of nonsense, eh?'

Hazel's face fell. 'So it's not true then?'

'No, of course it isn't,' said Barry, hurt.

'Oh well...'

Barry coughed. 'Well, it's nice to see you anyway, Hazel. Would you like a drink?'

'No thanks.'

There was an uncomfortable pause.

'I tell you what,' Barry said after a while, cheering up. 'I've still got this hire-car that me and the lads rented. Perhaps you'd like to come up into the Sierra with me tonight and have dinner looking out to sea?'

'I – I'm sorry, that's not possible,' Hazel told him.

'But Hazel, this is Spain!' he said. 'You're on holiday! Everything is possible!'

She dipped into her handbag, pulled out a brown official envelope. 'Not when you've been banned from driving for a year, Barry...'

If he – and the rest of the lads – had but realised it, the previous weeks' and months' chaos was perfect tranquillity compared with the destiny that now awaited them. Machinery had been set in motion. Dark, secret machinery. And the prime movers were no longer any of the Seven but sweet Hazel and the far from sweet Ally Fraser – not forgetting Kenny Ames.

The work went on, day after sweltering day, yet somehow, out here in Spain, it didn't seem to matter. With the beach and bistros close at hand, it was a long way from freezing Thornely Manor, or a building site in Byker with the wind cutting through your donkey jacket.

One morning, about half past ten, the lads had just knocked off for a break. They'd already done three hours' work, and the sweat was glistening on their shirtless skins. Oz toiled up from the chemical toilet that had been installed half-way down the hill. The experience had not been a pleasant one. Maybe it was the beer, or maybe it was last night's paella.

'I'd give it five, if I were you,' called Bomber, seeing the grimace on Oz's face.

'I'd rather go in the bushes than use that thing,' moaned Oz.

'The bloke I'm sorry for is the one who has to clean it out,' said Neville. But he didn't have to use it most of the time.

Moxey glared at him, and then at Dennis. 'It's all right for some,' he complained. 'Some of us are staying in the villa. Some of us have twenty-four-hour access to tiled bathrooms and soft toilet paper.'

'Which is a tossin' sight better than sharin' a sweat-box with eighty thousand flies,' Oz added ruefully.

Barry warmed to the theme. 'That pong could cause great

aggression and disharmony between us lot,' he observed.

Dennis got the point, but what could he do? 'We've put up with worse conditions than this, Barry,' he pointed out. 'We're not going to fall out over a Portaloo.'

'Well I like going in last thing at night,' Wayne chipped in. 'Mr Portaloo Sunset, eh?'

They barely bothered to groan.

'No I'm serious,' said Barry, pursuing his theme. 'It's the ferronomes, y'see.'

'No it wasn't,' Wayne cut in. 'It was the Kinks.'

'Not a lot of people know about ferronomes,' Barry ploughed on regardless. 'I only found out when I read this article in a magazine at the chiropodist's.'

'Footnote, was it?' muttered Dennis sardonically.

But Barry wouldn't be deterred. 'Look, if you don't want to hear it's no sweat off my arse!' he exclaimed irritably. 'Go back to your normal moronic topics of conversation – sex, relegation and the best pint I ever had.'

Oz had had enough. 'Come on, then, Barry, dazzle us!' he called.

Reassured that he had everyone listening, Barry took the floor.

'Ferronomes may well be a contributing factor towards football hooliganism, y'see.' (They didn't.) 'They're invisible entities which float off into the atmosphere when you pee. And they stimulate aggressive tendencies.'

He'd lost them already.

'Now at half-time, when everyone pees at once, massive numbers of ferronomes are set free. And that's why sixty-seven per cent of violence takes place in the second half.'

He gazed around triumphantly.

'I can believe that one,' said Oz, drawing on many years' experience of the lower depths of human depravity. 'I was at Villa Park once and this bloke peed in me pocket...'

Before he could go on, Vicki pulled up in her convertible and wiggled up to the villa. They watched every teetering step. Wayne clocked her the hardest and the longest.

'Off limits, boyo,' breathed Bomber.

But Wayne, once the sap was rising, wouldn't be deterred so easily.

'I'm not so sure,' he murmured. 'When we went to Ally's party, back in Geordie land, she definitely gave me a flash.'

'If you mess around with her and bollix things up for the rest of us,' threatened Bomber, 'I'll give you more than a flash.'

'Don't sermonise me, Bomb,' Wayne drawled easily. 'You're not above a bit of lechery yourself. I saw you with those two travel agents from Preston the other night down at the casino.'

Vicki came over to the pool and said hello. 'Eee, this place is coming on,' she exclaimed, appraising the work in progress. 'You'll be done here soon.'

'Aye, we don't hang about, us lot,' said Oz.

Vicki turned to him. 'What'll you do when the job's finished?' she asked.

'I'll just go home and face the grim reality of Thatcher's Britain. Unless your Ally coughs up a bonus . . . Then I might postpone the grim reality for a week.'

'And take off somewhere, like?'

'Aye, well, Barry an' me was goin' to meander slowly back through France. But his fiancée's showed up, so I suppose I'll have to elbow that. Be on me own as usual,' he added ruefully.

Barry was most put out. 'I'm very sorry if my plans have intruded on your plans, Oz,' he said.

'Not my plans, mate,' said Oz. 'You're the one that wanted to see the shite-houses of the Loire.'

'Chateaux, Oz,' murmured Barry. Why had fate cast him among swine?

'I've always fancied San Tropez myself,' tittered Vicki. 'I think there's more night life. I mean, it's more sophisticated down there.'

'Oh I agree,' cried Moxey manfully. 'Give me San Tropez every time!'

Vicki said goodbye, and went on to the house, from which promptly came the sound of little Debbie crying.

''Scuse me lads, won't be a minute,' said Neville, embarrassed that this should happen in front of his workmates with Brenda away for the morning.

The others looked at each other.

'I'll say one thing for my Marjorie,' observed Oz. 'She never wanted to be this close to me work.'

Everyone nodded sagely.

'You should get Hazel up here, Barry,' he went on. You could sort out your private life and screed concrete at the same time!'

'I'd like my private life to remain private, if you don't mind,' snapped Barry.

'We await developments with baited breath,' said Wayne to himself.

Later rather than sooner the end of the day's work came round.

'Right lads, knock it on the head,' cried Dennis, scurrying towards the cooler full of ice and beer that they always had ready for finishing time.

'Who fancies going down to the casino tonight?' said Wayne, pulling deeply on his can.

'Bomber'll be there,' leered the West Countryman. 'Lots of female tourists down the casino.'

'I'm on,' added Moxey. 'Me luck's gotta change sometime,'

Wayne turned to Barry. 'Are you coming?' he asked. 'Or is it dinner à deux with Haze?'

'It is, as a matter of fact. I managed to get a table at that place in the port. The one that's in all the guides. Where all the people off the yachts go,' he swanked.

'If that doesn't do the trick, nothing will,' said Oz to himself.

They made ready to go. Barry latched on to Oz as they made their way down the slope.

'I'm sorry if you're upset about that French trip,' he said.

'Aw, that's all right,' cried Oz, big hearted. 'I might go to Ibiza, actually. Got some mates down there who say they're out of their skulls twenty-four hours a day. And there's so much spare you're driven insane from choice. Sounds like the sort of place for a rest after this . . .'

'Obviously Hazel's arrival has put a whole new complexion on our relationship,' confided Barry. Oz looked pityingly at the pits and pockmarks on Barry's face. 'I didn't ask her, Oz, I didn't beg. *She* came to me!'

'Paid her own fare, like?'

'Oh yes! I mean, that tells you something, that.'

'It tells me she's got more money than sense.'

'Oh, no, Oz, don't put the mockers on it. You know how important she is to me. If it wasn't for Hazel us lot would never have got together again. We wouldn't be here!'

'True,' said Oz quietly.

'It seems aeons ago, doesn't it?' cried Barry warmly. 'When we were all reunited to renovate my love-nest.'

Oz could hardly blink back the tears. 'We did a cracking job on that plumbing,' he managed to say.

'You didn't labour in vain, Oz! I'm much more optimistic about the future now.'

'I still think you should have put in a bigger boiler,' Oz was careful to point out.

Beneath the outward calm, down at the casino the joint was certainly jumpin'. Hazel was watching the roulette wheel like a stoat observing a rabbit. Barry was trying to get her attention. He had no luck until the wheel stopped spinning and the croupier paid out the winners. Hazel was not among them.

'That restaurant I'd booked at,' he ventured. 'The one I told you about ... the one that's so difficult to get into ...'

Hazel wasn't interested. She was busy placing her bet.

'They've given the table away,' Barry went on undeterred. 'He says he can't guarantee another one before next August.'

'I'll be just as happy with a sandwich,' said Hazel, her mind elsewhere. 'And could you get me another tequila sunrise?'

'What's got into you, Haze?' asked Barry, confused.

'Oh I love this, Barry!' she cried. 'The atmosphere, the chandeliers, the green baize, the tension. It's so romantic!'

'How much have you lost?' asked Barry phlegmatically.

'I'm about a hundred and fifty up!'

'Pesetas?'

'Pounds.'

'Pounds! You've almost paid for your air fare then!'

Nearby Wayne and Moxey were busy playing blackjack. Wayne had just been dealt a two, and sucked in his breath.

We could be on here, he thought to himself as the dealer waited.

Just then Vicki came in, clad elegantly in a flimsy black number.

'Fold,' said Wayne simply, and put down his hand. Moxey and the dealer looked on in astonishment as he melted away.

'Surprise, surprise,' called Wayne as he sidled up on Vicki. 'Your old man let you off the leash, has he?'

'My old man kicked me out,' said a hurt sounding Vicki.

'Oh dear,' sympathised Wayne. 'Lover's tiff, was it?'

Vicki looked a bit lost. 'With Ally it's always business,' she said. 'His solicitor's down here. It's not for my ears, whatever it is.'

But Wayne was dismissive. 'You don't want to bother yourself with all that off-shore tax-shelter dialogue,' he urged her. 'What'll it be?'

From another blackjack table Oz and Bomber watched what was going on. Bomber picked up his chips and rose. Oz looked at him quizzically.

'Are you cashin' in?' he asked.

'Business,' said Bomber quietly, nodding towards Wayne and Vicki at the bar. 'Vicki's Ally's lady, and Wayne's Wayne. Right?'

'He never gives up,' said Oz, reluctantly picking up his chips. 'He's like one of them wire-haired terriers that keep humpin' your leg.'

They walked over to the bar. They could tell by Vicki's giggles and Wayne's lecherous leer the kind of patter he was giving her.

'Wayne, me old dear!' cried Bomber, clapping a heavy hand down on his shoulder as though he were hailing a long-lost friend.

'Oh, hello Bomb,' said Wayne with markedly less enthusiasm. He looked like a schoolboy who'd been caught scrumping apples.

'It's your lucky night, boyo,' Bomber boomed heartily. 'Those two travel agents have showed up. I think that Daphne's taken a right shine to you. No problem there,

Admiral,' he added nudging Wayne in the ribs. That'll cramp his style, he reflected.

'What are you on about?' asked Wayne peevishly.

Bomber leaned over to Vicki. 'I love the way this lad comes on all innocent and naive,' he said, winking roguishly.

'What's your game?' cried Wayne as Bomber steered him away from the bar.

'I'm protecting you from yourself, lad,' said Bomber quietly. 'And the rest of us at the same time. That Vicki's private property.'

'I know that,' snorted Wayne. 'D'you think I'm an idiot or something?'

'When it comes to skirt,' Bomber drawled laconically, 'I *know* you're an idiot.'

Vicki and Oz were left by the bar.

'So that was the rescue, was it?' she enquired, sounding slightly aggrieved.

'Sorry?' said Oz, trying to play the innocent.

'Howway!' she cried. 'I'm not daft!'

Oz decided a hint of diplomacy was called for. 'Look, we know Wayne,' he explained, 'and we know he can get out of order.'

'He's not so bad. He just saw I was down in the dumps, so he was offering friendship and conversation. It's just his way of trying to get in me pants ...'

There was more to this girl than met the eye, thought Oz.

Moxey, meanwhile, had just bumped into Barry, looking worried.

'I've never seen this side of Hazel before,' he admitted, nodding towards the roulette players.

'She's on holiday, Barry,' said Moxey, trying to placate him.

'But I've been on holiday with her before. This isn't unwinding – it's reckless abandon. She's just bet the down payment on a three-piece suite on number eleven.'

Moxey raised an admonishing finger. 'Hey, you haven't nailed her yet, kid,' he warned. 'It's her money, not your settee.'

And Barry knew he was right.

TWENTY-THREE

With the work on the villa nearing completion – and Hazel now on the spot, bringing Barry's personal drama to a climax – the plot thickened as quick as scalded cream.

After Ally's discussion with Kenny Ames at the Tennis Ranch, contracts between the Scots 'businessman' and Malcolm Harbottle suddenly became more frequent; disturbingly so. The news from Ally's pet brief was bad: the original Fraud Squad visits to Thornely Manor and Newcastle the other month had given way to a period of deceptive calm. But Inspector Morris and Sergeant Lawrence had not been idle, not at all. According to Harbottle, there were ominous signs that they had teamed up with investigators from the Inland Revenue and that soon they would be moving in on the Fraser Empire in a big way. In fact, the solicitor had told Ally in his latest, lengthy phone call that probably the only reason they hadn't moved in was because to do so would guarantee that Ally would stay in Spain. As things stood, it was pretty certain that as soon as Ally set foot on British soil, the machinery of warrants and charges would go into motion, passports would be confiscated ...

It was after this last conversation that Harbottle flew out to Spain for a crisis conference.

The solicitor was nervous as he toyed with his drink in the Club bar.

'Look,' he told Ally, 'it's obvious from the questions the boys from the Fraud Squad have been asking that there's been help from the local police here. I'd say the Spaniards have been keeping an eye on you.'

Ally tensed, but outwardly he stayed cool. He'd been in

jams with the law before – and he had always managed to avoid the worst through some bold stroke. He'd think of something, and if all else failed he could call in a few favours in the criminal community.

'So there's some co-operation,' he said with a frown. 'But how far off is an actual extradition treaty?'

Harbottle shrugged, loosened his tie. 'Who can say? You'll be all right here for a while yet, so long as you keep your nose clean. You . . . er . . . haven't actually done anything *illegal* in this country, have you?'

'There's the . . . tourists . . . I've been so hospitable to,' said Ally wrily. A very minor offence, of course, but you couldn't guarantee anything if the Spaniards were really hand-in-glove with the Fraud Squad. Any excuse would do.

Harbottle had read his thoughts. He smiled thinly.

'I'd get that work finished as soon as you can, and from now on take no chances, none at all,' he advised.

'And meantime I'm goin' to need some operating capital,' said Ally. 'I've got cash and negotiable bearer bonds in the UK that could be realised quickly here – but then collecting's a problem . . .'

'Can't help you there,' Harbottle said quickly. 'I have to be terribly careful, old chap. The Law Society can get very shirty when there's obvious bending of the rules, and of course I am known to work for you . . .'

Ally nodded wearily. Cynical thoughts coursed through his mind. He remembered sayings about rats leaving sinking ships, no honour among thieves . . . There was plenty of folk wisdom on the subject and it was *all* true.

'Fine, Malcolm,' he said crisply. 'I don't expect you to compromise yourself more than you need to. I'm sure I can make my own arrangements. Presumably you'd have nothing against simply handing over some . . . shall we say . . . documents from your safe keeping to the care of a trusted emissary?'

Harbottle looked doubtful, then nodded reluctantly. 'I can cover myself for that, yes. Not that anything untoward's involved, I'm sure. I have your assurance of that, naturally.'

'Naturally, pal. And you'll get your fees paid.'

'Fine. And who would this . . . emissary . . . be?'

'Oh, a chap I *know* I can depend on, Malcolm,' Ally answered with a hint of accusation. 'There are still a few reliable people around, y'know.'

Especially, thought Ally as they prepared to go into lunch, when those people owed you six grand. He'd been careful only to let Dennis off the interest on his debt at the time of the Thornely Manor 'strike'. Something had told him that, sooner or later, a little leverage was going to be very useful, and so it had proved to be.

'Everything seems to be goin' swimmingly at the villa,' said Ally warmly. 'Your lads seem to be able to just get on with it. All highly skilled men, y'see . . . I knew I'd done the right thing getting a highly motivated team over here, men you can just leave to do their jobs . . .'

Dennis looked sceptically at his boss.

'Aye,' he said. He gazed around the bar. 'So you invited me here after work just to praise the lads. That's very nice. Gracious, I'd say. And, if you don't mind me saying so, not entirely typical of your normal attitude as an employer. Would there, by any chance, be any other motive for getting me here and plyin' me with pricey alcohol?'

Ally smiled. 'You could say that.'

'Fire away. I promised Christine I'd be back for supper.'

'Well,' Ally began relaxing back into his chair, 'it's true that these past weeks and months you've been just my gaffer – a change from your former duties. What I'm asking you to do now is more in the old line, a bit of fetching – all expenses paid, scheduled flight, the works –'

'Back to bein' your go-fer,' Dennis said in bitter recollection.

'I'm short handed here so far as staff are concerned,' Ally said. 'And there's some delicate legal matters I need to settle. To that end, I need some . . . confidential papers . . . from home, and I need 'em fast. You'll take a morning flight to Newcastle, turn around and come straight back, with the documents. A bit of a break, a taste of the jetset business lifestyle, eh? And as you said, the lads'll just get on with the job. Hardly notice you're gone . . .'

Dennis decided not to argue about who had actually

273

claimed the lads would 'get on with the job'. He was pretty certain about what was actually going on here, and it stuck in his gut. But there might be some gains from this desperate measure on Ally's part, if he played it right.

Dennis agreed to fly home. First thing in the morning. Straight there, collect the case of 'papers', and straight back.

That same afternoon, Brenda was lining up a snapshot of Hazel standing in front of a luxurious yacht that was moored at the marina. Hazel had insisted she take it – 'just to show the girls back home!'

'You don't have to focus, Brenda,' she called, explaining the workings of the camera. 'It's all automatic.'

Brenda was all thumbs. Automatic or not, the little black camera seemed to bristle with buttons.

'Which thing do you press?' she wailed.

'The red one. And make sure you get lots of the yacht in.'

Brenda fired, and the camera whirred. Just then a handsome, elegant man in his early fifties appeared on the deck of the yacht. He watched amused as Hazel and Brenda changed places.

'Perhaps you like I take one of you both?' he called in a soft Italian voice.

Hazel shot away from the yacht's rail on which she had been leaning as though it were electrified.

'Ooh, I'm sorry if I was leaning on your boat,' she said, blushing hotly.

The man laughed pleasantly. 'No, please come aboard,' he invited them. 'I take the picture here.'

Hazel hardly hesitated. She was up the gangplank in a second. Brenda needed coaxing.

'I am Massimo,' said the Italian, greeting them decorously.

'Hazel Redfern. And this is my friend, Brenda Hope.'

'*Come sta?*'

'Very well, thank you,' said Brenda stiffly.

Massimo took the camera. 'You want I take you against the wheelhouse?' he suggested.

'Any time he likes,' whispered Hazel saucily.

They took up their positions, and Massimo framed the

picture. Another Adonis in designer jeans – younger this time, but with the same disdainfully elegant air of the Euro elite – came up behind them and put his arms around the girls' shoulders. The shutter clicked.

'I did not know we had guests, Massimo,' said the newcomer.

'These are my friends Brenda and Haz-elle,' he laughed.

'And I am Gunter ... *enchanté*.' He shook their hands lightly.

Massimo summoned his steward. 'You like champagne?' he asked the girls.

'Yes please,' said Hazel.

'No thank you,' said Brenda.

'Something else, per'aps?' offered Massimo, effortlessly glossing over the little *contretemps*.

'It's just a little early in the day for me,' Brenda explained. Massimo made a soothing gesture, and looked at his watch.

'In Hong Kong they are already having dinner,' he said with a roguish twinkle in his eye.

'C'mon Brenda, we're in no mad rush,' urged Hazel.

And Brenda agreed, a trifle reluctantly.

'Soon we put out to sea,' said Massimo when their drinks had arrived. 'We meet friends, we have lunch. We catch the sea bass. Alvaro is very special cook. Mmmmm – superb!'

'You join us, per'aps?' added Gunter.

Brenda looked alarmed.

'We'd love to!' cried Hazel, but Brenda was racked with guilt.

'Hazel, we can't,' she hissed, but her friend wouldn't be deterred. This was better than any paperback romance!

'Why?' she asked blandly. 'Wouldn't you rather go out on a beautiful boat than walk around the streets like a typical English tourist?'

Brenda was caught between the devil and the deep blue sea.

'Well ask him when we'll be back,' she said uncertainly.

Massimo overheard this, and laughed.

'You are English,' he cried, topping up their glasses. 'We have you back in time for tea!'

*

On the patio of the tennis club Kenny and Ally were sharing a drink.

'You're more worried than you let on,' Kenny was saying. 'I mean, three sets to love! I'm embarrassed to take your money, son.'

Ally shook his head sadly. He needed to talk through his problems with someone, even though he knew that hearing of his little difficulties would give Kenny Ames a great deal of sadistic pleasure.

'I sense that the solids are about to hit the air-conditioning,' he admitted at last.

'Fraud Squad? The Revenue? Her Majesty's Customs and Excise?'

'They could be bracing me. Maybe I should go back and tough it out.'

'But?'

'There's a few too many imponderables. All things considered, it may be best to stay a wee while and see which way the wind is blowing.'

'If you want to buy yourself some time, you'll need some readies down here. And if they're really on your case, they'll have your bank manager in tow. So any transfers of currency are out of the question.'

Ally raised his eyes to heaven. 'I've been round the block, son,' he said patronisingly.

'Okay,' said Kenny. 'But most of the people you'll need to bung down here won't take your Barclaycard –'

'I'm getting cash flown in,' Ally cut in.

'Carrier pigeon, is it?' asked Kenny. He was enjoying this. He flapped his arms about like an exhausted bird. 'He'll get a bit knackered across those Pyrenees,' he chuckled.

'Dennis is bringing it in.'

'What, your gaffer? You must trust him.'

'He doesn't know . . .' said Ally quietly.

Siesta time. The lads were scattered round the pool area, seeking whatever shade they could find from the noonday sun. At the edge of the still unfinished pool sat Barry, an umbrella over his head, his feet in a carrier bag. Neville was fanning himself with a days-old *Daily Mirror*.

'I envy Den,' he said languidly. 'He'll be in an English pub now, murdering an English pint.'

Moxey squinted at him. 'You're a strange lad, you are, Neville,' he murmured. 'As long as I've known you you've always wanted to be someplace else. There's people down here who've paid a bloody fortune to enjoy that hot Spanish sunshine.'

Bomber was more precise. 'He'd rather be drinking warm ale in some manky pub in Gateshead,' was his opinion.

'Ah yes,' noted Moxey, 'but if he was there he'd wish he was here.'

He lay back, too whacked by the heat to pursue this line of argument any further.

Oz and Wayne, meanwhile, were sharing a cool tube.

'I sometimes think Bomber's on Ally's payroll,' said Wayne. 'I mean, someone's made him my naffing chaperone. It was on last night with Vicki, I know it was.'

Oz knew all the answers. 'Look, obviously the lass has problems, right? Obviously she's vulnerable –' He paused and belched luxuriantly – 'even to your most transparent overtures. But it's not going to help us, and quite frankly it's not going to help the lass if you leap on her bones.'

'Oh, you've joined the moral majority, have you?'

Oz took another long swig. 'Wayne,' he said, chucking the empty can over his shoulder, 'your nuts aren't going to get rusty down here. I mean, there's Swedes, there's Germans, there's French –' his eyes grew misty – 'there's Danes, there's Brits. From Malaga to Gib it's wall-to-wall strump. So why Vicki? Is it the danger? Does the thought of getting your knees broke give you a giant stalker?'

He was just settling down for a swift forty winks when Nevil le gave his 'back-to-it-lads' call.

'Oh, deputy gaffer is it now?' asked Moxey.

Neville felt a bit embarrassed. 'Look lads,' he reasoned, 'if we start early we can finish early and have a few jars.'

This was what the troops wanted to hear. Grumbling a little, they got to their feet.

'Oh and by the way,' Barry chimed in, 'the drinks are on Hazel tonight.'

Everyone looked at each other, dumbfounded.

'She asked me to ask you, like, to join us for cocktails at the El Segundo.'

This made a change from Barry's customary invite – bring a bottle and a trowel. Moxey thought he'd twigged it.

'Oh, you've done it Barry! What a strike, kid!'

Barry hadn't a clue. 'Done what?' he implored.

'Barry and Hazel invite us for cocktails,' went on Moxey, ruffling Barry's hair. '"If any of you know cause or just impediment ye are to declare it".'

'Don't be coy, son,' added Wayne. 'An announcement is obviously imminent.'

'Have you fixed a date?' asked Neville after he'd politely offered his congratulations.

Barry was looking flustered. 'Look, I'm not getting engaged,' he said firmly. 'It's just that she won some money at the casino and wants us all to celebrate.'

'How much?' asked Oz.

Barry didn't know whether to be modest or to boast. 'Five hundred pounds,' he said finally, looking at his feet.

'Blow me, she's an heiress,' said Bomber. 'I'd shut the gate on that one if I were you.'

Wayne was already planning the evening's drinking strategy. A couple of Hawaii Honeymoons, a Long, Comfortable Screw or two, a swift snort of the old Harvey Wallbangers, and he'd be game for anything – especially another Long, Comfortable Screw, preferably shared with A Certain Party.

TWENTY-FOUR

Brenda had been a bit edgy when they set off for the El Segundo that evening – after all, she'd never had any secrets from Neville before. Hazel, of course, had been full of it.

'You Eengleesh girls, I love so much to touch your skin,' she giggled. 'Come into my engine room, I show you my peeston.'

Brenda tried to shush her, in case Neville overheard their girlish whispering, but Hazel wouldn't be deterred.

'I said to him,' she reiterated for the ninth time, '"Massimo, we may be three miles out but that doesn't give you territorial rights".'

Oh well, sighed Brenda, I shouldn't feel too bad about it. We didn't do anything really naughty, did we? It was all very innocent, really. And by the time they were settled at their table she'd begun to feel rather pleasantly vampish.

'Here's to Hazel – our Lady Luck,' Bomber was saying, raising his glass.

'I don't think she'll ever be that lucky again,' said Barry phlegmatically, urging them to make the most of it while they could.

'Oh, we were quite lucky today too,' babbled Hazel, fluttering her eyelashes at Brenda.

Brenda gave her a warning look.

'Why?' asked Neville. 'What did you do?'

Here we go, thought Brenda. He's hit the jackpot first time.

'Oh, we just enjoyed ourselves,' said Hazel coquettishly.

'Well, we're not going gambling tonight,' said Barry with some vehemence. 'We're going to have a quiet meal.'

That didn't sound like a barrel of laughs to Oz.

'If I were you,' he told Hazel, 'I'd go back to the casino and ride your luck.'

Barry protested, but Oz wouldn't be put off.

'No,' he argued. 'I mean, money's relative. Five hundred pounds sounds all right, but if you was to stick it all on one number and it came up... Now that could make a canny difference.'

Hazel perked up at this. 'How much would it be?' she demurely enquired.

'Thirty-five to one,' said Oz with years of practice at the bookie's streamlining his mental arithmetic, 'that's seventeen and a half thousand quid.'

'Don't even think of it,' Barry hissed in Hazel's ear.

'And even that's relative,' observed Moxey, warming to the theme. 'Look at all the affluence around us. Down here that would buy you half a bloody mast.'

By the time they'd worked out all the probabilities, Hazel stood to gain upwards of half a million.

'But would you be happy?' asked Wayne.

'Oh yes, definitely,' Hazel said without a moment's hesitation.

'I prefer money that's been made by honest graft,' muttered her intended.

'Me too,' Bomber concurred. 'Two hours toil of a Tuesday night on the pools – and eight score-draws come up.'

'So how did all these people get their money?' asked Brenda, indicating the world about them.

'Not through graft, pet,' Oz hinted darkly. 'Half those buggers out there are either embezzlers, arms dealers or drug smugglers – like them two poncin' down the quayside.'

They followed his nodded glance.

Oz took in the silk shirts and the Ralph Lauren sweaters tied casually around their waists.

'They've just got off a boat as big as a Channel Ferry,' he sneered. 'Now d'you think they got that 'cos for thirty years they ran a business in a shed in North Shields making vinyl roofing?'

To his surprise the pair waved towards their table and came over.

'Brenda! Hazelle!' they cried in unison. It was Gunter and Massimo. They bowed politely and kissed the girls' hands.

Brenda could have died. She rose unsteadily to her feet and made fumbled introductions.

Her husband couldn't have looked more astonished if she had climbed on to the table, stripped off all her clothes, and challenged everyone in the place to a limbo-dancing contest.

But later on, when he was rubbing sunburn cream on to Brenda's scorching shoulders in their bedroom, he'd managed to swallow his hurt pride.

'You really got burnt on that boat, didn't you?' he said.

'Mmmm,' said Brenda. He was a real pet, was her Neville. Lots of fellers she knew would have knocked their wives into the middle of next week. He'd taken it very well, considering.

'D'you think he's really a prince?'

'He says he is. And there was this coat of arms in the wheelhouse.'

'There's a coat of arms above the bar in the Fat Ox too. But it doesn't mean Alf Tonks is in line for the throne.'

'Anyway,' said Brenda. 'There's all sorts of counts and princes in Italy. It's not like having an English title.'

Neville looked slightly disappointed. But still . . .

'I hope Hazel's photos come out,' he said, 'or your mam will never believe it . . .'

Brenda sat up on the bed.

'She's a funny girl, that Hazel,' she said. 'Talk about hidden depths! I tell you one thing, Barry's got his hands full.'

In fact, it was more of a skinful as far as Barry was concerned right then. Though the waiter had hinted that it was time to go he'd insisted on yet another fundador, with a cappuccino for Hazel. They sat at a corner table in a hotel bar and pecked at each other miserably.

'It's long past your bedtime,' Hazel was saying, thinking of the hangover he'd be sporting come daybreak.

'There's a lot of things still to be resolved, Hazel.'

'I've told you – nothing happened. Prince Massimo was a perfect gentleman, much as you'd expect from royal blood.'

'You told me he'd invited you to Sardinia for a fortnight,' moaned Barry.

'Yes, but with a lot of other people. There'd have been a crowd of us.'

Drink had made Barry impetuous. 'Listen Hazel,' he snapped, 'if that's the life you want you'd better go after it. Let me tell you, sailing around the Mediterranean sipping cocktails and scuba diving is not *real*, y'know. You'd be a plaything to him. He'd probably dump you in Corsica with no ticket back. But *I'm* real . . . and I have feelings, and they're very bruised. You made me a laughing stock in front of me mates. They've watched me suffering while you make up your mind what you want out of life . . .'

He lurched unsteadily towards an abyss of self-pity. Then, with a superhuman effort, he rounded on Hazel.

'Well,' he announced, 'I'm sick of your evasiveness and I'm sick of your procrastinating.'

Hazel was lost for words. When the waiter arrived with the drinks, Barry tossed his fundador back in one and slammed his glass down on the tray.

'I'll have another, *por favor*!' he cried. The waiter slunk wearily off to the bar.

'Why have you never been like this before?' was Hazel's first question once she'd recovered some of her composure.

'Probably because I've never been so pilloxed around before.'

'You're so assertive and decisive,' she said without a trace of irony. 'And that's what I need in a man – 'cos I'm one of nature's vacillators.'

Hazel's praise had gone to his head. 'All right,' he said boldly, 'if it's decisiveness you want we're going to get married! And I'm not talking about a "prolonged engagement" with announcements in the local gazette. I'm talking about here, next week.'

Hazel's eyes lit up. 'All right!' she breathed excitedly.

'Sorry?'

'I accept! We'll get married here. It'll be ever so romantic.'

Barry slowly realised the error of his ways.

'Look, it doesn't *have* to be here,' he ventured, back-pedalling furiously.

'It's perfect,' said Hazel with a satisfied smile.

'No, but your folks wouldn't be able to get down. Nor would my mother, not with her hip. And your Auntie Nora and Jeffrey and Dominique and the twins.'

This was more like the Barry of old. But it was a totally new-look Hazel who took up the initiative.

'Sod the lot of 'em,' she cried with reckless abandon. 'I don't want a wedding like all our friends'. I don't want an accordion player and prawn vol-au-vents in the Bridge Street Assembly Rooms.'

Through the fundador fumes the harsh reality of what was being said began to dawn on Barry.

'Shouldn't we review this in the morning?' he asked nervously.

But Hazel wouldn't be put off.

'Oh no! Don't waver, Barry. Not now!'

'I'm not, I'm not. Just as long as you're serious.'

'Absolutely!' she said, leaning over and kissing him. 'And first thing in the morning I'll tell Massimo that Sardinia's out of the question.'

A little way along the street, in a discreet bar-cum-restaurant, another little drama was being acted out. Wayne, on the prowl, had just encountered Vicki, and she was far from pleased to see him.

'Hello,' she said flatly. 'What are you doin' here?'

'Why, is this bar too elegant for my kind?' asked Wayne the gallant. It was obvious he'd had a few, and now the sap was beginning to rise.

'I thought by this time of night you'd be checking out the discos.'

'I've done that – and they yielded nothing as delectable as yourself.'

Vicki looked irritable. 'Look, I'm just having a quiet nightcap,' she said crossly.

'Where's Ally?' asked Wayne, checking to see that the coast was clear.

'He'll be holed up with Dennis, I should think. He's due back at the airport about now.'

Reptile-like, Wayne slid in.

'That bloke don't half leave you hangin' around a lot of the time. It's either business or golf with him, in'it? Under the circs no one could blame a girl like you for... y'know... seeking the company of others. Albeit on a temporary basis, of course.'

Vicki instinctively looked in the mirror above the bar to check her appearance. With relief she noticed Bomber standing by the door, obviously having found what he was looking for. Knowing that help was at hand, she relaxed.

'How temporary?' she asked Wayne teasingly. He lit her cigarette and she looked up at him seductively.

'I can't promise to love you forever, but certainly till next Tuesday.'

'It's very tempting, Wayne,' she said playing with him like a cat with a mouse, 'but I think your minder's here.'

Bomber's enormous hand descended on his shoulder. 'By Jove, you almost gave me the slip there, you crafty little bugger!' he cried lustily.

Wayne's ardour, however, subsided as his anger rose. 'Look, leave it out, Bomber!' he exclaimed, stabbing the big man's chest with his puny finger.

'When's it going to get through to you that the lady might just want to be alone?'

Wayne was furious. 'I know the lads put you up to this but *I'll* decide if I want to be saved from myself, OK? The joke's over, d'you hear me?'

Bomber's response was to pick up Wayne as if he were a bale of straw.

'Say goodnight, Wayne,' he said as he hoisted him over his shoulder and carried him, kicking and struggling, out of the bar.

The smile had come back to Vicki's face. She gestured towards a dark corner of the room.

As if by magic, Oz appeared out of the shadows, and joined her at the bar.

'Close shave that!' he exclaimed.

'Another two here, Pepe!' called Vicki.

Oz admired Bomber's style in dealing with the problem. 'He's a right little lecher, that Wayne,' he added.

'Oh, don't mind him,' said Vicki, her knees brushing his. 'He just sort of got carried away...'

Dennis looked neither to the right nor to the left as he strode down the corridor that led to Malaga customs. The trip to Newcastle and back had been uneventful. The collection and everything else had gone smoothly, despite the need for one or two detours. Dennis smiled grimly, took a deep breath and turned into the customs area.

'Señor . . .'

A tap on the shoulder. Would the gentleman please step into the back room? Some formalities, understand . . .

The scene was like a dream: the humiliation of the body search, their thorough combing of his clothes, and finally the case.

'If señor will permit . . .'

Dennis nodded. The Spanish official smirked.

The smile on his face died when he opened the case and realised it was empty.

Yes, he had gone over to Newcastle to deal with some family matters, Dennis said, just as he had rehearsed it to himself all day. He had brought the case back with him because he might need it for his final return to the United Kingdom.

From then on, everything was even more extreme politeness, though he could see that the Spanish officials were both mystified and irritated. For them, a dead cert had failed to turn up, and for Dennis a suspicion had been confirmed in the clearest possible way.

An hour later, when he drew up outside the Marbella Club, complete with empty case, he was tight-lipped and determined. This was going to be the showdown, the end of Dennis Patterson's slavery. It had to be.

Ally was all smiles when he received Dennis in his suite, asking about the trip, hoping everything had gone smoothly.

'They took me apart at customs in Malaga, Ally,' Dennis said then. 'Took everything apart.'

Ally Fraser blanched. 'They... did what? So how...' He stopped himself, but Dennis filled in the missing words for him.

'So how come I'm here to tell the tale, Ally? Even though I was set up?' he said with a bitter smile. 'I'm here because I took the precaution of removing your "confidential papers" before I left Newcastle and putting them somewhere nice and safe. I didn't bother to count it, by the way – all I know is, there was a tidy few grand that the Fraud Squad and the Revenue would love to get their hands on. And if I'd been carryin' that lot goin' through Spanish customs, I'd have ended up in deep trouble.'

'Listen, pal...' said Ally, taking a threatening step towards Dennis. From smile to snarl in seconds, the classic psychopath again.

'No, you listen!' Dennis growled, standing his ground. 'You lay a finger on me, and there's six lads who'd do to you what they did to Big Baz and his mates – who don't happen to be over here to do your fightin' for you, *pal!* Not to mention the fact that they could bust you pronto to the Spanish authorities. You want to run the risk of being expelled from this country, Ally?' He looked tauntingly up at the Scotsman. 'Where would you go? The Costa del Parkhurst?'

Ally stayed where he was, his eyes smouldering with impotent rage.

'You couldn't give a rat's what happened to me,' Dennis continued with quiet menace. 'You'd shop your own granny for an advantage. But I've got wise. I've learned to protect myself, Ally – people do, even poor bastards like yours truly who have to graft for a living!'

'Dennis,' Ally said, switching back to a forced smile. 'Of course I didn't realise... Look, we can come to some kind of an arrangement...'

'First you let me off the six grand!' Dennis snapped. 'Plus I get back the deeds to my house. Then the lads get paid every cent owin' to them, guaranteed before they leave Spain. And we get tickets home, in our hands. *Then* you get your loot, Ally. Not before.'

'Be reasonable,' pleaded Ally. And already his mind was working like a computer, thinking out alternatives, ways to outflank fate.

TWENTY-FIVE

Ally Fraser slept badly that night. Even when he did manage to doze off, Dennis Patterson returned to haunt his dreams. There was no golf or tennis in the morning. By noon, the living room of his suite was thick with the fug of cigar smoke. The bottle of scotch on the coffee table was half empty already.

As usual, Kenny Ames was torn between solving Ally's problems and enjoying watching him dancing on the hook.

'I know it must go against the grain, old son,' he said, 'but you have to give your gaffer top marks for initiative.'

'If I ever get back to the UK,' growled Ally, 'I'll mark him for life.'

'He's pretty safe then, by the sound of it,' joked Kenny, puffing on his cigar. But Ally was in no mood for levity. 'All I'm saying,' Kenny went on, 'is that it don't look like you'll be seeing England's green and pleasant land for a while. Don't fret about the twenty-five gees. Look upon it as a blessing in disguise.'

Kenny's altruism was lost upon Ally. 'I find it hard to be that philosophical,' he snarled through gritted teeth.

'Now be fair! It tells you they're on your case. It's only a matter of time before they seize your books, freeze your assets and issue the warrants. I speak as a person with some experience in this area.'

'So what do I do?' For such a tough guy, Ally looked surprisingly vulnerable.

'You need to buy yourself some time, son. Spain may not be the haven you hoped for. Who knows, maybe ultimately you may be wiser to set us up in Costa Rica or the Mongolian People's Republic.'

Ally glared at him. 'Don't come the comedian with me, Kenny,' he snapped.

'Bear with me, son. The Brits will already be in touch with their Spanish amigos. So don't even think of using that route.'

'I have money in Switzerland.'

'That's better! Foresight, planning, the ability to think ahead. That's what separates us from the herd, Ally.'

'I'll have to go myself, though.'

'Then you get yourself to Tangier. I know this bloke with a boat. Don't worry, he's not a tan hand in a nightshirt with a flowerpot on his head. He's from Felixstowe, dead solid.'

'How much?'

'Twenty per cent.' Kenny's voice was deadpan.

Ally Fraser looked horror-stricken.

'Only 'cos you're my mate,' went on Kenny, really rubbing it in. 'And that's all-in. For that you get Bob Blues in Tangier, all overheads and the crew of the *Princess Di*.'

'We can argue about the numbers later,' said Ally gruffly. 'How do we get the ball rolling?'

'I'll need something up front,' said Kenny casually.

'I've got some cash in the safe up at the villa,' Ally told him.

Kenny rose smartly to his feet. 'Well, let's get up there and count it,' he said cheerily.

Ally paused in the act of putting on his jacket. He went through the moves in his mind.

'So I'm on Bob's boat, with me money in a suitcase,' he said at length. 'How do you propose to get me back on Spanish soil undetected?'

'We'll have to think about that one,' said Kenny smoothly, and opened the door.

Back on the site, knocking-off time was approaching. Behind the villa's living-room curtains, Christine, Brenda, Vicki and Hazel were giggling in a conspiratorial way. They had a big jeroboam of champagne and a trayful of glasses.

'All right, lads!' cried Christine, stepping out into the warm sunlight. 'It won't hurt you if you down tools ten minutes early.'

The lads gawped in amazement at the odd procession that trooped out of the house behind her.

'Just open that, Dennis,' said Christine, handing him the bubbly. ''Cos Barry's got an announcement to make.'

Right on cue – for they'd rehearsed this little episode at coffee-break – Barry slipped in alongside Hazel and raised his hands for silence. His voice was a mixture of embarrassment and pleasure.

'I am now able', he intoned like a town-crier, 'to put an end to all speculation concerning Miss Hazel Redfern and myself. Last night, I'm happy to tell you that she agreed to be my wife –'

A loud cheer went up. When Kevin Keegan first stepped out on to the hallowed turf of St James's Park, he could hardly have received a warmer salutation.

'There's more! There's more!' cried an excited Hazel, trying to hush them.

'She's in the club,' murmured Moxey.

'The nuptials will take place next Wednesday,' announced Barry. 'And needless to say, you're all invited.'

'She must be,' Oz concurred. There was no other explanation for such unseemly haste.

Ally and Kenny sidled up. Vicki – quite innocently – had put them in the picture, and now Kenny had a plan.

'Barry and Hazel!' called Dennis, raising his glass.

'Barry and Hazel!' chorused everyone. They clinked glasses – and none more enthusiastically than Kenny Ames and Ally Fraser.

Though the shadows had lengthened a little, everyone was still in festive mood. Apart from Dennis and Christine, who'd gone off to the supermarket, they clustered around the happy couple, making jokes, digging Barry in the ribs, offering advice. After all the vicissitudes of the last few weeks, it seemed as though he and Hazel might make it to the altar after all.

Bomber picked up the almost empty jeroboam of champagne.

'By golly,' he exclaimed. 'We did this quick enough. I

suppose the bride and groom should have the last drop.'

Hazel pushed her glass forward. There was a mischievous glint in her eye.

'You sure you should?' warned Barry. 'You get very silly on champagne.'

'I don't have it very often, Barry.'

'You had too much the first time we were engaged.'

'Here,' cried Moxey, 'How often have you two been engaged?'

'Three times altogether.' They were the Burtons of the building trade.

'Not counting this,' added Barry pedantically. ''Cos this isn't really an engagement. This is an announcement of our wedding.'

'I can't see the point of engagements meself,' said Oz. 'I was home the other week and me cousin Paul says to me "Me and Karen are saving up to get engaged." I said, "What are you talking about? You're either going to get wed or you're not".'

'Oh come on, Oz,' cried Vicki, laughing. 'Girls like that sort of thing.'

''Course they do,' agreed Brenda. 'They like getting the ring and they like showing it to all the other girls at work.'

Predictably Wayne had a less idyllic view. 'It's just a way of tellin' the world that a bloke is out of circulation six months before he walks up the aisle,' he sneered.

'Ee, you're so cynical,' squealed Vicki.

And Moxey agreed with her. 'I think the way Barry and Haze are doing it is great,' he exclaimed. 'Notwithstanding the three previous engagements, it's pretty impetuous, right? Here we are toasting the announcement, and by this time next week it's done.'

Oz picked up the bottle and held it to the light. It was empty.

'I just wish we had something to toast it with,' he said sadly.

As if by magic Dennis, Neville and Christine appeared from the house, laden down with six-packs, big litre bottles of supermarket plonk, and a supply of sandwiches and cocktail snacks.

'Don't panic,' called Dennis. 'The supply train got through.'

There were sighs of relif all round. It was thirsty work, this celebrating.

'Where's Ally?' Vicki asked Neville. The last she'd seen of him, he'd been in deep conflab with Kenny Ames.

'He's inside getting some papers from the safe,' Neville reassured her. 'He'll be out in a minute.'

'He's probably in tears at the thought of us takin' half a day off,' muttered Oz.

'I thought a whole day, meself,' said Barry. 'I don't want to spend the morning of the most important day of me life laying tiles.'

'No,' said Neville miserably. 'That comes later.'

'Neville!' snapped Brenda. Two years on, and he still hadn't started on their bathroom.

Just then Kenny Ames came wandering over.

'Planning a church wedding, are you?' he asked amiably.

'No, no,' said Barry quickly. 'A civil ceremony. You see, neither Haze nor I are great believers. Organised religion's responsible for most of the world's ills, I happen to believe.'

Kenny wasn't the kind to take up the theological gauntlet Barry had thrown down. He smiled blandly.

'Nevertheless,' Hazel chimed in, 'we'd like it to be somewhere picturesque, wouldn't we, Barry? Perhaps a nice little whitewashed restaurant in the hills, set among orange groves.'

'Or bougainvillea,' added Barry.

This was Kenny's cue to introduce the plan he'd dreamed up.

'Here!' he exclaimed. 'I've just had a thought! I have just had a thought.'

Everyone listened intently to what he had to say.

'What about a wedding at sea?' he said, wide eyed.

There was a stunned silence. Then Moxey spoke.

'I thought people got buried at sea,' he joked.

Kenny glared at him. 'People do many things at sea,' he said, trying to smooth things over. 'Including getting married. Now I have this yacht –' he paused for effect – 'and I can't think of anything more romantic than getting spliced on the blue sparkling Mediterranean. What do you say?'

Barry couldn't believe it. 'D'you mean you're offering to loan us your yacht?' he spluttered.

'Only on the condition that I get an invite,' laughed Kenny.

Barry thought about it for a moment.

'But there's the other guests, y'see.' After all, if he couldn't share the day with family, he wanted to have a few friends around.

But Kenny had an easy answer. 'They'll come too,' he announced. 'We'll have the reception afloat. Unless, of course, you've got planeloads of relatives jetting in from the UK.'

'We haven't,' said Hazel, thrilled to bits at the idea. First the Prince, and then this! 'That's the point of having the wedding down here, y'see. To avoid all that.'

Kenny Ames's smile got broader and broader.

'Then the *Sans Souci* is at your disposal!'

Barry was incredulous. 'Oh, I'm very touched, Mr Ames,' he burbled. 'It's very, very kind of you, but we couldn't possibly . . .'

'Yes we could!' said Hazel loudly. 'We accept!'

'Chance of a lifetime, pet,' murmured Vicki.

'I think it's lovely,' breathed Brenda. 'I wish we'd had a wedding like that,' she said to Neville.

'I just hope the weather holds,' said Neville, ever the romantic.

Dennis and the other lads crowded in to give their views.

'You are a good sailor, aren't you, Barry?' asked Dennis, exploring possibilities. Barry had a stomach like a kitten, and with all that booze . . .

'You're a lucky lad,' said Oz. 'Bloody sight more romantic than my wedding. Registry office in January. And I had to borrow twenty-five quid off me best man half an hour before the kick-off to buy a ring at Woolie's.'

'I remember reading about that in the *Tatler*,' Wayne put in.

Ally Fraser came out to join them. 'Let's go, then, Kenny,' he said, impatient to be off.

'Oh, I'm all right, Ally. I think I'll stay here and have a few jars with the lads. One of you can drop me off, can't you?'

There was a chorus of offers.

Ally looked nonplussed. 'Vicki . . .' he snapped.

This wasn't a question. It was a command. Vicki leapt to her feet and gave Hazel a kiss.

'I'm very happy for you both,' she whispered. But her face as she trooped off behind Ally was far from beatific.

Later that evening, Hazel, slightly hung-over, was sitting on the bed talking on the phone.

'Telephonio par Inglese, *por favor* . . . Oh! You speak English! I'd like to place a call to England.'

Barry came in from the bathroom.

'What are you doing?' he asked supsiciously.

'I thought I'd tell me mother,' retorted Hazel.

'You won't!' said Barry firmly.

'She'll be ever so thrilled, Barry,' trilled his intended.

'If you tell her, the whole ruddy family will know in five minutes. And then they'll all be upset.'

He took the phone from her.

'No, no, don't bother now, *muchas gracias,*' he said, and replaced the receiver.

Hazel looked more than a little put out.

'Maybe we should just ask my folks and your mother down,' she ventured.

'No!' Barry was putting his foot down. 'Everyone we don't ask is going to be terribly offended and they'll never forgive us.'

'You're right,' said Hazel, with a sigh. The yacht was a smashing idea, but . . . 'I suppose I feel it's going to be such a special day, I'd like them to share it.'

'They'll see the photos,' said Barry, trying to make up for her disappointment. 'We'll take lots of photos.'

Hazel brightened at this.

'I can't wait to see Valerie Nelson's face!' she exclaimed. 'She was so unbearable about her wedding, just because she had the reception at the Hadleigh Park Hotel. I'll be able to say, 'There's me, and that's Barry, and behind us is the coast of Africa"!'

Perhaps it wasn't such a bad idea after all, she began to think. But Barry had more practical things in mind.

'It'll save your dad a bob or two, not having to pay for a reception.' Then a dark cloud passed over his face. 'Mind you, we'll miss out on the presents. Though that's a very mercenary attitude,' he added, feeling guilty.

'No, you're not wrong, Barry.' The same thought had occurred to her, and she wasn't too happy about it either.

But such things would sort themselves out in the long run, she reasoned. Here we are in Spain, she thought, and it's like a fairytale come true. She was beginning to wonder how quickly she could have the wedding pictures developed when Barry suddenly jumped to his feet.

'Oh, God!' he cried.

Hazel looked at him in considerable alarm.

'Oh God! Oh God!' he went on. 'I've just thought of something. I've just thought of a *real* problem.'

'What is it?'

'Which one of the lads do I ask to be best man?'

As usual, Oz, Bomber, Moxey and Wayne were the last ones in the bar. Carlo, the barman, stood idly polishing glasses, praying that each round would be the last. A country where every public bar had by law to close by eleven seemed the ideal sort of place to make a living. But it was so cold in winter . . . and the food!

'Soon you finish work here?' he asked.

'Next week,' Moxey told him. 'Why?'

'My wife will be very happy,' said Carlo.

'What's your wife got to do with it?'

'Before you come here, I close bar early. Eleven thirty, maybe midnight. Now I go home two, three o'clock. She think I have another woman.'

'Aye, well, we're almost done now,' said Oz resignedly.

'Good!' Carlo muttered under his breath.

'Not here!' cried Oz, catching what he said. 'On the site! Four cervezas, Carlo, and two more fundadors!'

Carlo exhaled noisily, and went to get their drinks. Oz dug around in his pocket and pulled out a crumpled pile of paper. He dumped it on the bar.

'What's all this?' asked Wayne, holding up something. 'You must have a lot of dry-cleaning to collect.'

'Lottery tickets,' said Oz.

'He's been buying these since the first day we got here,' Bomber explained.

'Big prizes,' added Oz.

'In twenty-five years I win nothing,' said Carlo sadly as he brought their drinks.

'And what would you do if you did win?' asked Moxey.

'I buy my own bar and close at eleven.'

'What would you do?' Moxey asked Oz.

'I'd see you all right, Mox.'

'New passport, like?' Moxey liked the idea.

'If I win a small prize, aye. But if I win the jackpot you can have a new face!'

Moxey made to lay one on him. 'Hey! Hey! I've lived with this face a long time, I have,' he whined.

'I'm not denigrating your looks, Mox,' said Oz. 'I just thought that a fugitive from justice could use a new face.'

Moxey thought about it.

'Well, maybe a new nose,' he said finally. 'Sting had his done and I must say it's a definite improvement.'

'I'd have those ears fixed at the same time if I was you,' chipped in Wayne.

'And if I was you,' said Moxey evenly, 'I'd button my lip. Before I alter the shape of *your* nose.'

Bomber leaned towards the barman. 'You'll miss this, Carlo,' he chuckled, 'this dazzling repartee.'

Oz was off in a dream-world of his own. 'I'd buy me mother a bungalow,' he said to no one in particular. 'Somewhere with nee stairs. And then maybe I'd get meself a yacht and I'd race Kenny Ames to Gibraltar and back.'

'What d'you think about Kenny offerin' Barry his yacht and havin' us scruffs aboard?' asked Wayne, picking up what he said.

'He likes us, man,' said Oz, as though it were plain as the nose on his face.

Moxey looked puzzled by this.

'Because he's lonely,' went on Oz. 'All these villains here get like that. They're desperate for conversation. News from home, what's goin' on, how's the weather. They put up this front about livin' in paradise, but they're all fish out of water.'

'I suppose you're right,' pondered Wayne. 'He'd probably pay twenty grand to walk down Peckham 'igh Street and buy an *Evening Standard*.'

'Is this what's going to happen to you, Mox?' asked Bomber. 'When we've gone.' There was a note of concern in his voice.

Moxey didn't have an answer off pat. He thought about it for a while. 'Well . . . probably,' he said at length. 'I'll miss you lot, it's only natural. But I've been on me own since I was about three. Anyhow, I've got this idea. See, I met this bloke down the port.'

'You want to be very careful about blokes you meet down the port,' warned Bomber, and there was a big laugh all round.

The phone rang. Carlo went to answer it.

'No, no,' Moxey was anxious to point out. 'He was a Canadian. And he's been workin' his way round the Med. Crewing on yachts, like. I fancy that. Deck-hand, or steward for some Greek tycoon.'

'I'd still have your nose done first,' Bomber admonished him playfully.

'Señor Osbourne,' called Carlo, holding out the phone. 'Is for you.'

There was puzzlement all round. 'Who's giving you a bell at this time of night?' asked Wayne.

'Probably the lottery people,' murmured Bomber as Oz shuffled unsteadily over to the phone. Moxey resumed his story.

'Hello?' said Oz in the corner. 'Oh, hello, Dick! How are you, son?'

'Are you not alone?' It was Vicki.

'No, but it's all right.'

'I thought you might be there.'

'It's a fair bet. What's the matter?'

'I just wanted to talk. I feel a bit down, y'know. Been on me own all evening.'

'Where's Ally?'

'I just wish I knew where I was. Wish I could see you.'

'Aye, well, that would be a bit dicey.'

'He's going out tomorrow night. So maybe we could go somewhere.'

'Aye, well, we might be grafting late tomorrow. Y'know, to make up time for Barry's wedding.'

There was a brief silence. Then Vicki came back on the line.

'He's back,' she said hurriedly. 'I'll have to go. Tara!'

Vicki had just replaced the receiver when Ally came into the room. His face was flushed with the strain of a long, hard evening. He'd tucked quite a few Scotches under his belt.

'Oh!' she exclaimed, a bit flustered. 'I was just calling La Masia to see if you were still there.'

'I never went there,' growled Ally.

'That's what they said,' agreed Vicki, thanking her lucky stars her little white lie had been the right one. 'Where have you been then?' she asked trying to sound natural.

'Business.'

'You could have said, instead of leaving me on me own all night. I could have stayed up at the villa with the others.'

'The others? What d'you want to spend your evening with that bunch of no-hopers for? You think a bricklayer's going to take you to the Marbella Club?'

'I was thinking of the couples. I mean Dennis is very –'

'Him especially,' snapped Ally. 'I don't want you talking to him, I don't even want you mentioning his name.'

'But he's your man, Ally!'

'Not any more. Let me tell you, when the moment is right, Patterson has got it coming to him. But don't go shooting your mouth off about this to that Christine.'

'I wouldn't.'

'Oh, wouldn't you? So it wasn't you that told her I might be staying down here permanently?'

Vicki looked abashed. 'No! . . . well, I may have mentioned something casually in conversation.'

'Don't,' snarled Ally, the veins bulging on his forehead. There was an angry silence between them.

'Well, are you?' Vicki asked eventually.

'That's my concern.'

'Don't you think it's my concern as well?' she pouted. 'If you're deciding to live in Spain, don't you think I have the right to voice an opinion?'

Ally rolled his eyes towards heaven.

'Vicki, the only time I've ever heard you voice an opinion is in a boutique, between this dress or that one.'

'You can't ask me never to go home again,' she wailed. 'Never see me family and me friends . . .'

'Oh, of course!' cried Ally, heavy on the irony. 'I'm being selfish. I realise that all this isn't good enough for you. Christ, you must ache for the scenic splendour of that council estate in South Shields.'

Vicki burst into tears.

'How you must miss queuing in the supermarket for your baked beans and Bounty Bars,' he went on mercilessly. 'And those exotic Friday nights down the club with all the other scrubbers.'

'You're a bastard, Ally,' she sobbed. 'I'd rather go back there than take this.'

She stormed off towards the bedroom, but Ally grabbed her arm.

'*You* don't leave *me*,' he grated, thrusting his face right up close so she could smell the whisky on his breath. 'When you go, it's because I kick your arse out of here!'

She punched him. It was a hopeless gesture. Ally Fraser, veteran of many a tough street brawl in his youth, gave her a stinging backhander across the face.

TWENTY-SIX

The sun was well up in the sky, and Dennis was singing lustily in the shower.

'I've never heard that before,' said Neville as Brenda made coffee.

'What?'

'Dennis singing in the shower.'

'He's ever so cheerful, I've noticed that.'

'It's very worrying,' Neville fretted.

'Why, for heaven's sake?'

'What I mean is, I'm not just used to it.'

'I think it's Chris,' said Brenda in a whisper.

But Neville would have none of it. 'Aw, women always think it's women that cheer men up,' he declared. 'I think it's more than that.'

Brenda, a little miffed at having her bubble pricked, asked him what his theory was.

'I don't know,' he admitted. 'Maybe it's going home. Maybe it's because he's got another job lined up.'

'Say what you like. They seem very well suited. And she's a very nice girl.'

'I'm not saying she isn't.'

'You certainly got out of bed the wrong side this morning.'

'I'm sorry. I suppose it's the situation, livin' in such proximity with another couple.'

But Brenda tried to look on the bright side. 'We haven't had to pay for a hotel, have we?' she pointed out.

'I know,' Neville conceded. 'But it's a bit restricting in other areas.'

Brenda gave him a contemptuous look. 'You're so old fashioned in some ways, Neville,' she said. 'I know they're in he next room but you don't have to run both taps every time we make love.'

Dennis came in, a towel around his waist, his hair slicked down over his head.

'Can you believe it? There's no hot water again!' he moaned.

Soon the lads were hard at work. They sensed that special kind of job's-end urgency, the little fillip that you got when the finish came in sight.

'Could I interrupt the proceedings for a minute?' Barry asked, waving his arms in the air.

Dennis didn't pause from his labours. 'We've a lot to do, Barry,' he said tersely.

'It won't take a minute,' Barry persisted. 'And it's something I'd like to get settled.'

Reluctantly they downed tools and walked over to where Barry was standing.

'Y'see, I didn't sleep much last night,' he announced. 'I agonised.'

The boys looked at him askance.

'It's not off again, is it?' Oz asked impatiently. 'I've already rung Mercedes and they're delivering your present next Tuesday.'

'No, no, no, no,' stammered Barry. 'It is to do with the wedding, mind.'

'I thought it might be,' said Bomber in an undertone.

'I have to choose the best man,' Barry announced. 'From one of you, like. And the thing is, I'm very unhappy about not upsetting the unlucky five.'

Puzzled glances were exchanged. What on earth was he on about?

'Y'see, I've been very close to all of you collectively, and each of you individually,' he ploughed on. 'I thought of you first, Oz.'

'Me?'

'Think about it. When you've spent a few wet Sunday nights in Port Stanley, that does forge a bond, doesn't it?'

Oz was a bit taken aback by all this bondage stuff.

'Hey, let's put the record straight,' he protested. 'When he says we formed a bond it never went further than a few beers and a game of darts.'

But Barry wouldn't be put off. 'Nevertheless you are a contender,' he told Oz.

Now it was the turn of Dennis and Bomber.

'It's hard to separate you in my mind,' Barry's speech went on, 'because you have such similar virtues. Anchors, men of substance. Best man material if ever I saw it. And much the same could be said for you, Neville. In all the time we've known each other I can't recall us ever exchanging a cross word.'

'Bollocks!' snorted Neville.

Barry laughed. 'And your ready wit is one of the things I admire about you.'

'His ready what?' Moxey wasn't sure he was hearing right.

'And Moxey!' the chairman of selectors continued. 'I have to tell you that as of this morning Ladbrokes had you down as a 33 to 1 outsider.'

This was kid's stuff to Moxey. 'I've backed longer shots than that,' he called.

'Yet, I said to meself, in the early days in Germany, it was Mox and me who were the outsiders. We weren't in the Geordie Mafia, and it took a little while before we won the respect and affection of the others.'

Wayne couldn't take much more. 'Is this like Miss World?' he asked. 'You eliminate the runners-up before giving me the sash?'

'Wayne,' Barry intoned, his eyes half closed, 'you and I ... poles apart in so many ways. But no one ever offered me more advice than you. Not always taken. Not always wanted ...'

Oz looked at his watch. 'Be overtime tonight, Dennis,' he observed drily.

'Howway Barry,' called Dennis. 'The suspense is killing us.'

'Very well, then,' said Barry. 'I'll come to the point. I couldn't decide.'

There was a general groan. Someone threw a lump of earth at him.

'So what I thought was,' he said with his back turned, 'the

fairest way would be to draw straws.'

He turned round and held out his fist.

'The short one wins.'

Six hands reached tentatively out. But they would have to stay on tenterhooks for a while, for at that moment Ally Fraser turned up, looking hostile.

'Union meeting, is it?' he grimaced.

Barry hastily stuffed the straws into his pocket, and got back to work. What a shame! He was as excited as the rest of them to learn who the lucky one would be.

Ally Fraser was sitting behind a desk in the living room of the villa. In front of him was a big pile of paperwork. Dennis was standing behind him.

'I've been sorting out the invoices,' Dennis was saying. 'You'll have to settle with the local trade before the job's finished.'

'It will be finished, will it?' asked Ally sourly.

'What do you mean?' queried Dennis. As he was fond of saying, he'd never walked away from an unfinished job in his life.

'In the light of our current relationship, it wouldn't have surprised me if you'd told them not to bother. You do have me over the proverbial barrel, don't you?'

Dennis wasn't one to gloat. 'Look,' he announced, 'the lads came here to do a job. The situation between you and me's got nothing to do with it.'

Christine came in, having caught the tail-end of the conversation.

'I'm sorry to interrupt,' she said, 'I just wanted to ask something.'

'What's that, Chris?' asked Dennis.

She turned towards Ally, a puzzled expression on her face. 'Vicki was going to take Brenda and me to this ceramics place to buy a present,' she explained. 'But we can't get through to her.'

'Oh, maybe she's taken the phone off the hook,' Ally said smoothly. 'She wasn't feeling too good. I wouldn't count on seeing her today.'

Chris murmured her apologies and left.

Ally turned back towards Dennis, shaking his head. 'I can't see you making any deadlines with this bloody wedding coming up,' he said.

'Look, if we take Wednesday off, we'll make it up on Sunday. It might surprise you to learn that my lads take great pride in their work. Your job will be done on time and under budget. I guarantee it.'

Some time later, Kenny and Ally were on the yacht in the marina. It was blisteringly hot. Kenny had just gone down into the cabin for more champagne. Ally was looking worried.

'You must admit the wedding's a godsend,' Kenny said when he came back.

Ally still looked glum. 'Aye, but there's still a lot of imponderables,' he said quietly. 'The timings have got to be exactly right. I hate making crucial arrangements which involve seven hod-carrying lunatics.'

Kenny shrugged, and smiled. 'Don't worry,' he soothed. 'They'll be blissfully ignorant.'

Ignorant they certainly are, thought Ally. 'But I'm still concerned about the timing,' he maintained.

'I mean, how far will this boat be off-shore?'

'My man Bob Blues will be down tomorrow. He'll dot all the i's for you. A week from now your fiscal problems will all be over, son.'

But Ally still wasn't convinced, so Kenny poured him a glass of bubbly.

'To the happy couple,' said Ally grimly.

That evening Dennis and Christine were enjoying an intimate dinner in a little restaurant down by the port. A bottle of the local red stood on the table. The waiter had just moved off with their order.

'What time is it?' asked Dennis.

'I don't know,' Christine said automatically, and then wondered. Why would Dennis book a table for nine and then ask her the time?

'It always amazes me,' went on Dennis, 'that a girl like you, managerial class, runs a hotel, height of efficiency ... but doesn't wear a watch.'

Christine laughed. 'I've got three!' she protested. 'They just don't tell the time.'

'Aye, well, I got you this.' He passed a long, slim case across the table. 'Open it,' he motioned.

Inside was a sleek, expensive wristwatch. Christine was thrilled.

'Oh Dennis! It's lovely!' she cried, obviously touched. 'But you shouldn't have . . .'

'Well, I have.'

She leaned forward and kissed him. 'Thank you,' she breathed.

Dennis felt some explanation was called for. 'Well, this has been a strange holiday for you,' he began, 'what with me working and staying in a villa with seven brickies and no pool.'

'I've had a great time,' said Christine as she strapped on the watch.

'You've had to fend for yourself a lot.'

'Used to that.'

'Anyhow I'm glad you came and ... Well, you've no excuse for missing your plane tomorrow!' He said this rather sadly, knowing their time together would soon be over.

'I'm not going,' said Christine quietly.

'What?' gasped Dennis. He couldn't believe his ears.

'I rang the hotel, and they weren't panicked, and I thought it would be awful to miss the wedding, having got to know everyone.'

'Oh.' Dennis didn't sound too sure of himself.

Christine looked at him for a moment. 'You don't seem very pleased,' she said with disappointment in her voice.

'I'm just surprised.'

'Dennis, I know you, your face is an open book. And you don't seem very pleased.'

'It's just that things are heating up here the next few days and I'm more tied up than ever.'

'Come on, Dennis,' scoffed Christine. 'I'm aware of things.

I'm aware there's no love lost between you and Ally.'

'Never has been,' said Dennis out of the corner of his mouth.

'No, but now it's worse. I saw the way he was looking at you yesterday. As if he'd like to murder you.'

'Oh, he could,' said Dennis evenly. It was a prospect he'd considered more than once. 'But he won't.'

'You're not going to tell me, are you?'

'Not yet.' He put his hand on hers, and smiled. 'Look, don't worry, I'm fine. For the first time in years I've got my nose in front.'

She smiled too, and glanced at the classy new watch on her wrist.

Dennis caught her eye. 'What are you looking at your watch for?' he asked jokingly. 'You haven't got a plane to catch, have you?'

Now he knew he had the courage to see this one out right to the end.

Not many yards away, unbeknown to Dennis and Christine, another couple were sitting in the corner of a bar. But the mood around Hazel and Barry's table was very different. Hazel was dabbing at her eyes with a tissue, while Barry looked anguished and uncomfortable.

'I can't help it, Barry,' she sobbed. 'I'm devastated.'

'I know you are,' said a grieving Barry. 'But we must face reality. And in your heart of hearts you know I'm right.'

'I suppose so,' Hazel managed to splutter.

'In the morning you must ring Mr Ames, and tell him how much we appreciate his offer. And just explain it can't be . . .'

Hazel's reply was lost amid a flurry of choking sobs.

By the start of the following day's work, the doomy mood had spread. The lads were gathered disconsolately around Barry, Christine and Brenda among them. It was like the scene outside the gates after a factory closure.

'How's Hazel taken this?' Brenda asked Barry.

'Not very well. Distraught, in a word.'

'She was so excited,' Brenda recalled.

'We both were. But in the end she agreed with me.'

'We'd better phone her,' Christine whispered to Brenda.

Oz scuffed around in the dust with his boots. 'So it's off, then?' he shrugged. 'It's a good job we didn't get a present.'

'I just realised we were being very, very selfish,' Barry was saying. 'Y'see, weddings aren't for the bride and groom. They're for the relatives and friends. They're for old aunts and grannies who need days like that. I couldn't deprive them of it. Take my Auntie Lillian. This'll probably be the last time she leaves the house.'

'So instead of the Med, you've settled for Wolverhampton,' Moxey summed it up.

But it wasn't all bad news for Barry. 'It'll be at the Hadleigh Park Hotel,' he pointed out. 'It's in its own grounds, with a lake and swans, and it's not cheap, let me tell you!'

'When will it be?' enquired Dennis.

'That depends on the Hadleigh Park, doesn't it? They're in great demand. It'll be the first Saturday that their Jacobean Suite's available.'

'We're all still asked, aren't we?' Neville wanted to know. He'd bought a shirt for the occasion, and didn't want such an extravagance to go to waste.

'Of course you are,' cried Barry with an expansive gesture. 'You're my best friends in all the world!'

'So we've still got to settle the best man issue, right?' Wayne realised after a moment.

'That's true,' agreed Bomber. Now he'd had time to think about it, he quite fancied the idea. 'It doesn't matter what the venue is,' he said magnanimously.

'Oh no!' Barry quickly knocked that one on the head. 'If it's back home, I'll have to ask my cousin Martin. If I don't he'll be terribly offended.'

Which is exactly how Barry's six best friends in all the world felt.

Whatever the S.P. might have been on Bob Blue, he was far from your average villain in appearance. He looked like a retired solicitor's clerk, and spoke in a little mousy voice that was barely audible.

'More coffee?' Ally said.

'Yes please,' said Bob, whispering into his lap.

'Shall we what?' asked Ally, not catching what he said. On TV, old men were supposed to be funny, but Ally didn't see anything very amusing in this. He'd found very little to laugh at in the past few days.

'He says shall we run over the timetable one last time,' Kenny filled him in.

'Oh, for God's sake!' snapped Ally. 'I'm going to Zurich Wednesday. I pick up my money first thing the following day.'

'You then fly to Rome,' said Whispering Bob. 'And your connecting flight to Tangier arrives at ten to eight. I shall meet you there. And if you want dinner or a glimpse of the night spots, I'll be happy to oblige.'

'I'll not be in no mood for belly dancers,' Ally growled.

'Please yourself. Saturday's free – I've left one day clear for unexpected contingencies. Then if the wedding's at three we should cast off about ten – not too early for you? – and rendezvous with the *Sans Souci* about three fifteen. D'you have a lavatory?'

'What? On the boat?' asked Kenny. Why should he want to know that?

'No, here,' said Bob. 'I need to pee.'

'Through that door,' said Ally. He waited for the door to close before tackling Kenny.

'Is he OK?' he hissed.

Kenny made a dismissive gesture. 'Of course! I told you, top rank. For thirty-five years he worked in a merchant bank.'

This didn't do much to calm Ally's fears.

'His only ambition', went on Kenny, 'was to retire somewhere with his own boat and a massive income. So he kept his nose clean, took a lot of abuse and acquainted himself with all the company's financial transactions and how to plug in the computer. Three years ago he took a one-way ticket to Tangier, having first transferred a million and a half quid to his account there.'

A phone rang. 'Get that, will you?' Ally called into the bedroom. Then he levelled with Kenny Ames again.

'I grant you he's not flash,' he conceded, 'but neither does he look too nautical.'

'Oh, believe me!' insisted Kenny. 'Once he gets on that boat he's Long John Silver.'

Vicki came in from the bedroom. She was wearing dark glasses and a bathrobe. She trod very warily.

'Sorry to interrupt,' she said. 'It's Hazel. She wants to speak to Kenny.'

'Who the devil's Hazel?' thundered Ally.

'Barry's fiancée.'

'For God's sake, we're in conference here!'

'It's about the wedding.'

Kenny flashed Ally an anxious glance, and picked up the extension phone.

'Hazel,' he said in a playful voice that must have cost him a lot of willpower. 'Are you having second thoughts? Are you saying there's still hope for me?'

He listened intently for a moment. Then his jaw dropped.

'Off? What do you mean off?' All the bantering tone had vanished along with his smile.

Ally looked at him aghast. Now what the hell would they do?

They must have done some quick thinking, because not half an hour later Ally was sitting at a table outside a bar overlooking the port and Barry – still in his begrimed work clothes – was parked opposite him.

Barry couldn't understand why a chauffeur-driven car should have arrived at the site and whisked him off to meet Ally. Still less could he grasp the meaning behind Ally's big beaming smile as he pulled a bottle of white wine from an ice bucket.

'I love the port at this time of day,' reflected Ally as he poured the wine. 'I love that light, and the sound of the breeze in the rigging and the shadow of the masts in the water.'

Barry was acutely conscious of the sweat stains under his arms, of the dirty work boots that contrasted with Ally's white Gucci loafers. 'Yes, yes, it's lovely!' he stammered. 'Very picturesque, only I wish I'd had time to put clean jeans on.'

There was a pause. Then Ally leaned forward.

'You know, Barry,' he said warm-heartedly, 'I owe you a lot.'

'Do you?' asked Barry, mystified.

'Oh yes,' went on Ally. 'You're the person who brought all the lads together. And if that hadn't happened they wouldn't be doing this job down here for me now, would they?'

There was a certain logic in what he said. Barry nodded.

'You and me are the employers – the managerial class, so to speak. That's what separates us from the others. Not that I'm disparaging the lads in any way.'

'No, no,' Barry hastily concurred. 'But running your own business does have different burdens.'

'Exactly,' beamed Ally. There was about as much similarity between his operation and Barry's 'All kinds of Work Undertaken' as there was between the Grand Canyon and a drainage ditch. He offered Barry his cigar case.

'Ta very much,' said Barry. He didn't smoke, but he figured it was the right thing to do. 'I'll smoke it later, if you don't mind,' he said politely, and tucked the cigar into his top pocket.

Ally made a big show of lighting his own cigar.

'The reason I persuaded Kenny to offer his yacht to you . . .' he puffed – but Barry looked surprised. 'I didn't want any fuss, Barry,' he said dismissively; and continued, 'It was because I knew how much that would have meant to me at your age. And I see a lot of me in you. Yet now I hear you've changed your mind.'

A slightly sinister look came into his eyes.

'It was a very agonising decision,' blustered Barry.

'Oh, I know why you made it,' said Ally through a cloud of smoke. 'And I respect you for it. It's the old working-class guilt. The ties that bind.'

'In a way . . .' said Barry, not sure what was coming.

Ally made a big gesture with his cigar. 'Barry, son,' he said confidentially. 'People like you and me have risen above that struggle against the odds. And we shouldn't be ashamed of it. You canna' let your roots shackle you for the rest of your life. You have to look forward. Your only allegiance now is that you love Hazel. And in my humble opinion, your duty is to give her a day she'll remember for the rest of her life.'

Barry looked lost. He thought he'd thrashed it out with Hazel. He'd been pretty certain that they'd made the right decision in scrubbing the shipboard wedding. And now the whole thing was wide open once more...

By nightfall, though, he and Hazel had made up their minds – or rather, the seed that Ally Fraser had planted had germinated. They were drinking in a hotel bar with Oz, Bomber and Moxey. Hazel looked radiant. Barry was puffing away uncertainly on his cigar. How do you keep these things alight? he wondered as he struck yet another match. He was beginning to feel slightly queasy.

'If the wedding's on again, fine,' said Oz. 'But don't start telling us that Ally Fraser is a prince among men.'

Barry had been pursuing this line of reasoning ever since he'd rounded the lads up and herded them down to the bar to celebrate. 'It was the first time I'd ever really sat down and had a talk with the man,' he was saying. 'I'd always accepted you lot's opinion that he was some sort of monster. But you speak as you find and he seemed to me to be perfectly charming and very civilised.'

'I'm just thrilled he persuaded Barry, 'cos I'm over the moon,' chipped in Hazel.

'When we get back,' said Barry, 'we'll have a little party for family and friends.'

'Why?' asked Moxey, not really listening.

'It just seems the best of both worlds,' Hazel explained.

'No, I didn't mean that. I meant why would Fraser take all this trouble over you two?'

Barry was deeply offended by this. 'Oh thanks very much,' he said, looking pained. 'That's charming!' After all, he and Ally Fraser, being men of business, had a special relationship that none of the others could share.

Moxey apologised. 'But it does seem a bit queer,' murmured Bomber.

The conversation turned towards who would pay for the food and drink – especially the latter. But Barry and Hazel were indignant at the notion of Ally Fraser picking up the tab.

'It's coming out of my pocket, that is,' said Barry, his chest swelling with indignant pride.

'Of course if you took the boat out far enough,' said Moxey, 'all the drink'd be duty-free.'

Oz scoffed at the notion. 'Don't be a dickhead, Mox,' he exclaimed. 'You still have to buy it at the off-licence first.'

'The odds on you being best man have lengthened even further,' added Bomber.

Which reminded Barry ... 'First thing in the morning,' he announced, 'we'll pull those straws.'

'Count me out,' said Oz.

'Me too,' said Bomber.

'Yeah, I'm not keen,' Moxey added.

The three dissenters finished their drinks and stood up. Barry was a bit hurt by this.

'What's up with you lot?' he demanded to know.

'Fly your cousin Martin down,' said Oz huffily, and walked out. The others followed. It was all a puzzle to Barry.

'No matter how hard you try, Haze,' he reflected, 'you always end up offending somebody.'

He looked gloomily at his drink. So half the field in the best-man stakes had scratched even before the off. He sighed. His cigar had gone out again.

TWENTY-SEVEN

Ally's car was parked outside the club. The boot was open, and his driver was busy stowing away a pile of suitcases. Up in his suite, Ally was going through his briefcase, checking that he had everything.

'When will you be back?' asked Vicki. She was still wearing the dark glasses to cover the bruises Ally had given her.

'I'm not certain,' grunted Ally.

'I don't even know where you're going.'

'Don't need to know, do you?'

'So what about me?' asked Vicki, bravely sticking her neck out. 'Am I allowed to talk to people? Am I allowed to see the girls?'

Ally could live without this third-degree. 'Look, Vicki, it's a free country,' he told her. 'Do what you want. Mind you, if you took it into your head to hop on a plane to Newcastle, you wouldn't be able to do that.'

'Why not?' asked Vicki sulkily.

'Because I've got your passport,' he said, flourishing the vital document. He snapped his case shut and strode briskly out of the door.

Soon the car swept up to the villa. As the driver got out to open the door for Ally, Oz drove by in the minibus, leaving a cloud of dust in the air.

Once the lads would have jumped to attention and saluted when Ally put in an appearance. Nowadays he only merited a surly grunt by way of acknowledgment – except for Barry, who greeted him with a sunshine smile.

'Morning, Mr Fraser,' he beamed.

Ally nodded curtly, gazing at the almost completed pool.

313

To give them their due, they'd done a good job. There could be no grounds for complaint here.

'How'd you like it then?' asked Barry, rubbing his hands expectantly.

'Very nice. Very nice indeed. Job well done.'

Barry looked like the cat that got the cream. But Ally Fraser had other things on his mind.

'Dennis!' he called.

The gaffer looked up. Ally nodded towards the house.

'Your mate's gratitude is overwhelming,' Wayne murmured to Barry as the two of them disappeared indoors.

Ally Fraser was wasting no time. He opened his briefcase and took out his cheque book.

'I'm going away for a few days,' he explained, 'so I'm leaving you a few signed cheques for those outstanding bills you mentioned.'

'You still trust me then?' said Dennis, half-mockingly.

'I'd like to use your nuts for golf-balls, Dennis,' grated Ally. 'But yes, I do trust you.'

'There'll be no crap lying around when you get back,' Dennis promised. 'We'll clean up the entire area.'

'You're nothing if not thorough,' Ally retorted with heavy irony. 'Now what about the lads' recompense?'

'I'll take care of that.'

'Oh?' There was a note of menace in his voice.

'That money of yours I'm holding,' said Dennis casually. 'I'll pay them out of that – salary, overtime and bonuses as agreed. I'll post you an itemised statement accounting for every penny.'

Ally gave Dennis a cold, hard stare. 'And the balance, pal? The balance of *my* money?' he hissed.

'Where would you like it?'

'It's that simple, is it?'

'Aye. I've got it, you want it. I await your instructions. But I'll be keeping back three grand...'

Ally nodded. 'So that's your wee bonus, is it?'

'No, it's the approximate cost of six air tickets back here. Plus bed and board.'

Ally's face flinched slightly. 'I don't follow you,' he said.

'Well, just supposin' I'm leaving the pub one dark night and

two of your boneheads take me round the back. Or supposin'
someone throws a brick through me ex-wife's window. Or
puts frighteners on me kids or me girlfriend. I'd need that
cash, wouldn't I . . .'

Ally was none the wiser.

'. . . . so's me and the lads could come back here. Take apart
everything we've built for you. And afterwards take *you*
apart.'

Ally nodded. There was a tense, uneasy silence between
them. Finally Ally spoke.

'A man like you could have had a job with me for life,
y'know,' he said quietly.

Oz pounded on the open door. 'Vicki?' he called, peering
round into the empty suite. He didn't want to go charging in
on one of Ally Fraser's goons.

'Oz?' came a voice from the bathroom.

'Aye well, I was in town pickin' up some tiles and I knew he
was out of the way,' said Oz as he stepped into the room.

'I'll be through in a minute,' called Vicki.

'I've phoned you a couple of times, but Ally picked it up so
I rang off. But you've never phoned me. I heard you were
sick.'

Vicky came in, holding the robe against her. She was still
wearing the sunglasses.

'It's good to see you, Oz,' she murmured, her voice thick
and full of relief.

'I can hardly see you in those glasses – you look like Greta
Garbo. Den says Ally's away for a few days so we can have a
meal, right?'

Tears welled in her eyes. 'I don't know where I am, Oz,' she
murmured. 'Or what I should do.'

'What's been happening?' said Oz, concerned. With
surprising delicacy for such a big man, he reached up and
took off her glasses.

'Bloody hell!' he exclaimed. 'Did he do that?'

'Yeah,' she sniffed damply. 'And this.'

She pulled down her robe to reveal a nasty purple bruise on
her shoulder.

'Right,' said Oz evenly. 'I'll kill him.'

315

The minibus screeched to a halt in a shower of flying stones. Oz leaped out and ran towards the villa, not bothering to slam the door.

'Where is the bastard?' he cried. The lads looked up in surprise.

'Who?' asked Neville.

Oz pointed at Barry. 'His mate, Ally,' he said tersely.

'He's not my mate. I simply said –' Barry began to say, but Wayne cut him short. He could tell Oz didn't want a lecture.

'He's not here, Oz,' said the cockney.

Oz stormed off into the house and confronted Dennis, busy as usual with his paperwork.

'Where's Ally?' he demanded.

'Gone. Why?' asked Dennis. He'd never seen Oz so angry.

'Look, Den, I don't give a toss about who he is or what his reputation is. I'm going to nail the bastard to the floor, right?'

'What's all this about?'

'He's rich, he's got muscle and he's got gadgies like us kow-towing to him. But that doesn't give him the right to do what he did.'

'What did he do?' Whatever it was, Ally would get far worse in retaliation if Oz got his hands on him.

'He whacked Vicki about, that's what he did.' Oz was breathing heavily from the exertion of keeping himself under control.

'How do you know?'

'I've just been there.'

'You were supposed to be pickin' up tiles.'

'Never mind bloody tiles, Dennis,' raged Oz. 'That sod's been using Vicki as a punch-bag.'

Neville poked his head into the room. 'What's going on?' he asked. Dennis hurriedly told him to close the door.

'One thing I can't stand,' Oz fulminated, 'is blokes who duff women up. Especially someone I care about.'

'Who's this?' said Neville as he came into the room. Dennis looked equally taken aback.

'Vicki!' breathed Dennis. Talk about playing with fire!

'Since when?' Neville demanded. 'Did you know about this, Dennis?'

'First I've heard.' He couldn't get over it. He'd no idea!

'Look, I didn't broadcast it, all right,' Oz was careful to point out. 'I've got some sense of discretion.'

'First *I've* heard,' Neville said uncharitably.

'Anyhow, that's my business,' said Oz, keen to be off. 'Just tell me where Ally is.'

'He's gone,' said Dennis. 'He'll be at the airport by now.'

In the room next door Neville could hear Debbie start to cry.

'Right!' said Oz. 'I'll get him there.'

He moved off, but Dennis grabbed him. Before he could speak, Brenda came in.

'What's going on?' she demanded to know. 'Keep your voices down!' She started when she saw the scene in front of her.

'Can you just leave us a minute, eh, Brenda?' Dennis was quick to say. She complied.

'You're not going to stop us,' warned Oz as he struggled to be free.

But Dennis wouldn't let him go. 'By the time you get to the airport,' he reasoned, 'he'll be well away. Just calm down, okay?'

'He'll be coming back though?' said Oz as he quit bullocking about.

'I wouldn't bank on it.'

Neville's thoughts immediately flew to the money that was due to him. 'Where does that leave us?' he wanted to know.

'Well taken care of,' was Dennis's enigmatic reply. But Oz wouldn't believe him.

'Ally's going to get it,' he insisted.

'He's already had it,' Dennis was quick to point out. 'I've hurt him more than you and your Doc Marten's ever could.'

'How?' asked Oz, baffled by all this.

Dennis sighed, and began to tell the story.

'Right, this is between us three, OK? It goes no further,' he said. After he'd got their tacit agreement he went on. 'When I went home for him last week it was supposedly to get some contracts. But that was just a pretext. Harbottle gave me a bag to bring back. But I had me doubts, so I opened it.'

Neville asked the obvious question.

'Cash,' replied Dennis. 'He was trying to smuggle readies down here so he used me as his mule.'

'Pretty risky,' murmured Neville.

'Oh, it was. I got turned over at the airport.'

'So where's the cash?' asked Oz, looking worried.

'Back in Newcastle in a safe place. So don't worry about your wages, Neville. I've got Ally where it hurts.'

They gasped and slapped him on the back. What a brilliant stroke to pull! Dennis had got Ally by the short and curlies, all right.

'Me arse is covered too,' said Dennis, looking pleased as Punch. 'So whatever you're feeling, Oz, just put the cap on it, right?'

'Right,' agreed Oz.

'So let's get back to work, then,' urged Dennis.

Neville and Oz walked slowly back towards the pool. Neville coughed, and paused to look behind them.

'So how long's this thing with Vicki been going on?' he whispered innocently.

Late in the afternoon, a large group was standing by the pool. Everyone was smartly dressed. A fair number of empty bottles and cans was scattered about.

Dolled up in her best Princess Di outfit, Brenda was kneeling down with a trowel, laying the ceremonial last tile. She scraped off the cement and everyone cheered.

She stepped back, admiring her handiwork.

'Did I do it right?' she asked Neville.

'It hasn't fallen out yet, pet,' he said.

Then it was Dennis's turn.

'My lords, ladies and gentlemen, fellow brickies ...'

There was a loud chorus of jeers.

'...we are here at the completion of another shining example of British workmanship. I'm sure if our gracious benefactor Mr Fraser was here ...'

More jeers.

318

'. . . he would want us to celebrate the occasion in a suitable manner.'

He carefully put down his can – after all, he didn't want to waste it – and then, holding his nose, plunged fully clothed into the pool. A mighty cheer went up, and then everyone followed suit.

The celebrations went on well into the night. Midnight was approaching when the lads squeezed themselves into a tight bunch for Carlo to take a picture with Barry's camera. A couple of flashes went off and the group broke up.

'We won't be late tonight, Carlo,' said Barry as he put his camera back into its case. 'It's the big day tomorrow.'

'Tonight you drink till dawn. Is no difference for me.'

This was a turn-up for the books.

'You've straightened out the old lady, then?' asked Bomber.

'No,' said Carlo miserably. 'The old lady, she leave me.'

'Hey, well,' Oz broke in, 'I hope you're not putting that down to us, pal.'

'What's this?' said Dennis, coming back from the Gents.

'Carlo's wife left him,' said Oz. 'On the eve of Barry's wedding,' he added ominously.

'Bad sign, Barry,' murmured Wayne.

'Oh, don't be silly! I might have expected that from you.'

'We marry eleven years. My heart it hurt, y'know,' Carlo was saying. But Moxey reckoned he was putting a damper on things.

'Keep it to yourself till tomorrow,' he advised.

They went back to boozing and talking among themselves. They'd certainly help Barry see out his bachelordom in style.

Then Barry banged the table.

'Can I just say something?' he called over the hubbub.

A loud groan went up.

'. . . I suppose you think I'm sentimental, and I suppose I am really, but I always find it very special when the seven of us are together. And the fact that you're all together for my wedding means a lot to me . . . an awful lot.'

There was scarcely a dry eye in the place.

'Shouldn't you save your speech for tomorrow?' asked Neville.

'I've got one for tomorrow, all written,' called Barry to another chorus of groans. 'No, I wanted you to know that the best man situation has been resolved.'

'Who's the lucky feller?' asked Wayne, very off-hand.

Barry was a bit miffed. 'If you'd rather be down the port looking for tarts don't let me stop you,' he sniffed.

'It was only a joke,' Wayne protested.

'Well, I never know whether you're joking or not,' Barry said irritably. 'This is a moment of joy and celebration and I'd really rather like you to treasure it.'

He looked angrily around the group. Dennis told him to calm down.

'He's under a lot of strain,' Moxey whispered to Carlo.

Bomber yawned and looked at his watch. Barry fixed him with a glare.

'Am I keeping you from something?' he snapped.

Bomber protested his innocence, but Barry wanted to argue the point. Suddenly Oz grabbed him by the tie.

'We'd all like to treasure this moment,' he snarled with his eyes about an inch away from Barry's, 'but we don't want to do it for the next six hours. So who is it?'

'Well . . .' said Barry, smoothing his tie. It was the only one he had with him, since he hadn't expected to get married when he did his packing. '. . . It's all of you.'

A surprised murmur went up. Just like that Agatha Christie film, eh? Pretty smart thinking, for Barry.

'There's no rule says you have to have just one best man,' he was saying, 'so I'm having six of them.'

Carlo, lost in his own sadness, gave a little sob. Barry gave a start. Of course! He'd forgotten to include Carlo, and now he'd upset him.

'Look, I'm sorry if you're offended, Carlo,' he blustered, 'but let's face it, we hardly know each other.'

Carlo, mystified, raised a tearful face.

Just then a woman in her late thirties put her head around the door. She saw Bomber and waved.

'Right with you, m'dear,' he called.

They looked at him, curious. 'See you in church, lads,' he said and scurried off.

'Who's that, then?' asked Wayne. Bomber certainly was a dark horse, all right.

'I think she works in the cloakroom down the casino,' said Moxey.

'He must have put a few bob in her saucer,' observed Neville drily.

'Why don't we go down there?' suggested Wayne, seizing the initiative. 'We'll have a flutter, see what's about.'

'Not me,' said Barry, declining the offer. 'I'm taking a big enough gamble as it is.' He giggled inanely. No one else laughed.

'I'd better get home, actually,' said wet-blanket Neville.

'I'll come with you,' said Dennis. He liked the idea of Chris there waiting for him.

'Aw come on,' protested Wayne. 'You're off the leash for once.' At this rate he was fast running out of partners. But Neville and Dennis insisted, and left the bar along with Barry.

'I don't believe this,' Wayne continued, bitterly disillusioned. He looked at Moxey and Oz, his only companions.

'What a difference from how it used to be, eh? But anyhow, we're left. The hard core, eh?'

'No.' said Oz, knocking back his drink. 'I'm off too.'

It was unbelievable – Oz leaving a bar without being helped. The man who drank like there was no tomorrow and very little left of today, who every year, they reckoned, got a Christmas card from the directors of Scottish & Newcastle Breweries.

Moxey was the first to regain his powers of speech.

'Where are you going?' he asked.

'I'm going to see someone.'

'Well, who?' Wayne butted in. If Oz had a bit of totty stashed away somewhere, he had a right to know who and how and where and what was it like. He told Oz as much.

'You don't have the right to know anything, Wayne,' said Oz, cool as a cucumber.

'I thought you of all people would be up to a bit of mischief.'

'What mischief? What did you have in mind? D'you ever ask yourself, "What's the point?" What is the point in going down the port and having another drink in an empty bar? Or going down the casino watching a couple of old ladies playing blackjack? You're always chasin' around lookin' for something or somebody that's never going to happen, Wayne.'

And with that he turned on his heel and left. It was arguably the longest speech Wayne had ever heard the big feller make. It was certainly the most painfully perceptive.

'Well screw him, eh?' he said finally.

Moxey shrugged, and toyed with his drink.

'He's not wrong, kid. Times change. Nothing stays the same.'

Wayne brushed such theories aside. 'Oh, don't get all philosophical on me,' he protested. 'Top it up, eh, Carlo.'

They hunched down over the bar. Carlo quietly poured them fresh drinks.

'You've got to resign yourself to the fact that no dazzling event is going to happen and suddenly transform your life,' said Moxey.

Wayne shrugged. 'I resigned myself to that years ago,' he said leadenly. 'I don't want to transform my life. I'd just like a bit of action and some female company.'

There was a long pause between them. There was no one else in the place.

'Forget it,' urged Moxey. 'It's not on. It wasn't meant to be, right?'

They lapsed into silence. Behind them, four pretty airline stewardesses had come into the bar. They looked around, checking it out. The place looked dead. They shook their heads, and went somewhere else to try and get laid.

Oblivious of all this, the two sad drunks at the bar stared gloomily into their drinks.

Dennis and Neville tiptoed into the living room, careful not to wake the girls or the baby.

'D'you want a nightcap?' whispered Neville. His main reason for leaving the bar so early had been because he felt guilty about leaving Brenda and the bairn behind. He could use another drink.

Dennis refused a brandy. Beer was more his scene these days. He stretched out on the sofa and popped his can open.

'It's easy to get used to a life of luxury, isn't it?' he reflected. Swimming pools and cocktail bars made a big change from Arthur Pringle's pub and a shake-down on the floor of the old manor.

'But it's back to reality next week,' Neville pointed out, sipping on his beer. 'We'll just be another couple of unemployment statistics.'

'Mind, we'll have a nice tan down the dole queue.'

Neville paused. It was a sobering thought.

'What are you going to do?' he asked Dennis. 'Have you given it any thought?'

'I can't be a brickie again. I can't face a North-East winter on some desolate building site.'

'I've got no choice. That's all I am, that's what I do. And I'm not ashamed of it...'

''Course not. Nor should you be. I'm just talking about me. I need to change my life.'

'Does Chris figure in your plans?'

'I dunno ... Well, I'd like her to be but, till something materialises, I haven't got much to offer, have I?'

Neville looked at him. 'There's Ally's money,' he said quietly.

'What about it?'

'It's just sitting there, where you hid it. If I was you I'd be tempted to keep it and...'

'And what?'

'Well, maybe buy a little newsagent's.'

Dennis laughed. 'By the cringe, you don't set your sights very high, do you, Nev? I thought you were going to say "Take it and go to Brazil", not buy a bloody newsagent's.'

'There's not enough for Brazil, is there?' said Neville ruefully.

And there never would be, for either of them.

TWENTY-EIGHT

Vicki was standing in her underwear, holding up dresses. She couldn't decide what to wear.

'Did I read somewhere that green's unlucky for weddings?' she called. 'I mean, I like this one but it might be a bit diaphanous.'

Oz came sloping in from the bedroom, half-dressed, unshaven, a can of beer in his hand.

'Too what?' he grunted, admiring the view. Vicki was a big improvement on his Marjorie in her Marks and Sparks thermals.

'Flimsy,' said Vicki. 'I mean, there'll be quite a breeze out at sea, won't there?'

'I tell you one thing,' said Oz, 'there won't be money to spare for dresses like that back home.'

'But I've got car-loads of dresses,' protested Vicki. Oz didn't even have the car to put them in. The return home was looming ever nearer, and he didn't relish the prospect any more than Neville or Dennis.

'It's not just clothes you'll be giving up. With Ally you've had villas in the sun, first-class travel, room service, jacuzzi's. Let's face it Vicki, you've had everything.'

'Including black eyes,' she put in.

'I know, but you've got to be realistic.' Oz could see their future together, and it was the polar opposite of what Vicki had enjoyed – a council flat in Gateshead, the bus queue on a wet Monday, the chip shop, the launderette. 'If you go back home it's going to need a major readjustment,' he pointed out. 'There's nothing there for you.'

'There's you.'

'Aye, well, you'd better have your eyes open about me an' all,' he confessed. 'I'm hardly a prize catch, Vicki. I'm just a working-class gadgie. I was brought up in a desperate area. I've had no education. People can only understand me within a thirty-mile radius of Gateshead. I'm out of work next week. I've got nae money put aside and nae prospects. Howway, pet! What have we possibly got in common?'

'Everything,' said Vicki quietly.

There was a knock at the door. She jumped, pulling her dress around her breasts.

'Who can that be?' she whispered.

'Don't worry, I'll handle it,' said Oz, looking tough. 'Go make yourself decent.'

Vicki vanished into the bedroom and Oz, looking decidedly indecent himself, opened the door.

There were two Spanish policemen outside.

'Is Señor Fraser here?' asked one of them.

'No,' said Oz. He was always scruplously honest when dealing with the law.

'Can we come in, please?' the other asked, flashing his identification.

'Oh aye,' said Oz, showing them in.

'Where is Señor Fraser?' they asked when the door was closed.

'I don't know,' Oz admitted. 'He flew off a couple of days ago.'

'Are you a friend of his?'

'Not me, mate.'

'Why are you here?' asked the taller one.

That was a difficult one. In fits and starts Oz's powers of reasoning came into action. 'I'm here because I'm, ah, picking the young lady up to take her to a wedding,' he was eventually able to splutter.

The policemen looked at Oz in his socks and vest, and then at each other.

'Aye, well, we're all men of the world, aren't we?' Oz added, trying to brazen it out.

'Evidently you do not expect Mr Fraser to come back so soon,' said the tall policeman.

'No idea. What d'you want him for?'

'Questions.'

'I suppose the English police have been on to you, have they? Want you to check him out, do they? You should do, he's a slippery bugger.'

The other policeman had been idly gazing at the TV which flickered unattended in a corner of the room. Suddenly he envinced great interest.

'Look!' he said, 'the results are coming up.'

He turned up the sound.

'What's this?' asked Oz. Not checking their pools on duty, were they?

'Every Saturday at this time they give the winning numbers of the lottery,' the policeman explained, digging in his pockets for his tickets.

Might as well check mine too, thought Oz, reaching for his jacket. 'We don't have anything like this in England,' he said. 'We have Premium Bonds, like, but I've never known anyone who won more than fifty pound.'

The announcer was giving out a string of winning numbers. The two policemen reacted with resigned disappointment, just as they had done every Saturday for years.

Oz was scanning his own batch of tickets. 'One one three eight one two,' he muttered under his breath. 'Hey!' he shouted, nudging one of the Spaniards. 'Is this number here the same as that one there?'

The policemen looked at the ticket Oz was holding, then at the numbers on the screen. 'One one three eight one two,' they recited. Then realisation hit them.

'*Madre de Dios!*' they cried, pumping Oz's hand. 'One one three eight one two!' They slapped him on the back. The English, he wins the lottery! they told each other over and over again. Fortune shines on him! He has a lucky face, yes!

'What will you do with it all?' they cried, and hugged him close. They'd never known a winner before.

Vicki came into the room, and saw Oz locked in a passionate embrace with two swarthy policemen. 'What's going on?' she asked anxiously.

Oz seemed the calmest of the lot.

'Apparently I've just won eight million pesetas,' he said very coolly.

Then he went ape.

Minder

—back again

Anthony Masters

Terry McCann and Arthur Daley are the Laurel and Hardy of London's criminal fraternity. Arthur's the one with the silver tongue, he could talk his way past St. Peter at the pearly gates if he wanted to. They say he even charges his mum petrol money when he runs her home . . . And when Arthur's hot air finally blows cold, it's usually poor old Terry who's left to do the dirty work! If there's ever a fast buck to be made, they'll be there like a shot. The only trouble is, where Terry and Arthur are concerned, there's always a sting in the tale as well!

MINDER – BACK AGAIN is based on the smash hit Thames Television series created by Leon Griffiths, starring Dennis Waterman and George Cole.

TV TIE-IN/FICTION   0 7221 5823 8   £1.50

Also by Anthony Masters, available in Sphere paperback:

MINDER

NOCTURNE FOR THE

GENERaL

JOHN TRENHAILE

Stepan Ilyich Povin, the KGB general who featured in Trenhaile's highly acclaimed first two novels, has been betrayed by his deputy and is now cruelly entombed in an Arctic concentration camp.

He has suffered two years of beatings and interrogation and fears for his life. But the Kremlin have been secretly keeping him alive.

For Povin unwittingly retains the final link in a chain whose completion would be very useful indeed to his oppressors – and equally revealing to British Intelligence who draw ever closer to the deadly prison camp . . .

ADVENTURE THRILLER   0 7221 8647 9   £2.50

Also by John Trenhaile in Sphere:
A MAN CALLED KYRIL
A VIEW FROM THE SQUARE

A selection of bestsellers from SPHERE

FICTION

NOCTURNE FOR THE GENERAL	John Trenhaile	£2.50 ☐
THE BEAR'S TEARS	Craig Thomas	£2.95 ☐
HOTEL DE LUXE	Caroline Gray	£2.95 ☐
FUR	Jeremy Lucas	£1.95 ☐

FILM & TV TIE-INS

AUF WIEDERSEHEN PET 2	Fred Taylor	£2.75 ☐
LADY JANE	Anthony Smith	£1.95 ☐

NON-FICTION

HOW TO SHAPE UP YOUR MAN	Catherine and Neil Mackwood	£2.95 ☐
THE DUNGEON MASTER	William Dear	£2.95 ☐
1939: THE WORLD WE LEFT BEHIND	Robert Kee	£4.95 ☐
NO BELLS ON SUNDAY: THE JOURNALS OF RACHEL ROBERTS	Alexander Walker	£2.95 ☐

All Sphere books are available at your local bookshop or newsagent, or can be ordered direct from the publisher. Just tick the titles you want and fill in the form below.

Name _____

Address _____

_____

Write to Sphere Books, Cash Sales Department, P.O. Box 11, Falmouth, Cornwall TR10 9EN

Please enclose a cheque or postal order to the value of the cover price plus:

UK: 55p for the first book, 22p for the second book and 14p for each additional book ordered to a maximum charge of £1.75.

OVERSEAS: £1.00 for the first book plus 25p per copy for each additional book.

BFPO & EIRE: 55p for the first book, 22p for the second book plus 14p per copy for the next 7 books, thereafter 8p per book.

Sphere Books reserve the right to show new retail prices on covers which may differ from those previously advertised in the text or elsewhere, and to increase postal rates in accordance with the PO.